LADY DAIMYO

AND THE

SILVER LINING CURSE

Randy,
Thank you for being an
advanced reader for This
sequel. Appreciate your
comments on both This novel
and The firstone.
Enjoy Reading This. Tracy
may like This one too.
womenomics

Steve
1/4/22

S.J. FAIRCHILD

ACKNOWLEDGEMENTS

This novel could not have been written without encouragement, patience, and assistance from family, friends, and business colleagues.

Katherine—my literary muse for 58 years—read and edited. I am grateful for her patience and attention to detail. Beta readers provided excellent suggestions which I incorporated. Thank you, Antonia Fairchild, Mark Borroni, Stephan Witkowsky, Denny Holland, Carl McKinzie, Bob Williams, Randy Yale, Hanna Hasl-Kelchner, Jean Earnhardt, Paul Johnson, and Bill Balzer.

And special thanks to Lyn Fairchild Hawks who improved the content, understanding, and structure—and to John Jewell, Granville Hill, Ed Haugh, and Ben Rock who contributed insights into Japanese culture and literary references.

Once again, Streetlight Graphics assisted in the cover designs and formatting work.

To all of the above, I am indebted. Thank you!

"All warfare is based on deception. Hence, when we are able to attack, we must seem unable; when using our forces, we must appear inactive; when we are near, we must make the enemy believe we are far away; when far away, we must make him believe we are near."

Sun Tzu

"Do not regret what you have done."
"Do not fear death."

Miyamoto Musashi

"Quality is everyone's responsibility."
"If you do not know to ask the right question, you discover nothing."

W. Edwards Deming

"But make sure you don't make the same mistake twice."
"America looks 10 minutes ahead; Japan looks 10 years."

Akio Morita

JAPANESE TERMS

Daimyo: A powerful Japanese magnate or feudal lord
Sensei: Teacher
Hafu: Mixed race
Shogi: Japanese chess
Samurai: A Japanese warrior who served a daimyo
Gaigin: Foreigner
Debiddo: David
-chan: Suffix used to address a younger female
-sama: A respectful suffix for individuals of higher rank
-san: Suffix among equals
-kun: Suffix used to address/refer to males of junior status
Oji-san: Uncle
Hakase: Doctor
Kobito: Sweetheart
Arigato: Thank you
Hai: Yes
Sayōnara: Goodbye
Kon'nichiwa: Hello
Natto: Food made from fermented soybeans
Mevious: Japanese brand of cigarette
Ikigai: One's purpose in life (reason to live)
Kabuki: Classical Japanese dance-drama theater
Noh: Japanese theater involving music, dance, and drama
Mizu shobai: Water business
Yakuza: Japanese crime organization
Yamaguchi-gumi: Osaka yakuza

BUSINESS ENTITIES AND TERMS

Japan Technologies (JT)—An Osaka-based company founded by Kenji Kobayashi in 1950. It manufactures and markets appliance dissipater products; the first company to license the silver-lining technologies invented by International Protected Solutions (IPS).

Major JT customers include Japanese appliance original equipment manufacturers (OEMs)—Hondoya and General Appliance of Japan. Gano-Nippon competes against JT.

International Protected Solutions (IPS)—Company founded by Paul (Pug) James in 1989. It invented the silver-lining technologies—a series of patented thermal and acoustic dissipaters which revolutionized products for appliance and related industries. Major customers include American appliance OEMs—Exeter and General Appliance of the US. Lawrent competes against IPS.

Thermal and Acoustics Dissipater—A metal alloy and/or plastic combination that dissipates (or insulates) heat and noise from designated areas—an important technology for appliances, automotive exhaust systems, construction, and aerospace.

Brunei Investment Trust—An offshore investment trust owned by Kenji. This trust invests in real estate and technology companies. As of May 2002, it owned twenty-five per cent of IPS outstanding shares.

Delaware Plan—An IPS shareholder action plan to restructure IPS, remove Pug James from management, and allow JT to acquire IPS.

MatraScience--Silicon Valley technology company. Pug James, Michael Fields, and Jackson Huntley worked for this company in the 1980s.

FRIDAY, SEPTEMBER 20, 2002
SAN MATEO, CALIFORNIA

M ARCY JAMES TOSSED ASIDE THE *San Mateo Times.* She felt as if a load of bricks rested on her heart.

Surely, my so-called daughter-in-law could have confessed she killed Annie Burr. Oh, Skip! They gave you a life sentence for a murder you didn't commit! And your so-called wife confessed after you committed suicide!

Marcy poured a drink as tears rolled down her cheeks. Despite her disappointment at her son's behavior, he didn't deserve this.

She spoke to no one in particular, "Always knew in my heart Skip didn't kill Annie. It's all Pug's fault. He mistreated Skip when he worked at IPS, encouraged Skip's affair, and then accused Skip of betrayal."

A loud knock interrupted her thoughts. It was 9:30 in the morning. She opened the door and saw Pug.

He stared back with a big grin, as if he were really happy to see her after all these months. It was clear to him she wasn't pleased. Her slovenly appearance shocked him. She reeked of alcohol.

"Marcy, gotta talk with ya!"

"What for?" she asked.

"I got problems."

She held the door open. "Looks like you could use a drink."

"Just water." He entered and noticed the almost empty bottle of Jack Daniels. *She's snockered already.*

1

She brought him water and he watched her refill her glass, take a long swallow, and light a Marlborough.

"When'd ya start smokin' again?" Pug asked.

"Not that you really care; but let's see, after I saw that video of you screwing some Japanese babe like you used to screw Tiffanee."

"Hey, that wasn't me! I was ... uh. . . photoshopped!"

"Didn't look that way to me ... you were groaning out, 'oh, baby, oh, baby.'"

"Look, I wanna move forward. Got me some serious problems."

"What? You got problems? How about Skip killing himself in jail, and then his wife confessing to the murder? And don't forget Dave, your favorite son. He's arrested for bigamy and child abandonment. Like father, like sons. You can be proud of your fucking legacy!"

"I wanna talk 'bout gettin' back together. I could move in ... see a marriage counselor."

She laughed. "As you always said, 'Do my ears hear me?' You encouraged Skip to cheat on his wife, and you drove Dave out of the country. And to make matters worse, you forced Michael Fields to quit IPS and ignored his advice to save IPS. You've put a curse on everything you've touched. Hell, you don't need a marriage counselor, you need a psychiatrist!"

"Damn it! I fired Fieldsy's ass. That ain't fair. He deserved it. Come on, let's talk like adults."

"What's in it for me?"

"Look, I haven't felt this bad since Mom died."

"You should be crying for our two sons and your ten-year old daughter."

"What daughter? Has that Jack gone to your head?"

She handed him photos and a note. "Got these in the mail a few days ago. Take a gander while I go pee."

He stared at the photos. Duplicates of the ones he received.

Five minutes later, she returned. He was looking at the *National Inquirer's* cover page showing Ronald Blunt's photo and the quote, "Our Next Commander-in-Chief?" She heard him mumble something obscene about Blunt. He turned to look at her. The gun was pointed at his head.

1
MAY, 1985
OSAKA, JAPAN

"D EAR NATSU-CHAN," KENJI SAID, "YOU look worried."
Eighteen-year-old Natsu Nashakatani had begun a
weeklong break from her international boarding school.
She joined Kenji Kobayashi, her guardian and grandfather figure, at
his Osaka residence. They sat on the porch overlooking a verdant,
Nicklaus-designed golf course owned by Kenji's Brunei investment
trust. Kenji's chef slipped in to serve a breakfast of natto rice along with
small dishes of miso soup, grilled fish, pickles, and nori.

Natsu's jade eyes blinked at Kenji's penetrating stare as she hesitated
to eat. Tired and sad, she glanced at the food in front of her. She dared
not defy her guardian who sat so upright as if his spine were titanium.
She feared disappointing him.

At last, she found courage to speak. "*Sensei*, I do not wish to burden
your mind. My last year of school has been ... difficult. Students ridicule
me and say hurtful things."

"In what way?"

"They call me *hafu*. They joke about my unnatural eyes and different
hair color." She struggled not to cry. "They say I will fail because society
will not accept me, that I am not true Japanese."

Kenji sipped his miso soup. He placed the bowl on the table. "How
do you handle those classmates?"

"I ignore them and concentrate on my studies."

"You cannot win battles by avoidance and disappearing into books."

3

"But why do they torment me? I have done nothing wrong!" Her voice rose. "Will it always be this way?"

"Your distinctive attributes—intelligence, maturity, and fluency in English—create jealousy. Others cannot match your accomplishments in academics and school activities." He took a white linen handkerchief from his pocket and reached to dab at her tears. "Besides studies and extra reading, what other actions do you take?"

Natsu calmed and straightened her shoulders. "I interact with students from countries other than Japan. They understand and accept my appearance. We often play *shogi*." A slight smile played at her lips. "Sometimes, I let them win."

"Calculated defeats are acceptable, if your long-term goal is ultimate victory."

"You mean you allow your opponent to think he's winning?"

"Correct! Throughout your life, you will encounter adversaries. It may feel they have all the clocks, but you have all the time." Kenji smiled and pulled out a Mevious, tapping it against the case. He lit it and inhaled. "As for shogi, it teaches valuable lessons in deceiving one's opponent. I employ this strategy when confronting business competitors or personal adversaries."

Natsu reflected on this. *This is why Kobayshi-sama taught me shogi.*

"Sensei, I still worry I will not succeed at university."

"Your parents gave you talent and capabilities."

She felt tears rising again. "I envy classmates who know their parents. I know very little about mine!"

"You don't recall what I told you about your father?"

"Like him, I should photograph everything with my mind?"

"Correct. This is why you excel in science and math; hence, your decision to study engineering like him. He earned a doctorate in metallurgy."

"He did?" That her father earned an advanced degree was a revelation. "Knowing that gives me confidence when I attend Osaka University. And … my mother?"

Kenji reached for a folder, pulled out a picture, and passed it to Natsu. "This is your mother at age twenty-five. You have many of her lovely features."

"She is very beautiful." Natsu's eyes filled with tears again. *But my eyes and hair color, are so different. I am not as pretty as she.* "May I keep this?"

"You may. From your mother, you inherited excellent judgment. I predict you will have an entrepreneurial spirit like her."

"Entrepreneurial spirit?" Natsu asked.

"You undertake new challenges and risks like learning shogi and expanding your knowledge—important traits of an entrepreneur. Who knows, someday you may discover a new technology."

Natsu seemed confused about the new technology comment. She chose not to question.

"But Sensei, how does one prepare for such a role?"

"You have started your journey. You graduated first in your class and scored first on the entrance examination for engineering school—the first woman to accomplish this remarkable achievement. Forget your unfriendly classmates and look forward. You see why I delayed sharing more about your parents?"

"I am still unclear," she responded.

"You must experience life's obstacles to better appreciate your heritage."

She remembered her school headmaster announcing her valedictorian status. *A bright future may lie ahead if I overcome obstacles.*

Kenji interrupted her thoughts. "I have a special surprise."

"Surprise?"

"Something different. We will watch *Ran*, a new film directed by my close friend, Akira Kurosawa. This film has valuable lessons."

"You financed some of his films."

"Correct."

"I will be attentive." But she had questions. *What does this entertainment have to do with my parents? My future life?*

After viewing the movie, Kenji and Natsu entered a beverage shop to drink tea. While waiting for their drinks, Natsu exclaimed, "Oh, I just realized the plot of *Ran* is from Shakespeare's *King Lear*!"

"Very good, Natsu-chan. What lessons does the film teach?"

"Verify actions before trusting words! King Lear misread his daughters' intentions."

"Correct! That mistake proved costly. Never forget that. In your lifetime, you will meet people who resemble characters from Shakespeare's plays. Their stories are lessons that teach how to deal with life's struggles, tragedies, betrayals ... and to appreciate the lighter moments."

Looking bewildered, Natsu asked, "Sensei, how can I absorb all this?"

"Do not fret, Natsu-chan. You have plenty of time to become acquainted with more Shakespeare. My library is for you to use."

She couldn't wait to browse and read Kenji's extensive collection of books including Asian history and philosophers.

"Why did Kurosawa-san use *samurai* characters?" Kenji asked.

"I do not know."

"The samurai warriors followed a code of conduct and system of beliefs that reveres courage, respect, honesty, integrity, loyalty, honor, and persistence—important elements for your future success in life and business."

"But, all samurais were men."

"No, there were female samurais like Tomei Gozen. They trained in the use of weapons to protect their household, family, and honor in times of war. You need weapons and skills to defend yourself and attack when required," Kenji said. "For now, think of yourself as a samurai in training."

"Is that why you had me learn the art of fencing?"

"Correct. Later you will study samurai sword techniques. When you have acquired the necessary education and experience of a modern-day samurai, you can aspire to become a lady *daimyo*."

"Sensei, what is a daimyo?"

"For now, think of Okazaki-san and me as modern-day daimyos in industry. At a later time, I will instruct more about samurais and daimyos. Meanwhile, research the lives of Oda Nobunaga, Toyotomi Hideyashi, and Tokugawa Ieyasu."

She wrote the names on a tablet. "Why do I need to know about them?"

"These men were famous daimyos who helped to unify Japan.

Perhaps, one day you can unify something important to your life and career," Kenji added.

"Sensei, were there women daimyos?"

"To my knowledge, there were no true lady daimyos." He smiled and leaned forward. "One day you will become a true lady daimyo with loyal samurais serving you."

His confidence in her was heartening but at the same time challenging. She needed to know how Kenji had achieved his daimyo status. "Sensei, who are your trusted samurai warriors?"

"Two men come to mind, *Hakase* Yamura and Ashi-kun. Both have distinguished themselves by loyally serving me for many years. But there is a caveat to my statement."

"What is that, Sensei?"

"One must evaluate a samurai's actions each day. History indicates that even the most loyal samurais can betray their leaders. And betrayal may come with back up."

"What do you mean?"

"Adversaries may conspire against you."

"Why is this information relevant to my life?"

"Natsu-chan, you will experience conflict in life and in your chosen career. You must be prepared to defeat your enemies." He poured more tea for Natsu. "Now let us return to our discussion of *Ran*. Your turn: connect this film to your life."

Natsu spoke without hesitation. "When I return to class next week, I will evaluate classmates by assessing their actions before trusting their words. I will not make King Lear's mistake."

Kenji smiled thoughtfully. "These lessons will help you in school and later in your career. Your classmates and future colleagues will know your destiny and honor you. Twenty years ago, such aspirations for women were unthinkable. When you finish your engineering studies, we will continue our plans for your future."

At week's end, she drove to Osaka University to begin summer classes. The car's back seat held stacks of books from Kenji's library. She was determined to excel in her studies and to demonstrate to Kobayashi-sama that she was worthy of his trust.

But doubts lingered. With Kenji she felt safe; but, when away from him, she worried.

Sensei gives me good advice, but how will male professors and students treat me? I'm the only female admitted to the freshman class. And I am hafu. In this society, those are two obstacles.

Can I become the first woman daimyo in this country? A daimyo of what?

2
WEDNESDAY, MAY 15, 2002
BURLINGAME, CALIFORNIA

E NJOYING A PATRICK HENRY, HIS favorite rebel beer, Pug James sat at the end of the mahogany bar in Kuletos. Formerly known as the Velvet Turtle, this restaurant held special memories.

He was pleased to return to this favorite haunt, but that was about it. The last four months had been a disaster: he suffered a stroke, followed by physiotherapy, copious meds, and a stay in the VA hospital's mental ward. His wife divorced him, he lost his company, one son was in jail, and the other son, Pug declared a traitor.

But now, Michael Fields, his former colleague, gave him an opportunity to rebuild his life. Pug motioned to the barkeep to bring another bottle.

A new chance? Fieldsy thinks he saved me. Bullshit! Fieldsy doesn't know it, but he's gonna help me get my company and my silver-lining technologies back!

Pug swigged the pale liquid as he finished a sketch on a bar napkin, his thoughts operating at fiber-optic speed. He already had two solutions for the first project ordered by Michael Fields. He grabbed his beer, tossed a ten-dollar bill on the bar, and headed to the dining area.

As he passed by the opposite end of the bar, a familiar face stared back.

"Tiffanee?"

A slim blond stood and opened her arms to hug him. "Pug! It's you!"

9

In the fifteen years since their affair ended, she hadn't aged. A light scent of Nina Ricci perfume drew him in and brought him back to their first encounter at the Velvet Turtle. Her hair, skin, figure—as lovely as he remembered.

For a moment, he could hardly find words. "Great! Wow! Can't believe it's really you, Tiffanee! Hey, just headin' to dinner. Ya gotta join me!"

He watched her glance at her phone. "My friend's cancelled. Looks like I'm free." Her smile, and clear blue eyes sparkled yes.

After they sat, Pug blurted, "Tiff, you're still one beauteous babe!" *I could jump you right now!*

She laughed and touched his arm. "Pug, always loved your way with words. And hey, you're thinner than I recall. How've you stayed so fit?"

"Got me a personal trainer, doing lotsa exercise. Lost me fifty pounds. My doc told me to ease up cuz I'd been workin' so hard. Feelin' like I'm twenty again."

"I'm impressed. And you've kept your mustache!"

"Yeah, could use a little more hair on the top."

She threw back her head and laughed. That laugh was music to Pug's ears.

The server stopped at the table and recited the day's specials. Pug interrupted, "Hey honey, not ready to order yet, but bring us a bottle of Cakebread Chardonnay!" She departed.

"Pug! You remembered my favorite wine!" Tiffanee said.

He winked. "Gotta trapped-steeled mind when it comes to our history." He looked into her eyes. "Gosh, Tiff, this is like old times at the Turtle … when my inventions at MatraScience made it great." He shook his head. "Ya know, after I quit, company went to hell. I hear someone bought 'em on the cheap in '99."

"I think that was Zyco." Tiffanee leaned in and giggled. "Their executives went to jail."

Pug squirmed a little, a little too close to home with his oldest son's arrest and confinement.

She leaned back. By her smile, Pug could tell she was giving him a closer look.

"I remember your bar napkin sketch at the Velvet Turtle—back in 1987," she said.

"Yep, that was when I invented MatraConnect 5000 and sold it to Pacific Gas & Electric; the start of our great times together."

The server filled their glasses and took their dinner orders. He ordered his favorite: rare filet mignon, baked potato with bacon and sour cream, and a large Caesar.

Pug continued, "What happened after you left MatraScience in 1987?"

She took a while to answer. "Honestly, our separation devastated me, but I eventually accepted it, I guess. You had tremendous pressures from family, your father's mental issues, and your new boss."

"Yeah, I had my 'you-know-what' in a ringer. So, where'd you go after MatraScience?"

"Stayed with my parents in San Jose. Went to San Jose State for an MBA. Two years later, I graduated and joined a real estate firm in San Francisco. That's where I met Alan McIntyre, the firm's in-house lawyer responsible for commercial property deals. He taught me commercial property development." She tipped her head sideways and smiled. "I've always been attracted to more seasoned men."

"Alan was my age?"

"He would have been fifty-eight this year. After he became chief executive officer (CEO), his wife died in an auto accident. After a respectful time, we began dating. Soon we became serious, he proposed, and I accepted."

Pug detected sadness in her voice, watched as her eyes teared.

"He died unexpectedly," she continued, "but left me comfortable with a nice home. I now run the Alan McIntyre Charitable Foundation for heart disease research."

Pug could not believe his luck. *Still gorgeous, sexy, and got bucks.* Her next comment intrigued him:

"It's been lonely since Alan left. His son, Kevin, is grown and well into his career."

The server brought salads and refilled their glasses. Pug stabbed at his salad with gusto.

"Pug, what did you do when you left MatraScience?"

"Started my own business, invented the silver-lining technologies, made it successful, and then sold my company to investors. I call it my 'Pearl Harborin' Japan."

Tiffany looked askance. "Sounds like a story I need to hear, but what are you doing now?"

"Um ... just started a development lab to invent new stuff!"

"Sounds exciting."

"Uh, yeah ... um ... wanted to retire and play golf, but it's not in my Levis. I gotta be inventin' and fightin' to protect what's mine."

"Levis?"

"Ya know ... jeans."

"Oh, genes!" She laughed. "Always loved your clever words."

He loved her infectious laugh and the dimples in her alluring face.

When his filet arrived, Pug exclaimed to the server, "Hey hon, where's my sour cream for my potato? And bring a bottle of Stags Leap cabernet sauvignon."

"Excellent choice. Be right back, sir."

Tiffanee sampled her grilled salmon. "How long did you stay at MatraScience?" she asked.

"Left the joint in December 1989, after two miserable years of Fieldsy bossin' me around."

"Fieldsy? Oh, you mean Michael Fields?"

"Never gave me credit for my inventions, my patents, my customer skills, or my successful product launches. Found out later he stabbed me in the back."

"So, what did you do?"

"Invested in MatraScience put options. Made me a ton of money. Then bought me a business in South San Francisco (SSFO). Took on debt, personal guarantees, lotsa sacrifice. Fast forward couple of years, I had a bunch of inventions, patents, and ready-to-do commercial deals— start of my silver-lining technologies and 'Pearl-Harborin' Japan."

"This is getting interesting," she replied.

"It's a long story and requires another 'Yogi Bear' session."

"Yogi Bear?"

"Ya know, the baseball guy who said I'm doin' it all over again."

She laughed out loud. "Your Pug-speak is amazing."

Dinner finished, they lingered over espressos. Pug glanced at his watch. "Tiff, almost eleven. Waitress wants her tip. Better let you get home. Next time, I'll tell ya about my silver-lining technologies, my negotiatin' and inventin' laws, and Pearl Harborin' the crummy Japanese."

"You've mentioned the Japanese a couple of times. What's the deal with them?"

"Don't trust them people, an' they stole my patents!"

"Pug, come to my home in Hillsborough for dinner. I have a wonderful chef who does French or Italian."

"Italian, hands down. I'll spring for the Chianti." He hugged her. "Walkin' you to your car. Ya okay to drive?"

"Thanks, Pug. I'm fine and look forward to seeing you soon."

They approached her BMW 740. "Thanks for a fantastic evening, Tiff. Love your silver BMW—reminds me of my silver-lining inventions."

Tiffanee got into the car and clicked the seat belt.

"Drive careful, Tiff. Doors locked?"

She smiled. "Soon, Pug!"

Pug watched her drive away then strolled to his condo. *Wow! Like old times with Tiff! Shoulda dumped Marcy then.*

He plopped down on the sofa. Yawning, he stretched out, closed his eyes and reflected on the last eighteen whirlwind hours:

Michael Fields had checked him out of the VA hospital, drove him to Burlingame where Michael introduced Pug to his new home—a brand new Skunk Works lab with his own condo nearby. Kuletos Restaurant happened to be a short walk away and where he headed for dinner earlier.

Thoughts swirled as he drifted to sleep. *Tiff, you're my 'Yogi Bear' babe! Dammit! With you back in my life, I gotta get me that Niagra. And, Tiff, you beauteous, lonely babe who's lookin' for love ... you don't know it, but you're helping me get back my silver lining.*

3
DECEMBER 1988
MT. FUJI, JAPAN

K ENJI LIT A *MEVIOUS* AND sharply inhaled, his lungs emitting
a wheezing sound. He placed the cigarette in an ashtray and
held a handkerchief to his mouth. He coughed and cleared his
throat.

Natsu saw a distinct red stain on the handkerchief but said nothing.

"Natsu-chan, what do you see here?" He shoved a paper across the
desk.

Natsu looked at the schematic as her sleek, auburn hair fell forward
gracefully.

"Lots of words and concentric circles," she said. "A geometric puzzle that you will explain?"

"Of course." Kenji leaned back in his leather chair.

They were at his Mt. Fuji hunting lodge, a massive structure containing six guest rooms, a dining hall accommodating thirty guests, and a great room with two huge stone fireplaces. Hunting trophies from Kenji's African excursions hung on the walls along with paintings of the Rocky Mountains, gifts from his mentor. Evening advanced and a hint of stars appeared through the floor-to-ceiling windows. The chef quietly served dinner and cleared dishes.

"Natsu-chan, you worked hard these last few years. You graduated first in your engineering class, earning a double major in mechanical engineering and material science. My heartfelt congratulations!"

"*Arigato!* Engineering studies expanded my confidence. My male classmates show more respect and invite me to join their groups."

Kenji smiled, "Is that the only reason they invite you?"

She bowed her head, blushing. *A rhetorical question!* She raised her head and looked him in the eye. "In truth, I managed this situation quite well." She could see Kenji liked her reply.

Kenji coughed slightly and stubbed out his cigarette. "Now, let us discuss your *ikigai*."

She pointed to the middle of the schematic. "You refer to the center area?"

"Correct. In separate lessons, I will explain the four intersecting circles and the eight elements. The intersection of the four circles defines your purpose in life." Kenji paused. "Questions?"

"Very soon I start graduate business studies. I do not have time to think about ikigai."

"Natsu-chan, life is complicated. Understanding and practicing your ikigai will help. We will examine the schematic in logical steps." He pointed to the first circle. "Tell me what you love."

"That is easy. Math, material science, different cultures, shogi, fencing, Shakespeare, and *noh* theater. I can continue if you wish."

"Your love for continual learning and your diversity of interests impress me, but achieving your ikigai requires continual effort and diligence. As we review all eight elements in the four circles, remember ikigai can always improve from its current state. We will now discuss the remaining seven elements. Then you will begin to understand."

"Sensei, I cannot explain all these elements. You give me an impossible task."

"Patience, dear Natsu-chan. We will not finish today. I will give you questions to consider. Then, your graduate studies and business career will provide data and experiences for the other elements—passion, mission, profession, vocation, what you are good at, what the world needs, and what you can earn."

"This will not be a quick process."

Kenji laughed. A deep-chest cough ensued. He grabbed his handkerchief.

Natsu watched with concern. "Your cough would go away if you did not smoke."

"Natsu-chan, do not lecture! If you knew my stress as a young pilot training for my first *kamikaze* mission, you would understand why I smoke. It relaxed me then, and it relaxes me now."

"I apologize, Sensei. I will not raise this subject again." She knew how fortunate he was to avoid that mission. But why did he choose to mention kamikaze? Kamikaze pilots committed suicide for a cause larger than one's self and when the adversary had won.

"As to your observation, ikigai is never a quick process. A famous samurai, Oishi Yoshio, once said, 'The point is that once you know what you want, your reason to live, you must be prepared to sacrifice everything to get it.' What does that mean to you?"

"I am not sure. Don't let obstacles prevent you from achieving your ikigai?"

"Part of the answer. You must use all your capabilities to achieve your objectives and aspirations. Leave everything on the battlefield."

Three hours later, Kenji completed the tutorial. "You can now see why ikigai principles are crucial to your future success in life." He paused to light another cigarette. "You know about Shinzo Abe?"

"Hai, he is the current deputy chief and cabinet secretary for the Liberal Democratic Party. The press predicts he may be our future prime minister."

"I admire him as a shrewd political colleague. He believes women deserve equal opportunity to rise and succeed in the business world. He calls this idea 'womenomics.'"

"Womenomics?"

"The idea that women's economic advancement will improve the economy as a whole. Women in the workforce should be rewarded with jobs and salaries that match their skills, talents, and ambitions."

"But Sensei, what does this have to do with ikigai?"

"Natsu-chan, if you practice ikigai, you can be a leader for 'womenomics.'"

Natsu smiled. "An appealing aspiration for a future woman daimyo."

"Absolutely. If I am unavailable when an important decision must occur, rely on your ikigai."

Natsu saw Kenji's expression change. Concern clouded her thoughts. "Sensei, I cannot imagine you never being available."

"My favorite samurai warrior, Miyamoto Musashi, once said, 'There is nothing outside of yourself that can ever enable you to get better, stronger, quicker, or smarter. Everything is within. Everything exists, seek nothing outside of yourself.' You must have patience, discipline, focus, and commitment to become a modern-day daimyo. Your ikigai roadmap will guide you. One more thought. My business colleague of many years, Okazaki-san, was also mentored by my sensei. If for some reason, I am not available, you can rely on Okazaki-san. He fully understands what you and I have discussed." He gazed at Natsu and touched her face lovingly. "Natsu-chan, you will be the new symbol of Japan's future."

"Hai, Sensei. I will be mindful of all your lessons as I begin graduate business school. And I respect Okazaki-sama." *And I will talk with him to verify your words.*

Shiganari Okazaki's image flashed in her mind. She admired his distinguished manners, his handsome face and pewter-gray hair. He remained deferential to Kenji when they were seen together. Yet Natsu understood he was as successful in business as Kenji. She considered Shiganari more empathetic about her unique heritage. As a result, she felt relaxed around him. Perhaps that is why Kenji encouraged her to consult with Shiganari for another perspective.

"Now, Natsu-chan, on another subject, tell me what you learned about *kabuki* and noh theater."

"Watching these performances was a nice break from my studies. I much prefer noh over kabuki."

"Interesting. Explain."

Without hesitating, "Noh feels more traditional and conveys more thought. I enjoyed actors wearing masks instead of face paint. The leading actors require multiple skills, not only in performance but in management and production of the play."

"You have done your research and captured the essence of noh. Tell me why you didn't like kabuki."

"Kabuki relies on exaggeration and too much showmanship." She paused, then wrinkled her nose, "Much like those classmates I detest."

Kenji laughed. She could tell he knew her confidence had increased over the last three years. She looked forward to graduate business school and continuing her ikigai journey.

4
THURSDAY, MAY 16, 2002
BURLINGAME

I N THE MORNING, PUG, CRADLING his framed patents and pictures of his MatraConnect 5000 closure and IPS 10000 dissipater inventions, strode to the lab. Approaching the front, he glanced at the sign above the door, PSW II, in raised silver letters. Pug's mind flashed back to his first skunk lab he created at MatraScience. *But Fieldsy killed it, why?*

He entered the small reception *lobby and paused. Why didn't Fieldsy hire me a gal to answer the phones and make java?*

He moved past the receptionist's desk into the hallway leading to four offices, each fully furnished and occupant-ready. He headed to his office at the end. Inside, stacked boxes marked "Pug James" cluttered the floor. He placed the patents and pictures on a credenza. He examined folders Michael Fields had left. One contained details on ten projects. Another marked "confidential" described Michael's rules. Pug smirked as he reread them:

Rule # 1: Continue stroke recovery regimen. Take all medications prescribed by Dr. Tower —hydrochlorothiazide, lovastatin, Adderall, warfarin, and Lithium.

Rule # 2: No freelancing. Work on projects assigned by Michael Fields.

Pug mumbled, "Bullshit! I'll work on what I want!"

Rule # 3: If anybody asks, you run a contract development lab.

"Why the hell did he make me sign a non-disclosure agreement (NDA) and no-compete requirement? I own the inventions!"

He scanned the list of ten projects. "Boring! Same old thermal, sound, and dimensional problems for appliance devices. Fieldsy's got no imagination."

He opened a box marked "Lab Books" and leafed through them. One caught his attention. He spent fifteen minutes reviewing Dave James's lab notes from 1998. "Bingo! Forgot about his co-molded idea."

He glanced at his watch. "Oh shit, doctor's appointment at 9:00. Niagra here I come!"

Two hours later, he returned to PSW II. Tomorrow, there would be a prescription waiting at the pharmacy after the doctor reviewed blood tests. Pug managed to pass the physical by inserting a few lies along the way—such as—"Gosh, Doc, I've always been in good health!"

He sat back in his chair and mused, "What if I co-mold my silver-lining technologies with high-temp plastics? Brilliant! An' Fieldsy will never know."

5
MAY 1990
MT. FUJI

NATSU JOINED KENJI AT HIS mountain retreat. They met in the kitchen. On occasion, Kenji prepared their meal. Cooking was an activity he found relaxing.

"Welcome, dear Natsu-chan. Join me while I finish."

"What are you preparing?"

"We will start with crisp nori chips with toasted sesame oil, followed by miso soup and yakatori chicken with ginger, garlic, and soy sauce. You can help prepare the chicken."

"Sounds delicious." She put on an apron and followed his instructions. She smiled to herself. *Haven't I always been your dutiful sous chef?*

Before they began eating, Kenji raised his sake cup, "A toast to your success in achieving your MBA. Again, you graduated number one in your class. You achieved national recognition with your graduate thesis on entrepreneurship and disruptive technologies. You continue to honor your ancestors."

"Arigato, Sensei. My business classmates have been more accepting of me."

Kenji smiled, "Your classmates' respect correlates with your excellent academic achievements. Why do you think that is?"

"They are measured in their actions and possess multifunctional skills. They would excel at noh theater."

"What about those classmates whom do you not like?"

She smiled at his question. "They are definitely kabuki-types. They rely on exaggeration and showmanship to disguise their true motives. I remain wary of them."

"You have learned wise lessons from theater performances."

After dinner, Kenji retrieved the ikigai schematic and placed it on the table. "Remember when we discussed this and you articulated your mission in life? What did you say then?"

"I wanted to be a pioneer; the first woman in Japan to lead a global technology firm with disruptive technologies. After my business classes, I expanded it to include starting new businesses."

"A sign of a true entrepreneur. Your engineering degree, your patent, and now your MBA provide the education tools for two elements in your ikigai—profession and future vocation. Remember when Japan Technologies (JT) licensed your patent?"

"Hai. You only said my patent represented a remarkable technical achievement."

"Now that you have attended business school, why do you think JT purchased an exclusive license for your patent?"

"Licensing is one way to commercialize a technology and defeat competitors. I learned that in my entrepreneurship classes."

"Correct. JT used your patent to develop new products, open new markets, and keep JT's competitors away."

"I can see that now."

"Soon you will understand. Achieving your life's purpose requires such tools and weapons."

"I do not understand."

"A daimyo business leader needs technology like your patent along with samurai warriors who excel at product development and commercialization; more about this subject when you acquire business experience."

He continued. "It is now time to discuss your business career. First, you will learn about the Brunei Trust's outside and wide-ranging investments starting with restaurants, hotels, golf courses, and real estate holdings. You will start at appropriate levels and progress to more responsible positions. You will learn management techniques, both good and bad, by observing how others manage."

"But why can't I start at JT where there are customers, products and technologies?"

"Natsu-chan, listen carefully. Your first position starts at the Comfort Station restaurant and lounge. Suzi Yamamoto, your first manager, will teach you *mizu shobai*. Suzi is an extraordinary conversationalist. You will learn much from her."

"What does she or mizu shobai have to do with customers, technology, and products?"

"Mizu shobai is a place for facilitating business discussions. In Japan, important business transactions occur in informal settings such as restaurants and golf courses. In restaurants, you can also conduct the *natto* test. It measures a foreigner's commitment to do business in Japan. We challenge foreigners to eat the fermented soybean paste. Their reactions foreshadow if they can adapt and succeed in our culture."

"When I first tried natto paste, it looked, smelled and tasted unusual. Now, I am quite fond of it."

"Your mother excelled at mizu shobai, and she trained Yamamoto-san."

Remembering her mother's photo Kenji gave her, "That knowledge gives me comfort." She knew geishas were artisans, widely read, and proficient at conversation and hosting clients.

"Management and relationship skills fit into which ikigai circle?" Kenji asked.

"With more experience, it should improve 'what I am good at.'"

"Relationships are one of two elements of the commercial equation."

"What is the other element?"

"Technology—like for example, the metal alloy patent you developed in engineering school. When you work at JT, you will learn its business model. You will see the importance of relationships in commercializing technology and understand how to balance the two elements."

She pointed at the paper. "When I work there, will I expand the profession and vocation elements of ikigai?"

"Correct. I achieved my ikigai at JT. My close colleague, Okazaki-san, achieved his at Hondoya Appliance. Our American colleague,

Walter Marken, achieved his at Marken & Associates in Chicago. Hondoya represents a customer relationship, and Marken represents a trusted partner relationship. This knowledge will help you appreciate what the world needs and what you can be paid for."

She glanced once more at the schematic. "Those represent two more elements of the ikigai schematic. Now I understand why you had me work at Hondoya and at Marken & Associates during school recesses."

"Correct."

"Arigato for those opportunities. While at Hondoya, I had many conversations with Okazaki-sama. He answered all my questions and gave me excellent advice on my career aspirations."

"He is a wonderful resource for you," Kenji said. He then handed her a framed photo of four men dressed in early 1950's business attire. She recognized three of the four—Kenji, Okazaki-sama, and Walter Marken.

"Kobayashi-sama, who is the fourth person? American? European?"

Kenji replied, "One day you will learn his identity. For now, retain this photo."

"*Hai.*" *Why the mystery?*

"Now, we discuss other important subjects. You can determine where they fit within your ikigai."

Natsu nodded and made notes on her notepad.

"Men will expect your deferential actions because you are a woman hafu. Most will underestimate you. Business is war. Sometimes, people who appear as allies later become adversaries who will betray you. Can you think of examples from your readings that demonstrate this point?"

"You mean like King Lear who thought his two daughters were allies?"

"An excellent example," Kenji said.

He went to his library shelves and retrieved four books. He placed them on the table. "These are important books to study as you begin your business career."

She examined the titles—*The Art of War* by Sun Tzu, *Go Rin no Sho* by Miyamoto Musashi, *Out of the Crisis* by W. Edwards Deming, *The Japan That Can Say No* by Akio Morita.

"Study each carefully, and we will discuss later. For now, keep these key thoughts in mind: Sun Tzu said, 'All warfare is based on deception.' Musashi-san stressed the importance of a samurai's loyalty, duty and honor to his daimyo. Mr. Deming stated, 'Quality is everyone's responsibility.' Morita-san mentioned, 'America looks ten minutes ahead; Japan looks ten years.'"

"Sensei, you have given me much to consider." *I will learn and apply these lessons to my life and business career.*

That night she lay in bed and wondered if she should tell her sensei. Would he be disappointed or pleased? But she had earned samurai status. The last five years of higher education gave her mental weapons to deal with life's adversaries. In her spare time, she learned samurai swordsmanship techniques to complement her fencing skills.

On the inside of her upper left arm, she acquired a tattoo of Tomei Gozen in samurai dress. Later after sufficient business experience, she would acquire a female daimyo tattoo on the opposite arm.

6

FEBRUARY, 2001

OSAKA

ENJI AND NATSU RELAXED ON the porch overlooking the golf course. In the twelve years since receiving her MBA, Natsu's business accomplishments captured the attention and respect of JT colleagues and others in the business community. Her business accomplishments were one thing, but she had become a stunning woman. Her auburn hair, jade eyes, tall and trim figure turned heads.

Kenji had not aged well. He limited golfing, business travel, and spent less time in his office. A persistent cough rattled his chest.

He smiled at Natsu, looking at her with fondness. "My dear Natsu-chan, I'm pleased you joined me this weekend. I know you have been busy."

"I am never too busy for you. What a delightful winter day! A good day for golf on this beautiful course."

"It is unusually moderate for February," he said as he poured tea. "Now that you play golf, you see why Jack Nicklaus considers this one of his best designs."

"Hai! I enjoy playing this challenging course."

"Natsu-chan, golf allows you to conduct business in an informal setting and to assess the honesty of others."

"I have played with both honest and dishonest people. When I detect cheating, I let them win."

"Exactly. You practice Sun Tzu's deception principle!"

"Hai! I find his teachings most enlightening. I particularly admire his principle that the supreme art of war is to subdue your adversary without fighting."

"What have you learned from your study of samurai teachings?"

"I evaluate managers and subordinates according to loyalty, duty, discipline, and honor."

"And how about Mr. Deming's thoughts on quality?"

"I demand quality in every aspect of business, especially people's performance."

"Okasaki-san, Walter Marken, and I still practice these valuable principles."

She nodded. "Each of you has been successful in your respective business careers. You are my benchmarks." *And they all shared the same mentor. Is he the fourth person in that photo?*

"Natsu-chan, today the student controls the agenda. What would you like to discuss?"

"I have three topics, Sensei. The first involves technology. When I worked in JT's R&D division, the technology manager said JT licensed the silver-lining technologies from International Protected Solutions. What were the reasons for this transaction?"

"Our US resource discovered this company and knew the inventors of these technologies."

"Who was the US resource?"

"I will answer at an appropriate time."

She looked disappointed. *Why does he avoid certain questions?*

He continued, "JT realized the commercial potential of IPS technologies and purchased a license to use these technologies in Japan. Why do you think we did this?"

She thought for a moment. "Because JT had established deep relationships with important customers like Hondoya."

"Anything else?" he asked.

"Hai. JT didn't want to invest more money in development. A license was a cost-effective way to acquire technology to compliment JT's customer relationships."

"Correct. With IPS technologies and JT's relationships, we substantially increased revenues and profits. Because IPS desperately needed money at the time, *Hakase* Yamura and I structured the license agreement to include a twenty-five percent ownership in IPS."

"Why would you do that?"

"It was our first strategic step to merge JT with IPS and expand our market presence beyond Japan. You will be an integral part to complete this merger."

"Why hasn't the merger occurred?"

"Pug James, IPS's CEO and principal shareholder, ignored my merger proposal. He was afraid to lose control. He acted irrational according to our US resource."

"What do you mean irrational?" Natsu asked.

"He relied only on technologies and ignored customer and partner relationships. Then, he accused JT of violating the license agreement. He initiated lawsuits against US customers, competitors, and lawyers. He placed a curse on IPS and its silver-lining technologies."

"Sensei, you have always stressed the importance of strong relationships to facilitate introducing new technologies. Why would he make this mistake?"

"Only Pug James knows the answer. Perhaps he was arrogant, ignorant, or maybe sick."

She reflected on Kenji's comments. *Technology like the silver-lining patents could be one of my samurai swords. Another sword can be my relationship skills with customers and business partners. These swords will help me achieve my goal—to lead a company with disruptive technologies—a company that can unify the global appliance industry using JT's thermal and acoustic dissipaters. But first, I must destroy the curse.*

"Now, what is the second item you want to discuss?"

She answered, "The last twelve years have been rewarding but challenging. I have made mistakes and encountered setbacks. At times, I failed you."

"Natsu-chan, samurai warriors have a saying, 'You want to know the difference between a master and a beginner? The master has failed more times than the beginner.'"

"I remember reading that."

"And Morita-san stressed, 'But make sure you don't make the same mistake twice.'"

He coughed repeatedly then sipped water. "Thomas Edison, the famous American inventor, once said, 'I have not failed; I've found ten thousand ways that won't work.' So, you can see this wisdom is universal. What is your third item?"

"It involves my heritage."

"What would you like to know?"

"You told me about my parents and the traits I inherited. I feel there is much I still don't know. Have you shared everything?"

"Natsu-chan," he hesitated, swallowed hard and drank more water to clear his congested throat, "you have heard me praise my valued mentor, Patorikuku Hafati."

"Hai, the same person who mentored Okazaki-sama, Marken-sama, and Morita-sama?"

"Correct. Hafati-sama translated General MacArthur's vision into specific actions to rebuild our war-damaged economy. He provided wisdom, support, and connections to establish Japan Technologies."

"I know you have great admiration for your mentor." She looked down at her hands. He was avoiding her question again.

"What you do not know—my mentor was American, and his true name was Patrick Hafferty. He is the fourth person in the photo I gave you." Kenji sighed as if a secret burden had lifted from his mind.

Natsu thought, *Finally, the answer to my question. Why did Sensei take so long to share this?*

Kenji continued, "Patrick and his wife produced a son. His name is Seamus Hafferty. My mentor entrusted me to oversee Seamus's care if Patrick or his wife were unable. I accepted this obligation without hesitation."

"Sensei, excuse me for interrupting, but what does this have to do with my parents?"

"Be patient. After my mentor and his wife died in an auto accident, I sent Seamus to Denver, Colorado, Patrick Hafferty's home. There he finished boarding school, attended university, and acquired a doctorate in metallurgy at the Colorado School of Mines."

She sensed Kenji's emotions rise, the way his eyes looked moist and not from coughing. She waited for him to continue. *Sensei told me my father had a doctorate in metallurgy!* "During university summer breaks, Seamus worked at JT to retain his proficiency in our language and culture. One summer, he met a woman who worked at the Comfort Station. Their relations produced a baby girl." He swallowed, holding back tears. "She sits with me today."

Natsu's jade eyes widened. "You're saying Seamus Hafferty is my father? I thought his name was Shimasuhafati."

"One and the same."

"I can't believe this! Why didn't you tell me this before?"

"Natsu-chan, I didn't have to. You are intelligent enough to connect the dots. I am surprised you didn't question this before."

"But, Sensei, I didn't believe it was my role to question you."

"Now is your opportunity," he replied. "Remember what Deming said, 'If you do not know to ask the right question, you discover nothing.'"

She knew Kenji was challenging her to be more demanding. "What else do I not know about Seamus?"

"You met him at an Osaka restaurant when he visited last year."

She immediately recalled the dinner where she met Sean O'Leary. "Sean O'Leary is Seamus Hafferty who was Shimasuhafati?"

"Correct. We changed Seamus's name when he relocated to the states. This protected JT's future options. He became JT's US resource to identify technology partners. He introduced IPS to JT. In fact, he is a co-inventor of the silver-lining technologies."

The puzzled look on Natsu's beautiful face disappeared. Remembering Sean's image, she sighed. "Always wondered about the source of my auburn hair, different eyes, and height." She removed her glasses and dabbed at her eyes. Her voice resonated with anger, "You deceived me all these years?"

"Natsu-chan, my motives were honorable. Until you acquired more life and career experience, earlier knowledge would not benefit you."

She knew Kenji realized she did not accept this explanation. "What have you not disclosed about my mother?"

"Her name is Natsuko Nashakatani. After your birth, she left Osaka."

She sat silent, absorbing Kenji's new revelation. "I must meet her ... where does she live?"

"Dear Natsu-chan, most unwise. She is married and has grown sons.

Reviving such memories would benefit no one. All this information must remain secret. Is that understood? Public disclosure leads to unfortunate consequences."

She did not acknowledge his request. "What else do I need to know about my family?"

"Ashi-kun, my long serving operations officer, is your oji-san. He is the older brother of your mother. He was upset at your mother when she became pregnant. He felt your birth was a family embarrassment."

"That explains a lot."

"What do you mean?"

"He treats me differently than other male colleagues at JT. I respect his seniority and service; but honestly, he is difficult to work with. Why is that?"

"Ashi-kun considers you a threat. He suspects I am grooming you for the top position at JT. For now, we must monitor his actions with a careful eye. He may betray us."

"I will be cautious. I must say, while I learned JT's operations, his quality training was excellent."

"That is good to know. If you want further confirmation of what I have told you today, please confer with Okazaki-san."

"Sensei, I will think about what you have told me." *I will consult with Okazaki-sama. Fortunately, he answers my questions without hesitation or evasion.*

"Remember what I told you several years ago. You possess the best blend of your parents' and your grandfather's traits. Let us adjourn to the library where we can continue." He held a handkerchief to his mouth and coughed violently.

She grabbed his arm, feeling guilt for the anger she had unleashed. Alarmed at how much he leaned on her, she asked, "Have you seen a doctor about your cough?"

"I will, Natsu-chan, don't worry. Cold weather irritates my lungs."

"Hai, Sensei."

He stopped. "Now dear Natsu-chan, I have a proposal."

She smiled. "But you've already given me so many."

"This is for the one part of your life we have yet to discuss."

It wasn't just Kenji's health that alarmed Natsu as she traveled back via bullet train after a restful holiday in Kyoto. Kenji's latest directive worried her. She ordered a glass of wine to calm her nerves. *He has no natural heirs so why so adamant that I produce one? Kobyashi-sama is not in a position to give such advice. He has been successful without heirs. I can be successful too. When I asked him why he never married and produced heirs, he claimed he was too busy with war, university, business, being my sensei, etc. Well… I'm also busy.*

Kenji wanted her to establish a closer relationship with *Debiddo* James. He stated Hakase Yamura had fully vetted Debiddo's history. She observed Debiddo's progress and inventive mind, first at Soft Dev, JT's software subsidiary. There, he dressed casually and talked at a rapid clip. He often acted annoyed when people couldn't keep pace. After joining JT, he secured five patents for appliance applications. Now, he spoke at a more measured pace and listened in an attentive manner.

Natsu and Debbido developed good working chemistry at JT. Kenji knew Debiddo was the primary inventor of the silver-lining technologies. Since his father, Pug James, had contributed very little to those inventions—despite his name on the patents—so said Kenji—Debiddo and Seamus were the real geniuses for technical innovation. Debiddo impressed Natsu with his ability to lead product development teams. She appreciated he could focus on technical matters, listen well, and willingly cooperate with her unlike other Japanese male colleagues.

But she was confused. *What does Kobayashi-sama mean by closer relationship? Marriage or something else?*

Debiddo wasn't bad looking. She liked his tall, lean and wiry physique. His dark hazel eyes combined with an engaging smile captivated her. She imagined how their children might look—the best features of both parents like she inherited from hers. Her problem was she didn't know how to initiate a closer relationship on her own or even take the first step to find a partner. There had been no time for traditional dating. And she would never select anyone without Kenji's blessing. Now, Kenji claimed he'd found the right candidate. He made the stakes high cautioning that the silver-lining technologies came with a curse.

Natsu ordered a second glass. *What were Kenji's words? Debiddo can assist in defeating this curse and ensure we exploit the full potential of the silver-lining technologies on a global basis. The technology, combined with your metal alloy patent, will create other markets besides appliances. And ... a joint venture with Debiddo will ensure your legacy. Debiddo is the enemy of JT's enemy, Pug James.*

But what Kenji had said next made her nervous. "Keep your shogi strategy in full view. Having heirs remains paramount. Debiddo will never equal your daimyo spirit or intellect."

Were she and Debiddo mere board pieces in Kenji's business shogi game? His shogi strategy had been very successful to date. She would talk with Okazaki-sama to verify.

She sipped the last of her wine and sighed. "Perhaps," she whispered to the rice fields flashing past her window, "Debiddo can be one of my loyal samurais."

The next three months, Natsu increased non-work interactions with Debiddo. She lingered at the office and labs and happened to be near his office when he left for the day. She complimented his technical work and asked him about hobbies. She read *Cosmopolitan* and *Glamour*, searching for the strategies for attracting a man. At last, he invited her to have drinks and dinner, followed by several more social interactions.

They exchanged commitment vows in a private ceremony in Kyoto in June 2001. Three witnesses attended—Kenji, Shiganari, and Suzi Yamamoto who came from New York City. The night before the ceremony, Suzi tutored Natsu about intimacy. Natsu's knowledge of kabuki theater would facilitate her physical responses.

After a brief two-day holiday, Natsu's Osaka house became their official residence.

She conceived in December, 2001, and a son was expected in August, 2002.

7
FRIDAY, MAY 17, 2002
OSAKA

NATSU AND DEBIDDO LIVED IN a quiet, upscale residential community. Kenji gifted the house when she finished graduate business studies at the University of Osaka. The renovated residence included state-of-the-art conveniences and 24/7 security. Natsu's collection of modern Japanese art and stylish furniture displayed her refinement and elegant tastes. The noted interior designer and daughter of Katsutashi Nakasuki, Kenji's friend, personally selected the furniture for each room capturing Natsu's vision for home décor— simplicity, strength, and her favorite color schemes. Wall hangings throughout the common areas had hand-painted quotes from famous female samurai. One particular hanging described the key to harmony in one's life. The designer utilized *kanso*, the Japanese equivalent of *feng shui*, which is all about harmonizing oneself with one's surroundings.

Debiddo opened a Sapporo while Natsu reclined on a sofa. She glanced at a framed photo resting on an ebony credenza. Taken in the 1950s, it showed Kenji with the three men—one Japanese and two Americans. Debiddo would never know that one of the Americans, Patrick Hafferty, was her grandfather.

"Debiddo, tell me more about your latest idea."

"Several weeks ago, I reviewed my old IPS lab books from 1998— looking for ideas to develop new combinations of materials to improve thermal, acoustic, and dimensional flexibility for appliance dissipaters. I stumbled across my notes about co-molding high-temperature plastics with the silver-lining metal alloys."

"A novel approach! Maybe my metal alloy patent could be used as well."

"Absolutely," he said.

"Why didn't you continue working on that while at IPS?"

"Long story-short, I demonstrated proofs-of-concepts for patent filings. Then Pops killed the project, said it had no potential. This happened at the same time Soft Dev recruited me. I saw no future at IPS, so I quit."

She smiled at his last comment. *Kobayashi-sama's shogi strategy in action.* "What should we do with this idea?"

"If it's okay with you, I'll form a small engineering team to brainstorm possibilities."

"Good idea!" *And at the right time, I'll contact Jackson Huntley about patent strategy. Another enemy of Pug James will be our friend.*

"Natsu, we should think about what other markets this co-molding approach can open for JT."

"Like what?"

"One of our engineers used to work at Toyota. He said if we could improve thermal and acoustic performance on exhaust systems, automotive OEM customers would definitely be interested."

"Interesting." *Maybe we can integrate software capabilities too.* "How should JT quantify the opportunities in this market?"

"In the appliance world, we do appliance system analysis to understand customer problems and then develop solutions. Now, we'll do the same but call them AESAs (Automotive Exhaust System Analyses). In this way, we can specify proprietary technical standards using our solutions. This shuts out potential competitors."

"How so?"

"Our engineers write the OEM specifications with the AESA data."

"Debiddo, that is most clever! 'Specify in' JT and 'specify out' competitors! Any idea how big this market might be?"

"Billions!"

Natsu made a mental note to brief Kenji. Her technical instincts told her Debiddo had a novel concept. *He's definitely one of my key technical samurai.*

As she rose from the sofa, she grimaced and pressed a hand to her abdomen.

"What, Kobito?" Debiddo asked. "Are you in pain?"

"It's nothing, just indigestion. Nothing to worry about."

She sensed he didn't accept her explanation. But Kenji had taught her that a daimyo leader must never show weakness. More important, she needed to get this new project launched. The co-molding idea was truly revolutionary.

8
MONDAY, MAY 20
BURLINGAME

P UG ARRIVED AT 7:00 A.M., made coffee, reviewed project
notes, and outlined his testing work.

At 8:20, the buzzer rang. Pug opened the door, checked his
watch and announced, "'Bout time, guys!" He held it open and pointed
to the conference room. "In there. Sit your butts down!"

Pug plunked down at the head of the table. "Name's Pug James."
He pointed at the wall clock. "Don't know what Fieldsy told you guys,
but get one thing straight! When you're told to report at 0800 hours,
that means 0800, and not a second later! Anybody here been in the
military?"

No one answered.

"Didn't think so!"

Danny Sullivan spoke. "Michael Fields told us to arrive at 8:30."

"Fieldsy's not your boss! Clear? An' one more thing—see where
Elon Musk just founded Space X? Guy's a real winner. You stick with
me, an' we'll rocket to Mars! Now, gimme your stories. You, tall guy with
red hair, start."

"Uh, well, my name's Danny Sullivan." His fair skin reddened as he
spoke, his blue eyes wide behind thick lenses. "I have a mechanical arts
associate degree from San Mateo Junior College."

"Hope you're better than the guy I fired." Pug enjoyed the confused
look on Danny's face. *Danny-boy looks like that traitor, Sean O'Leary.*
"So, Danny-boy, what you good at?"

37

Danny paused. "Mechanical design, 3D printing. I have experience in thermal testing of high-temp metal alloys and plastics."

Pug scribbled on his pad. *Danny co-molded?* "Okay, hope you can tell me three ways heat can transfer between layers of very thin aluminum foil membranes."

"Um ... well ..."

"Not now! I'll know soon enough if you know your stuff." Pug took a sip of coffee and turned to a dark-haired, stocky fellow on his left. "So, what's your story?"

"Name's Pete Wycoff. I've worked in the acoustics field for the last fifteen years. I'm good at testing all types of materials and combinations for acoustics."

"Where'd you learn about noise?"

"I worked for acoustics consultants whose clients included automotive and appliances. I'm interested in plastics and how they integrate with other materials to improve acoustic performance."

"How come you're not still workin' for 'em?"

"My last employer sold his consulting business to a Japanese firm. Didn't get along with the new owners. The Japanese take forever to decide. I looked for a new opportunity."

"So ya don't like them guys, huh? Me too. They stole my silver-lining technologies, an' I'm gettin' it back and makin' it great again!"

The techs looked confused as Pug scribbled on his pad. *Pete co-molded, acoustics and non-appliance applications. Bingo, Bango, Bongo.*

Pug turned to the nervous-looking third tech. Sensing weakness, Pug said, "Gimme your pitch, an' make it quick!"

Voice wavering, he answered, "Name's Sam Flores." Pug watched him fiddle with his watch and ring. Sam's shaggy hair and oversized rimless glasses shouted coding nerd. "My college studies focused on statistics and computer science. I've consulted for some firms." He stopped, cleared his throat, and took a deep breath. "I've got good expertise in databases," he added.

Pug slapped the table. "Now listen up! Don't care what any of you guys did 'till now. Since I didn't hire ya, ya prove yourselves everyday if ya wanna keep your job. Understand? I developed ten projects. Study 'em, and we meet in two hours after lunch to divvy the load."

Pug handed out project sheets and directed each man to an office. He returned to his office and closed the door. He reread the ten projects and hummed his favorite melody, *Look for The Silver Lining*. First up, put the techs through a testing boot camp.

Later, the techs lunched at Applebee's.

"What do you think of General Pug Patton?" Danny asked after they ordered.

"He's certainly no shrinking violet," Pete replied. "But I think he knows his technical stuff."

"Yeah, but kinda rude," Sam added.

"Mike Fields didn't give much background on Pug," Danny said. "I looked at Pug's patent portfolio. He's definitely an inventor."

Sam swirled his glass of iced tea and took a long swallow. "But something bothers me. He didn't prioritize the projects, talked only about lots of testing. Pug strikes me as a micromanager."

"They say Steve Jobs was a pain-in-the-butt micromanager who drove everybody crazy," Danny said.

Pete replied, "If Pug James has ten per cent of Steve's creativity, I'll put up with a lot of shit. Danny, what's Pug doing while we're testing?"

"Who knows?"

Sam looked at his watch. "Better get back. Don't want to be court-martialed on our first day."

They all laughed.

When they re-convened, Pug announced, "Okay guys, let's hear it."

Danny spoke first. "All the projects involve appliance applications and have thermal requirements that look straightforward. No big deal."

"Like your confidence, but tell me somethin' I don't know, like what materials to use for the best thermal performance?"

"I assumed the right materials. Just common sense."

Pug scowled. "Pug's first law of invention: don't assume nothin.'

Second law: don't forget the first law. Ya'll learn all my laws. Never forget 'em!"

Pete interrupted. "Several of these projects have acoustic requirements. That means different materials and combinations needed to optimize the thermal, acoustic, and dimensional metrics."

"See, Danny-boy, Pete's nailed the big kahuna. In fact, he's struck silver—the key to me finding new combos to solve customers' problems, including ones they don't know they got! We're gonna run every possible heat and noise test known to man. Why? Cuz that's how I develop the strongest patents. Guys, ya just learned Pug's third law of inventin'—patents are king in my world and never, I repeat, never forget it. If I catch any secret material lying around, there'll be hell to pay."

Sam raised his hand.

"Speak up, Sammy—don't futz around."

"Well, I see tons of testing, analysis, and retesting given what you said."

"That's why I'm putting you in charge of the data collection, analysis and report generation. I'll put your skills to a test, real damn fast."

Sam's shoulders relaxed, relieved to know what Pug expected from him.

Pug continued, "Danny'll head up the thermal testing for all materials, do the design and prototype work. Pete, you'll do the noise, vibration, and metric testing. You two'll research plastics and metal alloys to see the combo possibilities."

He set milestones for each testing program. Each technician would report his progress directly to Pug, and then he determined the next day's assignments.

"One more thing. Don't discuss any projects outside of this lab. Otherwise, your days here'll be kaput! Now get to work!"

After the techs left, Pug reviewed the test plans, satisfied he had assigned the right techs to right tasks. But his personal challenge was tougher, finding ways to optimize the co-molding of metal alloys and plastics. For that he needed some secret money. His thoughts immediately focused on Tiffanee.

9
MONDAY, MAY 20
SAN FRANCISCO

A T NOON, MICHAEL AND ELLIE Fields arrived in separate cars and parked near Ristorante Sienna in Cow Hollow. Giacomo, the owner, greeted them.

"Buon giorno, Signore e Signora Fields."

"Ciao, Giacomo. Bottle of Pellegrino?" Michael said.

"Si, Signore!" Giacomo did an about-face and departed.

"I love this restaurant," Ellie said. "The food tastes like my Italian grandmother's cooking."

"We can thank Pug for discovering this place."

"The only good thing that asshole ever did for you."

"I quit, didn't I?" *She's in a piss-ant mood today.*

"Yes, but now you're back trying to save IPS after Pug destroyed it. These last ninety days have been a living hell for you!"

"I know, I know…"

"Michael you're looking old—gaunt, ashen, your hair's thinner and grayer. How much weight have you lost?"

"A few pounds."

"Give me a break! You've lost at least twenty!"

"I'll get back to a normal work schedule, diet, gym workouts. As for you, you're looking prettier than ever." *Let's bag this topic about me.*

"Michael, don't change the subject."

"But it's true. You look better than ever. You doing something different?"

"Let's order. I'm hungry!" she replied.

"Okay." He pointed to the wine rack bolted to the brick wall. "See that wine display? Pug bragged he offered Giacomo a patented earthquake-proof wine rack in return for free food year-round."

"Yeah, I bet Giacomo said no way."

Michael noted her angry tone. "Look Ellie, PSW II will produce huge dividends for IPS with Pug's new inventions."

Ellie threw the menu aside. "How can you trust him now after he's betrayed you? Remember, he was the one who refused to discuss the IPS merger with JT after Kenji made an attractive offer to combine resources. All the shareholders would have benefited. The only shareholder Pug ever cared about was himself. That's why you quit when the deal went sour!"

Michael knew she was right, but he was determined to salvage Pug's inventive talent.

"Look, Ellie, Pug has only one option, the new Skunk Works. His psychiatrist at the VA hospital agreed."

"You talked to a psychiatrist?"

"We discussed Pug's rehab program before he got released."

"I don't care! I see no redeeming qualities in Pug James! He's unpredictable and irrational. Don't forget—this is the same guy who squandered IPS's valuable silver-lining technologies! He ruined his two sons' lives and left Marcy destitute. And he's betrayed your trust at MatraScience and at IPS. How can you still believe in him?"

"The meds have softened his renegade behavior, but he still has that creative spark. He acted like a new person when he saw the labs and my project list."

"Good luck believing that. Isn't today when he meets his new staff?"

"Yes, I gave the techs no clues other than copies of his patents. I wanted unbiased eyes and ears to observe him." *Not telling her about Sam's special assignment.*

Giacomo brought the Pellegrino and took their food and wine choices. After he left, Ellie asked, "Any word from Kenji on status of the Delaware Plan?"

"Waiting for his lawyer to send authorization to vote Kenji's Brunei Trust's shares in favor of the plan. Once we get that, you can execute the legal actions to elect a new board. Then, I can assemble the management team and move forward with the merger with Japan Technologies. If the Brunei Trust shares don't get voted, we'll be short ten per cent of the 51% hurdle. Thank god Pug and Marcy divorced, and their sons are gone. No single James controls the family's entire thirty-four per cent."

"Where can we find the ten per cent, worst-case scenario?" she asked.

"Not sure yet. Meant to tell you, Marcy's got a new boyfriend."

"Who?"

"Jack Daniels."

"Sad, but understandable given how Pug betrayed her."

"She called the other day talking about financial problems Pug left her. Then she mentioned Skip's situation. Says the Los Altos DA will reopen the murder investigation and interview suspects with motive to kill Annie Burr."

"Will the detectives interview you again?"

"Your guess is as good as mine."

"What else did she complain about besides money and Skip?"

"She mentioned Dave's wife, Tina, has been visiting Skip in jail."

"You gotta be kidding me! Why in the hell doesn't she get a divorce lawyer and sue Dave's ass? The dysfunction in the James family is a bottomless pit."

"At least, Pug's family problems won't distract him at PSW II."

"Since Marcy now owns fifteen per cent of IPS, what if some third party bought her shares on behalf of IPS?"

"Good question." He watched her eyes roll in disbelief at his non-answer.

"How much time do you give Kenji's lawyer to vote the shares?" she asked.

"Maybe you could visit Japan and jump start this. After all, you designed the Delaware Plan to get Pug out of IPS."

Giacomo delivered pasta primavera and refilled their glasses.

"Michael, what's the status on Pug's stupid patent malpractice against Dexter-Foresman?"

"That's why you and Jackson Huntley will meet to discuss a settlement."

"Jackson's bitter about Pug suing for patent malpractice and unprofessional behavior."

"I haven't talked to him since Pug started that whole mess. You can offer Jackson a retainer and the prospect of future patent and merger work."

They finished their meal. Michael looked at his watch. "Don't have time for dessert. Need to get back to the office. I have two interviews for the Chicago sales engineers. See you tonight about eight."

"I'll sit a while and have an espresso," she replied.

Michael knew Ellie was rapidly losing interest in helping save IPS. She certainly wanted no part in rehabilitating Pug. Sending her to Japan would be key to determine how much longer she would participate.

Ellie ordered a double espresso, took her phone from her handbag and dialed.

Giorgio answered in Italian. "Been dreaming about you."

"And I about you, Sweetheart," she said.

She adored Giorgio's classic profile inherited from his Sicilian parents. Thick, wavy hair matched his ebony eyes. Daily workouts kept his body trim. She fantasized how handsome their children would be had she married him first.

Their physical attraction began when he persuaded her to join his law firm, a decision she never once regretted. For years, they maintained a light-hearted flirtatious office relationship. However, over the last six months, their relationship grew intense.

She continued in Italian, "Just finished lunch with Michael. I'm so fed up with the IPS crap and Michael's naivete about Pug! Still trusts that asshole. Worse, Michael gets home late, leaves early—works weekends."

"Sounds like he's joined a Pug cult," Giorgio replied. "It's time you stopped your pro-bono work for an insolvent IPS and join me."

"Darling, bear with me. Michael wants me to go to Japan and jump start the Delaware Plan. Good opportunity for me to assess Kenji's plans and see if we can leverage that."

"Don't go there by yourself. It's male dominated."

"Look, I lived in Asia for five years and dealt with Asian chauvinists. I'll put on my 'big-girl' panties, okay?"

"You know I prefer them off."

She laughed but turned serious. "While Michael babbled about IPS, I had an idea. Why not contact Danielo? I have IPS's shareholder list. We buy IPS shares on the cheap and QT, get control of the silver-lining patents, then flip IPS to a competitor like Lawrent or maybe even to Kenji. I bet he'd like to own one hundred percent of IPS. But we have to move fast before the merger happens."

"I'll get on that! Your brilliant ideas are just one more reason I love you so much."

"You've mentored me well. Time we made some money off the IPS carcass."

Giorgio called Dan Abrillo. "Ciao, Danielo."

"Giorgio! What's up, buddy?"

Danielo Abrillo was CEO of Technovenia, a venture capital company that bottom fished for privately-owned, undercapitalized American technology companies. Then they flipped them to the highest bidder. Rumors circulated that Technovenia dabbled in international money laundering. Danielo excelled at keeping things looking clean and legal.

"Got a line on an undervalued company with unique proprietary technology—a series of valuable patents. We can buy the company's shares, do a quick turnaround, and sell it at a huge premium. Got a reliable inside source."

Giorgio knew Danielo was the right man for this task and would ensure it happened smoothly with minimum scrutiny.

"Send me info. If it looks good, I'll move fast.," Danielo concluded.

"I'll send the financials and names of three key shareholders who might be interested in dumping their shares—two individuals and an investment trust. One more thought. How's Technovenia's relationship with our Staten Island contact?"

"Technovenia has parked a lot of bucks in his properties. The guy's always looking for quick cash."

"Good. Once I'm back from overseas, we might get him in the mix to create distractions."

Giorgio smiled and ended the call. *On our way! El and I will get a nice payday and revenge for her.*

10
MONDAY, MAY 20
SOUTH SAN FRANCISCO (SSFO)

D RIVING TO IPS's OFFICE IN South San Francisco (SSFO), Michael thought about Ellie. *She's done a good job helping me these last crazy months. Today, she seemed unusually angry. Need to call Kenji about Ellie's trip and update Jackson before the Stanford conference.*

When he arrived, Michael's assistant *looked up from her phone.* "Marcy James on line one."

He looked at his watch and sighed. "Thanks. Tell her I'll be right there."

He entered his office and closed the door. Poor Marcy. A few years ago, she was a pretty blond, fashionable and perky. Last time I saw her, she was dressed in baggy sweats, seriously overweight, and chain smoking. Everything about her cried unhappy.

She told Michael she had not talked to Pug since viewing the anonymously-sent video of his sex with an Asian woman. She refused to visit him in the hospital after the stroke and during rehab. Her lawyer handled all communications. With no contest from Pug, their divorce finalized in record time. She now owned fifteen per cent of IPS. Despite getting full title to the house, the mortgage and equity loans exceeded the current market value. Her small 401K had disappeared.

"Hey Marcy, how are you?" Michael asked.

"Honestly? Not any better since we last talked. Any good news for me?"

"As Doug Aldrich, MatraScience's CEO, once said, 'When you're up to your rear in alligators, hard to remember your goal was to drain the swamp.'"

"That bad, huh?"

"Yeah, incoming appliance orders and shipments have declined. A major customer still won't buy the company's IPS 10000 dissipaters. Until new sales guys are trained, we won't see much improvement. I'm cutting expenses just to keep IPS from bankruptcy."

"I guess, uh ... you can't loan me money like we discussed last time?"

"Marcy, I haven't taken any compensation. Remind me again, how much money you need?"

"About fifteen thousand for the next few months. As you know, he left me a terrible mess. What's he doing now?"

Right now, you don't have a need to know; besides not sure I can trust you. "Does Dave know anything?"

"I don't talk to him since he abandoned his family to work in Japan. With Skip in prison, he refuses to talk with me. The detectives who arrested Skip want to talk again. Not sure why."

"Marcy, last time we talked, you applied for work. Any success?"

He heard the sound of liquid pouring. *Is that booze?*

"I wanted to work at my old interior design firm, but can't afford a full-time caretaker for Skip's kid. I'm part-time at Walmart for pocket money," she said.

"You have your hands full." Michael suppressed a yawn and glanced at *The Wall Street Journal.*

"Michael, any chance I could sell my IPS shares?"

He quickly put the paper down. "Marcy, you can always sell if you find a buyer."

"What share price could I get?" she asked.

"Your ex always valued IPS at two and half times book value per share. That only works when the value is positive." He heard her gulp.

"What are you saying?"

"IPS has a negative book value. That formula produces a negative price."

Michael heard more liquid pouring.

Marcy whined, "What do I do? These shares are the only liquid asset I have left."

"How about an equity loan on your house?"

"The SOB used all credit line before his stroke."

"Tell you what, I'll check with other shareholders and see if they want more shares. Unclear anyone wants to invest in a near-bankrupt company. Here's another idea—maybe I can find someone to loan you money using your shares as collateral. What do you think?"

"Michael, I could really use any help. I'm losing hope."

"I don't want you giving up those shares. I'm determined to make IPS whole again. That's why I became the CEO after Pug's stroke."

"Yes, I supported that. I'm sorry he treated you so badly."

"If anyone approaches you to buy your shares, check with me first. I'll work like hell to get you a better deal."

"God bless you, Michael."

"Take care, Marcy."

Michael sat there thinking about how he did and didn't feel sorry for her. She enabled Pug's dysfunctional behavior and betrayals. Then the sex tape arrived.

And Marcy had just presented Michael with an interesting opportunity. This was Plan B in case Dr. Y. didn't vote the trust shares in a timely manner. With Marcy's shares, he could implement the Delaware Plan. Only Kenji and Jackson Huntley would know about Plan B.

SFO

Michael arrived home around 9:00 pm. He sat at the table while Ellie brought dinner and a glass of cabernet sauvignon.

"So, how'd your interviews go?" she asked.

Michael sampled the wine. "Two good candidates. Competent engineers with proven sales skills. Reminds me of guys I hired at MatraScience."

"How was the rest of the day?"

"One crisis after another. Keeping irate vendors at bay, calling customers about their overdue payments, etc."

"Like I told you many times, Pug left you a huge mess. When do you see him again?"

He took a few bites. "That reminds me to schedule the first project review at the Skunk. For now, he's off my radar for a few weeks."

"Have you talked with any of the James family besides Pug?"

"Only Pug." *Why do you even care?*

"At lunch, you said I should go to Japan. You know Japan is a male-dominated environment. Shouldn't you go instead?"

"I'd love to but can't afford the time away. You know the Delaware Plan backwards and forwards. Besides—we lived in Asia—you know the ropes and as Pug would say the 'slopes.'"

"Michael, don't use that derogatory word. It's like you calling Chinese chinks or Koreans gooks. You know better than that."

"Sorry, I was just quoting a pugism."

"Well, don't anymore. I have no respect for that bigot."

He continued eating. *Jesus Christ, what's got into her? She used to laugh at the pugisms.*

"I'm going to bed. Clean up the dishes before you come upstairs."

He poured another glass of wine. *Japan's on despite her comments.*

11
WEDNESDAY, MAY 22
SAN MATEO

M ID-MORNING, MARCY'S CELL PHONE RANG. "Hello," she said.

"Ms. James, this is Dan Abrillo."

"Who?"

"I represent Technovenia. My company would like to invest in IPS. Would you be interested in selling your shares?"

Marcy paused. "How do you know I own shares?"

"Ms. James, public records indicate you recently divorced. California being a community property state, I assumed you got shares in the settlement. If this is incorrect, I won't waste your time."

"Why not contact my ex-husband about his shares?"

"We would, but we can't locate him. Do you have his phone number?"

"No!"

"Okay. Would you be interested in selling some or all of your shares?"

"Mr. Abrillo, excuse me for a few minutes, my grandson's fussing. I'll be right back."

"No problem. Take your time."

She put the phone down and poured Jack Daniels into a tumbler. Five minutes passed. "Sorry for the delay, but you know how little boys are when they go potty."

"Absolutely."

"Mr. Abrillo, uh…"

"Please call me Dan."

"Okay. But as I was about to say, IPS is privately owned. So, how can you make me an offer … when you can't possibly know how good the company is?"

"An excellent question. Sometimes when financial data is unavailable, we consider other factors like technologies. We understand IPS has developed silver-lining technologies. Its patents have interesting potential in markets like aerospace, construction, and power. With an equity interest in IPS, we can leverage our expertise to enter those markets."

Marcy sipped from the tumbler before replying. "What price do you have in mind?"

"Three dollars per share. Think about it. I'll call back in a few days. Okay?"

On a notepad, she jotted *150,000 X $3.00 = $450,000.* "Give me your contact number."

"My cell is 201-438-8500."

"Thanks." She ended the call and slumped to the sofa. She dozed—dreaming what $450,000 could do for her. When she woke, she dialed Michael's number.

Dan immediately dialed Giorgio.

"Hey buddy, how'd it go?" Giorgio asked in Italian.

"Marcy didn't seem overly excited about three dollars a share."

"Probably surprised her. My source tells me she's not smart."

"Good to know. Makes my follow-up with her easier. How high do we go if she wants more?" Dan wondered.

"If she'll sell all her shares, we can go to four bucks. But before that, do a full-court press and threaten to walk. She'll panic when she sees $450K go bye-bye. In the meantime, contact Pug James and test his interest. Here's Pug's number. When I return from my trip, you can approach the foreign shareholder."

"On it."

An hour later, Dan called Pug.

"Mr. James, my name is Dan Abrillo. I represent a venture fund, Technovenia."

"Yeah, so what? And hey, you Italian? You got the name and accent."

"Yes, sir, I am … and I understand you own shares in a company called IPS."

"None of your business."

"Sir, you sound like a no-nonsense guy. I'll cut to the chase. Would you be interested in selling some or all of your IPS shares?"

"This is a special company, an' I know. How much ya talkin' 'bout?"

"Mr. James, let's meet and discuss what makes sense for you. We might be able to do an all cash offer. What would be a convenient time and place?"

"Gimme your number. I'll get back to ya." *How in the fuck did he get my name and why the interest in IPS? But hey, if Tiff doesn't put out, Techno-what's-its-name might.*

12

WEDNESDAY, MAY 22
SOUTH SAN FRANCISCO/OSAKA

As EVENING FELL, MICHAEL PLUGGED away in the IPS office, previously occupied by Pug. All evidence of Pug's presence had disappeared—framed degrees, patents, military awards, photos of his Green Beret unit in Vietnam.

Michael's only renovation was re-painting Pug's army-green walls a pale air force blue. His decorating style looked sparse and conventional: a simple oak bookcase containing reference books, Asian history books and works of philosophers. Selected Shakespeare plays rested on the top shelf. Orderly "file-piles" of folders and documents covered the desk, credenza, and floor.

A placard on his desk stated, *Don't Waste This Virgo's Time!*

After Marcy's call regarding Technovenia's offer and in spite of the time difference, he dialed Kenji's number. They spoke frequently since Michael had returned as IPS's CEO.

"Good evening, Kenji. Trust I'm not calling too late."

"Not at all, Michael. I have been re-reading my favorite book by Sun Tzu."

"His *Art of War?*"

"Correct."

"What is your favorite principle of Sun Tzu?" Michael asked.

"That is easy to answer … using deception to defeat one's adversary."

"Interesting." Michael knew Kenji to be a master of this strategy.

He recalled how Kenji compromised Pug at the Comfort Station in the early 1990s.

"Just talked with Marcy James. A company named Technovenia wants to purchase her IPS shares."

"What do you know about this company?" Kenji asked.

"It's an Italian-based mezzanine investor that searches for financially distressed companies with good patents. Their money sources are questionable."

Kenji lit a Mevious and slowly exhaled. "How did Ms. James respond?"

"She's inclined to accept because of her dire financial problems."

"Michael, do not worry. Pug's and her shares are pledged as collateral for IPS's loans with Silverado Bank. Pug accepted those loan covenants when Silverado refinanced the credit line. Impossible for Ms. James to sell her shares without bank's approval."

Michael thought, *How does Kenji know about this collateral?*

Kenji took another drag. "Recently, you asked why I transferred cash to IPS from my personal accounts."

"Yes, I never understood why Silverado bank accepted those payments and postponed IPS's foreclosure."

"I own a controlling interest in this private bank. It allows me to keep certain cash transfers secret."

Michael thought, *And one more example of your deceptive talents. Pug never connected the dots between Silverado loans to IPS and Kenji.*

Kenji continued, "We Japanese are very cautious. Before I trust, I verify actions. You're aware of King Lear's mistakes?"

Michael glanced at his Shakespeare books. "Didn't know you read Shakespeare as well, Kenji!" *One more thing we have in common.* Kenji's next comment surprised Michael.

"Michael, you demonstrate a measured and thoughtful approach to decisions and actions."

"I appreciate your compliment. Right now, I feel like the proverbial Dutch boy plugging holes in the dike. I fix one problem, and two more appear."

"Michael, you have risen to challenges very well. When Ms. James decides to accept this or any other offer, inform her about the lien."

"Understand."

"Ms. James can be part of our deception," Kenji said softly as if it were a pact between them.

Michael smiled. *Kenji has a long-term plan and will reveal it in due course. Good thing I'm patient.*

"Who else covets IPS besides Technovenia?" Kenji asked.

"I can think of several—competitors like Lawrent, disgruntled shareholders, former employees, etc."

"Ms. James will be our pawn in our shogi game with adversaries."

"Makes sense. On another matter, my talks with Jackson Huntley and Dexter-Foresman have gone well. Soon, we can eliminate that obstacle so the merger can proceed."

"Excellent."

"A more urgent matter. For three weeks, Dr. Yamura hasn't returned my calls about the paperwork to vote your Brunei trust's IPS shares."

Kenji coughed and cleared his throat. "My apologies, Michael. Hakase Yamura assured me the shares would be voted promptly. Most disappointing."

"As you can imagine, these delays compound IPS's problems. Ellie, my wife, can travel to Japan to assist Dr. Yamura. She understands the plan's complexities. I've authorized her to act on IPS's behalf. She can be in Japan in late May. Is that convenient?"

"I will clear my and Dr. Yamura's calendar for that period. Sun Tzu would approve of your decision to send her. What else would you like to discuss?"

Michael smiled at Kenji's Sun Tzu reference. He knew Kenji understood.

"How has Dave performed since he joined Japan Technologies?"

"He demonstrates creativity and proposes many new product ideas for appliance applications," Kenji replied.

"I know you expect him to take a leading role after the merger."

"Yes, he can make significant contributions to our technical position. His executive coach works diligently to improve his management potential."

Michael considered this last comment. *Kenji doesn't sound very enthusiastic about Dave's future.* He was interrupted by Kenji's next statement.

"On another subject, I have a request, Michael. Do you know a lawyer with expertise in commercial real estate acquisitions in the United States?"

"My wife has excellent legal contacts with experienced real estate lawyers."

"Please have her contact Nashakatani-san to understand our requirements."

"I'll ask Ellie to follow up. Goodbye, Kenji."

"*Sayōnara,* Michael."

His mind switched gears as he dialed Ellie's cell. When she answered, he said, "Just talked with Kenji. He's upset Dr. Yamura hasn't voted the shares."

"What happened?"

"Unclear. When I told him you developed the Delaware plan, he specifically asked you to come and help jump start the process. You're going to Japan the week of May 27."

"How will Kenji react working with a woman?"

Michael sensed her annoyed tone. "Hey, while you're there, you can discuss other options to acquire the shares if the Brunei trust shares don't happen."

"Anything else?"

"Look, this is a great opportunity to use your legal smarts on an important matter for IPS and me."

"So, what do you want me to do?"

Michael could tell she was unhappy. Right now, attitude was the least of his concerns. This trip would confirm his increasing suspicions.

"Call Nashakatani-san. Kenji wants recommendations for an experienced US real estate lawyer to represent him in the US."

"Real estate. What's that got to do with Dr. Y? And who's Nashakatani-san?"

"Kenji's business associate for real estate investments," Michael said. "Kenji said some New York City real estate mogul seeks Japanese investors for his Staten Island condos."

"Staten Island? Sounds like Ronald Blunt."

"Kenji didn't say. Call Nashakatani-san and get the specifics."

The call finished, Michael dialed a Palo Alto number and left a message. "Japan's on! Do your voodoo at Stanford."

13
FRIDAY, MAY 24
OSAKA

H AKASE YAMURA ARRIVED AT JAPAN Technologies for his morning appointment with Kenji.

Kenji's office was designed by one of Japan's premier architects. It appeared in architectural magazines with its floor-to-ceiling glass walls and a spectacular panoramic view of a nearby lake and beautifully manicured park. One-of-a-kind furniture pieces designed by the legendary artist, Katsutashi Nakusaki, added to the office's stunning ambiance.

An assistant invited Yamura to sit at the enormous glass conference table where a shogi set rested at the center. Carved from burnished paulownia wood, the intricate shogi pieces depicted samurai warriors. Yamura stared at the opposite wall where a woodblock print hung. It depicted Miyamoto Musashi, one of Japan's greatest samurai swordsmen. Next to the print hung an ikigai schematic with イキガイ in the center.

Natsu sat in an adjoining room where she would watch and listen. A video camera provided a direct view of Yamura's face. Kenji insisted she witness this specific encounter.

Yamura stood when Kenji entered. The elegantly dressed men greeted each other with deep bows. At 78, Kenji's former trim physique and erect posture had declined due to painful arthritis. He kept his neatly groomed hair dyed coal black. Hakase Yamura, unusually tall— six feet, three inches—towered over Kenji's five feet, seven inches.

Natsu considered Yamura's rimless spectacles and jaunty bow ties quirky, yet a bit endearing. She knew Kenji had never doubted Yamura's unquestioned loyalty and responsive service. For over thirty years, Yamura had been a faithful samurai warrior who fixed a myriad of problems with utmost discretion and precision.

"*Kon'nichiwa*, Kobayashi-sama," Yamura said. "You had a nice weekend?"

"I relaxed at Mt. Fuji." Kenji replied.

Natsu observed Yamura's subtle smirk when Kenji mentioned Mt. Fuji. She wondered what Dr. Yamura was thinking.

The assistant poured tea, offered biscuits, and departed.

"Hakase Yamura, we have important issues to discuss."

"Will Ashi-kun join us?"

"I will brief him after he returns from Hokkaido," Kenji responded.

Natsu thought, *Are you afraid Kobayashi-sama might discuss something with no witnesses?*

Hakase Yamura continued, "Understand. Ashi-kun has been your loyal lieutenant for over thirty-five years. He looks forward to undertaking more responsibilities when you retire. He has devoted every waking hour and sacrificed personal desires to help build a successful JT."

"Hakase Yamura, you need not tell me what I already know."

Natsu was pleased with Kobayashi's quick reply. *Hakase Yamura should apologize.*

"Ashi-kun's heavy smoking cannot be good for his health," Kenji added.

Natsu wondered, *Kobayashi-sama, you should follow your own advice!*

"How is Natsuko?" Hakase Yamura asked.

Natsu was startled. *Why does he concern himself with my mother?* She watched as Yamura's hand slipped into his coat pocket. She thought, *Yamura records conversations too. He must have studied Sun Tzu.*

"Ashi-kun reports his sister is happy with two sons and a caring husband."

Natsu pondered this last exchange. *That's exactly what Kobayashi-sama told me.*

"Has Seamus honored your agreement?"

She made a note to investigate this agreement.

"He ceased searching long ago," Kenji noted.

"Do you wish me to continue monitoring Seamus?"

"No."

Natsu laughed as she saw Yamura make a note on his legal pad. *Can't you remember a simple no?*

Kenji handed him a one-page document:

Delaware plan for IPS.

Succession plans for JT, Thermal Acoustic Device Association (TADA), and IPS.

Kenji lit a cigarette and sipped tea to clear his congested throat. "Let us discuss the Fields's Delaware Plan. You know the details."

"Hai, he devised a clever shareholder action plan to restructure IPS."

"As I already instructed, the Brunei trust must vote its IPS shares for this plan. Then, Mr. Fields can implement the Delaware plan and subsequent merger with JT."

"My apologies, but your other critical priorities intervened during the past weeks. I will attend to this."

Natsu thought, *What critical priorities?*

"Advise me when the shares are voted. Hostile forces, both known and unknown, want to destroy IPS and control its portfolio of silver-lining patents."

"Hai." Yamura responded.

"Let us review the succession plan. Natsu's son will arrive soon. She and her son will sustain the family legacy. She will oversee the development, growth, and management of JT and the eventual merger with IPS."

Natsu watched Yamura's eyebrows furrow as he drew a linen handkerchief from his pocket, removed his glasses, and wiped his eyes. She could tell he disagreed with Kenji.

"But with all due respect, Kobayashi-sama, a woman cannot provide face for a Japanese company."

Natsu thought, *There it is. Yamura is our enemy.*

"Debiddo will serve as face," Kenji said.

"They cannot handle such a challenge in our current business environment."

Natsu thought, *Yamura, you don't know this woman daimyo's capabilities.*

Kenji replied, "They can and will with you, Marken-san, and myself assisting."

Yamura nodded. "Does she know her true heritage?"

"She knows only how her parents passed."

Natsu remembered Sun Tzu's advice about deception. *It's clear my sensei no longer trusts Yamura.*

"Where does Ashi-kun fit into the future organization?" Yamura asked.

"With your advice, we will determine a suitable role."

"Hai, he wishes to assume more responsibilities."

Kenji coughed repeatedly. "You mentioned that before."

Natsu observed Yamura's expression of deference that disguised something else. This irritated her. She knew Kenji was annoyed with Jun as he constantly asked Kenji when he planned to retire. Kenji's confidence in Jun had deteriorated.

Kenji answered, "You and I will take steps to implement the succession plan. Give me your thoughts in five days."

Natsu couldn't wait to hear Yamura's specific recommendations. *I'm not optimistic.*

Both men stood, exchanged bows, and Yamura departed.

Natsu saw Kenji grab his chest and cough as if in pain. *The cough worries me.*

Kenji spoke out loud, "Well, Yamura, you must always do what your head *gesu yarō* wants."

Natsu chuckled as she left to attend a project review.

His cell phone rang. Kenji answered, "Kon'nichwa, Shiganari."

"Kenji, how was your meeting?"

"As we suspected, Yamura rejects the succession plan. He delays voting the trust's shares and offers only excuses. I now seriously doubt his loyalty."

"He violates the samurai code. What do we do?"

"Instruct your associates to accelerate their investigations. Research links between Yamura, our competitors, and a Technovenia venture fund. Also increase surveillance on Ashi-kun. He seems distracted and worried."

"Perhaps Ashi-kun realizes Natsu will succeed you. After you officially announce her role, maybe Ashi-kun will accept it and pledge his loyalty to her. She may find a suitable role for him."

"I have serious reservations. Ashi-kun attempts to deceive me with his sycophantic behavior, and he still harbors resentment towards Natsu. His seniority alone no longer entitles him for advancement. Natsu will lead JT and become one of Abe-san's pioneers for womenomics."

"I will alert the Yamaguchi-gumi boss. I suspect Yamura has contacted some of the boss's former associates who were expelled from the organization."

"I will talk with Debiddo then have dinner with him and Natsu." Kenji paused for a moment. "Another matter: Ronald Blunt will visit Osaka in a few days to discuss purchasing three of our properties." Kenji lit another cigarette.

"Are you smoking again? You know it irritates your lungs."

"I know, I know. Natsu will organize the Blunt meeting but will listen by audio link. Blunt has no need to know about our secret weapons in Osaka and in the US."

"Kenji, have you read Mr. Blunt's first book, *It's Not Stealing, It's Business?*

"No."

"Worth reading before you meet him."

Kenji eyed the book resting on his credenza. "I will consult Sun Tzu and not disappoint Blunt. We'll talk later this evening. Sayōnara."

Natsu returned to the video room to observe Kenji's next meeting.

At three o'clock sharp, Debiddo entered Kenji's office. "Kon'nichiwa, Kobayashi-sama. Always my honor to see you. How are you?"

"No serious complaints other than old age. My body declines faster than my mind." Kenji smiled tightly, suppressing a cough.

Natsu knew his chest discomfort had been particularly bad these past weeks.

"Cigarette?" Kenji asked.

"Natsu asked me to stop for our son's sake."

"I too, should follow her wise advice."

Natsu thought, *Kobayashi-sama, I wish you would actually listen to me.*

Tall and well-dressed in a dark blue suit and maroon tie, Debiddo appeared a respectable businessman, his hair neatly and professionally styled. Natsu was pleased Debiddo had matured. She hoped their son would inherit his best physical traits.

"Debiddo, give me your technical report."

"Sir, Natsu prepared this summary of my current projects for appliance applications. She outlined the status of each project in concise terms."

Natsu was pleased Debiddo publicly recognized her contributions unlike Japanese male colleagues.

"Her technical training gives her a unique perspective," Kenji said.

"Please review at your convenience. Natsu and I are looking at unique combinations of materials to improve thermal, acoustic and dimensional flexibility of appliance dissipaters—specifically co-molding the silver-lining technology metal alloys with high-temperature plastics."

"Debiddo, Natsu briefed me on this project. You are to be commended. Tell me from your perspective why IPS did not pursue this project?"

Natsu awaited Debiddo's response. *Will his answer be consistent with what he told me?*

Natsu observed a change in Debiddo's cheerful demeanor.

"After I demonstrated proofs-of-concepts for patent applications, my dad killed the project."

"Why would he do that?"

"He was jealous he didn't think of it first. Made me mad. Saw no future with IPS. All this happened about the time SoftDev recruited me."

Natsu knew this from the information furnished by Yamura. It was good to hear his honest feelings about his father. *Frankness: Americans can be especially direct and that is always advantageous for us.*

Kenji continued, "Let us discuss another matter. JT and IPS will merge to form a global entity. JT will completely own the silver-lining technologies. But there are adversaries who oppose us. Natsu will rely on you to combat these threats."

"I will support Natsu to my fullest ability."

Natsu smiled at Debiddo's enthusiastic reply. *This lady daimyo values your loyalty.*

"Sir, I have one question. Should I consult with Hakase Yamura and Ashi-san?"

Kenji did not hesitate. "No, for now, we keep this secret." Kenji glanced at his watch. "Time to leave for the restaurant. We will continue our discussions at the Comfort Station."

Natsu thought about Debiddo's last question. *Can we trust Debiddo to keep this secret?*

The Comfort Station began as a former rest and recuperation facility for the imperial army, a shameful footnote to its history of young Korean women forced to provide sex for the soldiers. In the early 1950s, it converted to a restaurant and private rooms for conducting mizu shobai. Kenji and Shiganari bought the business in the mid-1960s. It became their favorite location for facilitating after-hour business deals for JT and Hondoya.

Natsu enjoyed this restaurant for private reasons she never discussed with anyone. Here, she excelled at business transactions on an equal footing with male counterparts—unlike how women were treated in the early history of this location. Second, this is where she learned valuable relationship skills from her mentor, Suzi Yamamoto. Although Suzi now lived in New York, the two women maintained a close friendship and communications. Suzi advised her on managing men.

This evening she would continue honing her role as JT's future leader.

Kenji had booked his private dining room. Natsu arrived and greeted him with a customary bow.

"My dear Natsu-chan, your beauty always amazes."

"Kobayashi-sama, you are most kind." Natsu, quite pregnant, wore an elegant blue-green silk dress and jade necklace, one of Kenji's many gifts. She moved to Debiddo, who gave her a light kiss on the cheek.

She waited for Kenji's gesture to sit on the tatami. As she reclined, she felt a stabbing pain in her stomach. She showed no reaction.

The hostess brought Sapporos for the men and mineral water for Natsu. A tray of edamame and nori rolls followed. She did not wait for the men to start eating. During her pregnancy, she ate less to control her weight. As a result, she was constantly hungry. Her doctor advised her to eat more.

She smiled and said, "I remember my first business position at this restaurant. I have fond memories of that time and of my friends, especially my first manager, Yamamoto-san."

Debiddo asked, "Who was he?"

"She! Yamamoto-san taught me the importance of relationships in business—that success in business requires solid relationships with customers, partners, and government authorities. You must remember that." She noticed Kenji's subtle smile.

"My dad always said technology was king. Without that, there's no progress. He ignored relationships."

"That is why IPS never achieved its potential with the silver-lining technologies. We will not make that mistake at JT," Natsu said firmly.

She again saw Kenji's knowing smile and understood his concerns about Debiddo's general management potential.

The hostess brought the next course—the house specialty—Kobe beef. Side dishes of rice and vegetables accompanied the perfectly grilled meat.

"Debiddo, did you brief Kobayashi-sama about our special project?"

"I started to, but he said you already did that."

She sensed Debiddo's disappointment. She continued, "Kobayashi-sama, I will keep you informed of progress on this project." She noted Kenji's approving nod. "And Kobayashi-sama, what did you want to tell us about the future management of Japan Technologies?"

Kenji stubbed out his cigarette and emptied his beer glass. "Debiddo, you will oversee the technical operations. After the baby's birth, Natsu will return full time to direct all JT operations. But in Japan, for now, a man must appear as the business face. Natsu will direct but from a silent position. Debiddo, do you understand?"

"Yes, sir."

"Natsu-chan, your thoughts?"

"Arigato for the trust you have placed in me. I will not fail you."

Dinner finished and dishes cleared, the hostess served sake. Kenji raised his cup. "I propose a toast to your successful venture, your future, and your children." Debiddo raised his cup; Natsu raised a glass of mineral water.

Kenji continued, "Do not underestimate our many challenges. Michael Fields and Marken-san can assist."

Natsu again nodded. For Debiddo's benefit, she asked a series of rehearsed questions. "I understand Marken-san, but why Michael Fields?"

"JT and IPS will combine operations. Michael Fields will facilitate this merger from the US perspective while you manage Japanese considerations."

"What is the merger status?" she asked.

"An excellent question. Michael will send a legal representative to finalize plans. Until then, keep this information confidential. That is all for this evening. Return home and enjoy the rest of the evening."

They bid farewell and left in their chauffeur-driven cars. Natsu was exhausted and uncomfortable. She made it clear she did not want to talk during the drive home.

Her thoughts alternated between the pregnancy and her business duties. On the one hand, it was important to produce a natural heir, but she resented that it took nine uncomfortable months out of her life. Her condition prevented one-hundred percent concentration on business. Yet, she felt responsible for everything. Kenji had placed her in an impossible dilemma.

At home, Debiddo went to the kitchen to get a Sapporo while Natsu reclined on the sofa. When he joined her, he said, "Kobayashi-sama gave us much to consider." He put his arm around her. She pulled away.

"*Kobito*, what's bothering you?"

"Debiddo, it's so easy for you! You only have to worry about technical matters and act the face role for JT. This pregnancy is a burden you do not have to bear. It is most unfair!"

She watched his stunned silence. *He is at a loss for words.*

"What would you want me to do?"

"Do your technical job and make sure there are no surprises. I'll figure out the rest. We will follow Kobayashi-sama's direction without fail."

She saw Debiddo silently nod. She knew he would obey, confident he understood his role.

Later that evening, Kenji called Shiganari.

"Kenji, I expected your call."

"What more have you learned about Hakase Yamura?"

"Your suspicions proved correct. My associates report he frequently contacts two former subordinates of Yamaguchi-gumi's boss."

Kenji exclaimed, "When he accepted my employment, Hakase Yamura assured me he no longer associated with those people!"

"Hai! Perhaps, in hindsight, one never truly leaves. I suspect he uses those contacts to conduct nefarious activities."

"Why involve them?"

"I do not know, but we should prepare for uncomfortable consequences. It is important that Natsu have plausible deniability," Shiganari added.

"Agreed. We will increase our personal security details and for Natsu-chan and her son." Kenji's immediate thoughts turned to the Brunei Trust. *Has Yamura misappropriated our assets?* "Who else has he contacted?"

"My Hondoya associates report he met with senior executives at Gano-Nippon and General Appliance of Japan. You know what that means?"

"Hai! He reveals our commercial plans and secrets to appliance competitors and their *keiretsu* affiliates."

"This disrupts the merger plans with IPS and the supply of JT's dissipaters to Hondoya and other OEMs."

"This cannot happen," Kenji replied.

"We will increase our activities at Hondoya and JT to counter these threats. What about Ashi-kun?"

"I suspect Hakase Yamura has corrupted him. We must supplement your investigations of both men," Kenji concluded.

He left an encrypted voice message to Natsu. "Begin trust audit."

14
SATURDAY, MAY 25
MT. FUJI

K ENJI GREETED SEAMUS WHEN HE arrived at his lodge. "Kon'nichiwa, Seamus."

"Kon'nichiwa, Kobayashi-sama. Arigato for meeting with me."

Kenji was pleased Seamus spoke Japanese, indicating he retained his fluency.

Kenji coughed repeatedly. "I apologize for this head cold and sinus infection."

They entered the lodge's great room which displayed numerous souvenirs from Kenji's foreign travels and safaris. One wall contained a floor to ceiling bookcase with books collected over forty years. Atop gigantic Persian carpets rested rustic Indonesian furniture built to Kenji's specifications. Pictures on the tables testified to Kenji's close relationships with senior government officials. This room always impressed first-time visitors who realized the owner was well read, globally savvy, and well connected at the highest levels of business and government. It had been several years since Seamus visited here.

"Sapporo?" Kenji pointed to the bar fridge.

"Arigato." Seamus grabbed a beer, discarded his Nicorette gum, took a long swig, and sat opposite Kenji. Between them, a hand-carved marble samurai shogi set rested on a glass table. It complimented daimyo and samurai warrior pictures hanging on the walls. A picture of

Tokugawa Ieyasu hung prominently on one wall. He was a daimyo who unified Japan which led to two hundred years of peace.

"Seamus, I did not expect to see you again after our arrangement." Kenji studied Seamus's expression. Seamus's uncertainty was evident. Kenji would leverage that advantage.

"I seek your forgiveness," Seamus replied, diverting his eyes away.

Kenji drew a long puff and coughed. *A sincere request? Most unexpected.*

"Seamus, please explain."

"Until now, I believed you hid the truth about Natsuko and my daughter. I engaged a private detective to find the truth."

"And you did that despite my warning that revisiting painful memories created more problems? You accepted my payment and promised to cease searching." *Seamus, you betrayed me again.*

"Hai, I violated our agreement and now feel honor-bound to return the monies."

"Why did you disregard our agreement?"

"I needed closure on the most traumatic event in my life since my parents died. I grieved when Natsuko disappeared. She was my only true love. I did not know she was pregnant when she disappeared. I would have married her and taken her to the US."

Until now, Kenji hadn't considered Seamus's deep feelings for Natsuko. "Why did you choose to use a private detective?"

"Kobayashi-sama, I knew you and Hakase Yamura would monitor my activities. My detective located Natsuko in Sapporo, Hokkaido. After meeting her, I now understand."

Kenji remained silent letting Seamus continue. *Seamus has learned the intelligence trick of Hakase Yamura.*

"Natsuko explained what happened. First, she was deeply embarrassed at becoming pregnant. She refused your offer to stay in Osaka and expressed sincere gratitude for relocating her to Sapporo, finding her a job, providing financial assistance to start a new business, and most importantly for taking care of her daughter."

"All you mentioned, I remember. Did she tell you why she wanted to leave Osaka?"

"Hai. She said her oji-san Ashi claimed she humiliated the family name. He ordered her to leave Osaka. This compounded her own embarrassment."

"Most interesting." *Ashi-kun never discussed that with me.* "So, how did she react when you told her about Natsu?"

"I showed her pictures of our beautiful and intelligent daughter. I explained that Natsu is pursuing a business career. Natsuko said a huge burden of guilt had vanished. Finally, we agreed to maintain our secret so her husband and sons will never know."

"Good. What do you plan to do with your new insight?"

"Kobayashi-sama, I misunderstood your motives, but I now understand why you kept this quiet. You were protecting both mother and child. I didn't have the wisdom ... or maturity to appreciate that."

Kenji offered a cigarette to Seamus. Seamus declined. "You stopped smoking?"

"Hai. I quit a year ago."

"I too should follow your lead." He lit another cigarette and opened a new Sapporo. He knew Seamus wanted approval. He would not oblige.

"Please accept the return of the remaining monies." Seamus said.

"Seamus, I honor my agreements."

"But I'm duty bound to repay you."

Kenji paused, his thoughtful demeanor again interrupted by needing to clear his throat. "Seamus, let us continue this discussion over lunch."

They drove to a nearby restaurant without talking. After ordering Sapporos, Kenji said, "Seamus, you asked about repayment. I have some thoughts."

"I am at your service, Kobayashi-sama."

"Recently, I conveyed the truth to Natsu about her parents. She now appreciates her heritage and essential role in continuing your father's legacy."

"How did she react?"

"Debiddo never needs to know her true heritage. Understood?"

"Hai."

"However, Debiddo would welcome your technical collaboration. He always considered you his technical mentor."

"I can do that. What about Natsu?"

"She needs time to become comfortable with her heritage and

to incorporate it into her plans. She possesses wisdom to optimize the best outcomes. As for another repayment, I want you to act as her confidential commercial advisor." Kenji sensed Seamus's positive reaction. Kenji knew this played to his strengths.

"I would be honored to help her, and it's the least I can do for my daughter. Over time I hope to prove I'm worthy of her understanding and trust."

"That will depend on how she views your actions. Another repayment involves Hakase Yamura. He disrupts my succession vision by using adversaries to interfere … and to harm Natsu. That must not happen."

"What adversaries?"

"Gano-Nippon and Lawrent and possibly others. Your intimate knowledge of both companies can assist in defeating their nefarious actions. Hakase Yamura conspires with them to betray Japan Technologies and IPS. Meet Natsu at your earliest convenience to develop a response to Gano-Nippon. Likewise, work with Walter Marken and Michael Fields to address Lawrent's threat. These adversaries must not steal the silver-lining technologies."

"I welcome this challenge." Kenji could see that Seamus grew more excited. "What about Ashi-san?" Seamus asked.

"As you know, he blamed you for embarrassing the Ashi family. We suspect he conspires with Hakase Yamura and cannot be trusted. It is best you avoid direct contact with both. However, if you learn of any disloyalty, let me know."

"Sad that two of your loyal employees have disappointed you."

Kenji studied his face. *A most ironic comment coming from you. But I expect you will monitor Ashi-kun on my behalf.*

Bento boxes arrived accompanied by more beer. They began eating, dipping sashimi and sushi in soy sauce and wasabi.

Kenji placed his chopsticks on the edge of the bento box and spoke in a firm voice. "Now, comes your most important repayment. We enter dangerous times. There can be no hint or sign of corruption. Do not engage in any of your past activities—not only for Natsu's sake, but to respect your father's memory. Do I have your solemn vow?"

Seamus stared down at the bento box, his hand suspending the chopsticks. At last, he lifted his reddened face and looked directly into Kenji's eyes. "I will never again dishonor you, or Natsu … or myself."

To Kenji, Seamus appeared sincere. But once again, Kenji would not make the King Lear mistake.

"Excellent! Meet with Natsu as soon as possible. I will inform her of your commitment."

"Arigato, Kobayashi-sama. You have been very understanding."

"Let us enjoy our meal." They raised glasses.

Kenji knew Natsu would review the video and voice recordings of his conversations with Seamus. *Natsu will verify your behavior before she believes your words.*

15
SUNDAY, MAY 26
OSAKA

O N SUNDAY, NATSU WAS AT her office to catch up on work and to review videos and recordings from Kenji's meeting with Seamus. She knew Kenji wanted her to make an independent assessment. As she watched, she jotted thoughts on her note pad:

Seamus violated an agreement he struck with Kobayashi-sama. Can he be trusted with future agreements?

But if he hadn't violated this agreement, I would never know the complete story except for Kobayashi-sama's version.

Seamus did not know my mother was pregnant with me or what happened to her. I understand his subsequent actions. He loved her and felt betrayed when she disappeared.

I am impressed with Seamus's intellect and cleverness in discovering the truth. He knew Kobayashi-sama and Hakase Yamura would monitor him. I hope I have inherited these traits.

I must be careful about Oji-san. He, not Kobayashi-sama, was responsible for putting my mother in exile in Sapporo. I see why Oji-san despises me. Can we ever reconcile?

I can monitor Seamus's actions to verify his words. Kobayashi-sama gave him very specific assignments. I need to learn more about this corruption that Kobyashi-sama mentioned.

16

SUNDAY, MAY 26

HILLSBOROUGH, CALIFORNIA

AT HILLSBOROUGH'S FINE WINE & Spirits Store, Pug purchased a magnum of Chianti Classico Reserva and a bottle of Cakebread Chardonnay. At the florist next door, he selected a bouquet of fifteen red roses. As he paid, he exclaimed to the clerk, "I'm goin' over Niagra tonight!"

"Pardon me?"

Pug laughed. "Private joke."

The taxi eased along a two-block drive lined with giant palms. At the end, the drive circled around to a portico surrounded by elaborate landscaping. Stone steps led to the front door.

"Jesus Christ! What a palace! Must be 12,000 square feet and three stories high." Pug handed the driver a fifty-dollar bill. "Keep the change. This is my lucky night!"

Pug pressed the doorbell and waited.

"Pug! So happy to see you!" Tiffanee kissed him. "Such nice wine, and the roses are gorgeous!"

"Count 'em."

"There are ... fifteen?"

"Babe, fifteen years since you and me met."

"That's so sweet! Let me show you around."

Pug examined a tapestry hanging above a hall table. The intricate pattern had four intersecting, concentric circles surrounding the motif, イ キ ガ イ.

Where've I seen that? He racked his brain. *Maybe a Jap restaurant?*

Pug was awestruck as they toured the home with its massive rooms, vaulted ceilings, and ceiling-to-floor windows. The dining table could accommodate twenty persons. His engineering eye admired the construction. *If I got my name on this deed, I could take out a big loan!*

"Tiff, this house is top notch. These floors hardwood cherry?"

"Brazilian cherry."

"Love the crown moldings. The place's got my approval!"

"Glad you like it. The upper levels have bedrooms, sitting areas, a library, and three offices." She winked. "Show you later."

Pug smiled. *Babe, that's why I brought my Niagra!* "How long you lived here?"

"Alan bought this house in the early nineties. Previous owner went bankrupt, and as Ronald Blunt would say, a 'steal of a deal.'"

"You know Blunt?"

"Yes, he and Alan partnered on several California real estate deals."

"*Playboy* said he made billions doin' big deals."

"That's what the tabloids say."

"The guy speaks his mind and knows how to deal. Gotta love that!"

She laughed. "Pug, you're not shy either."

They strolled to the rear of the house passing through wide double doors. Comfortable chaises lined the glistening Olympic-sized pool. A fountain, banked by beds of impatiens, lobelia, and alyssum, splashed softly. Pug glimpsed, in the distance, the tennis court. He was astounded. *It's a fuckin' resort!*

"Rather than eating in the main dining room, I thought we'd enjoy dinner by the pool," Tiffanee said. The maid arrived with Prosecco and an antipasto platter. "Thanks Linda," Tiffanee said, handing a flute of bubbly to Pug. "I thought we'd start with Italian champagne."

Pug relaxed. "Babe, what a beautiful pool."

"Alan always enjoyed this area. He and Blunt sealed many deals here. At Kuletos, you said you bought a company in South San Francisco (SSFO), went into big debt, took on a lot of risk. Alan often said that's how Blunt did his deals."

"Sounds like he's my carbon copy."

"Always enjoyed watching Blunt in action. Reminded me of watching you invent and sell MatraConnect 5000 in 1987. A real thrill!"

"Tiff, gimme time, and I'll show ya I haven't lost a beat."

"Can't wait. So, tell me more about your bango and bongo."

With a full mouth of prosciutto and provolone, he answered, "Got me this company after tough negotiations. Owner wanted more money. We argued for weeks. Finally, usin' my sales skills, got 'im to lower the price near my first offer. He caved, an' best part, I made 'im finance the deal."

"Reminds me, I have something for you." She got up and headed into the house. Pug admired her shapely legs and curves conforming to the smart designer skirt. She returned with a book. "This is a fast, entertaining read."

Pug looked at the title, *It's Not Stealing, It's Business*. On the title page, he read the inscription: *To Alan and Tiffanee, You guys are terrific! Enjoy my masterpiece.* Signed in exaggerated script, taking over most of the page: *RONALD BLUNT.*

"Did you make Blunt a lot of money?"

"Yes…"

Pug interrupted, "How much?"

"Alan told me it was over a hundred million dollars."

"Whoa, nelly! What did you do with your share?"

"More property deals, and we even invested in non-real estate."

"Like what?" *Babe, I'm gonna tap you in more ways than one—money, lotsa rolls in the hay, who knows what else?*

"Alan liked Silicon Valley companies with new technologies. We took some excess cash, formed a JV— a joint venture—with Blunt to fund inventors with new technologies."

"JV's active?"

"Right now, it's dormant because Blunt wants to invest only in real estate. The JV's cash is currently in CD's. My stepson looks for investments but so far nothing."

Pug watched her pour more Prosecco. "You stick with me, Babe, and I'll show you some super stuff."

"Pug, you mean like you did in 1987?"

"Better!"

The maid announced, "Ma'am, Chef Sergio says dinner is served in fifteen minutes."

"Perfect. So, Pug, what happened after you purchased the South San Francisco company?"

"Time to start doin' my thing."

"You mean more bar-napkin moments?"

"Yep!"

"Like your MatraConnect 5000 invention?"

"Better, cuz I owned the patents, not MatraScience. I created IPS 10000—the first of my silver-lining technologies. I'm like Steve Jobs, know what customers need before they do. Totally interrupted the appliance industry with my dissipater products."

"Pug, I admire your 'can do' spirit! You said you 'Pearl Harbored' something. What was that?"

"Here's the deal: I'm at this Denver appliance trade show introducing IPS 10000 dissipaters and guess who stops at my booth? None other than an oriental who loves my silver-lining inventions, patents, and products. One thing leads to another, and soon he invites me to Osaka to strut my stuff to big wheels in the appliance industry. Couple of months later, he licenses my technology. Took the bucks I made on this deal and started my US business, an' bango, I'm off to the races. With money rollin' in, I invented more silver-lining stuff. Now, I'm attackin' other markets like water heaters, toasters, aerospace, construction. My company's sproutin' like Jack's beanstalk! The oriental guy comes back and makes me a 'Don Corleone' offer. Wanted to buy my company and all my patents. Did the deal and retired."

"What happened to the bongo part? Did I miss something?"

"Think about it. Bingo, I bought me the company by doing a fantastic steal. Bango, I got the Jap to give me the moola that funded my US startup. Bongo, I sold my company back to 'im who gave me the money to start the US business. Bingo, bango, and bongo! Pearl Harbored Japan big time with its own money! Laughed all the way to Silverado."

"Silverado?"

"The name of my private banker."

Tiffanee sat silent for a few moments processing his story. "Very impressive. What did you do with all your money?"

"Excuse me, Tiff. You got a gent's room?"

"Inside and turn right. Can't miss it."

"Be right back."

In the bathroom, he relieved himself and thought, *Fuck, what do I tell her? Think, Pug.*

He returned to the patio. "So, where were we?"

"I asked what you did with all your money after selling the business?"

"Oh, yeah. Well, I'm a generous guy. Shared my moola with the family, my loyal employees, my favorite charities. Took a three-month vacation."

"Pug, I'm impressed. I did the same when Alan passed. I set up a charitable medical foundation and donated to my church."

Pug grinned at her. "Babe, we are peas in a pod. Anyway, got bored and took some savings to start my Skunk 2. Needed to invent new stuff." *An' you just gave me a great idea to fund my Skunk 3.*

"Pug, I sense an encore coming. Hope you'll share it with me."

"Babe, you took the words out of my mouth. It'll be like 1987 all over." He saw her pleased expression. *My hook's been set. Now I'll reel her in slow but sure. Niagra! Do your job tonight!*

"May I ask you a personal question?" she asked.

"Shoot."

"What happened between you and Marcy?"

"Traveled a lot to get my company growing. One night, came home from a two-week trip, she slammed me with a two-by-four. Caught her cheatin' with my patent lawyer. I divorced her."

"I'm so sorry."

Pug felt good. *Sonovabitch, she believes me.* "Anyway, this all happened 'bout the time I Pearl Harbored Japan."

"Dinner is served," the maid announced. Tiffanee escorted Pug to a round table near the fountain. The table was set with colorful pottery and linens. A pewter lantern flooded all with a romantic, warm glow. Scented candles wafted in the air.

Tiffanee poured glasses of pinot grigio. "Pug, welcome to Villa McIntyre and back into my life."

"Like Schwartzy said in the movies, 'I'm b-a-c-k!'"

"Pug, I just love your way with words. I've really missed that."

Pug snapped open his napkin and tucked it under his chin. "Tiff, what does your stepson do besides the JV stuff?"

"Kevin's an engineer like you and also a lawyer. He spent three years as a United States Patent & Trademark Office patent examiner. He practices patent law in Silicon Valley."

"Can't wait to meet 'im." *Could be useful for me.*

"Always been proud of Kevin."

"Married?"

"No, still searching for Ms. perfect."

Pug took big bites of fettuccine. "Tiff, the chef's sauce is fantastic! Think he'll share the recipe?"

"Doubt that. Sergio guards his recipes like silver."

"Feel the same way about my silver-lining inventions."

"I'll invite Kevin to join us for dinner so you can meet. You two have a lot in common."

"Super." *Once more you stole the words right outta my mouth.*

"Pug, what about your children?"

"Let's see, uh, there's Darin."

"I thought you had two sons."

"Just one." *Not gonna talk 'bout Skip.* "Darin's like me when it comes to inventive Levis."

Chef Sergio served Veal Marsala. He poured the Chianti; Pug tasted and gave a thumbs up. The chef smiled and departed.

"What does Darin do now?"

"Got 'im a computer job in Osaka. Now he's a CEO."

"Any children?"

"Never married."

The chef presented the remaining courses—salad, followed by ricotta cheesecake along with several wine refills. Double espressos completed the dinner.

As they arose from the table, Pug said, "Tiff, great meal! I'm stuffed."

"So glad you enjoyed it."

They sat for a while, enjoying the pleasant evening and clear night sky. Pug stared at the bright stars.

"A penny for your thoughts, Pug?"

Pug smiled and gave her a big wink. "Just dreamin' 'bout the future."

"What's in that creative brain?"

"Before I tell, ya gotta sign my NDA."

She looked askance. "An NDA? You serious?"

"I make everyone sign one before I share my secrets."

"Well, Alan used NDAs in his business, so I understand. But can you share anything with me."

"For this one time, I'll make an exception. But ya gotta swear not to mention this to anyone, okay?"

"I promise."

"So, here's my dream: I wanna do a technology skunk works that creates new silver-lining technologies and products for all kinds of markets. I want my technology brand in every country, paying top dollar to license my patents, technologies, my know-how, my brand. I wanna be 'king of patents.' I'm makin' my silver-lining technologies great again."

"Can't you do that now … with Skunk 2?"

"No. I'm under contract to support a specific customer. Too limiting! Talkin' 'bout something much, much bigger, bolder. Like a Skunk 3 that goes after all kinds of markets and customers."

"Sounds so exciting! Love to be part of your new venture. I miss being in the business mix ever since Alan passed."

Pug kissed her and glanced at his watch. "Didn't realize how late. Better go."

"Pug, the night's young … and the hot tub calls." She gave him a mischievous wink.

They strolled arm-in-arm to the hot tub, undressed, and stepped in. They talked for another two hours and finished the magnum of Chianti.

At last, Pug slurred. "If I stay in this water much longer, I'm gonna shrivel up."

Tiffanee laughed. "In that case, I'll show you the rest of the house." They climbed out, donned thick terry robes and headed upstairs.

The next morning, Pug awoke when Tiffanee kissed him on the forehead. "Time to get up Mr. Pug Van Winkle. You really slept." She handed him a mug of steaming coffee.

Pug rolled on his side and gazed at her. "Well, ya certainly aided and abutted that." *Damn, Niagra stuff really worked!* "Last evening brought me back to 1987."

"Me too. Now get showered. We'll eat breakfast by the pool."

"Meant to tell ya ... after you fell asleep, stayed up and skimmed Blunt's book."

"Did you like it?"

"Yep! Marked a bunch of things." Pug grabbed the book and opened to page 39. "Here, Blunt says deal makin's in his Levis. Like me! On page 54, he says, 'I like thinkin' big.' That's me again! Small thoughts are for losers. Then on page 138, he talks about fightin' back. Don't let people run you over. Then on page 201, he yaks about fightin' after he got screwed. I did that when I battled crooks who stole my patents."

"Wow, Pug, you read that from end to end."

"Me and him take risks, act bold, fight when we hafta, tell it like it is, an' not afraid to hire legal gators and sue. 'Bout the only difference, he's got more hair. Won't hold that against 'im." Pug laughed. "Guy loves hangin' with good-lookin' ladies."

"Yes, you could say ladies distract him. Alan let him talk and talk. He can be exhausting."

"If I ever meet 'im, I'll give him a run for his words!"

Tiffanee looked at her watch, "Hey, get in the shower! Let's have some breakfast."

Pug headed to the shower satisfied he had accomplished his objective.

After Pug left, Tiffanee called Kevin. "Good morning, Kev! How are you this glorious day?"

"Great, Mom! Just getting ready for my Detroit trip to meet with Ford and General Motors. Representing a software client."

"Sounds right up your alley."

"I enjoy disrupting this market with new technologies. A few weeks back, I met this technologist, a guy named Elon Musk. He has a vision for electric cars in the future. He plans to start a new company in 2003. Could be a good JV investment. Anyway, what's up?"

"Speaking of new technologies, last night I reconnected with a friend from MatraScience. We had dinner and caught up after fifteen years. You should meet him."

"Why?"

"Well, he's very inventive, has several patents to his name, and just started a development company like Lockheed Aircraft's Skunk Works. Maybe there's synergy between Pug's activities and our JV. Worth thinking about."

"What's his name?"

"Paul James, but everybody calls him Pug. He reminds me of you— risk taker, thinks outside the box, extrovert, quick intellect, fun to be around, never a dull moment. Pug's full of life and confidence like you."

"Mom, I'm game. Set up a meeting."

"I got a better idea. How about dinner?"

"Mom, never turn down a Sergio meal. Tell me when and what wine to bring."

"Okay. Have a safe trip. Love you."

It had been some time since he heard her so excited. It reminded him of when she first met Dr. Taylor from that stupid church. *Sounds like this Pug fellow might be a good diversion.*

17
TUESDAY, MAY 28
OSAKA

ATSU JOINED KENJI IN HIS office at nine o'clock. They met each morning when Kenji was on site. Today after she updated him, he asked her to stay a few extra minutes before her next appointment.

"Natsu-chan, I recently met with Seamus Hafferty at Mt. Fuji."

"I studied the videos and recordings of that meeting," she replied.

"Meet with him as soon as possible. He has important information to share with you. You should listen to him."

"How will talking with him be of value at this point?" *After all, I have done quite well without him so far.*

"An excellent question. A direct conversation will assess his veracity. Consider your father a weapon for defeating adversaries. He has special skills that you can employ."

"Another samurai warrior for my team?"

"Correct. You have nothing to lose and everything to gain by meeting him and deciding how to utilize him. I have asked Seamus to call you. I suggest you meet at my residence to avoid scrutiny. Whatever you and Seamus decide, keep confidential."

"I await his contact." The thought of meeting Seamus both intrigued her but made her uncomfortable. This presented a unique challenge. Could she make him a worthy samurai?

Once more that stabbing pain returned. *Perhaps I should talk with Hakase Ishikara.*

18
TUESDAY, MAY 28
PALO ALTO

HOWARD RILEY, A VOLUNTEER MENTOR for startups, reviewed notes from yesterday's conversation with Pug. Howard called his IP attorney contact.

When Jackson Huntley answered, Howard wasted no time. "Hey Jackson, I'm mentoring a new client who says he's developed patented technologies for use in all kinds of markets—appliance, water heaters, power, and others."

"Who's the client?"

"Can't disclose due to client confidentiality."

Jackson laughed. "You're talking like a lawyer."

"What I can share, based on early due diligence, this client's a solid innovator in a variety of markets using material science and thermal/acoustic technologies."

"Interesting. Tell me more."

"Two things. First, if and when the client needs an IP attorney, can I give him your name?"

"Sure, always looking for a few good clients."

"Great! But I have some concerns. This client seems paranoid about his patents—makes off-hand comments about earlier experiences in suing competitors, licensees, and attorneys."

"Sounds unusual."

"Not a recipe for success, huh? If I see this client headed off course, maybe he'll talk with you."

"Sure, if you think I could help. Keep me posted. I'll send you a case study I'm presenting at an upcoming legal conference. May give you some insight on coaching this client."

After Jackson disconnected, he thought, *This should be interesting... appliance, material science, thermal and acoustics dissipaters.* He left a voice mail for Michael. "I think Pug may be starting a new venture. He's engaged a business mentor."

19

TUESDAY, MAY 28

SAN MATEO

A s promised, Dan Abrillo called Marcy. "Ms. James, hope you're ready to accept our offer."

Following Michael's advice, she answered, "Other buyers have contacted me with higher offers." By his temporary silence, she sensed surprise.

"Well, I'll have to check with my partners and see how high we can go. If I can convince them to go higher, ... it would be for all of your shares. How does that sound?"

She counted to ten, feeling her strategy was working. "Well, higher is better."

"How about this? Instead of selling now for whatever current offer appears best, Technovenia could give you cash now for an option to purchase your shares at a higher price at a later date. The option cash increases the longer the option period."

"Whoa, slow down. What?"

"We give you cash for an option to purchase your shares at future prices higher than three dollars."

She listened to him outline cash amounts for option periods of 30, 60, 90, 120, and 150 days. She became confused and more nervous as he talked. She blurted out, "How much time do I have to decide?"

"I'll fax the document today, and it will explain everything. This option idea is no risk to you. If we don't exercise the option, you keep the cash."

Feeling more relaxed, she twisted off the bottle cap of Jack. "Send me the fax."

"Will do, Ms. James."

Burlingame

Later, Dan met Pug at a Starbucks near Skunk 2. "Mr. James, appreciate you meeting with me."

"No problem-o, never turn down a free java. Tell me what you're all about; and by the way, call me Pug. So, I was right, you're Italian. Ya look like Michael Corleone from *The Godfather.*"

"People often say that," Dan replied. "As I told you earlier, my company wants to invest in IPS. As founder of the company and inventor of the silver-lining technologies, we feel you'd be a great partner."

"Not runnin' IPS anymore, but kept lotsa shares cuz of the great potential."

"Sir, perhaps you can help get other shareholders to sell. Then together, we can make IPS great again."

"That's what Ronnie said about America in 1980."

"Ronnie?"

"Ya know, Reagan."

"Oh. Anyway, together we can make IPS technologies great again and benefit other markets."

"Yeah, like what?"

"Well, for example … power markets, telecommunications, electronics …"

"Yep, current management's got no vista 'bout what can happen with my technology. I'd grow the hell out of those markets and others. Been there, done that!"

"Now you're talking! My partners have a clear-cut plan to get IPS growing and to become more valuable for an IPO."

"Like what I'm hearin.' I wanna kick out the damn foreigners who are destroying my creation."

"Technovenia would like you to lead that effort when we get control of the shares."

"Bingo! Now that's talkin' my lingo!"

"Good. We'll contact you soon to discuss the next steps."

"Don't wait too long. I got me several irons in the fire."

Pug thought to himself, *Watch me be the Ronald Blunt of the silver-lining technologies.*

20
TUESDAY, MAY 28
SAN MATEO/SSFO

"**M**ARCY JAMES, LINE ONE," MICHAEL'S secretary announced.

"Hey, Marcy."

"Michael, sorry to interrupt. Have a few minutes?"

"A few. Meeting with Silverado Bank to discuss IPS's loan default, one more financial headache. What can I do for you?"

"The Technovenia guy called again. I told him I wanted more than three dollars a share. After lots of arguing, he offered four dollars a share if I sold all of it. Told him I'd think about that."

"Good for you, Marcy. We'll see how serious Technovenia is. Remember he called you, so you're in the driver's seat."

"Maybe, but then he confused me. He said, if I wouldn't sell now, would I consider an option to sell later."

Michael listened to her describe the scenarios. "Marcy, sounds like they really want the shares. What do you think?"

"His four-dollar offer is certain; the option isn't. I'm accepting the four dollars."

"Marcy, I do have one question. How will you get Silverado to release your pledged shares?" Several seconds passed. "Marcy, you there?"

"I don't understand."

"You can't sell your shares without Silverado's approval."

Michael heard her pour liquid into a glass. *She's at it again.*

"Michael, what do you mean I can't sell them?"

"Your original shares were pledged as collateral for the bank loan from Silverado. Pug put up the shares as a personal guarantee. That was the only way IPS got the loan."

He heard her curse Pug's name. "Michael, I need help now! What can I do?"

"Have an idea. What if I talk to the bank and tell them about my restructuring plan to save IPS and increase IPS's future value?"

"How does that help me?"

"I need 51% of the outstanding shares to vote in a new board of directors who will approve my restructuring plan. If you vote your shares in favor of my plan, I think the bank will approve."

"Still don't understand."

"Bear with me. Maybe I can persuade the bank to give you a temporary loan with deferred principal and interest payments. The loan helps you immediately while my restructuring takes place. Once IPS operates profitably, your share price will be worth way more than Technovenia's offer or other offers that may occur."

"How soon can you pull this off?"

"The sooner you vote your shares, the sooner I can start. What do you say? Marcy, I won't let you down. I'll stop by tomorrow with papers for your signature. How much money do you need in the next ninety days?"

"Twelve thousand?"

"I'll bring a cashier's check tomorrow with the paperwork. Okay?"

"God bless you, Michael."

"Marcy, one more thing, I suspect you'll receive more offers to buy your shares from unknown sources. If you do, string them along like you're doing with Technovenia."

She hesitated, "What will that achieve?"

"There are several parties seeking to control IPS and its assets, especially its silver-lining intellectual property. We can't let that happen."

"Like who?"

"Several possibilities – Lawrent, Gano-Nippon, Kenji Kobayashi, and even your former husband. They'll use intermediaries like this Technovenia, so be careful. Do you understand?"

"Yes, Michael."

"Good. Don't discuss our agreement with anybody but me. If word leaks out, the bank will get cold feet and nix the deal; then bankruptcy. Everyone loses—you, me, and IPS. So, listen carefully ... " He gave her more instructions. "Any questions?"

"I understand, Michael."

"Take care, and I'll see you tomorrow. Goodbye."

Michael wondered, *Will she keep this quiet? I'll know very soon.*

Later that day, Michael met with Silverado. Thanks to Kenji, the bank quickly facilitated Marcy's loan documents and approved voting her 15% interest. Michael sent Kenji a coded message. *Got the 51% +, and Delaware is a go. Thanks for your help.*

Michael reviewed the Delaware plan for electing a new board of directors, officially removing Pug James from IPS, and reconfirming the merger tasks. As he studied the details, he thought, *My new chief legal officer will be a busy guy.*

21
TUESDAY, MAY 28
HILLSBOROUGH

A S THE TAXI NAVIGATED THE long driveway and drew up under the portico, Pug spotted a Porsche 911 parked nearby. "I like my future 'son-in-law' already," Pug told the taxi driver.

"Why's that, sir?"

"Classy car. My kinda guy!"

The maid escorted Pug to the terrace. Tiffanee rose to greet him. To Pug, she looked elegant in her colorful silk kimono and matching earrings. "Pug, good to see you again!" She kissed him on both cheeks. "I'd like you to meet my son, Kevin."

Kevin extended his hand, "A pleasure to make your acquaintance, Mr. James. Mom's told me lots about you."

"She's bragged on you too! Call me Pug."

"Be careful, Pug! She's biased."

"Okay, you two!" Tiffanee interjected. "Pug, what can we get you to drink?"

"Patrick Henry. No glass."

"You drink that rebel beer?" Kevin asked. "Mom, have Linda make it two."

"Okay, I'll be back in a bit. I need to speak to Sergio." She headed into the house but remained within earshot.

The maid arrived with beer and appetizers. "Here you are, gentlemen. Enjoy."

"Bring us another round in about fifteen." Kevin winked.

As she walked away, Pug said, "See ya got my engineering eye for nice shapes."

Kevin laughed. "You mean for women or cars?"

"Both. That your 911 outside?"

"Yes," Kevin answered.

"Your mom said ya consult for automotive companies."

"Yes, always loved cars, all kinds," Kevin said.

"You're a mechanical engineer like me."

"Yes."

"Why not work for Ford, GM, Chrysler? Ya know, where the action is."

"I'm not a nine-to-five guy. Representing different clients lets me survey the whole field, work on a variety of projects, and maintain independence. My law degree lets me see the patent potential in new technology commercialization," Kevin said.

"What kinda projects ya workin' on?"

"Several. I represent small tech companies that want to introduce new products to OEMs. For example, one of my clients has developed computer software to monitor acoustics and thermal performance of exhaust systems."

"Got any patents?" Pug asked.

"No, I don't invent. Mom told me you have several."

"Sure do, mostly in the appliance industry for thermal and acoustic dissipaters. I own a development shop that does technical work. I call it my Skunk 2," Pug continued.

"Sounds a lot like Lockheed Aircraft's Skunk Works for new technologies."

"Yeah, that's it," Pug replied. *What the fuck is that?*

"How long have you been doing that?"

"Retired after selling my business but got bored. Always dreamed about a new skunk."

"So, how's it going?"

"Okay, but I'm stuck with one client. Need me more flexibility, so's I can invent stuff, ya know, like—Steve Jobs does —before the market knows it needs it."

"How do you plan to do that?"

"A new skunk would develop products with nothin' to do with my current skunk."

"Can you share information?"

"I got this vista of inventin' a new co-molded technology using silver-lining patents. It'll revolutionize a bunch of industries. Hell, it might apply to automotive applications. Your mom said you gotta technology JV. Maybe we can match some ideas."

"Sounds interesting. I'll research your patents."

Pug knew Kevin was interested. Now he would reel him like his mom. "Hey! Why not stop by my skunk in the next few days. I'll show ya more."

"You're on."

"Here's 'nother idea. Thinkin''bout buying back my former company. I invented this super silver-lining technology. Can be used for lotsa different markets. Could get control of it for half a mill."

Tiffanee interrupted. "You boys hungry?"

"You bet! Me and Kevin talked up a good appetite." Pug watched Kevin nod in agreement. Now he knew Kevin was definitely interested.

"Sergio's outdone himself tonight," Tiffanee said. "Wait'll you see what he's prepared. Let's go to the smaller dining room."

The evening over, Pug headed home in the taxi. In his mind, mission accomplished! He had impressed Kevin and would close the deal when Kevin visited his skunk. He could see Skunk 3 becoming a reality very soon.

And the big bonus was sex with Tiffanee.

When Pug left, Kevin and Tiffanee sat in the library enjoying a 1975 Armagnac.

Kevin saw his mom smile. "Mom, I see what you meant about Pug."

"Just knew you two would have much in common," she replied.

"Pug's an interesting guy, definitely an out-of-the box thinker. I briefly looked at his patents ... quite impressive. His silver-lining patents look strong, and I liked his idea to acquire them to use in our technology JV. His new skunk idea is a perfect investment for our JV.

But we would need to dump Blunt. Can't let him think there's any future value in the JV. Otherwise, he'll want a huge premium to sell."

"Kev, I no longer trust him after he pulled that valuation scam on one of our property deals. Got Alan and me in trouble with the tax, bank, and insurance people. I don't want him in our lives anymore."

"I remember that, Mom."

"Kev, before we get ahead of ourselves, I want you to find out more about Pug. I need your judgment on how we can balance the legal, business, technical items, and my personal interests."

"Mom, at dinner, I noticed you, uh, enjoyed Pug's company."

"We had tremendous time together at MatraScience. Never a dull moment, he was a frenetic ball of energy. And he involved me in his business activities."

Kevin said, "You always enjoyed the business side of things. You and Dad were a great team in real estate."

"Kevin, I've never admitted this to anyone. At the time, I was ready to marry Pug."

"What happened?"

"He had issues at work with his boss and his father's mental health." An embarrassed look crossed her face. "And he was still married."

"Don't feel guilty. Heck, at the time you were young and infatuated. But be careful, Mom."

"Why?"

"Frenetic energy can implode … like a nuclear meltdown."

"Don't you worry, Sweetheart." She patted his hand. "Pug has changed—more calm, thoughtful, and he'll attend my church."

Kevin squirmed, "You know I'm not a fan of that megachurch. Doctor Taylor is taking too much of your money."

She frowned. "Okay, let's go back to my policy of not talking about that."

Kevin studied her, looking a little sad. "Well, anyway, 'bout time you found a fun companion. I know you miss Dad, but you need to move on. This is good, right? With Pug, you'll never be bored!" He stood and hugged her. "I better get going—got a full day tomorrow."

"I'm so proud of you, chairing that IP and real estate conference at

Stanford's Law School. But when I looked at the conference agenda, why didn't you tell me about the keynote speaker?"

"Don't you worry, Mom. His presence helped boost registrations. Thanks for introducing me to Pug. He's sending me his license model to look at before we meet."

"Wonderful, Kev."

She stood at the door and waved as he drove away.

As Kevin drove back to San Francisco, he thought about the evening. *Mom's definitely infatuated with Pug. At least he's a diversion—so Mom will spend less time with that megachurch Elmer Gantry.*

As for Pug ... a rare technologist and a visionary. A little weird, but so are Jobs and Musk. Need more due diligence before we get in bed with Pug.

22
WEDNESDAY, MAY 29
PALO ALTO

E LLIE FIELDS LOOKED FORWARD TO attending Stanford
University's annual law conference. The knowledge and
networking would enhance her skill set for future work at
Orlio & Associates. She would stay overnight in Palo Alto to avoid a
late evening commute. She looked forward to a romantic night at the
Four Seasons after the conference.

She entered the Sandra Day O'Connor ballroom, the venue for the
formal dinner and keynote. She felt upbeat. *This conference will be a nice
break from Michael and his IPS crap.* An open bar offered cocktails, and
servers circulated with shrimp and caviar appetizers.

She spotted Kevin McIntyre and approached feeling confident.
She had a new, sleek haircut and blowout, loving the subtle silver
highlights in her dark hair, matching her pearl necklace and earrings.
"Mr. McIntyre, my name is Ellie Fields. I understand you're chairing
this year's conference."

"Ms. Fields, my pleasure to meet you," he said shaking her hand.

She watched his eyes scan her from head to toe confirming she
made a good choice to invest in this ruby-red Oscar de la Renta dress
that hugged all the right edges. All thought of Giorgio faded briefly at
the sight of a handsome man at least ten to fifteen years younger. But
she would get back to reality later with Giorgio.

Finally, he looked at her name tag, "Don't tell me you work for that
legal scoundrel Gordon Orlio."

She grinned, "I plead the fifth. Please call me Ellie." She surveyed Kevin's handsome and youthful appearance. She noticed no wedding band and pronounced him an eligible bachelor with a sense of humor. *Wow, if I'd met him in law school before Michael.*

"What panels are you attending?" he asked.

"All the IP sessions. I see you're chairing the first one."

He nodded and glanced at the dinner tables. "Ah, how fortunate! We're sitting at the same table."

She didn't resist as he placed his hand on her arm and steered her there. Kevin pulled out a chair and sat next to her. She gave him a big, bright smile. "Kevin, may I ask a question concerning real estate matters?"

"By all means."

"I have a Japanese client who wants to invest in commercial properties in New York, New Jersey, and Florida. He needs first-class legal representation in the US. What firms would you recommend?"

"Well, my father worked with several firms over the years. He considered Kirkpatrick & Faircloth (K&F) the best."

Kevin took a business card from his coat's inside pocket of what she recognized to be a Brunello Cucinelli suit. With a gleaming Montblanc pen, he wrote names of the firm's principals. As he handed the card to her, he said, "Two of the partners from the New York office are at the conference. I'll introduce you."

She nodded at the server who offered wine, and said, "Red, please."

To Kevin, she said, "Thanks. Very kind of you."

He smiled and leaned closer, "Ellie."

"Yes?" she said, her heart beating faster. *It wasn't cheating to speak this close, was it?*

"Next time you talk with Gordo, tell him to call me."

"Oh," she said pulling back slightly and pretending it was to sip her wine. "Of course."

"I have information about a technology investment," Kevin said with a grin. "I know he likes to dabble in technology."

"My pleasure," she said smoothly while wondering. *What the hell's that about?*

After dinner, Kevin approached the speaker's stand. "Ladies and gentlemen, welcome to Stanford University Law School's conference. This year the conference focuses on two law areas—real estate investment and intellectual property. I have a surprise for you—a practicing expert who relies on legal advice for both matters. My father partnered with him on many successful real estate deals. Dad said when this man negotiated real estate deals, think Michelangelo painting the Sistine Chapel at fiber optic speed. He operates outside the box with his innovative licensing strategies; a master craftsman in deal-making and licensing one's brand. It is my distinct honor to welcome Ronald Jacob Blunt, this year's keynote speaker and a legendary mover and shaker."

Polite applause followed. Ellie looked around at the audience. They were exchanging glances. She like many of the lawyers in this room knew Ronald Blunt was allegedly successful, but not without controversy.

Ronald pumped Kevin's hand and gave him a bear hug that left Kevin's suit rumpled. As applause continued, he raised both arms, clapped along, and gestured with two thumbs-up.

"Ladies and gentlemen, tonight, I speak from my gut about my only passion: negotiating stupendous real estate and licensing deals. It takes smarts which I've got plenty!"

Laughter erupted. "Didn't expect that," Blunt said. Ellie watched him survey the crowd, looking a little confused. "Anyway, my legal bills—gigantic! You guys here got to love that!"

The audience applauded a bit awkwardly. Ellie had to chuckle.

Ronald continued, "Now that I have stroked your wallets, here's the real deal. Or should I say the real steal!"

For forty minutes, she listened to him speak about great deals done since his first best-selling book published. As he talked, Ellie remembered a *Wall Street Journal* article. *I wonder if all his lawyers agree about him paying his bills?*

At the end, Ronald announced, "Soon I'll fly to Japan and negotiate a spectacular hotel and golf deal. Just tremendous. You've heard about the famous Tower of London? Well, soon you'll be hearing about the famous Blunt Tower of Osaka and Blunt Golf Resort!"

Ellie saw him look at the audience with a satisfied smirk. He continued, "Stay tuned for the late-breaking developments. I will leave you with one more jewel. If your opponent brings one lawyer to the deal, you bring three."

The audience stood and applauded as Ronald hugged Kevin again before leaving with his security person. Ellie shook her head in dismay. She had a very different take on Kevin now. *Kevin knowing Blunt may be useful.*

That evening, she met Giorgio at the hotel. In their room, he opened a bottle of wine.

He asked, "How was the conference?"

"I would have enjoyed it more if you were with me."

"Wouldn't be prudent. How was the Blunt keynote?"

"Entertaining, at least. Never seen so many hand gestures. Hard to believe what he gets away with. But maybe we can use him."

"How so?"

"He could be a distraction and add confusion as we prosecute the Technovenia option."

"El, that's why I love you so much. Always thinking ahead."

"Giorgio, you're the one constantly stimulating my brain, not to mention other parts ... of me."

"My pleasure."

"Oh, before I forget, met your former student, Kevin McIntyre, quite handsome."

"Don't go getting any ideas; he's too young for you."

"Well, you better keep on your toes then. Kevin wants you to call him about some technology investment."

"Okay."

She gave him a mischievous look. "Hmmm, I've really missed you ... "

23
THURSDAY, MAY 30
TOKYO

HAKASE YAMURA RESERVED A PRIVATE dining room at Mizuwani Kojo, a Ginza-based restaurant. He provided favors for the owners; and in return, they accommodated his frequent requests for dining privacy. The room's wall panels had special acoustic abatement material that prevented outsiders from monitoring. He had summoned Jun Ashi to join him.

The hostess escorted Jun Ashi to the private room. "Hakase Yamura will be here in fifteen minutes. May I bring you a beverage?"

"A Sapporo, please." He sat cross-legged on the floor cushion at the table.

Jun devoted every waking hour and sacrificed personal desires to help build a successful JT. A nervous smoker like Kenji, he averaged three packs a day.

In his mind, something had changed. He had fewer interactions with Kenji and that left him uncertain.

The server returned with beer as Hakase Yamura appeared. Jun rose, and they exchanged greetings. A security aide guarded the door. Yamura told the server. "Sake, my usual." He turned to Jun, noting his unusual nervousness. "Ashi-kun, how have you been?" He observed Jun's tired expression and lethargic movements.

"I am very busy," Jun replied. "Kobayashi-sama's anticipated retirement gives me more duties, and I cannot disappoint."

"Your loyalty to Kobayashi deserves admiration. How long have you served him?" He already knew the answer but wanted Jun to confirm the years.

"I am in my thirty-fifth year," Jun replied.

"I too am in my thirty-fifth year of serving him." *But soon that will all change.*

"Hai. He relies on you for many critical services."

Hakase Yamura nodded and waited for the server to pour. After a small sip, he asked, "How is your sister?" He enjoyed using unexpected segues to keep people off balance.

"Arigato for asking. Natsuko is content."

"If you hadn't sent her to Sapporo, she would have suffered much humiliation." He knew Jun would be pleased with that compliment.

"Hai," Jun replied.

"To your knowledge, has Seamus Hafferty ever contacted her?" Yamura knew that mentioning that name always enraged Jun.

"That, that *gaigin* disgraced my family's name! I feel much shame. I encouraged Natsuko to work at the Comfort Station, where Seamus took advantage of her."

"Do not blame yourself. Kobayashi always staffed his restaurant with young, attractive hostesses."

"Hai, but he didn't have to use her for sex."

"No one expected her to sleep with a gaigin." *Jun, your memory fails you. Natsuko was not that kind of person. That is merely your rationalization. But for my purposes, you keep that fantasy.*

"Now the daughter repeats her mother's sin by taking up with a gaigin."

The first course of sashimi arrived, and each gentleman deftly swirled wasabi into soy sauce with the chopsticks.

"Now, to business, Ashi-kun. Kobayashi betrays you. You will never become CEO."

Jun dropped his chopsticks. "What?"

"Kobayashi lives in the past, consumed with Patrick Hafferty's legacy."

"But what has that to do with me?"

"Kobayashi wants Natsu to succeed him."

Jun trembled. "That cannot happen! A female hafu with no business sense cannot lead!"

"Kobayashi poisons her mind with destiny nonsense," Yamura added.

Jun stared at the food as he processed this comment. The server brought the next course and more sake. After the server left, Jun grew agitated. "What about my future?"

"Kobayashi would not say. That is why he never gave you any equity in Japan Technologies even though he did for me." He knew Jun would be upset at hearing this.

"What about Debiddo?" Jun asked. "He should be locked in a development lab like his crazy father!"

"Ashi-kun, you do not deserve such treatment. Kobayashi disrespects you." *Jun, you don't need to worry about Debiddo. He has his own history problems.*

Jun's shoulders sagged; he shook his head. "What do I do?"

"Work normally, so no one suspects. Report any unusual activities including Debiddo's technical projects."

"What will you do, Hakase Yamura?"

"Kobayashi now excludes me from many matters such as real estate. He acts delusional, not capable of leading. I will neutralize him." Yamura tapped the table as he spoke. "Rest assured, I support you and your future."

The server cleared the table, and the owner arrived. "Hakase Yamura, I trust the meal met expectations?"

"Hai! Outstanding, as always. Please bring a bottle of Baron de Cognac Platinum XO."

He bowed and soon returned with the Armagnac and two glasses. They raised their glasses. "To our collective health and futures."

They sat quietly, reflecting, drinking.

After Jun left the restaurant, Hakase Yamura continued enjoying the liquor and quietly contemplated his next steps. Jun would be a useful pawn and reliable spy to keep tabs on what Kenji, Natsu, and Debiddo were doing. At the right moment, he would launch his attack on several fronts.

Kobayashi isn't the only one who studies Sun Tzu.

24
THURSDAY, MAY 30
PALO ALTO

E LLIE ARRIVED EARLY FOR THE conference's second day. As she completed registration, she glanced around looking for Jackson Huntley. Michael told her he had an undergraduate metallurgy degree, attended Harvard law, worked three years as a USPTO examiner, and spent fifteen years as MatraScience's chief IP attorney. He then became partner in the law firm of Dexter-Foresman. There, Jackson filed patents for all the IPS inventions. In late 2001, Pug accused the law firm of patent malpractice and Jackson for alleged ethical violations. Dexter-Foresman and Jackson countersued, and a lengthy discovery continued.

Ellie recognized Jackson as he approached the registration desk: thin, gaunt, stark rimless glasses, receding hairline, and very large ears.

"Mr. Huntley, I'm Ellie Fields. I'm attending your panel today."

Jackson put down a coffee cup and shook her hand. "Nice to meet you. Are you a patent lawyer?"

"No, I specialize in securities law, but I have clients with patent issues. I'm on a steep learning curve, and this conference is an excellent learning and networking opportunity."

"Hope our panel discussion helps."

Jackson took a seat at the head table. Ellie sat front row center and opened her laptop.

She watched Kevin McIntyre gavel the session to order and introduce the panelists and describe their backgrounds. He noted Jackson's expertise in prosecuting and enforcing patents, commercializing new technologies for automotive markets, domestic and international. She was intrigued by Jackson's law school case studies, his novel about IP espionage, and his non-fiction work—*Managing Technical Renegades*. She thought, *I bet Jackson used Pug as one of his renegade examples.*

"Jackson, please begin," Kevin announced.

"Thanks, Kevin, for your generous introduction. My presentation today will be interactive. I've distributed a case study based on actual events. I'll talk through the scenario, pose questions, and then ask how you would represent the client in this case."

Jackson's deft presentation impressed her, and his case study sounded like a true business saga. She smiled to herself. *This is about IPS!*

At the panel's conclusion, Ellie approached. "Mr. Huntley, excellent presentation! I thoroughly enjoyed your case study."

"Thanks. Was it helpful for your future patent work?"

"Absolutely! Could you join me for lunch before the afternoon sessions start? I have several pertinent ideas to share with you."

Jackson looked at his watch. "We have a two-hour break. Meet you at the University Cafe on El Camino?"

"Excellent. I'll book a table."

She arrived at the restaurant and ordered a glass of sauvignon blanc. Opening her laptop, she reviewed her questions. Soon, Jackson arrived and sat across from her.

"Thank you for meeting me, Jackson. I'll get right to the point: you said your case study was based on a real client. Must have been a challenging engagement!"

"Understatement! The CEO's paranoia squandered the company's revolutionary technologies. He refused advice about patent filings, commercializing strategies, and filing lawsuits. Regrettably, the company never achieved its commercial potential. It's probably bankrupt by now."

Ellie paused, sipped her wine, pleased Jackson's comments reflected her views about Pug. "I know this client is IPS."

Jackson examined her name tag. "Fields. Any chance you're related to a Michael Fields?"

"My husband."

He frowned and stood. "This conversation is over."

Ellie stood and spoke softly, "Please, Jackson, hear me out! I can only imagine your anger. Michael authorized me to discuss ways to settle these unfortunate lawsuits."

"Better be convincing evidence, otherwise I'm leaving. Pug caused my firm and me unbelievable problems."

"Please, give me fifteen minutes."

"Fine."

They sat down again.

Ellie outlined IPS's current status, Michael's new role, and Pug's problems and exit from IPS. She described merger plans for IPS and Japan Technologies and stressed the benefits of an amicable settlement of the lawsuits.

Jackson's tense expression relaxed. "Sounds like you're offering an opportunity."

She smiled. "IPS can accommodate different relationships depending on your interests. In any case, Michael wants to meet at your earliest convenience." She looked at her calendar. "Are you available June 3 at your office?"

"Should be no problem."

"Perfect. With Pug gone, the decks are clear. Solving this legal matter would eliminate a major obstacle."

"Ellie, I appreciate your candor."

"My pleasure. Thank you for your understanding."

That evening, when Michael arrived home, he found Ellie in the library with her laptop. "Decided to come home early and take a break," he said.

"I'll get some refreshments. See you on the porch."

"What were you doing before I interrupted?"

"Recording notes from the IP panel discussions and my meeting with Jackson."

"Anxious to hear what he said." *Wonder if her version matches his?*

Michael strolled onto the porch, his favorite area of the house with its unobstructed view of the Presidio. The night was clear, cool and pleasant. Ellie brought wine and a tray of snacks. They clinked glasses.

"How did day two go?" Michael asked.

"Attended several panels. The first included Jackson. He discussed the dos and don'ts of commercializing new patented technologies."

"Anything useful?"

"Funny you should ask. Jackson presented a redacted case study, but I immediately recognized IPS as the company."

Michael noted Ellie's satisfied expression like she had discovered something. "What did Jackson say?"

"When he realized our relationship, he threatened to leave. Long story short, he agreed to meet and discuss settlement."

"Ellie, you must have charmed him." *Jackson told me you did good.* Appreciate you jumping into this IPS legal mess pro bono."

He waited for her to acknowledge his compliment. *Interesting ... no response. Her mind is elsewhere.*

25

FRIDAY, MAY 31

HILLSBOROUGH

PUG LEFT HIS DEVELOPMENT LAB at noon and headed to Aristotle, a Hillsborough Greek bistro. He needed a break from reviewing test reports. Danny's and Pete's testing of the silver-lining metal alloys and high-temperature plastics showed promising results about co-molding options.

He found Tiffanee enjoying a glass of wine at an outside table. He grabbed her glass and took a sip. "Ummmm ... tastes like that peanut griggo you served the other night. Love your taste in wine and ... me."

She laughed out loud; it pleased him she loved the way he spoke. He took the bottle from the ice bucket and poured himself a glass. Pug leaned near her ear, "What say I stop by later tonight?" He planted a kiss on her cheek.

"Absolutely!"

He wasted no time in pressing his advantage. "I told Kevin about buying my former company, ya know, the one where I invented the silver-lining technologies. This could be a great investment for your JV. Thought I could get shares at a cheap price cuz o' the company's financial problems. Shareholders want more."

"So, how much are you talking about?" Tiffanee asked.

"Maybe a thousand K."

"A million ... hmmm. I'll call Kevin and see if our JV can spare that amount."

"Means a lot to me if you can, Tiff. Be a great investment in a great company. Kevin told me my silver-lining patents are strong."

"Great, right now let's enjoy this beautiful day and order lunch."

Pug sipped his wine satisfied his plan was underway. *Tiff, you're my honey with the money. Niagra encore tonight.*

26
FRIDAY, MAY 31
PALO ALTO

KEVIN'S CELL PHONE BUZZED. THE caller ID indicated Orlio & Associates.

"This is your favorite law professor calling," Gordon said. "How's it going, Kev?"

"Gordo, great to hear from you. Sorry you couldn't be at the conference. Enjoyed meeting your associate; she's quite the eye candy."

"It's her mind that impresses me. She said you're looking for investors for a technology play. Tell me more."

Kevin quickly updated Gordon about finding an investor to buy Ronald Blunt's interest.

"Kev, send me the details, and I'll run it by our venture fund. They could be interested."

"Thanks, Gordo. Who will call me back? You?"

"Expect a call from Dan Abrillo, the fund's CEO," Gordon replied.

In Kevin's mind, Ellie's connection to Gordo could be an opportunity to get rid of Blunt and find a new partner.

Gordon called Ellie. "Hey, Sweetheart, just talked with Kevin McIntyre. You're not going to believe this, but his family wants to find an investor to buy Blunt's interest in a JV. Apparently, Blunt wants out."

"So, that's the opportunity Kevin mentioned! Let's get Dan on this right away. Another chance to get Blunt in the mix."

"Already on it. Your meeting Kevin at the conference was serendipity."

"The more I think about this, Kevin's an impressive fellow. You taught him well at Stanford Law. Maybe we can leverage his Blunt relationship."

After Gordon faxed Kevin's JV information to Technovenia, Dan Abrillo contacted Kevin.

"Mr. McIntyre, Gordon Orlio suggested I call about a possible investment in a technology JV."

"Did you have a chance to study the confidential information I sent Gordon?"

"I have. The JV's proposed technology investments are impressive, lots of potential upside. Our fund would consider investing. When can we meet to discuss the specifics, timing, and other related matters?"

Kevin suggested they meet at his office. He furnished the contact details for Blunt.

Kevin reflected. *Technovenia moves fast! That's a good sign.*

27
SATURDAY, JUNE 1
OSAKA

Natsu met Seamus at Kenji's residence. She felt anxious. At their first encounter, Debiddo introduced him as Sean O'Leary, his technical mentor. Then, she had no clue he was her father.

Upon greeting him now, she noticed physical changes. His pock-marked, sun damaged skin was much improved. He no longer wore thick glasses, and his once shaggy reddish hair was short, silvery, and neatly styled. He was more fit and slimmer than she recalled.

Natsu invited him into Kenji's library where tea was set. "Natsu, when will your baby arrive?"

"In ten weeks," she replied. "I look forward to producing an heir." She knew he didn't expect such a candid reply. She continued, "Kobayashi-sama indicated you have information about my mother whom I have never met. Please share." *I will carefully verify your statements.*

Sean sighed. "I had not seen your mother in many years until a few weeks ago. She had disappeared when I returned to Japan in 1968. No one told me what happened or that she was pregnant."

"Why did you not search for her then?" Natsu said, sounding skeptical.

"This happened during my last year of school for my PhD at Colorado School of Mines. I returned to the US to complete my studies but vowed to return to Japan once I obtained my doctorate in metallurgy. I was determined to marry Natsuko."

"But you didn't return, did you?"

"Hai. Kobayashi-sama asked me to stay in the states and become JT's technical resource to identify promising US technologies. He and Walter Marken encouraged me to pursue my career in the US." He shook his head sadly. "I had distractions that caused my memory of Natsuko to fade ... but, I never forgot her."

"What changed for you in 2001?" *Kobayashi-sama never mentioned these alleged distractions.*

"By then, I had enough financial security to resume my search for Natsuko. I wanted closure for this traumatic time in my life."

"So, what did you do?" *I will confirm your statements.*

"I hired a detective to search for Natsuko and found her in Sapporo. When I met her, I learned she lives with her husband of thirty years. She has two grown sons. By all accounts, she is well settled and does not wish to revisit a painful time in her life. After our long conversation, I realized she left Osaka on her own accord despite Kobayashi-sama's attempts to keep her in Osaka."

Natsu stared directly at Seamus. "Why did she leave and abandon me?"

"She was embarrassed to be unmarried and pregnant with a hafu child. Her oji-san Ashi pressured her to leave."

This last comment stung Natsu. She knew the stigma of bearing a hafu child. It must have been much worse thirty-five years ago.

"Seamus, this helps me understand the pressures she and you encountered during that time and your subsequent decisions."

"Natsu, I'm truly sorry we both learned this truth after so many years. I feel ... and hope. . . we can have a positive relationship. I've lost irreplaceable time as your father. I'll always regret that. Can you forgive me?"

Natsu took a moment to reply. "How do you see us working together?" she asked. *For now, your words seem sincere, but forgiveness must be earned with actions.*

"In two ways. First, I'll act as Debiddo's technical consultant. Debiddo and I had excellent technical synergy at IPS. We invented the silver-lining technologies. Second, I'll advise you regarding commercial matters. I know groups like Gano-Nippon and Lawrent. Hakase

Yamura is not the only one who can employ special means to gather information."

"Seamus, that is good to know. I appreciate your candid comments. I will consider your offer." *I like your confidence.*

"I'll work hard to accomplish any tasks. That's the least I can do. I have no long-term interest in returning to a full-time role with any company. That's why I accepted Kobayashi-sama's consulting offer."

"One caution I require: we must not share your role with anyone. Debiddo should view you as his technical consultant, nothing more. Meet him as soon as possible to discuss our latest project. As for any other tasks, only you, Kobayashi-sama, and I can know. Is this clear?"

"Absolutely."

"Seamus, another matter concerns me. Perhaps you can assist."

"What is it?"

"I worry about Kobayashi-sama's health. His respiratory problem is compounded by excessive smoking."

"I've noticed the same thing."

"We need to have him see a doctor. Can you encourage him to stop smoking?"

"Natsu, I'll try, but you know how stubborn he can be."

"Anything you can do will be much appreciated."

After Seamus left, Natsu collected her thoughts before calling Kenji. She was determined to meet her mother and to verify what Kenji and Seamus had related. *After all, Kobayashi-sama insists I verify actions before trusting all words.* As for Seamus, she would have plenty of opportunities to test his words.

She arose from the chair and doubled over in pain. Unknown to Debbido or Kenji, she would see her gynecologist on June 19. It couldn't come soon enough.

28
SUNDAY, JUNE 2
OSAKA

HAKASE YAMURA ROUTINELY MET THEM at different locations and only on weekends. Today, a 2002 Lexus LC 430 sedan with darkened windows waited at a subway stop. The driver wore a mask; Hakase Yamura slipped into the car and donned a blindfold. No words exchanged.

Forty-five minutes later, he entered a small windowless room. His blindfold removed, he was ordered to sit. Two masked men sat opposite and introduced themselves as Wan-san and Too-san. An elaborate tattoo depicting a great menacing shark decorated Wan-san's right arm. Too-san's muscular biceps displayed samurai warriors swinging swords. A missing finger on his left hand indicated he had committed a serious offense against the yakuza.

Yamura knew these men were rogue operatives. He chose them to ensure secrecy.

"Hakase Yamura," Wan-san asked, "why this urgent meeting?"

"Kobayashi will disrupt the Brunei Trust and prevent our money transfers." Hakase Yamura continued, "The Brunei Trust will soon fund substantial real estate investments making monies unavailable for our purposes. A female hafu will become involved, and this will expose our transactions."

"You are paid well to prevent such obstacles."

"Hai, Wan-San! Please accept my apologies. I request your assistance to prevent outside authorities' interference."

"How?" Too-san asked.

"Eliminate the dragon's head."

Wan-San added, "What about the dragon's tail and the hafu?"

"Without Kobayashi, the hafu will not survive. I will see to that. The tail is a weak link." The two laughed, finding his comment amusing. A sake bottle passed and glasses filled. Wan-san proposed, "To successful obstacle elimination! *Bonsai!*"

Hakase Yamura stood, bowed, and departed. Blindfolded and escorted to the car, he was returned to a different subway station.

Back in his car, he smiled at the thought of how well his plan had progressed. *Kobayashi should know better than to betray me. His shogi strategy will fail him. I anticipate his future moves. He thinks I am unaware of his disgusting relationship.*

29
MONDAY, JUNE 3
OSAKA

HAKASE YAMURA CALLED A NUMBER only used by him and Kenji.

"Kon'nichiwa, Kobayashi-sama. I want to brief you."

Kenji hit the speaker button and motioned for Natsu to listen. "Proceed."

"Regarding voting the trust shares, we encountered delays. The trust audit has begun. Auditors request suspending all transactions pending completion."

Natsu passed a note to Kenji. *The annual audit occurs after September 30.*

Yamura continued, "The reason for the accelerated audit is to ensure the trust's compliance with new government tax regulations."

Natsu wrote, *How convenient.* She noted Kenji's agreement.

Kenji replied, "Hakase Yamura, I pay you well to avoid such problems."

"I have ordered the CFO to find alternatives, but I'm not optimistic. He strictly adheres to tax regulations."

Natsu jotted, *Surely, they can find a simple solution to such a small obstacle.*

"Hakase Yamura, resolve this immediately!" Kenji demanded.

"Hai!" Yamura replied. "As to your other requests, my intelligence agents checked activities of Gano-Nippon and Lawrent. I saw no evidence these companies are trying to acquire IPS or its technologies."

Natsu made a note to confirm this with Okazaki-sama's investigators and to ask Seamus to verify. *Yamura has given a negative assurance which means he has done nothing.*

"Have Lawrent and Gano-Nippon abandoned their efforts?" Kenji asked.

"Hai! They expect IPS will go bankrupt and no longer threaten their commercial interests."

Natsu shook her head which told Kenji she did not believe Yamura.

Kenji took her cue. "Hakase Yamura, do you agree with your agents' findings?"

"Hai," he replied.

"That is good to hear." He winked at Natsu. "Hakase Yamura, tell me your thoughts about my succession plans?"

They heard Yamura rustle papers as if searching for a document.

"Kobayashi-sama, I believe you proposed the best course of action to honor Patrick Hafferty's memory. Debiddo will continue the legacy with his son and will rise to the challenge. I trust you will find an appropriate role for Ashi-kun given his loyal service."

Natsu saw Kenji's skeptical frown. She passed him another note. *Deception.* Kenji's smile indicated his agreement.

"Hakase Yamura, I appreciate your unquestioned loyalty."

Natsu smiled at Kenji's counter deception tactic.

"Arigato. It has been my honor and duty to serve you," Yamura said.

"We will talk when you have more progress to report. Sayōnara, Hakase."

"Sayōnara, Kobayashi-sama."

Natsu watched Kenji slowly put down the phone and crush his cigarette into the ashtray.

"Gesu yarō!" His cough made it difficult to speak. He took a sip of water and continued, "My formerly-trusted samurai has violated the code!"

Natsu responded, "And he underestimates me." She saw Kenji smile.

"Correct, my lady daimyo!"

"If you wish, I can come back later to update you on the exhaust system project," Natsu added.

Kenji drank more water. "Not necessary, proceed."

"After we met at the Comfort Station, I accelerated the exhaust system project. I have developed an aggressive plan."

"First, tell me your vision for this project."

"My vision: invent and commercialize a disruptive and proprietary co-molded technology for automotive OEM exhaust systems. The new technology will dominate the Japanese marketplace and later the global marketplace."

"An ambitious vision! How will you commercialize this technology?"

"As you have taught, I will balance technology and customer relationships to optimize outcomes at each customer—identical to what you achieved with licensing IPS's silver-lining patents. I will implement a licensing model that gives customers alternatives, and this will prevent competitors from entering the market with alternate solutions."

"Have you developed this license model?"

"Not yet, but I'm studying the model Pug James created but never used."

"Very clever, Natsu-chan, use an enemy's tool to defeat adversaries. Continue."

"The project will be located in a separate building adjacent to JT's main complex. Security protocols will prevent unauthorized access to critical areas."

"What defines 'critical' for this project?"

"There are three. The first involves the technical/marketing data obtained from analyzing customer automotive exhaust systems."

"What assistance do you need to facilitate this effort?"

Natsu bowed her head and asked demurely, "Could you contact your colleagues in industry and government to open the right doors at automotive OEM customers—so we may visit their technical and procurement functions?"

"Give me your specific OEM targets. When these meetings are scheduled, you will join me. This will prepare you to handle these relationships in the future on your own." Kenji coughed.

Kenji's cough worried Natsu and his comment had an ominous implication.

"What else do you require?"

She continued her deferential questioning. "Do you think Walter

Marken could provide similar information from the American OEMs?" She was pleased to see Kenji express agreement.

"Marken & Associates automotive JV should be able to accomplish that. I will call Walter to coordinate directly with you. What are the other critical areas?"

"The second will focus on design and proof-of-concepts for field trials. Field trial results when combined with the AESAs data will create solutions to customer problems. Then we develop specifications to obstruct competition. Kobayashi-sama, this particular area fulfills my ikigai intersection between what the world needs and what I can be paid for."

Kenji smiled. "A most astute observation, Natsu-chan. And the third area?"

Before she could answer Kenji, coughing and grasping his chest, excused himself to the rest room. She thought, *I must talk with Okazaki-sama. Sensei's cough worries me.*

Ten minutes later, Kenji returned and sat. "Natsu-chan, I apologize. For some reason, I cannot get rid of this terrible cold. Please continue."

She knew his medical condition was not a cold.

"The third section will focus on intellectual property. JT's patent lawyers will analyze the prior art and assemble the information for patent applications. With Michael Fields's assistance, we will enlist Jackson Huntley to facilitate global patent coverage. This can happen as soon as the Dexter-Foresman lawsuits conclude."

"Jackson Huntley is an enemy of Pug James. That makes him our friend," Kenji replied.

Once again, she sensed his satisfaction with her proposal.

He asked, "What other functions will be located in this facility?"

"One final area focuses on testing materials to select the best combinations of metal alloys and plastics. Debiddo's IPS co-molded work gives us a head start on selecting the optimal materials. I will contact my professors at Osaka University to recruit specialists in acoustics and material analysis."

"Will you be able to incorporate your metal alloy patent you developed at engineering school?"

"Hai. I will also incorporate the silver-lining technologies into the final solutions."

"Excellent idea! When the merger is completed, that will fit nicely with your project since we will control one hundred per cent of this technology. What other technical developments do you have in mind with this co-molded technology?" Kenji asked.

"I think we should examine integrating electronics to strengthen the patent claims. Debiddo's computer skills will contribute."

"Natsu-chan, electronics and software enhancements are most intriguing. I suspect the patent lawyers will consider this novel."

She was pleased with his praise.

"Discuss your human resource plans for this project."

Natsu was continually impressed with Kenji's questioning process. She vowed to adopt his style. She recalled Deming's advice about asking the right questions.

"I anticipate we will need a team of forty people, working two shifts, seven days a week. The challenges are many—thermal and acoustics performance, dimensional flexibility, model customizations, aesthetics, manufacturing ease, fuel optimization, environmental compliance, and costs. When required, we will recruit outside resources. I will conduct daily progress meetings with all four areas."

"Natsu-chan, you demonstrate you can organize and lead a complex project, a multi-person team. This will prepare you for CEO responsibilities."

"Arigato."

"How do you see Debiddo's role in this?"

"He will focus on technology, his core competency. Seamus and I agreed that he will assist Debiddo."

"Natsu-chan, I am impressed—your plan is comprehensive and well thought through. What is your commercialization target date?"

"Somewhere between September and October 2002. I will coordinate with Seamus's market and competitive intelligence."

"He can also assist you in opposing Hakase Yamura. Beware, Yamura will attempt to learn about your secret project."

"I have implemented strict security for this project. Oji-san Ashi will not have access to our facilities."

"I look forward to your updates."

Pleased, Natsu returned to her office. She felt he agreed with all her ideas.

However, she had two worries: Kenji's health and Hakase Yamura. Tuesday's call with the auditors would address Yamura's betrayal. As for the health concern, she would talk with Okazaki-sama.

30
TUESDAY, JUNE 4
OSAKA

THE INDEPENDENT AUDITORS SCHEDULED A conference with Natsu and Kenji.

"Good afternoon, Kobayashi-sama and Nashakatani-san. We agreed to report on our examination of the Brunei Trust transactions."

Natsu replied, "Arigato, Noguchi-san. Proceed."

"We must inform you of serious matters. First, the Brunei Trust's financial staff informed us that another audit had started—the reasons unclear. We could not talk with the trust's staff, and they refused all information requests without the CFO's approval. He was unavailable due to illness. Therefore, we resorted to alternative forensic methods.

Second, we have uncovered suspicious financial transactions—between the trust accounts and questionable offshore organizations. These transactions violate the trust's investment policies. We suspect these organizations have connections to companies associated with Osaka's yakuza."

Natsu breathed out. "Most alarming."

After considerable discussion, Natsu concluded, "Naguchi-san, please continue your investigation. I will provide further instructions. Sayōnara."

Kenji asked, "My dear Natsu-chan, what do you make of the auditor's report?"

"This confirms your suspicions. Hakase Yamura has corrupted the trust. What he did is contrary to your directives and possibly illegal."

"I will consult with Okazaki-san and decide next steps. It is best you have no detailed knowledge."

She understood and appreciated this protective shield.

"Natsu, you will replace Hakase Yamura as the third principal for the trust," Kenji stated.

"I will initiate the paperwork."

"We must proceed quickly now that Yamura is alerted."

"We will not let him prevail," she emphasized. *I will instruct Seamus to increase his surveillance of Yamura.*

31
TUESDAY, JUNE 4
PALO ALTO

Jackson Huntley welcomed Ellie and Michael to his large corner office on Sand Hill Road with its view of the Stanford University campus.

"Ellie, nice seeing you again." He turned to Michael. "Long time since you and I talked!"

"Jackson, great to see you … how long has it been?"

"By my count, three years, two months, four days and fifteen hours. A time seared in infamy in my brain!" He smiled, "But as a football coach once said, 'The future is now'."

"Tell us about your law practice," Michael said, surveying walls filled with photos of airplanes, expensive cars, and triathlon awards.

"You probably know I'm still 'of counsel' at Dexter-Foresman until the stupid IPS lawsuits conclude."

"Sorry you and IPS parted under such adversity. I quit IPS a few months before Pug initiated the lawsuits."

"Yeah, Pug bragged how he 'Pearl-Harbored' people. I'll never forgive his betrayal after doing all his patent work. And to pour salt in my wounds, he never paid on time, then sued us for damages, claiming fraud."

Michael replied, "Can't disagree with your feelings. Without the board's approval, Pug initiated those lawsuits and killed merger negotiations with JT. Several board members resigned after that."

"Wow, I had no idea that happened. Thought he had board approval."

"Jackson, that's behind us now. By the looks of things, you have done well since then."

"Yes, I have several prompt-paying clients, and I've built a solid reputation."

"Sorry to dredge up bad memories, but Pug's one of the subjects we wanted to discuss. Can I bring you up to date?" Michael said.

"Okay, and as Pug often said, 'Do my ears hear me? So, fire, aim, ready.'"

Michael laughed. "You even remember the pugisms! But Jackson, I'm the new IPS sheriff, operating under a ready, aim, fire protocol."

"A refreshing change."

Michael noticed Ellie did not share Jackson's enthusiasm.

"Stop me if I cover redundant ground."

Michael overviewed events since IPS sued Jackson. He covered IPS's disastrous financial situation, Pug's health issues, and his family problems. He outlined Pug's current status. Michael noticed Ellie's annoyance. He knew she had already covered these topics in her previous meeting with Jackson.

Jackson listened, occasionally rolling his eyes as Michael ticked off the topics. "So, let me understand, Pug's an independent contractor working on development projects for IPS, but no official connection to IPS?"

"Yes, and I developed the Delaware plan to form a new board of directors and eliminate all James family's involvement and other shareholders who support him."

"And I'm coordinating with Kenji Kobayashi," Ellie interjected. "That's why I'm going to Osaka tomorrow to jump start this process."

"Interesting, Pug always accused Kobayashi of stealing the silver-lining technologies," Jackson added.

"One of Pug's many conspiracy theories. When I became interim CEO after Pug's stroke, I met with Kenji and cleared the air. He supports my goals," Michael noted.

"He does?"

"Kobayashi still wants to merge Japan Technologies with IPS to form a global company—to dominate the appliance dissipater markets. My near-term role will facilitate this merger. Ironic part is, Kobayashi will use Pug's son, Dave, in Japan to lead the technical function for this global entity." Michael smiled. "Jackson, I see your skeptical look. Dave was 'Pearl Harbored' by Pug. That's why he quit IPS and left town."

"Yes, I remember the arguments between Pug and Dave about whose name should be on the patents."

"I never knew that," Michael replied.

"Just one of Pug's actions seared in my memory. But why do you want Pug working for you?" Jackson asked.

"Pug's brain can still invent new products for IPS. He's working at a small, private development lab with very focused projects and tough ground rules."

"How's it going so far?"

"Slow, but Pug's health and financial issues have impacted him. Give him time, and he'll be back to his old self. You know—the one we remember from MatraScience and the early IPS days. We can't afford to lose access to his creative mind."

On cue, Jackson looked skeptical. "Hope you're right about that."

"It's a risk worth taking," Michael said. "What questions do you have?"

"At the legal conference, Ellie outlined some interesting ideas. Could you get more specific?"

Ellie started to answer but Michael interrupted. "Yes." He pulled a document from his briefcase and handed it to him. "Take a few minutes to scan this. It explains my proposal." He knew Ellie hadn't seen the final document.

Jackson read two pages:

Mutual settlement of lawsuits with minimal adverse financial outcomes. Jackson's future role as an independent consultant to assist in the merger of Japan Technologies and IPS.

Jackson to assist related entities with patent filings and commercialization agreements resulting from development work at IPS, Japan Technologies, and PSW II. Opportunities for equity participation in the combined entity.

Option to join the combined entity as chief legal officer, if desired, at a future date.

"What's your timeline?" Jackson asked.

"Would yesterday be too soon?" Michael said with a wide smile. Ellie's anxious to return to law full time and cease her charity work for IPS.

"Give me twenty-four hours."

"Excellent, Jackson. If you say yes, I'll bring paperwork for your signature." Michael stood. "This has been an excellent meeting."

"It's a reasonable start, Michael. Not to embarrass Ellie, but she is an excellent legal counsel and a great diplomat. If I'd seen you at the legal conference, we wouldn't be talking today."

"That's why I sent her to soften you up."

As they walked to the cars, Michael wondered aloud, "Is he with us?"

"I am going home to pack," Ellie said.

"Okay, I'll call you this afternoon with last-minute instructions. If you have extra time, enjoy the local culture."

"No time. Gordon wants me to see other clients in Tokyo."

Michael wondered, *Clients in Japan?*

Back at his office, Michael called Jackson. "Hey Jackson, how do you think it went?"

"Pretty well. Hope I fielded your questions okay."

"Loved your comment about not embarrassing Ellie and dissing me. Well played."

"Ellie didn't look like she agreed with your comment about access to Pug's creativity."

"Yeah. She doesn't understand technology and how you manage technical renegades."

Jackson smiled. "Understand. So, what next?"

"I'll come by to complete the paperwork. Ellie's Japan trip should tell us a lot about what we do next."

32

TUESDAY-WEDNESDAY, JUNE 4-5
SAN FRANCISCO/TOKYO

ELLIE RUSHED HOME TO PACK and then headed to the airport. She seethed all the way to SFO Airport's International departure lounge. After boarding Japan Airlines, she settled into business class. *How dare Michael ignore me during the meeting with Jackson! He gave me zero credit for all I've done for IPS ... then he does all the talking and implies he's the one who developed the Delaware plan!*

The flight attendant brought champagne. *Ellie's anger began to fade. Calmer, she opened her laptop and viewed her itinerary. Added a night in Tokyo to get over jet lag before Osaka.*

She reviewed her work agenda:

Meet Kenji – Delaware plan.

US real estate lawyer.

Dinner with Ms. Nashakatani and David James.

Dr. Yamura.

Decide next steps with Kenji.

She closed the laptop, took a sip of champagne, and reached into her handbag for a letter handwritten in Italian. She smiled.

Amora mia,

Negotiating with Japanese men, you'll be breaking the Nippon garasu tenjo (glass ceiling). You're a pioneer in gender disruption in the land of the rising sun! Bonzai! And brava rising lady!

I pray for your successful trip.

Ti amo, Giorgio

She relaxed. *At least Giorgio respects me.* In her mind, she knew she could handle any challenge including dealing with chauvinistic Asians. *Japan here I come, ready or not!*

She closed her eyes as the plane took off. *Maybe I should join Giorgio's church. Not into evangelical babble, but it would give us more time together. I'll get him to dump that religious nonsense.*

She arrived at Dai-ichi Hotel and checked into Room 514 where Giorgio waited. The next few hours flew. On the way to the Imperial Gardens, they walked along a street parallel to the imperial palace. They held hands and chatted in Italian or English depending on the topic.

They strolled through the palace gardens, enjoying the beautiful evening. He looked at his watch, then the map. "I've booked a restaurant near here."

The hostess escorted them to a private room. Once settled, he said, *"Watashi wa karera ni karera ga hajimeru koto ga dekiru to itta."* The hostess bowed and departed.

"I didn't know you spoke Japanese!"

"A little. I told her we can start."

"You amaze me with all your talents. Should we order?"

"Relax and enjoy our special time. I've taken care of the details," Giorgio said.

"Thank you, Sweetheart." She observed the surroundings and recalled her first dining experience in Tokyo with Michael at a noisy *robatayaki* restaurant. "You're so considerate to select such a delightful and quiet atmosphere."

They enjoyed a variety of specialty dishes accompanied by sake. They concluded with a glass of Fuoco Sicilia liquor over ice. The hostess presented the bill.

Ellie reached for it, but he grabbed it. "My treat … your expense report would raise suspicion." She leaned over and kissed him. "Thank you, Darling."

As they walked back to the hotel, Ellie said. "This has been a fantastic evening." This trip confirmed what she already felt. Michael was in her rear-view mirror. The only decision would be when to go public.

When they arrived at the hotel, she whispered, "Room 514's minibar is full and needs our immediate attention."

"Hey, why not? Morning's still young."

As they sampled Cognac, she said, "Giorgio, by your look, something's on your mind."

"Do you think Michael suspects?"

She laughed softly. "Not a chance! His mission impossible to save IPS completely consumes him. I'm just his pro-bono pawn. Michael has been negligent and missing in action for a long time."

He leaned near. "Our Kyoto weekend will settle the final details."

"I'm ready to bolt as soon as Technovenia gets control of IPS." She gave him a passionate kiss.

33
THURSDAY, JUNE 6
OSAKA

JUN ASHI'S ANGER INTENSIFIED AFTER learning about Kobayashi's betrayal. Paranoia consumed him; his chain smoking rose to four packs a day. He called Hakase Yamura for frequent reassurance, and today was no exception.

Jun asked, "Hakase Yamura, when will I become CEO without interference from Kobayashi, the hafu and gaigin?"

"Ashi-kun, plan on two, perhaps three months. In the meantime, monitor activities at Japan Technologies. Has anything changed with Kobayashi?"

"He suffers with a chronic respiratory infection and spends more time at Mt. Fuji."

"Good. Gives us more time. Stay alert—and be patient—Ashi-kun. What about Debiddo?"

"He pursues a secret project. Access to the building is severely restricted."

"Investigate if Debiddo plans to incorporate the silver-lining technologies in this secret project."

"Why is that important?"

"This project may increase the value of the silver-lining technologies for other interested parties."

"Hai, Hakase Yamura. I will do my best to obtain information."

"If you need help to get access, I have special resources that can disable security systems."

Yamura felt comfortable with his overall plan. He had covered his bases with *yakuza*, the auditors, Ashi-kun, and his own intelligence operatives. Debiddo's new project intrigued him, and Kenji's health gave him another aspect to investigate. But most important, he had a nuclear option to defeat Kenji if needed.

34
THURSDAY, JUNE 6
OSAKA

ELLIE CHECKED INTO HOTEL OSAKA and then taxied to Japan Technologies. Kenji's assistant escorted her into his office. He stood, suppressed a cough and greeted her. "Welcome to Osaka and Japan Technologies. I apologize for my face mask. I recover from a chest cold." He directed her to a small table in front of the windows. "Your journey was pleasant?"

"Yes, Mr. Kobayashi, extremely pleasant. It's an honor to meet you. Michael speaks highly of you." The face mask hid his expression which made her uncomfortable.

"Thank you, Ms. Fields. But I am not worthy of such compliments."

She quickly surveyed the three floor-to-ceiling glass walls. "You have an impressive office. The views remind me of a William Turner or a Frederick Church painting."

"You admire landscape painters. My architect made this view a key focus in the office design."

She knew Kenji was quick on the uptake. *Better be careful.* She glanced at an ornate shogi set at the center of an enormous glass conference table. "You play chess, Mr. Kobayashi?"

"Most observant. I do—one of my true passions. In Japan, it's called shogi. We like to think it's more difficult than American chess."

"Perhaps if time permits, we can engage in a friendly contest. I haven't lost a chess match in quite a while." She couldn't tell if he was impressed as his eyes remained passive.

"That would be most interesting," Kenji replied. "Shogi rewards strategy and foresight. I will test your skill on my samurai battlefield." Kenji offered her a cigarette and a light. She accepted despite detesting this nasty habit and smokers.

She opened her briefcase. "Mr. Kobayashi, let's discuss status of the Delaware plan. The Brunei Trust shares have not voted. Until they are, my Delaware plan is stalled."

Kenji coughed. "As I told your husband, our discussions must be confidential. Only you and Mr. Fields need know. As a lawyer, you understand."

Ellie nodded. "Certainly, sir." *But I have attorney-attorney privilege with Giorgio.*

"My legal representative did not execute my directives in accordance with my agreement with Mr. Fields. The transaction should have occurred weeks ago."

She took a few puffs before placing the cigarette in the ashtray. "Can you elaborate?"

"Our investigations so far have found no acceptable reasons. In Japan, we avoid accusations and prefer discussions. When we exhaust them, we take other prudent measures. Your presence here is one measure."

"Thank you for your confidence."

"Dr. Yamura's reasons needs further examination. Proceed with caution because he oversees many critical matters besides my trust," Kenji cautioned.

"I see. For tomorrow's meeting, what do you recommend?" *What's with the caution stuff? Not my style.*

Kenji coughed again. "I told him you will meet with all IPS shareholders to discuss the Delaware plan. Approach him in a direct but polite manner; determine his reasons for delay. Offer him assistance to complete the voting action. He may ask unrelated questions. He excels at deception."

"I understand, sir." *I like the direct part. Polite will depend.*

"Now, let us discuss real estate." Kenji said. Natsu appeared at the door. He motioned her to enter. "Ms. Fields, I would like you to meet Nashakatani-san who joins our real estate discussions."

Ellie immediately recognized her mixed-race beauty—alabaster skin, tall stature, and penetrating green eyes. *Very pregnant, but no wedding ring? Did Michael mislead me?*

"Ms. Nashatani, my pleasure to meet you."

"Thank you, Ellie. We need not be so formal. Please call me Natsu."

You mispronounced my surname. Not a great start.

Natsu could tell Ellie was pleased at her offer of informality. Natsu's time in the US prepared her for such occasions. Put a potential ally or adversary at ease at the start.

An assistant appeared with fresh tea. Stirring his, Kenji said, "Nashakatani-san manages my real estate investments. She will represent my interests."

"What information about lawyers do you have?" Natsu asked. She knew a sudden segue would test Ellie's mental agility.

"I thoroughly researched legal firms to represent your interests—specifically with experience in helping offshore entities invest in US properties. I recommend Kirkpatrick & Faircloth, known as K&F."

Natsu was impressed at her quick reply.

Ellie handed a package to Kenji who immediately gave it to Natsu.

"I will examine this and recommend the next steps," Natsu said. "Summarize why you recommend K&F?"

"I have personal knowledge of this firm and have vetted two of the firm's partners," Ellie replied. "My law school alumnus partnered with Ronald Blunt on several property investments. K&F represented them on many successful investments."

Natsu's instincts told her Ellie's explanation seemed exaggerated. She would verify these words. "Ellie, our sources tell us Mr. Blunt—how can I say this—acts unpredictably when doing real estate deals."

"Not to my knowledge. Study my information, and let me know your questions."

"Thank you, Ellie," she said. "I appreciate your diligence. Tell me what we owe for your research. I will execute payment today." Natsu thought, *It's clear that she hasn't studied Mr. Blunt's actual history. I would have expected more. Perhaps she underestimates us.*

"Not necessary. I'm pleased to do this for you."

Natsu paused. "Very well. Ellie, I have arranged for us to have dinner."

"Thank you. If your assistant could call a taxi, I'll return to the hotel. I'll see you this evening."

They stood, shook hands, and Ellie departed.

"Natsu-chan, what do you think of Michael Fields's wife?"

"My research indicates she has excellent credentials. Her legal experience is difficult to ascertain because she has worked part-time for many years. I felt at times her statements seemed superficial."

"You mean she exaggerated her knowledge?"

"Hai, she would excel at kabuki."

"I expect a full report about Ms. Fields. Knowing marital relationships helps us better understand Michael Fields's value for our long-term requirements. Also get the name of that colleague who recommended K&F."

"Hai!" With that, she kissed him on the forehead and departed.

Relaxing in the hotel room, Ellie dialed Michael's office and left a voice mail. "Had a very good talk with Mr. Kobayashi. Clear he doesn't trust Y and concerned about the vote delays. Y's involved in activities that don't concern IPS, and Kenji wants me to proceed with caution. After I meet Y, I'll talk again with Kenji. This evening, having dinner with Natsu. I'll get information about her and Dave. Later."

She freshened up and booked a taxi. When she arrived at the restaurant, the hostess escorted her to a private room where Natsu waited.

Natsu wore a fashionable kimono and complimented it with understated makeup. Her earrings and jewelry matched the colors in her dress. If she weren't expecting, she could be mistaken for a Vogue model. She greeted Ellie with a bright smile.

"Natsu, I'm pleased we have some private time together. This is an interesting restaurant."

"I use this restaurant for business entertainment," Natsu said. "Kobayashi-sama knows the owner."

Ellie surveyed the surroundings. "Love the décor and ambience. I imagine businessmen enjoy this restaurant."

Natsu let her comment pass.

"David mentioned he worked for your husband at IPS. Called him the best manager he ever had."

"Michael considers him a very bright inventor, especially his silver-lining technologies."

"We are pleased with David's technical progress at Japan Technologies." Natsu saw the quizzical expression on Ellie's face. *She's not sure who reports to whom.*

"How did you get to know Mr. Kobayashi?" Ellie asked.

"He knew my parents. After they died in an unfortunate accident, he became a mentor and teacher."

Natsu knew Ellie was confused. *She's wondering about me! How did I get here? Ellie, you don't know it yet, but you have met your first lady daimyo!*

The server entered and took their drink orders. Natsu suggested Ellie start with white wine; she ordered appetizers—natto, sushi and drunken prawns, and sparkling water for herself.

Each sampled the natto dish and then watched live prawns squirm in the boiling alcohol.

Natsu was amused at Ellie diverting her eyes from the live prawns boiling. She watched Ellie struggle to swallow the natto.

"So, Natsu, what are your current responsibilities?"

"Besides assisting with Kobayashi-sama's world-wide real estate holdings, he instructs me about Japan Technologies's business model. These last few years have allowed me to apply my education."

"That must be quite a challenge given your condition. When do you expect?"

"My son arrives in two months."

"How wonderful for you and David. Will I meet him?"

"He's in Tokyo." *Why would you ask? It's not relevant to your visit.* She could tell Ellie was unsure of what to ask next.

The server entered the room and presented the menu. Natsu placed the order in Japanese and issued instructions. "I told our server to have the chef prepare a special meal for my honored guest."

"Very kind of you!"

"Now Ellie, tell me about you. Why did you choose the legal profession?"

Ellie took a sip of wine. "Law is in my DNA. Both parents and two uncles practiced law. I watched my dad in the courtroom and found it fascinating. I graduated from Northwestern with a degree in accounting, and both parents encouraged me to attend law school; finance and law, a powerful combination they said."

Natsu asked, "Where did you attend law school?"

"Stanford University."

"One of the top-rated schools in the United States."

"Yes, I think Stanford is number one."

"So how did you meet Michael?" *She doesn't lack confidence.*

"At Stanford."

"Oh, a lawyer too?"

"No, he attended graduate business school. We met at a joint-school social. Our undergraduate accounting degrees bonded us over spreadsheets."

Natsu laughed. "How Excel!" Her comment elicited a smile from Ellie.

"We married six months later," Ellie said. "Michael had a military obligation with the Air Force requiring him to spend time overseas. I worked full time as a lawyer during his absence."

Natsu knew that answer was false.

"With your academic credentials, I assume you work for a large firm like K&F?"

"No, I chose a small firm. The managing partner convinced me I would have more responsibility quicker. And I have never regretted the decision."

"Do you miss working full time?" Natsu asked. *I will research this managing partner.*

"I have the best of both worlds right now. Our daughters are grown, and I'm doing part time legal work while assisting IPS."

The server brought the food and arranged dishes. As she explained each course in Japanese, Natsu translated. "Ellie, would you prefer a fork?" *You flunked the natto test, the living in Korea test, and now for the key deception.*

"Thank you, that would be helpful." The server poured more sake.

"Natsu, tell me your aspirations for work and family after your son arrives," Ellie asked.

Natsu turned serious. "I will repay my obligation to my heritage and ensure my son continues our legacy."

"How does a woman acquire an important senior management position in Japan?"

"An astute observation," Natsu noted. *She's finally asked the key question about who am I.* "I have different plans. It is my ikigai." She observed Ellie's confusion. She expected Ellie to ask for clarification, but there was no follow up.

The main courses finished, the server brought a selection of fruits and desserts.

"Natsu, this has been a most enjoyable dinner and stimulating conversation. And the best part, we didn't talk business!"

Natsu smiled. "I could not have said it better. In Japan, good relationships lead to successful business outcomes." She looked at her watch. "I know you have a busy day tomorrow with Doctor Yamura. I offer a suggestion. Listen carefully to what he says and do the reverse of President Reagan's comments about nuclear agreements."

Ellie took a moment to respond. "Oh, you mean 'trust but verify?'"

"No, verify then trust. My chauffeur will take you to your hotel."

"Thank you."

Natsu called Kenji from her car.

"My dear Natsu-chan, I expected your call."

"As instructed, we did not talk business."

"Did she pass the natto and drunken prawns test?"

"She failed the natto test. She couldn't hide her distaste. She didn't like watching the prawns die in the boiling alcohol. But overall, she will deceive Hakase Yamura with her intellect, articulate speech, and her aggressive questions."

"What else did you learn?"

"She has excellent academic credentials, graduated number one in her law class. Asked questions like conducting a deposition. She definitely values legal career over marriage. She talked little about family. Speaks warmly about her legal mentor."

"How would you assess her honesty?"

"I saw deceptive behavior like refusing to use chopsticks despite living in Asia for five years. And she lied about practicing law when she lived in Korea."

"Important to know."

"She also attempted to engage me in talking about Debiddo and the silver-lining patents. I did not indulge her. I want her to underestimate me."

"Interesting and a wise course," Kenji replied.

"Kobayashi-sama, I practiced Sun Tzu's principles at dinner. When you let the other person talk, sooner or later they make mistakes. We will watch her actions with Hakase Yamura and determine if we can trust her words. I'll say good night."

"Good night, dear Natsu-chan."

Natsu looked forward to viewing the evidence from Ellie's meeting with Hakase Yamura. Both would be on trial.

Ellie found Giorgio watching CNN International. She kissed him and plopped down next to him. She whispered, "God, I've missed you today. Talking with Japanese can be exhausting."

"Tell me all about the meetings."

"Let me get comfortable." She kissed him again and headed to the bathroom.

She returned wearing only an oversized Stanford Law T-shirt, joined him on the sofa, and poured herself a glass of wine. She took a big sip.

"How did your meeting go with Kenji?" he asked.

"We got off to a good start. I controlled the meeting from the start to let him know I was in charge."

"How did he react to that?" Giorgio asked.

"He was polite and deferential. When I challenged him to a chess match, he seemed surprised but pleased. He liked my take-charge style."

"There you go again, charming the pants off older men. I'm jealous."

"Sweetheart, trust me. Kenji's not my type. And his office reeks of those smelly Japanese cigarettes!"

"What did you decide about the Dr. Y meeting?" Giorgio asked.

"Kenji offered obvious advice on how to handle Dr. Y. Tomorrow's meeting will be a piece of cake. But, then something strange happened."

"What do you mean?"

"Kenji asked me about real estate and before I could answer, in walks this young woman—mixed-race, I think. Oh, and pregnant. From that point on, Kenji stayed silent. The woman, Natsu, ran the rest of the meeting. I didn't expect that, especially in Japan. Anyway, no big deal, I got the real estate stuff under control. Thanks for your fast-due diligence."

"And you had dinner with this ... Natsu?"

"The meal started off on a sour note," Ellie said.

"What happened?"

"The restaurant served this natto shit. Couldn't finish it. Anyway, I confused her when I used a fork and not chopsticks. Didn't want her to know I lived in Asia."

"Good for you!" Giorgio said. "That way she'll underestimate you."

"Natsu looked way too thin for being so pregnant. Hope she has a competent doctor. She's definitely not the stay-at-home, submissive type. She asked good questions. I felt like I was being cross-examined. Call it female intuition but ... she barely mentioned Dave. No way to assess his role. She's not in a typical marriage. Doesn't use his surname, no wedding ring."

"Maybe she's the alpha in the relationship," Giorgio added.

"She knows a ton about Kenji's real estate world. She asked me several interesting questions. Her questions about Blunt confirmed that Kenji may invest in Blunt's properties."

"Interesting. Dan and I discussed getting Blunt involved."

"Perfect, Blunt's notorious for his triple D—distractions, deceit, and disorder."

"What's the story on her relationship with Kenji?"

"She said Kenji mentored her after her parents died. Not sure what that meant."

"Weird. I'm surprised an unmarried Japanese man would mentor a mixed-race girl. Japan's not known for diversity, accepting mixed races, or promoting women."

"One thing did piss me off. She had the audacity to tell me how to handle the meeting with Dr. Y. She has no understanding about how you negotiate with lawyers."

"Has Michael told you everything he knows about Kenji's past?"

"I always thought Michael was an open book, but the last several months I wonder. Michael asked me to follow up on the progress on the silver-lining technologies. Natsu wouldn't discuss. Probably doesn't understand technology."

He gulped the last of his wine. "Enough about Natsu. So, let's talk about tomorrow's meeting with Dr. Y."

She yawned. "I don't see him until one o'clock. Let's wait until breakfast."

He pulled her up from the sofa. "Know how often I thought about you today?"

She wrapped her arms around him and whispered, "No, please do tell."

She sighed as they got into bed. "We need to think about when we go public, and we need to clean up loose ends with this IPS mess and get Technovenia in full motion."

Giorgio snuggled close to her. "Everything is underway—Marcy. Pug, Dr. Y."

"Excellent. Then we can test Kobayashi about selling his shares too or doing some kind of deal. Do it before or after merger?"

"The longer we delay the merger, the more flexibility we have."

"Quit reading my mind, you clever devil," she said.

35
FRIDAY, JUNE 7
OSAKA

IN THE EARLY MORNING, KENJI and Natsu met in his office to watch last night's hotel-room videos.

Natsu anticipated his question. "The registration indicates Giorgio Orliani from Palermo, Sicily. Last night's intimacy and conversations suggest Ellie's in a serious affair with this person. We will have more evidence from the next few nights."

"I know how passions can remain secret," Kenji said. "For now, we keep this quiet. At the right time, we will inform Michael."

In Natsu's mind, she considered Kenji's comment unusual. Was he referring to something besides this video?

Natsu concluded, "The video indicates they conspire against IPS and JT, and Technovenia is part of their conspiracy." She watched Kenji nod in agreement.

"I'm starving," Giorgio exclaimed as they entered the hotel restaurant.

"We burned a lot of calories last night in bed … and this morning in the shower," she added in a flirtatious voice.

"I plead guilty, amora mia."

She examined the menu. "The server recommends we start with a traditional dish of natto along with miso soup. Sweetheart, no natto. Natsu ordered that crap last night."

"What the hell. When in Japan, go local."

"You've been warned. Okay, let's talk about Dr. Y."

"Bet he hated a female telling him where and when to meet!"

"Too bad! I'm ready for a contentious deposition."

"More like the Spanish Inquisition?"

Ellie, her eyes crinkling, laughed out loud. "Si, Signore. Kenji said be forceful but polite. Forceful yeah, polite depends."

The server brought the first dishes, and they began to eat. Giorgio frowned, "Oh my god, you're right! This stuff tastes ... ugh!" He pushed the plate aside.

"Let's order scrambled eggs and toast. Next time you'll listen to me."

Seamus eagerly anticipated meeting with Debiddo. Kenji's request gave Seamus an opportunity to return to his technology roots. It had been years since he worked in a development lab. He fondly recalled days at IPS when he and Dave co-invented the silver-lining technologies despite Pug's interference.

At the entry door, Seamus noted special security protocols. His first thought, *Impressive, but I could override if needed.*

Debiddo welcomed him. Seamus felt Debiddo's excitement at seeing him again.

"Kobayashi-sama told me you'd assist me in our development project."

"Debiddo, can't be full time. Kobayashi-sama gave me other tasks, but I'll do as much as I can."

"Whatever you can spare. It'll be like old times at IPS. We were a great team."

"Okay, let's get to it. Show me what you got."

"Some of my engineers worked at automotive OEMs. When I told them about my co-molding idea, they said the technology has great application for exhaust systems. I have a plastic engineer who understands high-temp plastics."

"Co-molding allows more design flexibility. Makes the silver-lining patents even more valuable!" Seamus added.

"Got another thought. We can integrate software and electronics enhancements to make the systems perform above expectations."

"Novel twist ... adding electronics! Good patent potential."

"That was Natsu's idea."

Seamus smiled. *Like father, like daughter.* "How do you assess the market potential?"

"Missionary marketing—like we did at IPS, but here I'm calling it Automotive Exhaust Systems Analysis (AESAs)."

"That'll help identify, prioritize, and clarify demand."

"Hai! Then we can spec in our technology to preempt competitors! Kenji arranged for high-level contacts at the OEMs to open political doors."

"Debiddo, before I forget, don't mention Sean O'Leary to anyone, okay?"

"You got it—no problem. We got to move fast to get the patents filed!"

"Natsu's exact words," Seamus added. *She's definitely my daughter.* "By the way, tomorrow's the big solar eclipse."

"Hai. Supposed to be visible throughout Japan."

"Maybe it'll bring good fortune to this project."

For the next two hours, Debiddo showed Seamus the different sections for the project's activities. At the end of the tour, Seamus commented, "Debiddo, you've done an amazing job in a short time. I'm impressed. And I'm not easy to impress."

"Thanks, Sean—I mean, Seamus. Natsu's been a great help. Your buy-in means a lot to us."

"Right!"

Seamus reflected on Debbido's work in progress. *And if this exhaust system project is as good as I think, it's an opportunity to make some money on the side like I did with the IPS patents.*

For the Dr. Y meeting, Ellie booked a small meeting room—no windows, air conditioning off, and furnishings removed except for a small rectangular table and two uncomfortable straight-back chairs.

The drab room with its beige walls simulated a law enforcement interrogation room.

When Hakase Yamura arrived, Ellie wasted no time. "Mr. Yamura, my name is Ellie Fields, IPS's legal counsel." She grabbed his hand with a firm shake and presented her business card. He did not reciprocate.

He glanced at his watch. "How long will this take? I have more important appointments this afternoon, and by the way address me as Doctor Yamura."

She looked at her watch. *Okay you arrogant asshole! No more Ms. Nice Gal.*

"This meeting should have started earlier, but you were late." Pursing her lips, she added, "And there would be no need to meet, if you had executed Mr. Kobayashi's instructions."

Ellie observed his elegant attire and impeccable grooming. Despite that, she sensed his discomfort as sweat beaded on his forehead.

"For your edification, the Delaware plan was never a high priority," he replied.

She interrupted, "Let's place our lunch orders before we continue. What do you drink?"

"I do not drink alcohol or smoke, but go ahead if you need it."

"I do." *And your nicotine breath says otherwise.* She called the server, ordered lunch, and a Grey Goose vodka martini with three olives. She lit a Mevious cigarette and exhaled towards him. "Back to business, why have you delayed voting the Brunei Trust shares?"

Smirking, he replied, "Why didn't you ask Kobayashi?"

"He clearly stated this is your responsibility," she said.

"Ms. Fields, must I explain how business is done in Japan? You gaigins, so eager to transact business. If you spent more time in my country, you would know better."

Ellie interrupted, "I have lived in Asia and have a deep understanding of the cultures, business, and legal matters. I resent your implication. I repeat, what caused the delay?"

He shifted his lanky body in the chair. She had him on the defensive.

"The trust's accounting staff caused serious problems with the trust assets," he explained.

"Have you informed Mr. Kobayashi? Yes or no?"

"You imply I haven't?"

She stared at him. "Is that a yes or no?"

"I have not."

She watched his lips tighten.

"And I won't until I identify the problem's cause. Auditors examine the books, and I have notified law enforcement. This will delay conducting all financial and legal matters associated with the trust assets. Anyone with the slightest knowledge of Brunei trust matters would know this."

She watched his self-satisfied smile. She pressed on. "But why wouldn't you inform Mr. Kobayashi?"

"Until we know causes and possible solutions, we do not involve others. I will not waste my valuable time educating you in our business practices, especially for someone allegedly familiar with Asia."

Ignoring the insult, she continued, "Besides this alleged accountant problem, what other reasons caused this delay?"

"That is enough reason. But there may be others."

She lit another cigarette blowing smoke towards him. "Do share." She watched his face reddened with anger.

"You are not authorized! The trust's principals already know." He looked at his watch. "I have an appointment. I am leaving."

"I will communicate our discussions to Mr. Kobayashi."

"Do whatever you must—assuming you know what you are doing."

"Rest assured I know what I'm doing. Do you?"

"I warn you. Informing him without proper knowledge will initiate dangerous consequences!"

"Duly noted. After I report to Mr. Kobayashi, we'll meet again."

"Speak for yourself!" He stood, walked to the door, and slammed it behind him.

Ellie felt she had won. She could leverage his non-cooperation to buy more time for her and Giorgio's plan. This would fit nicely in her goal for return visits to Japan.

Hakase Yamura returned to his office and locked the door. He opened his computer and focused on One-San's latest instructions—transferring more Brunei trust funds to offshore affiliates. Each transaction required special care to avoid red flags alerting authorities in Japan, Brunei, and elsewhere.

Ellie returned to the hotel room about 4:00 p.m.

"El, thought you'd be gone longer. How'd it go?" Giorgio asked.

"Didn't let the SOB up for air. He lied through those nicotine-stained teeth—not to mention his bad breath and arrogance. I wanted to punch him in his ugly mouth. But after the meeting, I had an idea. Maybe we can use Dr. Y once Technovenia puts him in play."

"How so?"

"For some reason, Kenji doesn't trust him which means Dr. Y is up to something. If we can find out what, we could leverage that knowledge."

"I'll brief Dan so he's on board before he contacts Dr. Y."

Ellie described the meeting. She concluded, "The bastard deserved my inquisition. No way in hell an ethical lawyer would not inform his client. If there are financial irregularities and he did not disclose them, he would be committing legal suicide unless ... "

"Unless what?" he asked.

"He orchestrated the corruption in the first place, a CYA? Could be why he said the trust principals knew about other problems with the trust; like blaming others."

Giorgio leaned closer. "Maybe the principals are conspiring to hide big secrets."

Ellie replied, "Fair point. Raises another question—can I rely on what Kenji told me?"

"El, maybe Kenji's playing good cop and Yamura's the bad cop. Or maybe it could be 'The enemy of my enemy is my friend.'"

"Interesting thought. Who said that?"

"Don't know, but that would mean Dr. Y could be a potential friend if he's truly Kenji's enemy."

"I thought of another angle to play so we have maximum leverage," Ellie said.

"What's that, babe?"

"I'm telling Michael I'll have to return to Osaka because Dr. Y is causing problems and Kenji needs more help in sorting this out. If I play my cards right, I can delay the merger while you and Technovenia do your voodoo getting the IPS shares. I'll record my meeting notes for Kenji."

"You got it, sweetheart. Meanwhile, I'll finalize our Kyoto trip. I've booked a room at that hotel Natsu recommended. What will you tell Michael about the meeting?"

"That Yamura acted like an asshole, and it requires more off-site consultations with Kenji and his lawyers. Beyond that, no need for him to know what goes on behind our closed doors."

Later that afternoon, Seamus secretly contacted Gano-Nippon technical leaders to gather information about competitors to help with Natsu's commercialization strategies.

Preliminary inquiries revealed no one knew about his Sean O'Leary activities with Gano-Nippon or Lawrent. Over the next several days, he would conduct clandestine meetings with selected people who worked on thermal and acoustic dissipater projects. He would offer minor technical points from Debiddo's project to encourage their cooperation. In return, he would receive information about the companies' procurement activities. Seamus relied on his photographic recall and no written records would exist. Following Kenji's instructions, he would periodically update Natsu.

An unexpected surprise awaited him when he interacted with contacts at Gano-Nippon. It had been several years since he participated in his lucrative side hobby.

Ellie sat cross legged on the bed recording summary notes on her laptop while Giorgio opened a bottle of wine, poured two glasses, and settled next to her. She felt a soft kiss on the back of her neck.

"Stop that, you devil! I'll never finish these notes!"

"Can't resist you."

She turned and kissed him. "Now, listen to what I wrote: 'Dear Mr.

Kobayashi, Below find my summary notes from meeting Dr. Yamura. I apologize for not meeting in person. I leave early tomorrow for an urgent client meeting in Tokyo. Dr. Yamura and I had an unproductive meeting. I solicit your guidance regarding next steps. He acted uncooperative and avoided answering direct questions. According to him, trust accountants corrupted the books. He claims major asset shortages have occurred. He is investigating. It is unclear when this was discovered and when investigation concludes. All trust transactions have ceased. He stated he will not inform you until solutions are found. I found this answer suspicious. When asked about other reasons for delay, he suggested the trust's principals know them. He refused to elaborate. He unilaterally ended the meeting under protest. I welcome your advice as to Dr. Yamura's veracity. It is imperative we consider alternative actions to find sufficient voting shares for launching the Delaware Plan. Michael asked that I remain your sole contact to avoid confusion in future communications. I will call from California next week to agree on next steps. After you have thought about this, I will return to Osaka and assist you in resolving this matter. I truly appreciate your generous hospitality. Please give Natsu my thanks for the lovely dinner at the Comfort Station. Sincerely yours, Ellie Fields.'"

She sipped wine waiting for his approval. "What else should I add?"

"Perfect! Dr. Y might have been more honest if you had been a man."

"I kept the bastard off balance like Kobayashi wanted. Yamura deserved zero politeness! I rest my case. But, I appreciate your honest opinion, so unlike Michael."

As they lay in bed, she asked, "How's Technovenia progress?"

"Dan thinks Marcy will sell; and if she doesn't, he'll follow up with Pug and then Dr. Y. Among the three, we should be able to get enough shares to put IPS in play and sell to the highest bidder."

"Darling, we pull off this IPS deal, we're looking at a nice payoff."

36
FRIDAY, JUNE 7
PALO ALTO

IT WAS URGENT FOR MICHAEL to settle the Dexter-Foresman lawsuit. That's why he initiated confidential discussions with Jackson three months earlier. The sooner Jackson got on board, the better.

IPS and Dexter-Foresman signed a memorandum of settlement. Jackson would terminate his relationship with Dexter-Foresman and become the legal consultant to a newly formed entity, JT-IPS, Inc. Later, Jackson could exercise an option to become chief legal and IP officer for the combined entity at a future date, pending JT-IPS board approval.

In Jackson's office, Michael handed him a confidential memo. "Take a look at this before I shred it." Michael knew Jackson was a quick study.

Jackson took a few minutes to scan the document.

Learn IP aspects of Pug's PSW II and any off-site activities. Monitor Pug James's activities to ensure compliance with NDAs, employment agreements, and contractual obligations.

Finish the Delaware Plan and complete the merger; relieve Ellie of all duties.

Travel to Osaka to learn details about Dave James's development project and to coordinate IP efforts with the Japanese lawyers for patent filings.

Using Pug's licensing model, develop a commercialization strategy to preempt competition.

"Questions?" Michael asked.

"How do I get information about the skunk works?"

"Sam Flores, one of the techs, will keep you apprised of each day's activities. I'll supplement whatever I can. Our goal is to protect the silver-lining technologies and to find ways to make it even more valuable. JT is following a similar course."

"Understand. I'll check my professional network to see if any other IP attorneys are involved with Pug. When will Ellie transition out?"

"When she returns from Japan, I'll announce your role. She'll be pleased to return to full time legal work at Orlio & Associates. Before I forget, see what you can learn about Gordon Orlio beyond his legal work."

"Any particular areas?" Jackson asked.

"For example, is Gordon involved with an offshore venture fund called Technovenia?"

"Got it. When I get up to speed, then I'll book a trip to Osaka and review Dave's work."

"I'll alert Kenji. He and Natsu look forward to your involvement," Michael said.

"Thanks. I'm already familiar with Pug's license model and have ideas to improve it. It made a hell of a case study I wrote for Harvard Law."

"Ellie talked about that after attending your panel. Pug never could implement the model. Thanks for facilitating this lawsuit settlement. Appreciate your lobbying for minimal monetary damage to IPS."

"Dexter-Foresman is glad to have this resolved. It can now merge with K&F. Thank Kenji for his offer to use K&F-Dexter's IP services. It facilitated the settlement and keeps me in good stead with my former employer."

"Agreed. Kenji always sees the big picture and the importance of relationships. As you complete the tasks, I'll keep JT informed," Michael added.

"As for me, I'll maintain my personal countersuit against Pug."

"Good idea. That'll keep him off balance."

"Sorry you and Ellie have been having problems. Hope you two can reconcile."

"Jackson, doesn't look good for us. But I needed to be candid with you before you accepted the new role. Ellie did a good job so far, but her motivation has seriously deteriorated. I won't let emotions or personal problems get in the way. I have employees and shareholders to consider."

"Michael, I appreciate your honesty. Needless to say, I won't discuss this with anyone."

"Thanks, Jackson. I'm on my way to a project review with Pug. I'll mention co-molding and see where that leads."

Burlingame

In the afternoon, Michael arrived at Skunk 2 for the first project review.

Pug yelled as Michael entered his office. "Darni! Bring us two javas, black as the ace of spades!"

"Who's Darni?" Michael asked.

"My new temp. She does the admin stuff—ya know—phones, coffee, toilets, and office ticky-tack." Pug expected Michael to react, but he didn't.

She arrived with steaming mugs of coffee. "Darni, say hello to Fieldsy. Him and me go way back. Taught 'im everything he knows about business."

"Nice to meet you, Mr. Fieldsy," she replied.

Michael replied, "Likewise, Darni … ?"

"Darnisha Washington." In her mid-twenties, she wore a short, snug skirt and see-through blouse. Every inch of her five-foot-ten, statuesque figure was on display.

"Please call me Michael."

She handed each a coffee and left. Pug watched her leave. After the door closed, Pug asked, "Whadya think? Not bad, huh? Danny says she looks like a tall Halle Berry."

"She's gorgeous. Where'd you find her?"

"Lives next door to me. Saw her at the coffee shop a few days ago. Just laid off from—guess where—MatraScience. If she passes my muster, I'll make her permanent." Once more Pug expected a reaction from Michael but got nothing. This gave him more confidence. *I'm gonna run rings around 'im.*

"How's she doing?" Michael asked.

"Everybody loves her. She's bright as hell, an' I'm moldin' her into a good assistant."

Michael scanned the office. "What's with the cot?"

"Readin' all them lab reports and thinkin' about testin' makes me sleepy. Need a quick nap. Like when Jobs created Apple, he slept in his office."

"Hope you produce like he did. Anyway, let's start so you guys can get back to real work."

Michael's comment about the Jobs comparison didn't faze him. Pug changed the subject. "Have you read Blunt's book on dealin' and stealin'?"

"Heard about it. Literary critics called it a ghost-written memoir-work-of-fiction about a tabloid celebrity of suspect credibility."

"Ya gotta admit Blunt's a top-notch can-do guy. When I get my inventions goin', you'll see me wheelin' and dealin' like him." Pug saw Michael smile. He knew Michael admired his inventive skills and expected an innovation encore.

They headed to the conference room and joined the three techs and Darnisha.

"Hey guys, you all know Fieldsy. Darni, take notes."

The three techs and Pug watched Darnisha settle in the chair and open her laptop. Her perfume wafted in the air.

Over the next two hours, Danny and Pete presented test data compiled by Sam. Frequently, Pug interrupted to add his views. At the conclusion, Pug announced, "Okay, rest time's over. Back to work. Darni, bring more java."

Back in his office, Pug plopped into his chair and put his feet up on the desk. "So, Fieldsy, whadya think?"

"The guys have done a lot of testing. Very impressive."

"Ya gotta build the data before decidin' materials. I'm layin' me a foundation."

"Okay, but when do I see your bar-napkin magic? You know, like the MatraConnect 5000 and IPS silver-lining dissipaters—three solutions for every problem?"

"Christ on a crutch! You can't rush a Steve Jobs to invent overnight. And by the way, I've been in the hospital ya know."

Michael smiled. "Okay, I'm impatient. How are the three techs doing?"

"Danny and Pete doin' fine. Don't hover over 'em like a hawk. They remind me of Darin."

"Darin?"

"Meant Dave." Pug knew he misspoke. He needed to be more careful. "Anyhoo, I give 'em the goal and let 'em go. Sam's slow. His get up and go has got up an' gone."

"I hear you. Next time I stop by, we'll check their progress. How about I come back in three weeks?"

"Good for me."

"Have to go. Before I forget, remember Dave's idea about co-molding—the integration of plastic materials with silver-lining metal alloys? Any possibilities for using that material combo for the ten projects?"

"Way ahead of ya. Pete tested a bunch of high-temp plastics integrating with metal alloys. A lot of dead ends." *Why the hell's Fieldsy askin' about co-molding?*

"Too bad ... always thought Dave's idea was clever. You know, like Steve Jobs's iPod invention about seven months ago?"

"Hey, co-molding was my idea, not Dave's. But to satisfy you, I'll have Pete keep testin'. Don't hold your breath."

Michael left, and Pug returned to his desk. He murmured, "Just wait Fieldsy, ya technical moron! Skunk 2's never gonna see my co-molded."

Pug left the Skunk and walked with Darni to their condos. He didn't notice Sam's car parked nearby.

Michael remained in the SSFO office until nine o'clock. He phoned Sam.

"Sam, wanted to check in about today. I'm confused. I heard a lot about testing and analyses, but couldn't connect the data to the ten projects."

"Pete, Danny, and I have the same question. Pug's got us testing and retesting—thermal, acoustics, vibration, materials analyses, dimensional and running costs, etc. Then our results disappear into his office black hole. We think Pug is doing something with outside groups, but he hasn't shared it. Darnisha spends a lot of time on the phone with molding vendors."

"Molding vendors? That's weird. Does Pug say what's the end goal?"

"Not really, other than he needs solid baseline data before Danny and Pete start designing and testing prototypes," Sam replied.

"Sounds ass-backwards." *Maybe Pug has a new innovation approach.*

"The three of us are confused too. We're running in testing circles. Oh, one more thing."

"What's that?"

"One of my duties includes cleaning the labs before we leave each day. Came across unusual lab notes left on one of Danny's test benches. He's doing plastic material testing."

"I thought Pete did that?"

"Pug's got them both on it."

"Okay, what's unusual?"

"Looked like old lab notes belonging to someone else. DJ initials were on each page, followed by dates from 1998. The notes were about integrating plastic materials with metal alloys using a bunch of different molding techniques."

Michael knew that was the same year Dave quit IPS. "Could you get me a copy of the notes?"

"Not sure. The next day, they were gone. I remember Pug screaming at Danny for leaving something out on the lab bench. Danny couldn't talk about it."

"Okay, tell you what: recall what you can and write me a summary. Tonight, Okay? Email it. I'll pay you extra."

"Will do."

"How are you and the other techs getting along with Pug?"

"Danny and Pete are okay. Pug doesn't bother them. Me, I'm in his daily cross hairs."

"Why's that?" *Wonder if Pug suspects Sam?*

"Well, I'm responsible for collecting, analyzing, reporting test results and formatting them into Pug's simplistic graphs and pictures.

He hates reading words. When the results don't match his expectations, he explodes, blames me—not the person doing the tests. Then he tells me to order them to redo their tests or whatever. Pete and Danny resent that."

"Sounds like he's putting you in a no-win situation." *Pug's old habits haven't changed. Management by chaos. I can put up with this if I see some "bar napkin" innovation like the old days.*

"In fact, yesterday, he told me Darnisha would start processing the test data and analysis. Not sure what I'll do when that happens. Pug says she's good at numbers."

Michael thought, *Yeah, and I'm sure the only numbers he's looking at are 36-22-36.* "Pug can be paranoid. Just go along with his demands and keep me posted. If he pushes beyond reason, call me. I'll introduce you to Jackson Huntley, and I want you to share with him what you just told me. He's working for me on related projects. Expect to chat with him periodically over the next several weeks. But don't mention his name to anyone at Skunk 2, especially Pug! Understand?"

"Okay, look forward to hearing from Jackson."

"One more question. What's the scoop on this Darnisha?"

"You mean Pug's WMD?" Sam laughed. "Woman of major distraction."

"Good one," Michael said. "Pug's not lost his ability to spot attractive ladies."

"She seems smart and motivated. She quit college, claimed she was bored. She confided that she left her last job because she was harassed by her boss. But here's the interesting part. Each night after work, they walk to Pug's condo."

"Aren't they next-door neighbors?" Michael asked.

"Yeah, but she always enters his apartment and spends the night."

"Keep me posted. One more item, what was Pug's reaction to your suggestion about the business mentor?"

"I gave him Howard Riley's phone number. Beyond that, don't know."

"Thanks, Sam. Talk with you later. Excellent work. Send me a note on the hours you've worked, and I'll cut you a check."

"Thanks, Michael. The extra money has really helped."

Michael checked his voice mails before leaving. He listened to Ellie's latest message about the Dr. Yamura meeting. *Wonder how her follow-up meetings went with Kenji. I hope they overcome the Yamura hurdle.*

But at this point, Michael wasn't sure.

37
SATURDAY, JUNE 8
OSAKA

NATSU ENTERED KENJI'S OFFICE AND gave him a transcribed copy of Ellie's voice mail. She remained silent while he read it twice. When he glanced up at her, she spoke—having gained confidence to control conversations with men. She knew he encouraged that skill.

"Hakase Yamura engages in misleading information and outright lies. The meeting video confirms this. The trust accountants would not conduct themselves this way unless they were directed."

"I agree, Natsu-chan. What other thoughts do you have?"

"Ellie ignored your advice. She acted forceful but most impolite."

"Michael said she has a strong, independent personality. That worked to our advantage," Kenji said.

"In that regard, she did not disappoint. Ellie is intelligent. However, her actions will make Hakase Yamura more suspicious. Using her as a deception tactic probably confused him. We should let him think Ellie will return and be a continuing problem for him."

She could tell Kenji was pleased with her assessment. "Kobayashi-sama, I have a question. What did Hakase Yamura mean about 'the trust's principals' knowledge of other problems?'"

Kenji answered with a shrug, "He offers distractions."

"A counter deception by him?"

"Correct, it is one of his many skills."

She wasn't satisfied Kenji had answered her question. "The only principals are you, Hakase Yamura, and Okazaki-sama. So, why did he refer to all three?"

"Hakase Yamura disagrees with my succession plans. He wants the merger with IPS to fail. He resents your increased role. That's why he delayed voting the trust's shares. His tentacles extend far and wide. I arranged additional security for you and myself. This weekend we meet at my lodge to discuss next steps."

"This is a complex puzzle. It is becoming personal for me. We must employ our best shogi skills to defeat him."

"Now to the other matter. What do the hotel room and breakfast videos reveal?"

"Mr. Orliani failed the natto test," Natsu replied. "Neither he nor Ellie understand what it means to do business in Japan. Both possess a narrow legalistic view of Japan. As for their room videos, they spent another active night and morning together. They left for Kyoto not Tokyo. Their affair is serious. We should inform Michael about the videos."

Natsu felt uncomfortable with Kenji's seeming reluctance to address this situation.

"Natsu-chan, when I inform Michael, you will be involved. I meet Hakase Yamura in a few minutes. Please observe our uncomfortable conversation."

"I am eager to see the battle joined."

Hakase Yamura arrived an hour later at Kenji's office.

Before he sat, Kenji demanded, "Give me your written report."

"Kobayashi-sama, I planned a verbal discussion."

"Have the trust shares been voted as instructed?" Kenji asked.

"We encountered complications with the trust finances. It appears there are problems with certain transactions, and—."

"And you did not know this ten days ago?"

Natsu heard Kenji's voice rise in response to Yamura's answers. She thought, *This is most unusual for Kobayashi-sama.*

"After our last meeting, I immediately instructed our CFO to vote the IPS shares in accordance with your instructions. He did not comply," Hakase Yamura said.

"Why did you not inform me then of his insubordination?"

"Kobayashi-sama, you know I am meticulous. I am investigating this matter and suspended the CFO until our investigation concludes. The CFO has taken to his sick bed."

Natsu made a note to check on the CFO's health.

"What happens in the meantime about voting the shares?" Kenji asked.

"The police will investigate. They ordered the trust cease all transactions until this matter clears."

"Surely, voting IPS shares cannot be a significant transaction."

"The auditors say trust assets have been misused. Voting rights attached with stocks cannot be transferred. The CFO may have inflated the share value of IPS stock to support more trust borrowings. And he has understated the trust income for tax purposes. Trust principals could face serious penalties."

"How could this happen without a principal's knowledge?"

"We have discovered forgeries of our signatures."

"By all means, my good doctor, obtain the truth." Leaning toward Hakase Yamura, he ordered, "Resolve this problem!"

"Hai." Hakase Yamura bowed and departed.

Kenji did not return the courtesy.

Natsu joined Kenji after Hakase Yamura left. She asked, "What is your next step?"

"Contact Okazaki-san and instruct him to have his investigators increase their surveillance. Everything Yamura said and did will be carefully vetted."

"I will instruct Seamus to supplement Okazaki-sama's efforts."

"Now, listen to my next phone call."

When Michael answered, Kenji stated, "Michael, I have important confidential information about Hakase Yamura and your wife. Nashakatani-san will send you documents and pictures. She will initiate weekly updates to keep you informed about this and other important matters. Do not discuss these matters with anyone except Nashakatani-san and myself."

"I will. I'm talking with Dave in few hours to discuss a technical issue," Michael said.

"Understand, Michael. I will instruct Nashakatani-san to join that discussion."

After Michael disconnected, Natsu said, "Arigato for allowing me to work with Michael. I look forward to getting to know him better."

"You will find Michael a trusted ally."

On his way to his office, Hakase Yamura spoke with Jun. "Ashi-kun, an urgent task for you."

"What is that?" Jun asked.

"Need more information about the gaigin's secret project. Obtain evidence of new patent filings, invention notes, prior art research, marketing analyses, customer contacts, interview notes, and the like. Determine if the silver-lining technologies are involved."

"Hai. I will immediately attend to this request."

"You and your colleagues will be rewarded for the quality of prompt information."

At his office, Yamura jotted thoughts about the recent developments.

Kobayashi no longer trusts me.

The recent visit by the Fields woman was part of his plan to distract me.

What is Kobayashi's next move?

My intelligence sources indicate Debiddo's project is high priority and considerable resources are involved. This makes my control of JT more important than ever.

38
SATURDAY, JUNE 8
SFO/OSAKA

ICHAEL VIEWED THE VIDEOS AND considered Kenji's comments regarding Dr. Yamura.

Michael realized Yamura had become Kenji's mortal enemy and now worked to sabotage the plan to merge JT and IPS. Michael's empathy for Kenji increased. Both had been betrayed by formerly trusted persons.

The videos confirmed what he suspected. He wasn't surprised Gordon was Ellie's lover, but he didn't realize how serious the affair was. He now knew why she delayed divorcing him. Their recorded conversations revealed plans to control IPS.

As Michael dialed Dave's phone number, he felt conflicted. Until now Michael assumed Kenji knew about Dave's history before coming to Japan. When should he inform Kenji about Dave's wife and son in the US? The sooner, the better—but first, Michael had a Pug matter to clarify with Dave.

When Dave answered the phone, Michael wasted no time. "Hey Dave, sorry to bother you on the weekend."

"No sweat! Always happy to talk with my favorite boss. What's up?"

"I'll get to the point. When you worked at IPS, you had this clever idea about co-molding high-temp plastics with silver-lining high-temp metal alloys."

"Michael, I'm putting you on the speaker phone, I want Natsu to join this conversation. She has a technical interest in this subject."

After Michael and she exchanged pleasantries, Dave continued. "Always thought my idea had great potential."

"Why didn't you pursue it?"

"Remember, that happened about the time I got the SoftDev offer, and Pops treated me like shit? That's why I quit. It was like he put a curse on every invention I did."

"Do you still have your original lab book?"

"Yeah, in fact I looked at it a few weeks ago. Why?"

"Two days ago, I talked with your dad about your co-molding idea. He claimed it wasn't worth the powder to blow to hell. He said his recent testing proved it."

"Bullshit!" Michael could picture Dave's red face swelling like Pug's often did. "Pops had zero, nada to do with it!"

"I'm confused. Apparently, there's another copy of your notes floating around. Did you make any copies?"

"Honestly, I don't recall. My lab assistant may have made an extra copy since he did the tests. If my crazy dad's using my idea, he's gonna pay!"

Michael thought, *Like father, like son—inventor paranoia.* "Do you still have plans for your idea?"

"We just started a new project using the co-molded concept to see where it leads. But it pisses me off that my dad ... "

"Dave, hold on for a moment. Do you have testing results to determine the optimum mix between plastics and metal alloys?"

"I have enough test data from my IPS days to develop proofs of concepts to show customers. I need more customer input about specific problems they want solved. Then I'll choose the right combination and molding processes."

"Makes sense—determine their problems, needs, pains—and then propose solutions. If you want, I'll send you whatever testing Pug's doing to help your project."

"Michael, right now it's not necessary. I have enough data to do the product design work. Maybe later."

"Which appliance customers are you targeting—Hondoya, General Appliance?"

"Yeah, those, and who knows—there may be other markets too. It's really shitty that my dad would try to steal my idea."

"What other markets besides appliance?"

"Automotive. Kobayashi-sama has already introduced us to OEM contacts."

"Sounds intriguing. Keep me posted. Have to take another call. Thanks for your update."

"Wait, Michael, keep me informed about what my crazy dad does. He's not stealing my idea!"

"You got it." *Natsu and I should have an interesting first call. This co-molding concept must be important to both Dave and Pug.*

Debiddo looked at Natsu. "Well, Kobito, what do you think? Pisses me off Pop's stealing my idea. I'll stop him in his tracks!"

"Call Seamus and see what he thinks."

He called Seamus as she listened.

"Hey, Debiddo. You're calling late." Seamus replied.

"Hope I'm not interrupting anything,"

"No problem, just watching a special video from one of my former colleagues. What do you need?"

Natsu noted that comment. She would tell Kenji.

"Pug's stealing my idea about co-molding plastic with metal alloys. He's the monster who won't die! Rises from a stroke to screw over his own son! It's like he's put a curse on my new project." Debiddo was shouting.

"Debiddo, calm down!" Seamus said.

"You're right, Seamus. Sorry about that."

"Tell me how Pug's planning to do this?"

"I don't know for sure. I think he has a skunk works doing contract development. No way he's gonna beat me!"

"Debiddo, I understand your anger, but think long term. Finish your project before you exact revenge. Then you have the advantage before you confront him."

"You make sense, Seamus. I was acting like my dad—fire, aim, and ready. With your help, I'll beat 'im to the finish line!"

"Debiddo, I look forward to helping you get there!"

Debiddo grabbed a beer and sat next to Natsu. "Seamus made sense, didn't he?"

"Hai. He can accelerate your project. As for your father, remember revenge is a dish best served cold."

"Yeah, that's why Seamus says finish the project first."

"I'm exhausted, Debiddo. Going to bed now." Thoughts swirled: *Have Seamus investigate Pug. Alert Michael. I'm glad Seamus followed my requests about Debiddo. Seamus is performing as hoped, but his video comment needs verification.*

She went to the bathroom to get ready for bed. As she removed her makeup, she experienced another stabbing pain; much worse than previous ones.

39
SATURDAY/SUNDAY, JUNE 8/9
MT. FUJI

K ENJI ENJOYED SPENDING QUALITY, UNINTERRUPTED time at
his Mt. Fuji lodge. He wanted a few more happy days with his
companion before admitting unpleasant news.

He poured two tumblers of Johnnie Walker Blue, raised his glass,
and said, "To the memory of Hafferty-sama, our valued mentor and
sensei."

Shiganari replied, "To Hafferty-sama! He introduced us to ikigai,
Sun Tzu, and the samurai philosophy."

"Hai, our weapons in the wars of business and overcoming personal
challenges."

Shiganari nodded. "He gave our lives meaning and courage to
survive and prosper while protecting our secret."

The weekend marked the 54th anniversary when Kenji and
Shiganari first met Patrick Hafferty. He had recruited both in 1948
to join General MacArthur's economic reconstruction teams. Patrick
recognized their sharp intellects, insatiable curiosities, work ethics,
and passions for business. He helped Kenji launch an Osaka company
to supply dissipaters for appliance OEMs. He assigned Shiganari to
Hondoya Appliance. They would become CEOs of their respective
companies. Along the way, they made shrewd investments in real estate,
hotels, restaurants, and golf courses. In 2002, they ranked among the
one hundred richest men in Japan.

Kenji continued, "That is why we honored Hafferty-sama when he died in 1968. At that time in Japan, few would undertake such a risky commitment."

"Hai, at that time, we did not know Natsu's capabilities. Hafferty-sama's granddaughter was only one year old then," Shiganari added. "But thanks to your excellent mentoring, she will sustain Hafferty-sama's legacy."

"Shiganari, you have been my trusted partner in this effort. Together, we trained her to combat prejudices—whether it be one's sexual preference, racial differences, the status of women. And you counseled Natsu to be empathetic. You have complemented my mentoring by providing Natsu a sympathetic ear.

"You had the foresight to hire an English nanny from Norland College in Bath, England to teach English to Natsu and to monitor her progress during the first fifteen years."

"Hai. The nanny introduced her to Shakespeare, kabuki and noh theater." Kenji added. "Natsu exceeds our demanding expectations. She will succeed as a woman CEO in global business." Kenji sipped scotch and smiled, "Her hafu heritage will be an advantage, and adversaries will always underestimate her!"

"Indeed!" Shiganari added. "And she constantly improves her knowledge. She understands the equation between technology and relationships."

Kenji was quiet for a long moment. "Hai. Natsu took Debiddo's co-molded technology idea and organized a comprehensive development and marketing effort."

"Very impressive. She demonstrates her leadership abilities."

"She's no longer a lady samurai. It's clear she can be a lady daimyo." Kenji's expression turned serious. "If for any reason I cannot continue as her sensei…," his voice wavered. "I know you will be there for her."

Kenji knew Shiganari suspected he had little time left. His pride or stubbornness prevented him from admitting defeat and revealing the sad truth even to his loyal companion.

"I will follow your example to guide her to be practical, forgiving, and … unforgiving when required."

"Hai!"

"When will you tell her about our relationship?" Shiganari asked.

"I have thought long and hard. It weighs on my mind. She probably suspects. I will inform her after her son arrives."

"Wise counsel. I trust she will accept our relationship just as her grandfather accepted us."

"I hope she finds her true long-term partner who matches her intellect and purpose in life, someone who respects her and treats her as an equal, someone who is more measured with a long-term perspective to help her achieve and sustain her ikigai."

Shiganari sighed. "We hoped Debiddo could fulfill that role; but unfortunately, his talents are limited."

40
SUNDAY, JUNE 9
HILLSBOROUGH

P UG'S SOLE INTEREST IN ATTENDING Tiffanee's megachurch was to understand why she donated to this church and learn the church's tricks to tap Tiffanee for money.

They sat in the first row. Pug joked loudly, "This whole dang pew donated by the Alan McIntyre Foundation?"

Tiffanee gestured to keep his voice down. Others in nearby pews looked askance at him.

Pug craned his neck to look at the vaulted ceiling and sparkling stained glass, his eyes surveying the entire interior. "Tiff, one impressive structure! Whoever designed this had my engineer's eye."

"Pleased you like it," she whispered. "You'll love my minister too. I just adore him."

"If he's good for you, that's 'nough for me."

Tiffanee laughed and squeezed his hand. "I will say, there's pressure to tithe. So, don't throw any quarters in."

Pug laughed and searched his pockets. "How 'bout a Patrick Henry cap? My favorite currency!" Pug squeezed her hand. He was pleased the way his plan was progressing. Attending this crazy church was more cement in their relationship.

She rolled her eyes. "Only if your caps are pure silver."

As the church filled to capacity with nearly 900 people on the main floor and 200 on the mezzanine, Pug scanned the congregants, many who were expensively dressed.

Pug thought, *Look at these wealthy nut jobs ready to hear this BS!*

The minister greeted the standing congregation. "Good morning, my beloved faithful! I'm Dr. Taylor. Please be seated." As they sat, he continued. "I see several newcomers today. Welcome!"

Pug could hardly stand it. Sonovabitch! Guy looks like Burt Lancaster! Same toothy smile, bushy head of hair, doesn't look a day over forty.

The minister engaged the audience with a spell-binding, upbeat sermon.

Pug glanced at Tiffanee. *She's really into this horseshit!* He began to worry. *Seemed like a sane broad 'till this moment.* But, at the same time, he felt that if she could fall for this BS and give money to this fast-talking huckster, he could get her to shell out lots of bucks to him.

After the service, they exited to greet the minister. Pug watched Dr. Taylor hug Tiffanee like a long-lost relative. "Tiffanee, wonderful to see you this fine Sunday morning. Praise the Lord! Thank you for coming today."

"Dr. Taylor, I thoroughly enjoyed your inspirational message."

"And Tiffanee, we thank you for your recent generous contribution to our building fund."

Pug thought, *Babe, hope you'll be as generous with me.*

"My pleasure, Dr. Taylor. I'd like you to meet my special friend, Mr. Paul James."

Pug extended his hand. "Doc, loved your talk—'specially 'bout takin' risks for God and protectin' your beliefs from the devil. My kinda principles!"

Tiffanee interrupted, "Paul is an entrepreneur who invents for a living."

"Mr. James, welcome! Our church needs more innovative Christians."

"Count me in! Anyone ever tell ya you look like that actor, the one in *Here's the Eternity?*"

"People tell me I resemble Burt Lancaster." Pug could see Doc Taylor appreciated the compliment.

Dr. Taylor turned to Tiffanee. "Before you go, there's someone I'd like you to meet." He motioned to a man nearby. "Tiffanee McIntyre,

I'd like you to meet our newest member, Gordon Orlio." She shook hands and introduced Pug to Gordon.

Dr. Taylor continued, "Gordon volunteered to join our fund-raising committee. You two need to talk."

Tiffanee looked pleased. "Gordon, always looking for help for this important project."

"Gordon and your son, Kevin, have a lot in common," Dr. Taylor interjected.

"What's that?" she asked.

"Stanford Law."

Pug was fascinated. *So, Gordon knows Kevin. Maybe another gator I can use.*

"You're Kevin McIntyre's mother?" Gordon asked. "Wow, what a small world! I taught him contract law. He chaired this year's successful legal conference."

"Yes, he's my superstar. I'll tell Kevin we met!"

Pug was jealous. He couldn't get a word with others dominating the conversation.

At last, she and Pug headed to her BMW. Pug sulked, but Tiffanee didn't notice. After strapping on the seat belts, he asked, "How'd ya meet Doc Taylor?"

"He coached my recovery after Alan passed. Gave me perspective on living life and introduced me to ikigai—my personal philosophy— my reason for being. I use it when I have a serious personal crisis or critical decision."

"Sounds like EST stuff the MatraScience guys used to yak about— back in the early 80's."

"No, no, Pug! Very different."

Pug smiled to himself. *Yeah, wonder if you slept with him too. You're into this guy big time. Better watch my step.* "Babe, Doc Taylor's speech got me thinkin' 'bout bringin' more pizzazz to my skunk works ideas." *Tiff baby, stick with me, and I'll be your sticky guy.*

"Pleased you enjoyed it, Pug." Pug caught her sly smile. "Thinking about a little vacation. Could you take a few days off for some fun in the sun?"

"Gimme the dates, and I'm yours."

Tiffanee directed the BMW along the tree-lined drive to her home and pulled in under the portico. "After lunch, let's rest and maybe take a dip. How's that sound?"

"Let's do it, babe!"

Pug knew the next few days would be critical. The fun-in-the-sun vacation would firm up his plans. He was closer to accessing Tiffanee's bank account. He wasn't sure how to involve Gordon.

41
SUNDAY, JUNE 9
PALO ALTO

THAT EVENING, KEVIN CALLED JACKSON Huntley. "Jackson, thanks for taking my call on a Sunday."

"No problem, Kevin. By the way, thanks again for inviting me to the Stanford conference. Really enjoyed it."

"Pleasure's mine. Your panel discussion got rave reviews." Kevin had researched Jackson's background before asking him to speak at the law conference. He knew Jackson had a stellar reputation among his legal colleagues.

"I had great participants who were really engaged," Jackson said.

"Their feedback praised your case study. Was it based on a true event?"

"Yes, I altered names and places to protect the innocent, and," Jackson chuckled, "the guilty, depending on one's point of view."

"Your key message resonated—about balancing technology and politics when commercializing. And, of course, to avoid litigation if possible."

"Especially true when you're involved with foreign entities. Relationship politics can be crucial. Naïve businessmen think technology or market brand rules; then they squander or lose their advantage because they ignored the politics of relationships."

"So, the reason I called," Kevin said, "and by the way, I'd like to keep this confidential; a professional courtesy?"

"No problem."

"I've been doing patent research on technologies developed and owned by two companies—MatraScience and IPS. You were the patent attorney-of-record for both."

"Yes."

"Well, I represent a client who wants to work with the inventor responsible for these patents. What can you tell me about Paul James?"

"A rare technologist who comes along once in a great while," Jackson answered.

"Sounds like an endorsement. Should my client consider him a good business partner?"

Jackson paused. "Pending litigation prevents me from discussing."

"I'm really only interested in personal traits like judgment, ethics, etc., nothing proprietary or business related."

"Nice try."

"Okay, any suggestions of people to contact?" Kevin asked. He thought Jackson's comments contradictory. *The pending litigation must be serious.*

"Contact Michael Fields. He might give you some insight. He once worked with Paul James at MatraScience and IPS."

"Thanks, I'll do that."

At home, Kevin sipped a coke and thought about Jackson's comments. *What legal problems between Jackson and Pug?*

42
SUNDAY, JUNE 9
SAN FRANCISCO

ELLIE ARRIVED AT SFO. WHILE in the passport queue, she checked voice mails. She listened to Giorgio's message. "Amora mia, guess who I met at church today, none other than Pug James. He was with this very attractive lady named Tiffanee McIntyre. Didn't you once tell me that was the name of Pug's mistress at MatraScience? Anyway, she's the mother of Kevin McIntyre, my former law student, the one you met at the legal conference. Here's the good news. Dr. Taylor wants me to join the church fundraising committee chaired by her. I'll find out what Mr. Pug's doing. Maybe we can involve Kevin in our plan."

Ellie was intrigued. *Maybe Giorgio's church connection paid off after all.* With luggage in tow, she met Michael at the arrival curb.

"Welcome home, El. Get any sleep on the plane?"

"Ambien helped."

He noticed she didn't react to calling her El. *She's got on her poker face or jet lag.*

"Hungry? We'll go to our favorite North Beach bistro, Alberellos."

"Okay," she responded in a bored tone.

Traffic slowed as they drove north on Highway 101. "Looks like an accident ahead. You'll be starving by the time we get there."

"No hurry."

Michael glanced at her. *Her mind's on someone else.* "While you were gone, Skip James's public defender called."

"What'd he want?"

"Updated me on Skip's situation. Doesn't look good."

"Well, maybe Skip's guilty. At this point, I don't care. He has no one to blame but himself, and of course Pug."

"But this will further depress Marcy when she hears it."

"She's as guilty as Pug for the way Skip turned out."

"Before I ask about the trip, I had the first project review at Skunk 2. I expected to watch Pug's innovative brain in action. Instead, he deluged me with test data, lab reports, and analyses. Bottom line, not the Pug I knew at MatraScience ... or IPS."

"You know the definition of insanity ... hate to tell you, but I told you so. Maybe the stroke did more damage than you realize," Ellie said.

"Possible, but why the flurry of activity going nowhere fast, unless ..."

"Unless what?"

"Pug's got some temp, a gal named Darnisha, to do the admin stuff. Didn't ask my approval."

"Since when does he ask for approval ... or forgiveness?"

"Don't remind me. He's probably having an affair with her."

"Michael, technically it's not an affair since he's divorced. Marcy can't cry foul like she did with that Japanese gal. What's your evidence he's screwing this Darnisha?"

"He's got a cot in his office."

Ellie yawned. "Maybe he's teaching her the fine art of on-site inventing, like he did with Tiffanee at MatraScience."

Michael stared straight ahead. He wondered, *What's with the Tiffanee reference?*

Neither spoke for a few moments. "Something else bothering you?" she asked.

"Yeah, Pug's lying. When I asked him about a project involving Dave's co-molding idea, he denied it. But lab notes confirmed it's still active but unrelated to my project list."

"So, what does that mean?"

"Who knows?"

Michael saw her irritated look. He knew she hated his incomplete answers.

"Got great news. Jackson and I finally resolved the legal issues between IPS and Dexter-Foresman. You're off the hook."

"Good. Now, I can devote more time to completing the Delaware plan and the merger."

"Not necessary. You can return to the law full time. No more pro bono for IPS."

"Hate to leave at such a critical time. Tell Jackson to contact me for any transition help."

"Will do." Michael expected more of a reaction to this change. "Tell me about your trip." *Okay, it's your turn. Can't wait to hear your version.*

"Kenji and I had a good strategy meeting. Told him I would handle Yamura. Then, I talked real estate with Kenji and Natsu Nashatani. Gave them my K&F recommendation; they seemed pleased. Kenji offered to pay, but declined his offer like you suggested."

"The least IPS could do." Michael added.

"First evening in Osaka, had dinner with Natsu. She's impressive. Dave couldn't join. Traveling, she said."

"Look forward to meeting her. Only know what Dave's told me."

"She's involved in Kenji's real estate deals. Now, she's working in Japan Technologies."

"What does that mean for Dave?"

"She's the power partner in whatever relationship they have."

"Oh look, we just passed Kuletos, the former Velvet Turtle hangout for the MatraScience gang."

"Pug's favorite place where he met Tiffanee."

"Can't recall, it's been fifteen years." *Tiffanee again?*

"Here's an interesting comparison, you're exploiting Pug's technical mind at Skunk 2, and Kenji's manipulating Dave's technical brain; like father, like son."

"Hadn't considered that." *Talk about an out-of-left field segue.* He knew his non-response annoyed her.

They passed the exit to South San Francisco. "Traffic's better; won't be much longer. How'd it go with Dr. Yamura?"

"He's like Dr. No in that James Bond movie—one big asshole, totally uncooperative. Clear he hates women, especially an American who speaks her mind."

"El, good for you! Did you let Dr. Y have it?" he asked.

"You should have been there. I didn't let him up for air."

"When you met with Kenji the last two days, what options did you discuss?"

"Nothing conclusive. We brainstormed various alternatives. Kenji dithered, couldn't decide. He wanted to consult with some unidentified colleague. He agreed I should return to Japan and keep the pressure on Dr. Y."

Michael slapped his hand on the steering wheel. "Damn it! I'm sick and tired of all this delay. We need those trust shares voted now! I'm calling Kenji tomorrow!"

"Michael, don't do that!" she replied. Michael sensed her agitation. "Why not?"

"He requested I check with him for an update before deciding the next steps. I need to send him my detailed report next week. If you call now, it'll confuse him. You know Japanese don't rush to decisions. I'll take the lead and finish this trust voting. It will require some return trips to Osaka. Make sense?"

"I like that. Jackson has enough on his plate." He exited on the Embarcadero, drove to Columbus Avenue and parked in front of the bistro. They entered Alberellos, and the host directed them to their favorite table.

Michael excused himself. In the restroom, he stared into the mirror. He knew their marriage was over.

When they arrived home, Ellie announced, "I'm going to the drug store to pick up my blood pressure meds. I ran out while in Japan."

"You're tired and need to relax. I'll go."

"No, Michael, you've already had long day, and I'm not really tired."

He watched her leave. He knew she would be calling Giorgio to discuss accelerating their plans.

Michael would propose a trial separation to begin immediately. At a minimum this would disrupt their plans.

His last thought before falling asleep, *Okay, Marcy, time to do your thing.*

43
TUESDAY, JUNE 11
SAN MATEO

E LLIE LOOKED AT HER CALLER ID. *Not again. She's testing my patience.*

"You have a moment, Ellie?" *Marcy said, sounding tearful.*

"Sure. How are you doing?" *As if you haven't told me several times.*

Marcy took a moment, "Uh … good as can be, I guess. Taking care of a small child at my age wasn't in my plan."

"I don't envy you." She yawned as she glanced at the front page of the SFO Chronicle.

"Ellie, I got this call from a company called Technovenia. They want to buy my IPS shares."

"Have you talked to Michael?"

"No. He's got much bigger problems than mine."

"How soon do you have to make a decision?"

Marcy began to sob. "I'm three months behind on the home mortgage, the two credit cards maxed out, and I have unpaid medical bills. Don't know how much longer I can hold on."

Ellie looked at her calendar. "Before you make any decision, I know some investors who might be interested."

"Ellie, you're an angel. That would really help me."

"Marcy, take care of yourself. I'll call in a few days. I'll talk with Michael; no need to bother him."

"Thanks, Ellie. I feel much better now."

Ellie dialed Giorgio's number. "Marcy just called about Technovenia."

"Think Michael knows?"

"She called me first. I'll string Ms. Dummy along for a while."

"Right, my pretty lady! We'll get another party to call her with a better offer to confuse her even more," Giorgio said.

"Great idea. I think she's getting desperate, so we'll need to move fast."

"Have the trust shares voted?"

"No, thank Dr. Y for that. He's acting like the enemy of our enemy."

"Okay, here's what I'm thinking ... "

Ellie listened to his ideas on the next steps involving Marcy, Pug, Yamura, and Blunt. She felt confident the plan progressed nicely.

At the end of their call, she stated, "The three Americans will be our useful idiots. Dr. Y could be a useful ally."

44
TUESDAY, JUNE 11
BURLINGAME

AT THE END OF THE work day, Pug watched the three techs leave Skunk 2. He told Darni he'd see her about 9:30 after he met with a visitor.

An hour later, the buzzer rang. "Kevin, glad ya could make it. Come back to my office. Got fresh coffee."

Kevin sat near the cot. Pug came back with two cups and handed one to Kevin.

"You sleep here?" Kevin asked.

Pug grinned. "Something like that. Ya know Jobs slept in his office at Apple? Want cream?"

"Nope, like it black."

"My kinda guy! Drinks Patrick Henry from the bottle, no cream in your java, a mechanical engineer who loves technology and good-lookin' ladies!" He saw Kevin smile.

"By the way, studied your licensing model," Kevin said.

"So, whadya think?"

"Very clever. Your multi-phased model allows licensees to go fast or slow, and it gives them multiple options to get new technologies into the marketplace. I have some ideas to improve it."

"Hey man, hard to improve perfection! But before we get specific, sign my non-disclosure form."

"Sorry?" Kevin asked.

"Simple. Before ya hear my secret ideas, ya gotta sign my non-disclosure. Put your J. Henry on it. Bein' a lawyer, you understand secrecy."

Pug watched Kevin read the document twice. *Kevin knows I'm serious.*

Kevin handed the signed document to Pug. "Let's talk."

"You're no nonsense like me. My mentor insisted on usin' NDAs."

"Mentor?"

"One of my techs told me about these retired dudes who help small business start-ups. Figured it was a good way to get free advice. So, I met this Howard Riley. He's an engineer like me and has me doin' a business model. Ya know, things like what customer problems need solvin', who are they, what's your value proposition, who's your potential partners, blah, blah, blah. Hell, I'm gettin' a real-life MBA. Best part, he listens, never interrupts—my kind o' guy."

"Okay, tell me your ideas." Kevin requested.

"One other thing. My mentor gave me a case study written by Jackson Huntley. Asshole wrote this case study about my former company. It's all fake crap! I sued the bastard's law firm for corruption. Now I'll sue him for defamin' me."

"You have a copy of the case study?"

"I'll get it before you leave."

"So, back to your ideas," Kevin continued.

"'Member when you told me there's been no real disruptin' in exhaust systems for the last thirty years?"

"Yes."

"For years, had this idea about inventin' a modular thermal-acoustic integrator to control heat and noise." He handed Kevin a lab book. "Look at my 1995 notes about co-molded technology."

Pug watched him examine the cover page, Paul James's Lab Notes, 1995. Each page's lower right corner was missing; where the inventor's initials normally appeared.

"Pug, the sketches and designs are very interesting. It looks like you designed an all-in-one dissipater comprised of co-molded high-temp, heat resistant plastics with high-temp special metal alloys. Your sketches show how it applies to auto exhaust systems."

"Kevin, by gosh, ya got it!"

"How'd you come up with this?" Kevin asked.

"Look, I'm great at solvin' customer problems and patentin' solutions. When we got more time, I'll tell you about my MatraConnect 5000 and silver-lining inventions. Anyway, when you said automotive OEM's want new solutions, it hit me. They want lighter-weight materials, more flexible dimensions, better heat and noise control, and modular flexibility. Goes without sayin' they want lower bucks, maintenance, all that … an' my solutions can be customized!"

"How's that?"

"By specing my solutions for each customer like I did at MatraScience."

"Sounds intriguing. But how do you customize the solutions?"

"VSA's," Pug replied.

"What that?"

"Vehicle System Analyses."

"So, how do you deal with competitors?" Kevin wondered.

"With VSAs, you're first to hear and see the problems. Bingo! First to invent a solution. Bango! First to set the spec standard, so bongo! First to commercialize, bongo again!"

"But … competition?"

"Piece o' cake! If customer wants multiple suppliers, my licensing model lets the competitors share my technology. No need to develop their own solutions. Bingo, bango, bongo, bongo, and bongo again! Everybody's happy."

"You sound like a can-do guy, a real visionary!"

"When I was Green Beret in 'Nam, anyone tellin' me it can't be done, I told 'em, you're right, you can't do it, but I'll get someone who can."

"Semper fi."

"Well, I'll be a sonovabitch. You a Marine?"

Kevin rolled up a sleeve to reveal a tattoo—an eagle atop a world globe.

"Oorah!" Pug exclaimed. He watched Kevin grin.

"So, Pug, you've outlined an all-in-one modular structure exhaust system of co-molded plastic and metal alloys that meets stringent design specs and cost targets."

"Well, almost. Done lots of preliminary materials testin' and my proofs of concepts need more work, but I'm on my way, baby!"

"How about meeting national certifications for safety, quality, and environmental standards?"

"What?"

"Certifications like Underwriters Lab and similar European ones would increase the acceptance of a new technology," Kevin replied.

"Should be a piece o' cake. See why I need more space to do all this stuff?"

"How do you see us working together?"

"First, you call on automotive customers and find customer needs and problems. Ya know, mission marketing for my VSAs. My mentor says do the research to find customer segments, size of opportunity. Right up your alley! Every OEM needs a separate VSA. Customers get committed to my solutions from the get-go."

"Makes sense. Besides the introductions and getting the VSA's launched, what else?"

"I need a separate company and location to finalize the designs, proofs of concept, and field testing. This location sucks. I'm under contract with another firm who ain't in the auto world. Besides, not enough space and techs."

"Space won't be a problem. Mom's broker license is still active. What I need from you is a list of requirements—space, capital equipment, etc."

"Great and you, my semper-fi buddy, will file the patents and do licensing deals after I invent."

"Before we continue, need you to sign my NDA." Kevin pulled a five-page document from his briefcase.

"Huh?"

"Like you, I have proprietary ideas that could enhance your idea."

Looking skeptical, Pug scanned, then signed it. "Okay, whadya got?"

"I'm always looking for ways to introduce other capabilities to improve vehicle performance, acoustics, and emissions. Your modular exhaust system concept could be strengthened by adding electronics. It allows drivers to monitor, adjust and optimize the thermal and acoustics operating performance—not to mention better fuel consumption, diesel combustion and emissions, catalytic burn-through, and controlling carbon monoxide dissipation."

"Whoa there! That's a mouthful! Like adding Jobs and Gates to my invention."

"Absolutely! No one has ever looked at the entire exhaust system in a holistic way. Imagine if there were a technology that could sense overheating in the exhaust system and then automatically initiate cooling."

"Hey, there is! My former company, MatraScience, has this neat stuff called cool trace which does that—cools hot areas."

"Great, I'll check that out. Also, I think there's another technology for noise trace. I know an Australian acoustics engineer who invented this for Japanese OEMs."

"The more, the better. Gettin' electronics into my invention needs more test equipment, resources. See why I need more space and special equipment?"

"What else do we need to discuss?"

"Bucks to get started?"

"How much can you invest?"

"Me and my mentor guy are doin' a business plan." *When in doubt just wing it.*

"When you got some numbers, I'll talk with Mom. Should she sign an NDA?"

Pug laughed. *She and I don't hide anything.* "Hey man, this has been a good meeting. Oh, one more thing: 'member when I told you about a company with neat silver-lining technology?"

"Yeah, I think you also mentioned that to my mom."

"I still have a nice hunk of shares in this company. The foreigners who control it are lettin' my technology die on the vine."

"So, what do you propose?"

"If we can round up enough money, I can approach each shareholder with an offer they can't refuse. Ya know, get the company on the cheap and use the silver-lining technologies for my project. I'll get ya the details."

"Thanks."

"Before I forget, there's another group interested in buying my shares. It's some foreign venture fund. Maybe we can deal them in."

"Who's the fund?"

"Technovenia. Here's the contact guy."

"Thanks, Pug. By the way, Mom seems like a new person since you and she reconnected."

"Yeah, I feel like I'm back in 1987 when we first met," Pug said.

"She loves being back in the business mix and that makes me happy."

"What do you mean?"

Pug saw Kevin's knowing grin as he heard him say, "It means she spends less time and money with Dr. Taylor."

Pug laughed. "You and me see eye-to-eye on that!"

Kevin left at 10:30. Pug was ecstatic. Kevin was on board. In his mind, he had hit the trifecta, Tiffanee's money, Kevin's automotive and IP knowledge, and great sex.

He locked the building and walked to his condo. Darnisha was watching Fox news. Pug announced, "Honey, I'm ready for that steak and more of your lovin' feelin'."

As Kevin drove home, myriad subjects flashed through his mind. Working with Pug would be fun. He didn't think Pug had much money to invest in this project so McIntyre control would be required. In Kevin's mind, that was fine because he could control the project's pace.

Pug's ideas about the co-molded technology felt revolutionary. They were definitely applicable to the OEM's exhaust system. Kevin realized his own ideas about electronics would strengthen the resulting patents.

Concerning legal matters, he chuckled at Pug's NDA. Easy to ignore if push comes to shove. But he would investigate Pug's lawsuit threat.

The Technovenia connection was another mystery. Was it a coincidence that both Gordon and Pug communicated with this group?

One thing bothered him. When he entered Pug's office, he smelled a woman's perfume near the cot. If Pug were involved with another woman, it would devastate his mom.

He left a voice mail for Tiffanee. "Just finished meeting Pug. He's a ball of energy, full of innovative ideas. Pug's project looks exciting, and I'll talk to you about locations, funding, and other matters—patents, legal structure/control and ownership, and the JV."

45
WEDNESDAY, JUNE 12
NEW YORK/OSAKA

RONALD BLUNT RELAXED IN AN oversized chair aboard his private 727 jet as it sped toward Osaka. The flight steward had just served him a double cheeseburger, French fries, and diet coke. After dousing them with ketchup and mayonnaise, Blunt took a huge bite and looked at Doug Stiller, his legal advisor. "What's my agenda for this Koby guy?"

"Didn't you read my memo?" Doug replied.

"Fuck no! Too long! I know these guys are tricky. You never know who decides what. Always babbling in their fuckin' language. Damn it, speak American! They lost the war for chrissakes."

"Ronald, Japanese prefer consensus," Doug said. "We have to be patient."

"You gotta convince 'em all or they don't deal. How many will we meet?"

"Not clear. A guy named Nash did all the arrangements."

"Whatever, I'm not losing to them. Tell me about this Koby guy. Any dirt on him?"

"Suzi Yamamoto says Kobayashi is very cautious, but she thinks you'll beat him hands down. She says he's a weak negotiator." Stiller took a deep breath and continued reading. "General MacArthur got Kobayashi started in the appliance industry. Kobayashi became the CEO of Japan Technologies, a major vendor for all appliance OEMs. He's also leads the Hondoya keiretsu."

"What-the-fuck's a kudzu?"

"Sorry, Ronald, I meant cartel. Bottom line, he's very successful and quite wealthy. Our source says billions with no debt."

"I'm worth billions too!" Blunt's marketing brand required this continuing fiction.

Doug swallowed hard and continued. "Later Kobayashi got into real estate—specifically hotels, golf courses, condos. Hence the reason for our visit."

"Can we trust our source?" Ronald wadded up the burger wrapping and tossed it on the tray.

"Absolutely! Yamura's intelligence is first rate."

"Okay, cut to the chase, Dougy boy. How do I deal?"

"We studied our current financials and the three properties Kobayashi offered for sale. Makes no sense to buy the hotels. Our banks won't finance."

"How's 'bout my German bank pals?"

"They got serious SEC and justice problems. Meantime, we let Kobayashi think we want a purchase deal. In the end, you finesse Kobayashi with a premium license to brand and manage their hotels, a win-win. They get your brand; their cash goes straight to your bottom line."

"Hell, tell me somethin' I don't know. How about the golf course? I wanna own that."

"Follow the money!" Doug smiled.

"Right! I get him to invest in my US condos in New York, Jersey, and Florida. I bet he'll love cleaning his excess cash in my properties. Okay, heard enough. I'm ready to rock and roll." He yelled at the flight steward, "Hey, another cheeseburger!" He looked at Doug. "Any Koby weaknesses I can leverage?"

Doug handed him a thick report prepared by Yamura and Associates. Blunt tossed it back. "Tell me—twenty-five words or less."

"With more money, Yamura will create fake dirt about dark secrets."

"And why should I believe this Yamura? I'll see how the meeting goes before I bribe more losers. Shit, they couldn't win a war if they tried. I'll nuke Koby by myself."

Doug chuckled. The steward returned with cheeseburgers and Cokes and announced, "Sir, Captain says we land in 45 minutes."

"This golf game with Koby is important. I need to beat him so he'll deal."

"No problem, Ronald. I sent your official handicap to Kobayashi. He'll have to give you strokes."

"Good. When he realizes he's losing the match, that'll soften him up. I hear these guys don't like to be embarrassed."

That evening, Shiganari called. "Kenji, what did the pulmonologist say?"

"He took an x-ray to see if I have infection. I should know soon. Do not worry."

"But I do worry."

"He will prescribe antibiotics like they always do." Kenji knew that soon he would have to admit the truth.

"What do you think of Mr. Blunt's proposal?" Shiganari asked.

"His initial offer for hotels is insulting, not serious."

"Suzi says he always starts with ridiculous offers. In the end, he just wants to license his brand and management services."

"Will licensing increase the revenue for our hotels?"

"Natsu's research indicates no history of similar Blunt deals in Japan. We would be charting new ground."

"I'll take advantage of that point," Kenji replied. "What about the golf course?"

"That's different. Suzi says he will buy it if he can find financing."

"I predict that, during our game, he will reveal his true intentions."

"Natsu developed scenarios for us to consider. She suggested we purchase Blunt condominiums in the US. Suzi agrees."

"That makes sense," Kenji said. For him the more disturbing news was what Suzi told him about Yamura's report. More evidence that Yamura was actively involved to disrupt his plans.

Shiganari added, "Should be an interesting round of golf. Blunt sounds like a checkers player. Natsu arranged for the natto and drunken prawns tests at the Comfort Station."

"I will promise Blunt to do my best regarding his requests. Like I did for Pug James."

"Hai, let him think you will take care of it." They both laughed. This was code for delaying without insulting the other party. But in this case, he might surprise Blunt by making haste quickly.

Later, a limo delivered Kenji to the hotel. He and Blunt would meet on the first tee at eight o'clock in the morning. The golf course would be closed except for Kenji and Blunt.

That night in bed, Kenji read quotes from his favorite samurai warrior, Miyamoto Musashi. The one quote he loved best, "Truth is not want you want it to be. It is what it is, and you must bend to its power or live a lie." Before he closed his eyes, another thought hit him. *I suspect Mr. Blunt lives a constant lie.*

46
WEDNESDAY, JUNE 12
ST. MAARTEN/ST. MARTIN

TIFFANEE'S PRIVATE JET LANDED AT Princess Juliana Airport on the Dutch side of St. Maarten. She and Pug whisked through private customs and passport control where Alfred, her housekeeper/cook/driver, greeted them.

"Bienvenue à Saint-Martin, Madame McIntyre."

"Merci, Alfred, wonderful to be back. I'd like you to meet Monsieur James. He'll be staying at Maison de McIntyre."

"Bonjour, Monsieur, my pleasure to make your acquaintance. Your first visit to our lovely island?"

"Sure is. I hear you have some great rum." Pug smiled at Tiffanee and added, "This lovely lady told me this is where genius goes to relax. I'll dream big here."

"Oui, Monsieur. St. Martin will not disappoint. Please follow me."

Alfred opened doors to the silver Mercedes 520, then slipped into the driver's seat. Tiffanee opened chilled Champagne and poured two glasses. "Here's to five days of fun, great cuisine, and ..." She leaned close and whispered, " ... other things."

Pug raised his glass. "Babe, I'm all yours!" *And you're my silver-lining key!*

Pug enjoyed the drive to Tiffanee's villa. Alfred's smooth-as-silk navigation of winding roads and hairpin curves impressed him.

When they arrived, he was amazed by Tiffanee's enormous hill-top home overlooking Orient Bay. The luxurious interior extended out to a terrace with a swimming pool that appeared to hang over the cliff. His engineering eyes took it all in.

"We'll lunch on my private beach, Pug, Fair warning! No clothes allowed."

"Umm ... before we go, I better use the restroom." *It's Niagra time.*

He returned just as Alfred emerged from the kitchen with a picnic basket.

Tiffanee led him down a sloping path to stone steps leading to white, pristine-clean sand. Pug stopped in his tracks. He marveled at the blue water, the waves gently crashing. A huge blue umbrella—the same blue as the sky and the water—awaited them. He drew in the warm air and felt sun on his naked body. *Chrissakes, can't get better than this!*

They cooled off in the ocean and then returned to the beach. He poured Champagne while Tiffanee spread out the lunch.

"Tiff, been thinkin' 'bout our future since we connected."

"Like what?"

"Me and Kevin could start us a skunk business bringin' my inventions to all kinds of industries, startin' with automotive. Kevin'll do missionary marketing. I invent, Kevin patents, then we commercialize. Best of all you'll be with me for the ride of your life!"

"You mean like what we did at MatraScience?"

"Much better! I'm talkin' a bunch of customers, industries, the whole nine yards."

"Sounds like you need another entity to accomplish this."

"Bingo!"

"A Skunk 3?"

"Bango! I'll call it Pug's Silver-Lining Works 3. All the new products will use my silver-lining technologies."

"And what's the bongo part?"

"Takin' Skunk 3 public."

"That sounds exciting! How much money will you need?"

Pug knew he'd hooked her. Now, reel her in. "I'm thinkin' at least half a mill to get things rollin.' That doesn't include a facility."

"Probably not unreasonable if the market opportunity supports it. Have you done a business plan?"

"Tiff, right now it's all in my beautiful mind, so need someone like you to ask questions and take notes. May need more cash to buy that company I told Kevin about. Kevin loved my idea."

"Kevin and I have already discussed this."

Pug felt he had both McIntyres locked and loaded. Time to strike while the iron was hot. "But more urgent, I need to speed my co-molded idea, but it can't involve Skunk 2. My client won't fund this cuz it's not related to their business."

"What do you mean?" Tiffanee asked.

"I need outside technical work to get the best molding techniques to combine plastics and metal alloys. For the next six months, my excess cash is tied up in real estate."

"So how can I help?"

He topped off her glass.

"You think you can invest some bucks to get this work done on the QT?"

"How much?"

"For starters, I'm thinkin' around 200K."

Pug saw her pause before replying. Had he overplayed his hand?

"I can swing that. Won't bother Kevin with such a small amount."

He couldn't believe his good luck. She was totally committed. "Tiff, you're one special doll." *And a very easy mark. Doc Taylor's got nothin' on me!*

She leaned toward him. "Pug James, I love your mind, your way with words, and most of all being with you. You've given me so many exciting things to think about. I love being back in the action with you."

"I wanna propose a toast. To the next phase of our beautiful relationship ... our bingo, bango and bongo."

"To our bingo, bango, and bongo," Tiffanee responded, laughing. "Let's finish lunch and relax for a while. Later, I'm taking you to my favorite restaurant in Coco Bay."

At the restaurant that evening, the owner brought the first course, a delectable seafood salad featuring ten different local fish.

"Pug, today with you on the beach was wonderful. Your enthusiasm, ideas and dreams have me excited beyond belief. I'll talk with Kevin when we return. We three will be a great team!"

"You got it, sweetheart."

"Meant to ask you, you remember when Dr. Taylor introduced us to Gordon Orlio when we attended church?"

"Yeah."

"Gordon works with me on the church's fund-raising committee. For some reason, he seems very interested in you."

"What'd you tell 'im?"

"Nothing really other than you work in product development. I hope I didn't betray your confidence."

"Nah. All them gators are nosy. If he keeps asking, you let me know." *Why's this dude checking on me? Didn't Fieldsy tell me one time his wife worked for some guy named Orlio?*

They enjoyed glorious days sunbathing, picnicking on the beach, boating to nearby islands, and dining in St. Martin's finest restaurants. For a change of pace, Tiffanee took Pug to a public beach near the Esmeralda Resort on Orient Bay—swimsuits optional.

Settling in beach chairs under a colorful umbrella, they watched people stroll by, many naked. Pug could hardly stand it. "Some of them gals are lookin' pretty darn good," he chortled, "but some just oughta cover it up."

Tiffanee suppressed a laugh. "Ditto for the fat dudes too." She removed her dark glasses and looked over at him. "Oh, forgot to tell you. I got a message from Kevin about our technology JV. You know, the one we might use to facilitate the new skunk works."

"Right. What'd he say?"

"Well, we have this partner we need to dump from the JV so we can move faster with your idea."

"Who's the dumpee?"

"You're not going to believe this, but it's Ronald Blunt. Think I told you he and Alan started the JV, but it went dormant after Alan passed. Blunt's not interested in technology."

"Lemme know when he's gone, so me and Kevin can get crackin'."
No way Blunt gets in the way of my deal. Screw 'im!"

Tiffanee smiled. "Kevin likes your idea for buying the IPS shares. We can do it if you'd put up collateral for your share of the purchase."

"No problem-o. I'll pledge my IPS shares and personally guarantee the loan. How's that sound, babe?"

"Perfect."

Pug smiled broadly at her. In his mind he had found his Tiffanee silver mine. His only question was how much money he could extract. He couldn't wait to leave Skunk 2 and put Michael in his rear-view mirror.

47
THURSDAY/FRIDAY, JUNE 13/14
OSAKA

KENJI AND RONALD MET ON the first tee of the challenging five-star golf course owned by Kenji's trust. The course featured narrow fairways, considerable water hazards, deep sand bunkers, and tricky undulating greens. Expensive to join, membership included top business executives and government officials—Blunt's type of club.

"Mr. Blunt, a pleasure to meet you," Kenji said, offering his hand.

"Likewise. Do me a good deal, and I'll invite you to my 'Big Apple' as my special guest!"

Kenji knew from Natsu's brief that Blunt often used this term. He conveyed a confused look prompting Blunt to add, "'Big Apple' ... my private brand for the greatest city in the greatest nation in this world. Means big opportunity and big bucks if you bite my 'Big Apple!'"

Kenji nodded and smiled. *This gaigin has no problem praising himself.* "I appreciate your invitation to the ... uh ... large apple. Shall we begin?"

"You bet. Up for a little wager?"

"Perhaps," Kenji mused, "but you are almost a scratch golfer, and I will need strokes."

"Don't believe what you hear in the fake news. When I got my MBA at Harvard, I shot close to par. Now it's closer to fifteen, because I don't practice. Too busy wheelin' and dealin'."

"I have a ten handicap, so I'll give you five strokes." Kenji knew from Natsu's report that Blunt was notorious for cheating, and he did not graduate from Harvard.

"Deal!" Blunt replied.

"As my guest, you have first honors," Kenji said.

Blunt blasted a 275-yard drive slicing sharply into heavy rough. "Reaching the green from there is almost impossible," Kenji remarked. Kenji placed his drive down the middle, just left of center, at approximately 225 yards.

Blunt, driving the cart, dropped off Kenji near his ball then continued down the pathway to find his. Kenji watched him search and called out, "Do you need help?"

"Nope, found it!"

Kenji took a five-iron shot, and the ball landed pin high about fifteen feet left of the hole. He watched Blunt take seven practice swings, pause, and adjust the ball's lie. The second shot landed on the green about five feet from the hole. Blunt drove towards Kenji and yelled, "See that? Tiger showed me how to play the rough. Ever played golf with him?"

"You play to a fifteen handicap?" Kenji asked.

"Feel like I'm back in my Harvard groove."

Kenji smiled at him. *Not bad for someone who went to CUNY on Staten Island.*

They finished the first hole with Blunt's birdie. Kenji managed a respectable par. Over the next seven holes, Kenji tested Blunt's intentions regarding the purchase of the two hotels. By the ninth hole, he knew Blunt wouldn't buy. Instead, Blunt proposed a licensing deal plus a substantial management fee but still wanted to buy the golf course.

After the first nine holes, they strolled to the restaurant. Kenji ordered beer, and Blunt requested a diet Coke. Kenji raised his glass. "Mr. Blunt, to a successful conclusion of both golf and business. May our second nine be as interesting."

Blunt replied, "Looks like I'm three up on you. How 'bout we double the bet so you can recover your loss?"

"Okay."

"Great! Now let's talk business. So how do you like my latest idea?"

"I think I could consider a licensing option. Perhaps that might work well for our hotels."

"The Blunt name is pure gold! You'd be first to enjoy my brand in Japan. You can take that to the bank!"

"Your licensing and management fees exceed traditional Japanese business norms. I require a substantial reduction before proceeding. How much discount can you offer?"

"What about the golf course? You willing to finance my purchase?"

Kenji remembered Suzi telling him Blunt often changed the subject to avoid answering hard questions "First, in order to finance your purchase of the golf course, you must forgo your hotel license and management fees as installment payments for the golf course."

Blunt thought for a moment. "Not sure I like that. Any other ideas?"

"Yes, but it would require investing in your American properties. If I were to buy several New York and Florida condominiums at acceptable prices, this could provide funds for your golf course purchase."

Blunt glanced down at his Kobe burger. He picked up the ketchup bottle, slapped it hard, and smothered the burger and fries. "If we can agree on prices, I can live with that."

Kenji took out a note pad and wrote the numbers 28%+ (NYC) and 35%+ (Fla). He handed the pad to Blunt and watched him do a quick mental calculation. Kenji knew Blunt was multiplying the prices times the number of units.

Blunt displayed a big toothy grin. "You just made a fantastic deal. I'll get Stiller to work the details. When we finish the second nine, we can wrap it. Okay for you?"

"Agreed," Kenji replied.

"You wanna know why I liked your second idea?"

"That would be most helpful."

"Don't like to mix my golf course business with my hotel deals. Your second idea did just that." He wadded up his napkin and tossed it on the table. "Say, any chance you're interested in technology?"

"What did you have in mind?" This surprised Kenji.

Reaching for a folder, Blunt replied, "Take a look at this, and we'll discuss before dinner."

In the lounge after they finished the round, Stiller presented a draft MOU and explained the revised deal numbers. Kenji excused himself to take a phone call. When he returned, he suggested minor revisions to the MOU before he and Ronald initialed each page and signed the last one.

Kenji proposed a sake toast; Ronald raised his Diet Coke. "To a successful deal that will be win-win, as Americans say."

"You won't regret this, and there's more deals like this ahead."

"Let us return to our rooms and prepare for dinner," Kenji concluded. "I hope you will enjoy our dining celebration at the Comfort Station and the special after-dinner entertainment."

"Great! Any questions about the JV investment?"

"If I understand, you wish a cash buyout of your 50% interest in this JV?"

"Yeah, just enough to recover my initial investment."

"Why sell?" Kenji asked.

"My original partner started this several years ago. He died before I got this venture runnin.' Between you and me, technology's not my thing. But, tell you what, having a JV in Silicon Valley is a huge opportunity to find new tech for your appliance businesses. Can't go wrong."

"I would like to talk with the other partner before investing. Would you put me in contact?"

"Hey Stiller, connect Kevin McIntyre with this fantastic guy. Tell 'im Kenji's got Blunt's seal of approval."

Kenji asked, "The name is Kevin McIntyre?"

"Yep, you're gonna love working with them McIntyres. Just so you know, I've already been contacted by Technovenia wanting to invest in this JV. So, don't linger. Much rather do a deal with who I know than who I don't."

"One more question, Mr. Blunt. You do not wish to continue any equity interest in this JV?"

"No."

With that, they agreed to meet at eight at the Comfort Station.

Natsu called Kenji and asked, "How did your discussions go?"

"Blunt thinks he just did a win-lose deal, but surprised at how fast I agreed."

"Kobayashi-sama, are you happy with the licensing deal?"

"Since we are the first hotels in Japan to license the Blunt name, I made him defer the first four-years' payments until the Blunt brand proves it increases our hotel revenues above the last four-years average. Natsu-chan, your deferral idea was very clever."

"Arigato, I will investigate this JV and see if it makes sense. We can reimburse Blunt for the verified original amount plus some nominal interest."

"Excellent," Kenji replied.

"I arranged extra-special entertainment for him tonight. We have three beautiful Geishas. It was Suzi's idea. The cameras are in place." Natsu said.

"Sun Tzu would be most proud of you both."

The next morning, Kenji accompanied Blunt to the airport in a stretch limo. On the way to the tarmac, Kenji listened to Blunt brag about his New York City limos. They stopped next to Blunt's plane.

Blunt turned with a big grin. "Kenji, your hospitality's been super huge. Last night's entertainment was fantastic. Loved doing karaoke with those hostess gals—first-class babes, with special moves. I should put them in my annual beauty contests."

"Pleased you enjoyed them." Kenji glanced down at his phone and read Natsu's text:

Photos and video will be ready when you get back.

Blunt grabbed Kenji's hand dragging him forward slightly. "Look forward to doing more win/win deals."

Kenji shook his hand and extricated himself. "I agree."

Blunt groaned as he got out of the limo suggesting he was exhausted from last evening's entertainment. Kenji watched Blunt's three hundred-pound frame slowly climb the stairs. He turned and waved at Kenji before entering the plane.

Kenji texted Natsu. *Contact Kevin McIntyre and update Suzi. We have just bought Mr. Blunt like Japan bought President Reagan.*

He pulled out a handkerchief and coughed. His latest pulmonary tests weighed heavily on his mind.

48
SATURDAY, JUNE 15
SSFO/OSAKA

THE NEXT MORNING, NATSU AND Michael held their first of the scheduled weekly phone conversations.

"Natsu, good to finally talk with you in private. I apologize for not visiting Osaka earlier, but things have been very hectic at IPS."

"Understandable, Michael. I look forward to our talks. What would you like to discuss?"

"As you know, I settled the IPS lawsuit with Dexter-Foresman. Jackson Huntley has agreed to take over Ellie's work. This couldn't happen soon enough."

"Wonderful news. Using Jackson is a smart move."

"Jackson will complete the Delaware plan and assist in the planned merger. I've asked him to learn the IP aspects of Skunk 2's projects. When he gets firm data, he will visit Osaka and provide an in-person briefing for you and your IP lawyers."

"That will be most helpful for our patent work in Japan. When he is here, I will show him our automotive project."

"I've also asked Jackson to take Pug's licensing model and develop a commercialization strategy for new technologies. He has considerable experience in such matters."

"That will help us develop a global IP strategy for commercialization. When we next talk on June 22, I will have an update on JT's automotive project."

Natsu felt good about this first call. *We are off to a good start. Kobayashi-sama's advice seems prescient. Michael's actions verify that he can be trusted.*

49
MONDAY, JUNE 17
OSAKA

Following Kenji's instructions from their last meeting in Mt. Fuji, Seamus met Kenji at his Osaka residence. Seamus had compiled sufficient intelligence to warrant an initial report. In anticipation, Kenji asked Natsu to observe the conversation in an adjoining room. She had been monitoring Seamus's activities for the last two weeks.

"Kon'nichiwa, Kobayashi-sama."

"Kon'nichiwa, Seamus."

Kenji took a slow sip of Johnnie Walker Blue. "I'm drinking scotch. You prefer Sapporo?" Kenji coughed and the rattle in his chest preventing him from speaking.

In the other room, Natsu looked on with renewed alarm.

Seamus retrieved a Sapporo from a bar cooler.

Kenji dabbed his mouth with a handkerchief. "Seamus, what have you learned since we last talked?"

Seamus opened his brief case and removed documents. "As you requested, I've investigated Gano-Nippon and Lawrent, the respective competitors of JT and IPS. It took longer than expected because I used intermediaries. They are slower than I." He handed Kenji a copy of his report.

"I understand the precautions to avoid meeting any prior associates," Kenji said, as he scanned the index. "I will share with Natsu. She will discuss details with you at a later date. Seamus, please summarize the key points."

"First, Lawrent still dominates the dissipater market at General Appliance of the US and is seriously attempting to steal IPS's Exeter business. Lawrent will cut dissipater prices to put more pressure on IPS's profits. Also, Lawrent bribes Exeter's procurement people. When IPS loses the business to Lawrent, it will then raise prices with procurement's blessing."

"So, Lawrent will sacrifice short-term profits to steal IPS's business," Kenji said as he tipped his glass and drained it. "Has IPS responded?"

"From all indications, IPS is holding its own. It hired new sales engineers to supplement Marken's political efforts. IPS offers new silver-lining technical solutions to problems that Lawrent ignores or cannot offer. Exeter seems content for now, thanks to Marken's political relationships."

"I'll have Marken offer incentives to counter Lawrent's. Did you learn anything about Lawrent's attempts to acquire the IPS technology and patents?"

"Apparently, it still wants control. It hired Technovenia, an Italian venture fund, to secretly buy IPS shares. Lawrent's former CEO is one of the fund's principals."

"Interesting." Kenji's face did not reveal his first thought: *Hakase Yamura lies again.* "Seamus, find which IPS shareholders have been contacted and who are Technovenia's other principals and its law firm." He looked forward to checking Seamus's information against what Michael had already reported. "Now, Seamus," he said, smiling, "let us discuss Gano-Nippon and General Appliance of Japan."

Seamus thumbed through his paperwork. "As you suspected, Gano works with General Appliance of Japan to undermine both Japan Technologies's and Hondoya's positions in the dissipater markets. Their combined efforts started when Hondoya's CEO and you announced your respective retirements."

"That is why we will now unofficially delay those actions."

"That's prudent. Lawrent and Gano-Nippon know about the Delaware plan and the merger. Hakase Yamura has met with senior officials from both General Appliance and Gano-Nippon. These photos prove this."

Kenji replied, "Then we must provide more corrupt intelligence compliments of an unwitting Ashi-kun." He looked at his watch. "Seamus, would you join me for an early dinner?"

"May I postpone your kind offer? It's been an exhausting two weeks."

"Of course, Seamus. Arigato for your hard work on this sensitive matter. We will talk again in a few days. May I ask how you and Debiddo are coordinating?"

"His progress is quite impressive. Natsu also makes significant contributions to this project."

"That is good news, indeed. You can be most proud of your daughter."

Seamus nodded and excused himself.

Kenji thought, *Why doesn't Seamus express more pride in his daughter? I'm sure Natsu noticed this.*

As soon as Seamus had left, Natsu found Kenji refilling his glass of Scotch and lighting another cigarette.

"Kobayashi-sama, I wish you would not smoke so much. You ignore your doctor!"

"Natsu-chan, I know, I know. Smoking is my one vice that provides immediate satisfaction. What are your thoughts about Seamus's report?"

She was frustrated by Kenji's continued smoking. He ignored her pleas by changing the subject. "We are fortunate for Seamus's assistance. However, it pains me to say this ... I still do not trust him nor my oji-san Ashi."

Kenji massaged his arthritic hands. "Your instincts are correct. In the past, Seamus has betrayed many. Recently, Ashi-kun has also exhibited betrayal. Has your independent monitoring discovered any unusual activities by the either of the two?"

Natsu's lovely face grew sad. "During Seamus's off hours, he spends considerable time watching videos with a former Gano-Nippon associate." She saw a look of concern cross Kenji's face. "I will continue to monitor him to verify his words. As for Oji-san, I will monitor him as well. He talks frequently with Hakase Yamura. This causes me concern."

"What else do you plan?"

"I will keep Seamus focused on very specific targets—assisting Debiddo on technical matters and assisting me on marketing intelligence. At the appropriate time, I will ask him to monitor Pug James."

Kenji sipped more Johnnie Walker and added, "I will have Seamus coordinate with Okazaki-san on monitoring Hakase Yamura's activities."

"Hai, Kobayashi-sama. That is exactly what Sun Tzu would advise. Meanwhile, my weekly communications have started with Michael Fields. I now see why you trust Michael unconditionally." She updated him on her last call with Michael. When Kenji coughed, she waited then asked if she could bring him tea. He signaled no.

"Excellent summary," he said, swallowing hard, suppressing a cough. "Michael continues to exceed our expectations. He will be a very important ally."

Natsu rose from her chair, leaned over, and kissed Kenji on the forehead. She whispered in his ear. "I admire and love you so much. I will let you rest, and we will talk in the morning. Good night."

As she returned to her office, she felt sad. Okazaki-sama confided that Kenji's health had deteriorated. She could tell that the latest news about Seamus and Ashi-kun greatly disappointed him. As for herself, her stomach pains had worsened. A terrible thought crossed her mind. *What if Kobayashi-sama were unable to continue leading JT? Am I ready?*

50
MONDAY, JUNE 17
NEW YORK CITY

I N HIS BLUNT TOWER APARTMENT, Ronald inhaled a Big Mac
with American cheese, along with fries, and a 24-ounce Coke. He
belched as his personal bodyguard handed him a decrypted memo.
He swore as he patted around for his trifocals and finally located them
on top of the Big Mac wrapper.

He scanned the first bullet point: K2 engaged in unacceptable
relationship.

He almost choked on a fry. His bodyguard lurched toward him.
Blunt swallowed hard and yelled, "Get away! This is private!"

The bodyguard backed out of the room, softly closing the door.

"This is fucking huge!" he yelled. "Man-o-man! Big-time leverage!"

Then he read the second point: *Beware of spies.* "What the hell?"
he said.

The third and final point: *JVMc will betray.* "What the fuck?"

He pressed the button next to his bed, known to all as the Big Mac
button. He shoved everything off his gold lame comforter and paced
the room until his assistant brought him another Big Mac and Coke.

"I know what that goddam Yamura's doing!" he screamed at his
assistant.

"Sir?" she said, startled.

"Trying to scam more money with fake dirt. That's what!"

When all she did was stare, he waved his hand at her. "Get the fuck
out!"

He took a bite of the burger and called Stiller. "Get your ass up here! Now!"

Within minutes, Doug hustled in. "You sound upset, Boss!"

"Goddam right! I got a spy in my company! Check out everybody, and I mean everybody!"

"We did a complete review two months ago; investigators found nothing."

"Do another one! Tell Suzi to come here now!"

Stiller left and dialed her number. "Boss needs you on the 35th right away."

"About what?"

"He's pissed about some spy thing."

The guard winked at her as she entered Blunt's apartment—five floors below the penthouse occupied by wife number three.

She found Blunt sitting on the bed exposed in an open robe. Three TV screens displayed *American Idol*, *The Bachelor*, and a rerun of *The Amazing Race*.

"Suzi, grab a Coke and watch my favorite shows."

She sat down next to him, "Ronnie, have you ever thought about hosting a reality show? Audiences will love you."

"Suzi, you see the real me. Got feelers out to the major networks to pitch my idea."

He put his arm around her and whispered. She went to the bathroom, and when she returned, he was under the sheets.

Today, however, their encounter seemed rushed. She asked, "Ronnie, you seem worried."

"Can't hide anything from you. Must be your far-east thing. Someone's betraying me!"

"Want me to look into it?"

"There's something else … my potential Japan real estate partner is queer."

"Queer?"

"Koby's a homo."

"Such relationships are illegal in Japan. He would be arrested."

"Whew! That's a relief!"

"Rest assured, Ronnie, Mr. Kobayashi is not gay. I have known him

213

for years. Seen him with many different women. He bribed pregnant women to disappear. We women know when men are unnatural."

He felt her hands massage his shoulders. He began to relax.

"What kind of reality show would you like to do?" Suzi asked.

"A show about doing real estate steals. I'm the greatest, so why not show it? Great for my brand. Whadya think?"

"Brilliant!" she replied.

"Suzi, your loyalty means a lot to me."

"Thank you for rescuing me from Japan." Her enticing smile always excited him.

"Okay, Suzi. I got things to do." He waved her away.

Suzi returned to her fourth-floor office and locked the door. She signed on to a VPN known only to her and sent an encrypted message with photos.

51
MONDAY, JUNE 17
BURLINGAME

S INCE THEIR SKUNK 2 MEETING, Kevin's subsequent Detroit
trips included contacting OEMs to discuss the exhaust system
project. His extensive contacts facilitated the missionary
marketing process.

Kevin's goals at each customer visit—document technical problems
with exhaust systems, discuss improvements, and determine market
potential. With his engineering and legal background, he performed
the VSAs in a systematic and thorough manner. Kevin updated Pug
after each visit.

After several visits, Kevin met Pug at a Burlingame Starbucks.

"You're stirrin' up things in ol' Detroit!" Pug said, slapping him on
the back. Pug felt Kevin cringe. *Oops, better not manhandle this Marine.*

"Thanks, Pug. Every engineering group I've met confirms
dissatisfaction with current exhaust systems. All want better thermal
and acoustic performance. They want better 3D metrics—less weight,
less cubic volume, more flexibility in design configurations. Honestly,
their feedback fits perfectly with your ideas about the modular and
customized designs! I can confirm we have tremendous opportunities
to incorporate electronics and software for reliability, safety, emission
controls—you name it!"

"Bingo!"

"With the right solutions, we can take serious market share from
incumbent suppliers. We can set prices on value and lowest life cycle

costs. Pug, bottom line, the market potential in the US alone is several billion dollars. When you consider the global market, both Asia and Europe, multiply by two or three X."

"Right! Now, I'll start writin' the specs."

Kevin smiled. "Give me a few more visits, and I'll get solid numbers on market potential and beachhead targets."

"My mentor buddy'll be impressed! Hey, ya know a guy named Gordon Orlio?"

"One of my law school professors. Why?"

"Your mom told me he's been askin' about me. How come?"

"No clue. Want me to talk with him?"

"Nah." Pug thought he detected a moment of concern in Kevin's face.

52
TUESDAY, JUNE 18
OSAKA

NATSU HAD SPENT A RESTLESS night. At three a.m., severe contractions racked her body. "Debiddo! The baby's coming!"

"But you're not due for another two months."

"Do not argue!"

He called her doctor, dressed, grabbed her overnight case, and gently hustled her into their Lexus. Thirty minutes later, they arrived at the hospital.

Debiddo hovered near her bed. "How's the pain?"

"Terrible!" She groaned at another sharp contraction. "Call Kobayashi-sama! Now!"

Debiddo quickly dialed Kenji's number. "Kobayashi-sama! Natsu's in labor! We're at the hospital waiting for the doctor."

Kenji paged his driver and dressed. An hour later, he arrived and found Debiddo outside Natsu's room. "What did Hakase Ishikara tell you?"

"She's definitely in labor. There are problems."

Kenji lit a cigarette. Dave pointed to a sign, and Kenji extinguished it just as Hakase Ishikara appeared. They exchanged bows. The doctor had delivered Natsu thirty-five years earlier, and he and Kenji remained close since.

"Kobayashi-sama, I apologize we meet under difficult circumstances."

"What can you tell me?"

"Simply put, the placenta and umbilical cord are not supplying needed blood and oxygen to the baby. Premature labor often occurs."

"Is she in danger?"

"We don't think so. However, if the labor persists beyond twenty-four hours, we will do a caesarean section. Right now, she's sedated."

Debiddo collapsed into a chair and covered his face with his hands. Kenji looked annoyed at his display of weakness.

Seven hours passed. Kenji and Debiddo paced, spoke little. The nurse informed them that Natsu was in surgery.

Two hours later, Ishikara appeared, looking disheveled and exhausted. He motioned Kenji and Debiddo to sit.

"We could not save the child. I apologize. If he had survived, there would be severe and permanent brain damage."

"What about Natsu?" Kenji demanded.

"She had a difficult time with considerable blood loss, but now she rests comfortably. She should stay here until her vital signs stabilize. She must avoid all stress during the next several days."

"Thank God she'll be okay," Debiddo exclaimed, tears rolling down his face.

"Debiddo, control your emotions!" Kenji snapped.

The doctor interrupted, "There is one other issue."

"What?" Kenji demanded.

"There was permanent organ damage. We had to perform a complete hysterectomy."

Kenji muttered, "No!"

The doctor leaned close to Kenji and whispered, "I am truly sorry we could not save the baby. Natsu became our first priority. Natsu told me she had been experiencing problems for several weeks."

Kenji abruptly stood and departed.

"Hakase, when can I see her?" Debiddo asked.

"She will remain under sedation for several hours. I will call when she wakes."

"Arigato, Hakase Ishikara." Through tears, Debiddo said, "We planned to honor Kobayashi-sama—our son's name would have been—Kenjiro Kobayashi James."

Heartbroken and fighting tears, Debiddo headed to his car. He sat for a moment then called Seamus. "I got sad news." His voice broke. "Natsu went into premature labor. Our son was stillborn."

"Oh, my God, … my grandson." Seamus paused for a long moment. "But Natsu will have more children."

Dave sobbed. "No! She suffered permanent damage! Our relationship is cursed. Kenji will blame me for this."

"Does Kenji know?"

"Hai. He wants you to call."

53
TUESDAY, JUNE 18
BURLINGAME

ICHAEL ARRIVED AT SKUNK 2 with low expectations. Despite that, he would revisit the co-molded mystery.

Darnisha greeted him at the door. According to Sam's background report, she attended college for two years demonstrating excellent skills in both Excel and PowerPoint. Her sexual harassment lawsuit against MatraScience was true. Rumors indicated she received a nice settlement.

"Good morning, Mr. Fields. Nice to see you again. Pug's been on the phone all morning with molding vendors, but he'll be available soon."

"I'll wait in the conference room." *Molding vendors?*

Michael watched her saunter away. Sam's WMD comment flashed in his mind.

Soon Pug emerged. "Fieldsy, you ready to rock and roll?"

"Can't wait. The techs joining?"

"Nah, I'll do the updates; no need for them to listen to me yak about stuff they've done." Pug grabbed a pile of lab reports from the nearby table and handed Michael the first one. "'Member the last project review and told ya about test data baselines? Well, this first report is the latest example. Got me twenty-five more right behind this one. Darni did these reports, and they're super. She's now permanent."

Pug waited for his reaction but got nothing. It confirmed Michael remained clueless. Darni would continue to be a great distraction.

"Pug, before you start, let's look at the original project list. Tell me the status on each one and then cross-reference the test reports with projects."

"Dammit, Fieldsy! Ya sound like a guy who's never invented one fuckin' thing in his entire life. Without testin', ya can't decide what kinda materials, let alone designs and proofs of concept. Ya gotta understand the materials!"

"I'm not arguing about how products get invented. Right now, it looks like you're managing a test lab. For chrissakes Pug, if Edison or Jobs followed this approach, we'd never have a light bulb or Apple II. I want your bar napkin days back! Those ten projects I gave you represent real appliance customer problems with real revenue potential. You of all people should understand that! How do you think I can pay for this lab without revenue flowing in from new products?"

Pug started to speak, but Michael continued, "You solve customer problems with designs and proofs of concept! You know that! Then you test alternative material combinations to see which works best. That's how you invented MatraConnect 5000 and then IPS 10000. So, where's all this testing going if you can't match with customer problems?"

Pug stood up and walked to the door and slammed it shut. "This'll be a short meeting cuz I was gonna review them test reports to show what I've done. You've screwed my presentation. What the hell you want from me?"

"Let me understand. After five weeks, you can't talk about progress on any of the projects?"

"Like I told ya, we've been testing, retesting, and summarizing. But ya don't wanna hear that. So, until I match this data with the ten projects, ya gotta wait!" Pug watched Michael thumb through the pages of the first lab report. "So whadya want me to do?"

"Okay Pug, we'll schedule the next meeting date right now. When will you be ready to match all this testing with the ten projects I assigned?"

"Gimme a few days, an' I'll call ya. Your projects resulted from some douchebag's opinion about customer problems. How in the fuck do I know they're real? Until I talk to customers, I won't know what's real or fake."

"So, why don't you validate those problems so your development work can focus on solving problems?"

"Now you're talkin'!" *I got 'im by the short hairs!*

"Pug, why didn't you complain about this in week one and save us five weeks?"

"Didn't think I could change your sacred project list."

"Pug, since when have you ever let an obstacle get in the way of your 'can do' spirit?"

"Lemme think about visiting customers and make sure I'm workin' on the right problems. May come up with better ideas. Gimme a few days dependin' on who's available, blah, blah, blah."

"I'll call you next week to schedule the next review."

"Ya got it!"

"One other question before I leave. How are the three techs doing?"

"Pete and Danny, they're hummin' on all eight cylinders. Sam's still a slow poke. Frankly Scarlett, I should fire his ass and get a new tech like Pete and Danny."

"I'll talk to him. I hired all three and take responsibility for hiring and firing."

"I'll give Sam other stuff and see how he does." Pug smiled slyly. "Maybe have him report to Darni. If she has problems, I'll let you know." Pug saw no reaction from Michael.

"Okay, let's talk in a week. One more item—remember I asked you about your co-molded concept?" Michael asked.

"Yeah, it's dead. Danny's plastic testing proved it."

"Just wanted to confirm you haven't changed your opinion."

Pug laughed. "If I do, which I never will, you'll be the first hear about it. Okay?"

"Couldn't ask for more, I guess. I'll see myself out."

Pug motioned to Darni to come to his office. "Got some great news, babe. Fieldsy demanded I visit customers to verify problems for these ten projects. You're joinin' me for the visits!"

They reviewed the project list, the customers to visit, and a tentative travel schedule. "So, make the reservations ... and uh, to save money, we only need one room."

"I'll get working on those reservations," she replied without her usual air kiss.

Pug thought she would be more excited. *Maybe she's under the weather.*

Driving back to SSFO, Michael called Jackson. "Hey Jackson, just left the skunk works after another disappointing review." He described the meeting.

"Sounds like Pug's unpredictable as ever; his strength and his weakness," Jackson said.

"Got this feeling he's doing something on the side with the co-molded idea he stole from Dave. Can't prove it yet. I'll have Sam Flores call you with more details. Then call Natsu at Japan Technologies, she'll update you about Dave's project."

"Got it. Michael, I admire your tolerance and patience with Pug's behavior."

"I hate losing access to that inventive mind, but not sure how much longer I'll tolerate this."

"Michael, you know what accountants say about sunk costs?"

"Yeah, they shouldn't affect future decisions."

Now, Michael would decide how much more rope and time to give Pug.

54
WEDNESDAY, JUNE 19
OSAKA

THE NEXT DAY, KENJI VISITED Natsu in the hospital. He wanted private time with her. She appeared pale and exhausted but pleased to see him.

"Kobayashi-sama, I appreciate your visit. But you have more important things than worry about me."

"Nonsense, Natsu-chan. What does Hakase Ishikara say about your recovery?"

"I can go home in five days."

"Excellent. Hakase Ishikara told me you experienced problems before and did not consult with him. Why didn't you tell me?"

"Kobayashi-sama, I did not think it was serious. I had too many other tasks to worry about." She sensed his disappointment. "I will be fine. However, I have second thoughts now I cannot have children. This partnership with Debiddo feels cursed."

"Natsu, I am responsible for encouraging this relationship."

"This event will not defeat me. As Sun Tzu counsels, I will be agile to overcome this obstacle."

She sensed Kenji seemed relieved; however, she worried. Had Kenji disclosed everything about Debiddo?

Later, Seamus arrived at Kenji's Osaka residence and found him in the library.

"Kobayashi-sama, my deepest sympathy. I share your sadness."

Kenji sighed. "Seamus, we suffer mutual loss. When appropriate, notify Natsu's mother."

"I shall."

They sat on comfortable overstuffed chairs around an elegant teakwood table Kenji had brought from Jakarta. He opened a fresh bottle of Johnnie Walker Blue and filled two tumblers. He raised his glass, "To Natsu-chan's health and prosperity. May she overcome this tragedy and continue honoring your father's legacy." Kenji knew mentioning Patrick Hafferty's legacy always resonated for Seamus. The recent tragedy increased the stakes for Seamus's cooperation.

"Hai, to Natsu-chan and my father." He took a long swallow.

"Seamus, you must increase your assistance to Natsu."

"I can, but what about Debiddo's role?"

"Ensure the exhaust system project gets completed on time."

"I will," Seamus replied.

Kenji recalled Michael's phone call informing him about Debiddo—his marriage and child in the US. He would wait until Natsu fully recovered before sharing. He wondered why Seamus never mentioned Debiddo's marriage.

Kenji continued, "Assist Natsu-chan in commercializing the new technology. With Marken-san's help, monitor Gano-Nippon's and Lawrent's behavior and propose counter measures." He poured himself another drink. "What questions do you have?"

Before Seamus could respond, Kenji began coughing uncontrollably. He held his linen handkerchief to his mouth, and with the other, grasped his chest.

Seamus saw blood on the handkerchief. "Are you okay, Kobayashi-sama?"

He waved the concern away. "I can't seem to shake this nasty cold."

Seamus stared in disbelief.

55
FRIDAY, JUNE 21
SSFO

ICHAEL READ THE LATEST ORDERS and shipments summary and absorbed the good news that IPS business had rebounded—thanks to Marken's new business leads and reentry to General Appliance. Despite this encouraging news, it was hard to concentrate. His mind alternated among pressing issues—Ellie's betrayal, Pug's disappointing progress, and now Kenji's information about Natsu's miscarriage. Michael knew, when Natsu learned the truth about Dave's first marriage, that would compound her misery.

His secretary interrupted. "Kevin McIntyre on the phone. Says it's important."

"Put him through." He answered, "This is Michael Fields."

"Good morning, Mr. Fields. My name is Kevin McIntyre. I'm a patent attorney with McIntyre & Associates. Jackson Huntley gave me your name. I understand you worked with a Paul James at both MatraScience and IPS. Is that correct?"

"Why do you ask?"

"I'm checking references for a client interested in working with Mr. James."

"Who's your client?" Michael asked.

"Can't disclose that, however, I can say, the work involves business development."

"Mr. McIntyre, I appreciate your attorney-client concerns. Send me a written list of questions on your firm's letterhead."

"Is that necessary?"

"With all due respect, I don't discuss such matters unless I understand the total picture. Fax me a list."

"Could we meet for coffee near your office and discuss?"

"I want to see those questions first."

"I'll fax you a list."

Thirty minutes later, Michael grabbed Kevin's fax and scanned the points: *Describe Paul James's innovation process. Is he a technical collaborator or solo operator? Cite examples of his most innovative creations. What have been his innovation mishaps? Cite examples of successful commercialization of new technologies. Assess his management capability. Does he follow legal advice?*

Michael reread the items and jotted his thoughts: *Kevin's questions confirm my and Jackson's suspicions about Pug. What is this new business development and Kevin's involvement? Does this involve the co-molding idea? Are competitors involved? Who else? Sam needs more time to investigate Pug. Update Natsu.*

Next, Michael called Jackson. "Kevin McIntyre called like you predicted."

"Kevin's a great patent lawyer. Met him at the Stanford Law Conference."

"Claimed he's doing background checks on Pug for a client's business development project. Any idea what this is?" Michael asked.

"No, told him I couldn't talk about Pug because of outstanding legal matters."

"Great response! That'll make Kevin suspicious."

"What are you thinking, Michael?"

"If Pug is pursuing outside work while under a three-year, no-compete contract with Skunk 2, he violates his employment contract, confidentiality agreements, and NDA. And ... he may be committing IP espionage!"

"What would you like me to do?"

"Sorry to give you another task. Get me more information about Kevin. See if you can determine his specific involvement with Pug. Offer Kevin some quid pro quo bait about Pug and see if he reciprocates. When you learn anything, give me a call."

Michael leaned back in his chair. *The noose around Pug's neck has just tightened another notch.*

56
SATURDAY, JUNE 29
SSFO/OSAKA

H ER MISCARRIAGE DELAYED THEIR WEEKLY conversations by one week. Both were at their respective offices.

"Good evening Natsu. Kenji informed me about the unfortunate event. I'm so sorry and extend my condolences. I hope you've recovered," Michael said.

"Physically, I am doing well thanks to my excellent doctors. Mentally, I seek comfort in rereading Sun Tzu's works, Shakespeare, and samurai teachings. They give excellent advice about confronting setbacks. Kobayashi-sama and I have had many shogi matches during my recovery. All this practice enhances my skills. I am able to play Kobayashi-sama to draws now."

"Good for you! Do you feel up to talking business?"

"Yes, I have had rest and time to think. Let me update you."

"If you feel you need a break, don't hesitate to stop," Michael cautioned.

"First, I would like to tell you about our development project. I sent you photos and information about the project's location, facility and resources. Debiddo and JT's team have done an excellent job getting the project underway."

"The facility looks impressive; you have state-of-the-art equipment. How many resources are working on this project?"

"As of yesterday, we have forty individuals not counting consultants and university students. We operate two shifts, seven days a week.

Kenji's donations to Osaka University opened doors for professors and students to participate in our effort."

"Doesn't surprise me, given Kenji's relationship network."

"Speaking of that, we have enlisted Marken & Associates to evaluate what US OEMs do in the exhaust system area. As for our facilities, we have four different sections devoted to technical marketing, materials testing, design and proof of concepts, and IP work."

"Jackson Huntley's recent visit to your facility confirmed this; he's very impressed with your progress and the initial patent work."

"Yes, he also shared your Skunk 2's material testing results. That helped Debiddo accelerate his testing and selecting the right combinations of materials. That will strengthen our patent filings."

"What is your target date for commercialization?"

"Based on our best estimates, we plan for August or September of this year," she responded.

"That's quite aggressive."

"We make haste slowly." From Michael's chuckle, she knew he liked that expression. "What do you have to report from your efforts in California?"

"I have done two project reviews with Pug James. Right now, he's focused only on testing materials, and you saw those results from Jackson's visit. Frankly Natsu, I'm disappointed because Pug does nothing but testing and hasn't progressed on the ten projects I assigned. He denies pursuing co-molded testing. Evidence suggest otherwise."

"Debiddo was quite upset when he heard about his father working on his idea without his permission. I persuaded him to focus on getting his project done before confronting Pug. To ensure there are no surprises, I have assigned a resource to investigate our competitors, Gano-Nippon and Lawrent. We also suspect individuals within Japan Technologies plot against our interests. I will brief you when we have credible information."

"All prudent actions on your part," Michael added. "A Kevin McIntyre contacted me about Pug James. He's checking references on Pug for an unidentified client. Jackson will look into that because Pug may be violating Skunk 2's employment agreement and NDAs. When we next talk, I may have additional information."

"Michael, I am a bit tired now. May we talk again later?"

"By all means. We'll schedule the next call when more progress occurs."

Natsu considered Michael's comment about Kevin. *Mr. McIntyre's visit next week should be most interesting.*

She appreciated Michael's timely and discrete manner in sharing the disturbing information about Debiddo's first marriage. Since she hadn't met Michael in person, his decision to inform Kenji was the correct sequence. She would thank Michael when they met in person.

57
TUESDAY, JULY 2
SFO/OSAKA

ENJI WELCOMED KEVIN INTO HIS office and introduced Natsu. They sat at the enormous glass conference table while an assistant served coffee and biscuits.

"It is my honor, Mr. McIntyre, to welcome you to Osaka," Kenji began. "I trust your flight was satisfactory and you slept well last evening."

"Thank you, Kobayashi-san. I enjoyed your gracious invitation to dine at the Comfort Station. An excellent dinner!"

"We appreciate you coming on short notice and so close to your national holiday."

"I'm not much for celebrating holidays when a business opportunity appears." Kenji noticed Kevin staring at the framed picture directly behind Kenji's desk. It depicted four intersecting circles. The center contained the words イキガイ. "I see you are looking at my ikigai picture."

"Yes, the schematic is identical to one my mother has in her home."

"She and I share a common bond," Kenji said. "A good omen. Now, let us discuss business." He glanced toward Natsu. "Regarding our current and future investments, Nashakatani-san manages and represents my interests. Going forward, if we agree to invest with you, she will be your contact. Now, she will provide an overview of our investments."

Until that moment, Natsu's dark green eyes remained fixed on

Kevin. She took his measure and used this tactic when first meeting a man with whom she would discuss business matters. She considered this an advantageous opening to take control. She knew Kevin would be confused by her hafu heritage, another advantage.

"Mr. McIntyre, we understand you know the K&F law firm. We are considering them for advice about investments in the US. What can you share about this firm?"

"My father's real estate company used K&F for many years. They proved reliable and competent."

"We understand Mr. Blunt no longer uses this firm. Why?"

"K&F and Mr. Blunt had serious disagreements and have severed all relationships. K&F was unhappy with Mr. Blunt's payments for legal services. Therefore, if you choose to work with this law firm, it will pose no conflict when dealing with Mr. Blunt. In fact, it could improve your negotiating leverage."

Natsu smiled at Kenji. Then she provided a project summary of possible US real estate investments. She peppered Kevin with smart questions and solicited his opinions and advice. She felt Kevin's answers were frank and knowledgeable. After two hours of discussion, Natsu suggested a break.

While Kevin was in the men's room, Natsu said, "Kobayashi-sama, I could tell Mr. McIntyre is confused about why I discuss real estate and not the JV investment."

"I agree. If he is clever, he will realize you are testing him."

When they reassembled, Natsu continued. "Mr. McIntyre, we will now talk about Mr. Blunt's interest in selling his JV investment." She saw Kevin relax indicating he was pleased to talk about the JV.

"Before we get into specifics and in the interest of full disclosure," he said, "there is another party interested in purchasing Mr. Blunt's interest."

"Can you disclose the possible competition?" Natsu asked.

"That would be unethical. But I can tell you it is a foreign-based venture fund that seems very interested in investing in Silicon Valley technologies."

"Thank you for that information. We understand the McIntyre

family shares equal ownership with Mr. Blunt. Please provide background on the JV's origin and current status."

"If I may, I have a brief presentation." Kevin inserted a flash drive into the computer. On the screen, the PowerPoint slides described the JV's original purpose, the activities since inception, and the reason for dormancy. "This Silicon Valley JV is nicely positioned to identify new companies needing financial resources to commercialize their technologies. My consulting work for automotive clients confirms this." Kevin concluded the presentation. "Mr. Blunt wants to sell his interest because he has no future interest in technology investments."

Natsu asked, "Why wouldn't he approach your family and give you right of first refusal?"

"Ma'am, Mr. Blunt probably believes he made a mistake with this investment, but he won't admit that. He just wants his money back. Whenever I talked to him about potential technology investments, his eyes glazed over and he delayed approval. Frankly, he didn't want to invest more money in technology. Real estate is his only interest."

"Does the McIntyre family think this investment was a mistake?" Natsu asked.

"Absolutely not! With the right technology-savvy partner, the JV has excellent potential."

"Interesting, seems foolish for him to not keep this investment," she added.

Kenji observed, "Mr. Blunt knows licensing, trademarks, and those kinds of intellectual property matters."

"True, but that involves branding, name recognition, and marketing promotion; that's much different from complex research, development, and commercializing technologies. Mr. Blunt prefers short-term transactions," Kevin responded.

Natsu saw Kevin glance at the shogi set in the center of the table. Kevin continued, "You know, like the difference between checkers and chess. We McIntyres prefer chess."

Once more, Natsu smiled at Kenji before replying. "We understand Mr. Blunt's disinterest; but for us to invest, we need to understand the JV's future."

Kevin described five different small privately held companies offering exciting investment possibilities. Then he described two unique opportunities. He alluded to discovering a Steve Jobs-like inventor who had a revolutionary idea to disrupt the current automotive industry that depends on fossil fuels. Also, he met a real visionary who plans to introduce a new concept that eliminates fossil fuels as an energy source. These are two examples of near-term and long-term investments.

He concluded, "I am a strong believer in supporting new technologies that can disrupt an industry."

During a break, Kevin went to an adjoining office to make calls. Kenji and Natsu conferred. "Natsu-chan, what is your opinion regarding this JV investment? Should we buy Mr. Blunt's interest?"

"Perhaps ... but let's learn more about how the JV would operate. Fifty-Fifty ownership means no one decision maker. Unacceptable." She smiled slyly. "This lady daimyo must be in charge. If we proceed, we should buy Blunt's interest and at least one per cent of the McIntyre's share."

"A good opening offer," Kenji replied. "Let's see where that leads. What do you think about his description of the automotive sector projects?"

"Mr. McIntyre's near-term investment involves exhaust systems, similar to our project, but we need to learn more. It could be an excellent way to expand and diversify on a global basis. I will talk with Marken-san about this. Michael Fields indicated Kevin had contacted him about Pug James. He said Pug may be involved with a development project unrelated to Skunk 2. I will monitor this."

They reconvened, and she began, "Mr. McIntyre, your information about the JV intrigues us. We will consider purchasing the entire 50% interest, however—"

"You have concerns?" Kevin asked.

"Equal ownership means no one decision maker. This is not acceptable unless the McIntyre family would sell at least one per cent or more interest in the JV."

Kevin nodded. "I may have an alternative—two entities."

They listened as he proposed McIntyre family operate in the Americas and Europe with a 51%/49% ownership while JT operated in the Asia and South Asia with a 51%/49% ownership. He handed them a draft MOU.

Natsu read the terms while Kenji continued discussion with Kevin. She was impressed with Kevin's preparation and anticipation of partnership scenarios. The MOU stated that upon the purchase of Blunt's 50% interest, the parties would revert to the agreed split of geographical ownership. After a few clarifications from Kevin, she and Kevin signed the MOU which would take effect once the Blunt sale concluded.

Natsu took Kevin on a brief tour of JT's facilities excluding the separate facility where the exhaust system project resided. Natsu subtly implied critical development work was occurring that may be of interest to Kevin. She would discuss more openly at a future date.

At the end of the afternoon, the three celebrated the deal with a sake toast. They would meet later that night for a celebration dinner.

Before departing, Kenji and Natsu discussed their meeting.

"What do you think of Mr. McIntyre?" Kenji asked.

"Quite articulate and perceptive. Based on my research, he possesses excellent credentials, both technical and legal. He gave an excellent presentation and suggested interesting ownership possibilities. He came prepared and ready to deal. He definitely wants a partner different from Blunt."

"What do you think of his judgment?" Kenji asked.

"Although unmarried, he declined the Comfort Station hostess's tempting offer. She tells me he passed the natto test and didn't hesitate to eat the drunken pawns; good omens."

"Why do you think Mr. McIntyre told us about the foreign-based venture interested in Blunt's interest?" Kenji wondered.

"An honest disclosure to let us know there is competition. He even gave us a clue. This could be another reference to Technovenia."

Kenji lit a cigarette. "I suggest you get better acquainted with Kevin. He could be a long-term ally in many ways."

"Interesting thought. I suspect he would excel in the art of noh theater. He takes a measured approach in presenting his ideas," Natsu replied.

"Correct. As you develop a relationship with him, it will begin transactional. Then explore strategic possibilities."

"What do you mean?"

"Get to know him on a more personal level, perhaps show him places like Kyoto so you can understand him as a human being and what truly motivates him. Does he have what it takes to do business in our country? What is his general management potential? Are your philosophies compatible?"

She knew what Kobayashi-sama was suggesting.

58
FRIDAY, JULY 5
PALO ALTO

B ACK IN HIS OFFICE, KEVIN reflected on the Osaka visit with Kenji and Natsu: *Kenji's an impressive person; Mom will be pleased he shares her ikigai passion. More impressive is Ms. Nashakatani. Did not expect a woman to take the lead. She's sharp, knows her material, not hesitant to demonstrate it. At times, Kenji acted deferential to her. Didn't expect that. Hope to know more about her if we become JV partners. She signed the MOU, so her position is important.*

Expect Kenji and Natsu to move fast if Blunt agrees to sell; the sooner, the better for us. Getting rid of Blunt makes the JV more valuable.

Japan Technologies could be a great technology partner. Their manufacturing facilities and development labs—first class, clean, quiet, well organized, state-of-the-art, quality emphasis everywhere. No wonder Japan is way ahead of the US.

When I mentioned the automotive projects, they both seemed intrigued. Do they have something similar? Opportunity to collaborate? Curious about the development work in that separate building.

He looked at his to-do list. The first item involved Pug's business mentor. Kevin constructed a ruse to contact the mentor.

During the course of his conversation with Howard Riley, Kevin learned interesting facts even though Howard had not mentioned Pug's name: Riley had been working with Pug for about two months. Riley considered Pug a difficult client because of his inventor paranoia, impatience, unpredictability, and inability to listen. Despite these traits, Riley considered Pug innovative and an out-of-the box type of inventor. *Riley knows Jackson Huntley from previous relationships. Double back with Jackson to corroborate information.*

59
SATURDAY, JULY 6
OSAKA

KENJI AND NATSU READ SEAMUS's confidential update supplementing his last conversation with Kenji: *Lawrent— with Gano-Nippon's support—engaged an Italian venture fund, Technovenia, to purchase IPS shares. Still researching the fund's legal counsel and principals.*

Technovenia separately contacted Marcy James and Pug James offering to purchase their shares. So far, she declined; not clear what Pug has decided. Technovenia will probably contact other IPS shareholders.

"What do you recommend?" Kenji asked.

"Through third parties we should provide intelligence to encourage Technovenia to approach Hakase Yamura. I will instruct Seamus to continue monitoring all adversaries seeking IPS shares."

New York City/Palo Alto

Kevin's cell phone buzzed with a familiar New York number: Doug Stiller.

"Hey Kevin, how you doing? Been a while since the law conference. Great event, by the way."

"Thanks, Doug. How's everything at Blunt Company?"

"The usual. Blunt keeps me hopping."

"What can I do for you?"

"Blunt asked me to tell you he sold his interest in the JV."

"To whom?"

"A very rich Japanese who made him an offer he couldn't refuse."

"Doug, Mom'll be disappointed Blunt decided to leave the JV."

Damn! Kenji and Natsu moved fast!

"Hey look, Blunt wanted you to know he agonized a lot. You guys deserve a real technology partner."

"Appreciate that." Kevin rolled his eyes in disbelief. "How much did Blunt sell for?"

"Two hundred and fifty large ones above his investment—enough to cover lost interest and opportunity costs. Anyway, the signed paperwork's coming."

"Thanks for the heads up. Tell Blunt we're sorry he's leaving, but maybe he's on to something. Mom said she may sell her interest too. We'll explore that."

"Off the record, if she's thinking about selling her interest, I have someone who may want to talk with her."

"Who?"

"Company called Technovenia approached Blunt, but the Japanese outbid everybody. I'll send you the main guy's contact info. Gotta go, Kev. Let's get together when you're in the 'Big Apple'."

"Will do."

Kevin considered all that transpired so fast. *Wonder if Blunt bothered to look at the original JV terms. McIntyres had right of first refusal on any offer. Oh well, one less lawsuit. So, both Doug and Gordo are pushing this Technovenia angle. Interesting. Need to alert mom. She'll be pleased Blunt's out. And I'm pleased I can spend more time with Natsu.*

60
SUNDAY, JULY 7
OSAKA/SFO

"MICHAEL, THANKS FOR TAKING MY call on short notice," Natsu said. "I have interesting information to share."

"No problem. What's up?"

"You mentioned a Kevin McIntyre. He visited us in Osaka. He is an impressive person—an engineer and lawyer familiar with automotive markets in the US. His family and Ronald Blunt jointly owned a Silicon Valley technology JV. We have purchased Mr. Blunt's fifty percent interest in this JV."

"Ronald Blunt? That is interesting!"

"When I showed Kevin around our facilities, he spoke of a client who has an exhaust system project for the US market. The more he described this project, it sounded similar to ours. Kevin alluded to a co-molding breakthrough."

"How can I help?" Michael asked.

"Could you investigate Kevin and see if there are any problems or conflicts of interests?"

"I'll have Jackson investigate. Jackson and I think Pug may be involved too."

"On another matter, Seamus Hafferty, obtained intelligence about Lawrent's activity in the US dissipater market. He'll brief you."

"I don't know that name. Is he American?"

"I'm sorry. Seamus Hafferty's American name is Sean O'Leary. Seamus is the son of Kobayashi-sama's mentor after the great war."

"Thanks for clarifying, Natsu. Appreciate all this information."

"Sayōnara, Michael."

She realized Michael was unaware of Seamus Hafferty's alias. Going forward, she would be more transparent. In her mind, she needed Michael's unconditional trust. She knew the co-molding reference would allow Michael to connect the dots to Pug.

Natsu entered Kenji's library and found him in deep thought. She waited until he motioned her to sit. Next to Kenji's chair, she saw an almost full wastebasket of stained tissues. Kenji's cough had not improved. In fact, his breathing appeared labored. She noticed an oxygen tank in a far corner of the library.

"Welcome, dear Natsu-chan. How do you feel?"

"The doctor has praised my fast recovery, Kobayashi-sama. Why is there an oxygen tank in here?"

"My doctor insists it will help my breathing. But it's just a medical nuisance."

She knew it was unproductive to question him further.

"Would you like tea?" Kenji asked.

Natsu noticed the Johnnie Walker Blue bottle. "I would enjoy what you drink."

"Excellent." He poured her a full tumbler and refilled his glass. He swirled his glass and took a long swallow and cleared his throat. "I have been thinking a great deal—how very fortunate in my business career to have a certain loyal friend and colleague since 1948. Hafferty-sama introduced us when we graduated from university."

"You refer to Okazaki-sama?"

"Correct. We think and act as one. Hafferty-sama recognized our special bond and never once passed judgment."

"Kobayashi-sama, I admire what Okazaki-sama and you have accomplished. You share many common experiences and challenges. I know you have been caring and loyal to one another. Private relationships should be irrelevant in business decisions. As a female hafu in Japan, I am most empathetic. One day our culture will be more accepting, and I intend to lead this reconciliation effort. You've given me education and samurai skills to fight this cultural challenge."

Kenji paused to light a cigarette. He coughed, took another sip of scotch, and once again cleared his throat. "You truly possess your grandfather's prescient wisdom."

"A generous compliment. I wish I had known him."

"Shiganari has observed your development over your thirty-five years and has expressed much pride in your success. He knows the lessons I have taught. If I cannot continue as your sensei, he will be there for you."

"I pray that will not be necessary." She felt a chilling concern.

"My dearest Natsu-chan, you blessed us when you came into our lives. You've become our lady daimyo." She was pleased. His official recognition of her daimyo status confirmed an earlier decision to get the second tattoo inside her upper right arm. It depicted a female in a traditional daimyo dress.

"And you, dear Sensei, have always been my hero. You taught me important lessons based on the art of war, the samurai code, and ikigai philosophy. Okazaki-sama listened to me and taught me to be understanding and empathetic, and you both provided me my dear Nanny who helped perfect my English and encouraged my love of literature." She raised her glass. "To the memory of my grandfather and to my beloved guardians. You've prepared me well."

"Let us adjourn for dinner, and we will discuss another matter. Hungry?"

"Hai."

At the restaurant, the manager greeted Kenji with a low bow. A waiter brought sake and Natsu's favorite appetizers.

"Kobayashi-sama," Natsu remarked, "you always know what your dining companions enjoy."

"Your grandfather taught me to pay attention, to observe people's habits, tastes, strengths, weaknesses—and most important: to listen first, observe second, and then speak." He poured sake into the cups.

Natsu braced herself as Kenji lowered his head.

He whispered, "I have unpleasant news."

Natsu's heart pounded. "What is it?"

Kenji said, his eyes brimming with tears, "I have congestive obstructive pulmonary disease which has become stage-four lung cancer. My doctors say it is incurable."

Natsu's hands flew to her heart. "No! No! Not true!"

Kenji, his voice weak, said, "My dear Natsu-chan, it is true. I received the diagnosis weeks ago. My time is short." He took another sip of sake. "The doctors will arrange palliative care so I remain reasonably pain free, mentally alert, and as comfortable as possible."

"I wished you would have told me sooner." She removed her chic designer eyeglasses and searched for a tissue in her handbag.

"I did not want to burden you before the birth."

"How long do you have?" she asked, struggling to regain control.

"Three months, probably less."

"Radiation, chemotherapy? Surely something to prolong your time!"

"Sweet Natsu-chan, my doctors researched this and consulted with esteemed oncologists. The side effects including experimental drugs make one's remaining days unacceptable. Palliative care is the only sensible option."

Natsu clasped her hands, vowing to stay calm, stoic. She knew she had disappointed Kenji with her tearful reaction. Her mind raced. *Finally, he tells me what I suspected! I must talk with Okazaki-sama.*

Collecting her thoughts, she asked, "What do I tell Debiddo and Seamus?"

Kenji paused. "They must not know about my condition. Shiganari will discuss these matters in more detail. He is your next sensei."

"I am overwhelmed." She dabbed her eyes and swallowed hard. "But I will follow your instructions to the best of my ability. I will not disappoint. I will honor your legacy."

"Dearest Natsu-chan, I know you will."

Eating little, they finished their meal in silence. She knew JT's leadership had officially transferred to her. Despite uncertainties ahead, she felt a surprising calmness and readiness to prove she was worthy of Kenji's confidence.

61
MONDAY, JULY 8
PALO ALTO

KEVIN INVITED TIFFANEE TO HIS office. He was eager to tell her about Osaka and Skunk 2. Kevin's office reflected his personality and robust life style. Framed photos everywhere—his family, his sports activities along with his academic degrees, certificates, and awards. Triathlon and swimming trophies were wedged among legal and engineering books.

"Mom, thanks for coming. Sorry for the short notice."

"No problem. I'm in the neighborhood anyway. I meet later with Gordon Orlio about the church building fund."

"Mom, let me know if he asks anything else about what Pug's doing."

"What do you mean?"

"Did Gordon ask you about Pug and what he's doing at the Skunk?"

"Yes, why do you ask?" She seemed surprised.

"I don't like other people nosing around our confidential activities."

"I understand. I will discourage him. So, tell me about Japan and your Pug visit."

"When Kobayashi realized I had recommended K&F, we immediately bonded. I also met a very sharp lady, a Ms. Nashakatani. She's Kobayashi's right-hand man—I mean, woman."

"Kevin, there just might be a woman or two in this world who meets or exceeds your high standards."

"Anyway, she's knowledgeable about all subjects we discussed and a key contact going forward."

"Isn't that unusual in Japan?"

"Yes, she is the first woman I've met where I felt an immediate intellectual bond."

"Kev, don't get any physical bonding ideas. We don't need a business conflict of interest. Why are you smiling?"

"Mom, how about you and Pug?" Kevin noted her embarrassed expression. "Anyway, I think she's already spoken for. Now, talk about serendipity! Blunt recently visited Mr. Kobayashi to discuss licensing deals for hotels and purchasing a golf course. Blunt asked Kobayashi if he wanted to invest in a Silicon Valley technology venture. Blunt claimed he wanted out. He gave him our names as the other JV partner. That's why they invited me to Osaka ... part of their due diligence."

"How much did Blunt want?" she asked.

"Stiller told me Blunt got $750,000. He called me two days ago to confirm Blunt sold his interest. We will get the paperwork soon."

She laughed. "That's $250,000 above his original investment! That guy never misses an opportunity to scam a buck. Guess he thinks his brand carries over into non-real estate deals."

"Blunt didn't have the decency to call us—probably embarrassed. When I talked with Doug Stiller, he mentioned some other firm wanted to invest in the JV."

"Who?"

"Technovenia, a venture fund. They called me after Gordo referred them for finding an investor to buy Blunt's interest. Looks like Kenji beat Technovenia to the punch. Anyway, back to Kenji and Natsu. I gave them my JV pitch, told them our plans for the JV and why this would be a good investment. Both realized this would be an interesting partnership if the right technologies could be found, developed, and commercialized."

"How did you resolve the ownership interest?"

"Told Kobayashi we can execute a MOU to immediately negotiate a 51/49% for the US markets and a 49/51% for Asian markets. They agreed."

"Your father trained you well. Will Mr. Kobayashi be a good partner?"

"Absolutely, Ms. Nashakatani took me on a brief tour of Japan Tech's plant. They focus on the appliance industry. And, guess what—some of their patent licenses come from Pug's former company. Can you guess which one?"

"MatraScience?"

"Nope, IPS. They licensed the silver-lining technologies and successfully exploited it."

"Goodness! Truly a small world! Pug never mentioned this to me," she said.

Kevin thought back to Pug's interest in purchasing IPS. *Now it all made sense. Pug wanted control of the silver-lining technologies to use in Skunk 3. In Kevin's mind, this was a smart move. Pug had told her he sold IPS to the Japanese. But Kenji and Natsu only mentioned a license. So, who purchased IPS from Pug? More investigation required.*

"Probably slipped Pug's mind," Kevin answered. "I piqued Natsu's interest when I mentioned the JV's potential investment in an automotive exhaust system opportunity. She said her company also has a major R&D effort focused on similar applications. They've assembled a talented technical and marketing team to accelerate development—probably way ahead of Pug's efforts. We have a possible competitor or maybe an ally to exploit fossil fuel-based exhaust systems."

"What do you mean?"

"First, with a twenty-year patent life, we can exploit the current market until at least 2022-2030. After that, new technologies will eventually obsolete fossil-fuel exhaust systems. Second, alternative energy solutions like electric-powered autos will radically change exhaust systems. Elon Musk wants to produce an all-electric vehicle. His progress will dictate when transition from fossil fuel to electric technology occurs. This gives us time to develop other technologies for electric vehicles. Third, if Japan Technologies becomes a good partner, we have more global opportunities to exploit disruptive technologies. And my ideas about using electronics, software, and artificial intelligence will fit nicely into that next wave."

"Kevin, I'm so proud of you! You see around the curve to predict the future. Just like your dad did in real estate."

"You deserve equal credit with Dad. I'll develop a project plan and get Pug's buy-in. Have you found any locations?"

"Yes, one of your father's real estate colleagues owns this SSFO building, and we can buy or rent for a reasonable amount. The building requires minimal renovations, pretty much move-in condition. I'll give you the address."

"Great, Mom, I'll start the legal work to set up the entity and how we share ownership. I'll organize a separate LLC holding company that'll own the assets and IP. With the JV clear of Blunt and ownership interests settled with Kobayashi, the JV can be a subsidiary of the LLC and Japan Technologies."

"How do we share ownership with Pug?"

"The McIntyre Charitable Foundation will be the majority owner of the LLC holding company with its interest in the JV. We'll control voting shares much like Sergey Brin and Larry Page structured Google's ownership. A separate legal entity, Skunk 3, will oversee development and commercialization. For appearance, Pug can own 50% with you owning the other 50%. All funding will come through the LLC for tax reasons, and all the IP will be owned by the holding entity. All this is above Pug's pay grade. Mom, your mission is to keep Pug focused on his core competency."

"I will." She smiled slyly. "You know I'm no longer a virgin in such matters."

"You're the best, Mom. The LLC will do big deals like strategic alliances, licensing, and whether or not to go public or stay private. Again, all above Pug's pay grade."

"Wish we could share more with Pug."

"Mom, I realize you like him a lot, but let's take a cautious approach until I learn more. Pug's impatient to act, but we have to get our diligence ducks in order. Okay?"

"Yes, Kevin, that will probably frustrate him, but thank you for all you do for me."

"You took care of me after Dad passed. I can never repay you. I have to get moving fast on Pug's invention idea. Hopefully when we sign all the NDAs, we can sit down and develop plans with our Japanese partner. By the way, don't mention this to Pug."

"Why not?"

"Pug hates the Japanese. He's paranoid about working with them."

"I'll keep quiet."

"Mom, what's Pug like now you've seen him up close and personal."

"Absolutely wonderful! His coming back in my life is too good to be true! We had a super time in St. Martin. Every Sunday he joins me at church. Dr. Taylor adores him, especially his sense of humor and his pugisms. Pug makes me feel very special."

"What do you mean by 'pugisms?'"

Tiffanee laughed. "Pug's mind is quicker than his tongue. He thinks faster than he speaks. His words come out funny and quirky." She looked away for a moment. "Pug's brought a new energy into my life like your father did for me."

"I'm pleased you've found a companion, but please let me know before you do anything permanent. I don't want you hurt."

"Rest assured, darling Kevin, it's only companionship, not marriage. I'm excited to get back in the business like I did with your father. Let's move fast on this opportunity. If for some reason, he and I part company, you and I will still control."

Kevin opened his briefcase and pulled out a notepad. "I want to update you on what I learned about Pug. I did a pretty exhaustive review of his patents from his days at MatraScience and IPS. He invented products for a variety of industries—power, telecommunications, appliance; his novel patents are quite impressive for thermal and acoustics applications. I even found one that involved infringement. We call that a 'silver bullet.'"

"Why's that?"

"The real test of a patent's strength determined by courts. Lawrent, an IPS competitor, challenged his IPS 10000 patents. The appeals court reaffirmed its validity." Kevin smiled, "So, the silver-lining technologies are silver bullets."

"What more did you learn about the IPS company where Pug worked?"

"At IPS, he invented appliance dissipaters that captured a significant piece of a global multi-billion-dollar market. That's why Pug wants the silver-lining technologies integrated into our auto project."

"Did you learn anything about the other IPS shareholders?" Tiffanee asked.

"No, but Pug will contact them separately to purchase their shares. So far, my research found no game stoppers. The patent attorney of record wouldn't talk because of attorney/client privilege. He referred me to a Michael Fields, and I talked with him."

"I know him. He used to be Pug's boss at MatraScience."

"That's interesting," Kevin said. *No wonder Michael was so coy with me when I asked him about Paul James.*

"How do we know if Pug's latest ideas have real market potential?"

"I'm doing the missionary marketing in Detroit," Kevin added. "That said, this project will require substantial up-front investment."

"Is Pug prepared to invest an equal share?"

"My gut tells me he doesn't have ready cash given his illiquid assets. Claims he's working on a business plan with a mentor."

"What's next?"

Kevin paused. "Pug's current company, Skunk 2, can't support the development and commercialization of his project because of limited space and resources. The property you found in SSFO sounds ideal for the Skunk 3. I'll take care of the entity formation, share ownership, patent ownership, and licensing models. Our JV, along with a new wealthy partner, could really influence global markets. Time is of the essence."

"That's what you gators always say."

"Gators?"

"Pug's term of endearment for all lawyers." She laughed. "I just thought about Blunt. When this JV becomes successful, he'll sue us. And you know what that means?"

"Yep, see you in court. As Dad liked to say, 'With Blunt, have your lawyer on standby 24/7.'"

62
TUESDAY, JULY 9
OSAKA

HAKASE YAMURA SAT AT HIS desk reviewing recent transactions for the Brunei Trust when his assistant interrupted. "Hakase Yamura, a Danielo Abrillo wants to talk to you about the Brunei Trust. He says it is extremely important."

He nodded. "Put him through."

"Doctor Yamura, thanks for taking my call. I am CEO of Technovenia, an Italian venture fund."

Yamura interrupted, "I am not familiar with this firm. Why are you calling?"

"We invest in undercapitalized, privately-owned companies with interesting technologies. We would like to purchase IPS shares."

"Mr. Abrillo, I do not own shares in this company."

"Yes, sir, but I understand you manage a trust that owns shares, and you can authorize investment transactions."

"And the source of your information?"

"I cannot reveal this due to a non-disclosure agreement. Would you be interested in selling the trust's IPS shares?"

"Send me a proposal on your company letterhead which describes what you desire, due diligence requirements, and price per share. Also, send me any information about your fund so I can assess your credibility. I will then discuss this with the other principals."

"Sir, I will send that immediately."

After they disconnected, Hakase Yamura penciled thoughts on his pad: *Technovenia could be useful in forestalling the merger. Discuss with One-san and Two-san to see if they want to participate. Investigate Danielo Abrillo. Can he be compromised? Who else is he working with? Interesting his call came after meeting with the Fields woman.*

63
TUESDAY, JULY 9
CHICAGO/OSAKA

N ATSU, WORKING IN A SMALL office adjacent to Kenji's, heard her assistant announce, "Walter Marken is on the phone. Kobayashi-sama is away. Will you take the call?"

"Hai," Natsu replied.

She knew Walter as a close colleague of both Kenji and Shiganari. Their personal and business relationships started in the early 1950s. Natsu met Walter when she worked for his company in Chicago during a summer break from business school.

"Kon'nichiwa, Marken-sama. Kobayashi-sama is unavailable. Your call transferred to me."

"Natsu-chan, wonderful to speak to you! I trust Kenji is well. Last time we talked, he had a terrible chest cold; his voice sounded weak."

"He has a respiratory ailment; currently resting at Mt. Fuji."

"Yes, his wonderful mountain retreat. I've been there many times. Glad he relaxes. He works much too hard. Give him my best wishes."

"I most certainly will."

"I trust you've recovered well," Walter added.

"Marken-sama, I appreciate your kind sentiments and the beautiful flowers. I'm fine. When will you honor us with your presence?"

"I'll visit in two months. Kenji invited me to a golf tournament."

"Wonderful! I look forward to seeing you." Her heart heavy, she knew this golf event would not occur.

Walter continued, "I have news. A while back, our company formed a venture to pursue opportunities in US automotive markets. Kenji indicated Japan Technologies looks at similar opportunities."

"Hai!"

"Our OEM contacts at Ford and General Motors informed us about an individual who visited Detroit several times to conduct technical and marketing surveys. He claims his company—or client—possesses a revolutionary co-molding technology for exhaust systems. Allegedly, it'll solve many current problems. If true, it will significantly advance the performance of exhaust systems. I believe similarities exist between this and JT's development project. I'll send an encrypted comparison."

Natsu's curiosity rose. "And the name of this individual?"

"Kevin McIntyre. We know him only by reputation—a very sharp engineer and patent lawyer—well respected in Detroit. He assists clients in introducing proprietary technologies. He has negotiated several licensing relationships for his clients."

"Sounds as if your venture might find him useful."

"I'll definitely consider that. But I wanted to alert you, Natsu-chan, since it may impact your development project."

"I will inform Kobayashi-sama when he returns. We may have more questions. Do you have any information about the company or the client Mr. McIntyre represents?"

"Not at this time," Walter replied. "On another matter, Seamus contacted me about Lawrent's former CEO. Apparently, he's an active investor in a foreign fund, Technovenia. They're sniffing around to purchase IPS shares and even contacted us because of Marken & Associates's close relationship with IPS."

"I will inform Kobyashi-sama. Arigato for your information. Sayōnara, Marken-sama."

She turned on the recorder and replayed the phone call. Later, she sent an encrypted message to Kenji. Questions raced through her mind: *Pug's involvement? Kevin's project related to Skunk 2? Kevin planning to use our JV? Does Kevin know Pug stole Debiddo's idea? Can we trust Kevin? How would Sun Tzu counter Technovenia? How much time do I have given Kenji's health?*

She called Michael Fields.

"Michael, I just talked with Walter Marken. He told me about Kevin McIntyre's activities in Detroit. From his description, it sounds like Kevin is working on a project with Pug."

"That explains why Kevin contacted me. Pug is definitely pursuing something beyond Skunk 2."

Natsu sensed Michael's concern. "Agreed. Walter also told me Technovenia contacted them about buying IPS shares."

"Technovenia is one active group. Have they contacted Kenji about the trust shares?"

"At this point, I don't think so. Hakase Yamura is the official contact for trust matters." She knew that if Yamura had been contacted, he would not share this with Kenji. "Michael, please contact Walter about the Technovenia and brainstorm the next steps. Explore how Marken and Kevin might work together. It could buy us some time."

"Natsu, this gets more complicated by the moment. I'll follow up immediately."

Natsu dialed Kenji at his Mt. Fuji lodge. She knew that although he was feeling unwell, he would insist on learning this latest information.

64
TUESDAY, JULY 9
NEW YORK CITY

B LUNT SCHEDULED DINNER WITH SUZI at Bluntasaka, the
Japanese restaurant in Blunt Tower on Fifth Ave. Whenever
they dined here, Blunt bragged about the restaurant's Michelin
two-star rating. Publicly, he ignored Suzi's contributions. She had hired
the architect who designed the restaurant, recruited the chef—a protégé
of Hisao Nakahigashi, the world-class chef from Japan—and found
Japanese women hostesses that Blunt insisted on privately interviewing.

Today's agenda covered the status of the five Japanese restaurants
Suzi established in Blunt hotels in New York, New Jersey, and Florida.
All five received critical acclaim for outstanding cuisine, service, and
ambience. Most important, her restaurant business knowledge brought
clout to the Blunt brand.

She handed him a one-page summary on each restaurant's financial
results.

"Suzi, I love your reports. No unnecessary stuff to distract me from
making fast, great decisions."

Suzi, an accomplished business woman, had given birth to a
daughter ten years earlier but kept her petite figure trim and youthful.
She was in the Blunt Tower gym early every morning. During business
hours, she wore fashionable clothing from top Japanese designers. Her
dark eyes and creamy complexion enthralled Blunt. She tolerated his
huge ego and never interfered with his other love interests. Jealously
was never a concern given her multiple roles.

As the dinner courses arrived, she ate traditional fare while Blunt consumed the usual—charred Kobe cheeseburgers, fries, and Cokes. She outlined the financial performance of each restaurant, the green card status of each chef, and plans for opening two more restaurants next year. She intrigued Blunt with her proposal to franchise and license additional Japanese restaurants beyond Blunt-owned properties. Once the meal concluded, he announced, "Suz, I'm giving you a h-u-u-ge bonus for what you've done for my brand."

"It is my pleasure to make your restaurants a great success."

"Let's go to my room. Gotta special gift for suggesting I contact Kenji to unload the JV."

In his private elevator that took them to the top floor suite, Ronald asked. "See where Dick Cheney was president for twenty-four hours?"

"Yes, President Bush underwent a colonoscopy on June 29."

"Too bad he recovered. Dick's our real president not that daddy's boy. Dick takes no prisoners."

"Ronnie, have you ever thought about running for president?"

"All the time."

Twenty-four hours later, Natsu sat in her Osaka office and reviewed Suzi's encrypted email and video. As she watched, *I now understand why Kenji never asked me to do what Suzi does. He had different plans for me. Suzi is one of my most valued samurais.*

Natsu typed an encrypted reply, highlighting the need to report any Blunt communications with Technovenia, Yamura, and/or Pug.

65

WEDNESDAY, JULY 10
BURLINGAME

A S THEY SNUGGLED IN BED, Darnisha whispered, "Pug, I got a wonderful surprise."

Pug, half asleep, muttered, "Huh?"

"I'm pregnant."

He bolted upright, threw back covers, and jumped from the bed. "What! You can't be! You're on the pill for chrissakes!"

Shocked, she blurted, "You. . . you told me you wanted to get married!"

"Shit! You don't have time for a baby. I need you full time at my new skunk!"

Darnisha pulled the covers to her face and sobbed. "But, I thought you would … "

"For chrissakes, stop crying!"

"What do I do?" she wailed.

"Get a fuckin' abortion!"

"I can't do that!" She turned over and cried into the pillow.

Pug paced, more agitated with every step. He lowered his voice. "Honey, do this for me, an' then we'll have lotsa babies."

She calmed down, "You promise?"

"Ab-so-frig-gin'-lute-ly!" He smiled and sat by her. "I promise on my mother's grave."

He stood, pulled on shorts and headed to the fridge. He snapped open a Pat Henry and took a long swig. *She fuckin' betrayed me. No way*

I'm having a kid, a half black one. How do I know it's mine? Who else she been screwin'?

Darnisha appeared, still teary-eyed. He wrapped his arms around her shoulders and spoke softly. "Sweetie, you'll not regret this." He gently wiped away her tears and held her tight.

She asked, "We'll marry then?"

"You betcha, as soon as Skunk 3 goes public." He knew she didn't understand what that meant. "Sweetie, go shower, take care of this, and send me the bill."

He popped open another Pat Henry and plopped on the sofa. *Shit, fool me once …* He glanced at a pile of unopened mail and started thumbing through envelopes. He tore open one with a Denver, Colorado address.

Four photos fell from the envelope along with an unsigned note. It read, *She is looking for you.* The photos showed a girl about ten years old. She looked Asian, perhaps mixed parentage.

66
WEDNESDAY, JULY 10
HILLSBOROUGH

LATER THAT DAY, PUG ARRIVED at Tiffanee's for their regular weekly dinner. Pug looked forward to discussing his Skunk 3. Pug felt he had her and Kevin wrapped around his finger, and they were totally clueless.

They relaxed on the terrace. "Pug, I've found the ideal property in South San Francisco, and it meets your criteria."

"Tiff, how'd you get that done so fast?"

"Called in a few markers from my former real estate colleagues." She handed him a package of 30 photos, mostly interior shots, along with the building's specifications.

"Looks perfect! When can I move in?"

"Immediately! It's been unoccupied for about six months but needs no renovation."

"Looks like I'll be spending lotsa nights and weekends there. I'll get me a cot to sleep over and save time."

"Make sure it's a king." She winked.

"Kevin's missionary marketing is gettin' me great info for my bar napkin voodoo," Pug said.

"That's wonderful," she replied.

"I'll control the destiny of my success!" When he saw her expression change, he quickly recovered. *Whoops!* "Couldn't happen without you, Babe! King cot will be busy."

He saw her smile return, "Kevin says he'll file your patents as soon as you're ready."

"I'll keep 'im so busy, he won't have time for nothin' else."

"In the meantime, I've asked him to set up the new entity for Skunk 3. When I told him about your holding company idea for the patents and an LLC operating company for the development, manufacturing, and marketing functions, he thought that made sense. You and my JV will each own fifty per cent of Skunk 3 with you as the CEO."

"Kevin thinks like me." She refilled their glasses. Pug toasted, "To Skunk 3." He took a long swallow. "And many more."

"Kevin will bring the paperwork tomorrow for our signatures so we can go live with the new organization. You'll be very pleased he's following your instructions."

"Me and Kevin are on Elon Musk's rocket ship to Mars."

The maid announced, "Dinner is ready."

As they walked back into the house, Tiffanee asked, "Can you stay over tonight, Pug?"

"Babe, I'm all yours!" *I'm impressed. Tiff is really involved. But not sure I want her around after I take Skunk 3 public.*

67
THURSDAY, JULY 11
HILLSBOROUGH

TIFFANEE CALLED KEVIN THE NEXT morning. "Kev, my meeting with Pug went well. He liked the property we selected, and he's eager to start. He'll visit the facility tomorrow. He gave me a list of equipment to order and job descriptions for technicians he wants to hire."

"Can we use the techs from Skunk 2?"

"Pug wants the two operations completely separate. He's very paranoid about confidentiality. I think he read Andy Grove's book *Only the Paranoid Survive*."

"Mom, Pug's no Andy Grove, but your point's correct. The last thing we need is a lawsuit about IP theft."

"Pug would never violate confidentiality."

Kevin replied, "So, what else did you discuss?"

"Told him you were ready to file the patents."

"One of my associates will do the detail work. In addition to Pug's contributions, my software enhancements will make the patent applications stronger. Later, I'll file continuation-in-part applications to improve the original patents, independent of Pug's."

"Kev, Pug says the patents should be in his name only."

"I won't disappoint him." *With my clever legal word-smithing, he'll think he's the sole owner.* "I'll update him about the work to create the separate entities. I have to admit, his suggestions made sense—to separate operations from technology, patents, and licensing. Like I told you before, the McIntyre family will control the voting shares of the holding company and ultimately control the IP, the funding, any mergers and acquisitions, and all major investment decisions." *And his fifty per cent ownership interest in Skunk 3 will be pledged as collateral for any loans, past and present.*

"Sounds good. Kev, but I'm a little concerned about Pug."

"Why?"

"I don't know … yesterday and last night something felt strange. Pug acted distracted and just going through the motions. Totally different from the fun we've had in St. Martin and at church."

"Don't worry. You gave him a lot to think about last night. Creative guys go through down time. Mom, I'm proud of you for following my plan."

"Hope you're right," she said.

Tiffanee's concerns bothered him. He made a mental note to check with Jackson to see if he would share more about Pug's past. The two had been informally exchanging confidential information as Jackson became more comfortable with Kevin's questions. Kevin considered hiring Jackson to help with Skunk 3's global patent work.

68
THURSDAY, JULY 11
PALO ALTO

A MONTH HAD PASSED SINCE THEIR trial separation began. Michael proposed he needed time to think through his future with IPS and their marriage. She agreed. She rented an apartment in Palo Alto while working full time at Orlio & Associates.

On July 11, they met at Starbucks near Stanford campus.

"How's work?" Michael asked.

"Busy. Traveling a lot for my New York clients. You?"

Michael noticed she seemed happy, a different person. *Sex with Giorgio must be good.* He replied, "Nothing new to report on IPS or Skunk 2. Pug's still Pug. What can I tell you?"

"Michael, for your physical and mental health, I hope you put him in your rear-view mirror and soon. I have."

He smiled as if agreeing. "Hey, got some documents for you." He handed her a manila folder. "I talked with our daughters. They said I owed you this courtesy. And they were shocked to hear my side of the story."

She scanned the first few pages. "You sure you want to do this now?"

"Ellie, did you expect something different?" He handed her photos from Osaka and Kyoto. "You and Giorgio, or is it Gordon, darling El?"

"Michael, it is what it is. Frankly, no regrets. Cut to the chase. What do you want?"

There she said it. Michael knew his decision was right. "A clean break with no assets going to you other than a quarter interest in the house for which I will pay you a nominal amount."

"You think Gordon and I won't contest?"

"El, give it your best shot after I give the judge and our daughters those videos and recordings from Japan as well as Palo Alto."

"Wow, Michael, you and your spies have been busy beavers."

He gave her a knowing smile. "It's not only about cheating on me. You betrayed IPS too. Didn't realize that when you were doing pro bono work for IPS and "pro boner" work with Gordon. If you contest, worse dirt will come out. Your Italian buddies opened a lot of possibilities. You two could be disbarred. For God sakes, spare our daughters a public divorce scandal during discovery. Your choice." Michael knew he'd hit the mark when her smugness vanished. She wouldn't want her relationship with Gordon to crash in a shameful and nasty legal and marital scandal.

"I see you hired a high-powered law firm," she said.

"Yep, thanks to your and Giorgio's due diligence."

"Who can I thank for these photos? Let me guess ... "

"Team effort. I expect to hear back with your signed agreement to my terms in twenty-four hours. As Giorgio would say, 'Ciao, baby, my amora mia.' Oops! Meant ex-amora mia."

Without waiting for her reply, he left. Driving back to his office, he felt relaxed—a burden lifted. For the first time in many weeks, he could focus one hundred per cent on saving IPS and working with Natsu. They could work to defeat adversaries who wanted to block their objectives. Two adversaries had just been neutralized.

69

THURSDAY, JULY 11
BURLINGAME

B ACK IN HIS OFFICE, MICHAEL heard his secretary announce, "Pug James on line one."

Michael picked up the phone. "Hey, Pug."

"Fieldsy, got great news! In my off-hours, I'm doin' some bar napkin thinkin'."

"Pug, as you always said, 'Do my ears hear me?'"

"They do. I got this idea for an appliance device usin' co-molding—a portable oven with a high-temp plastic outside and high-temp metal alloy inside using my silver-lining IPS 10000. The surface is cool to the touch even tho' the inside's cookin' hot."

"Now, that's my old Pug!"

"But … it's not on your precious project list. So, whadya think, Fieldsy?"

"Show me proof-of-concept along with test results."

"Ya got it!"

"By the way, how are the customer visits? Getting good data to use on the ten projects?" Michael asked.

"Yeah, but findin' more stuff that'll change the development time. Need more time to finish the visits."

"Give me specifics, and we'll find the time."

"You got it. Talk to ya soon."

Pug smiled as he hung up. *I just bought me two more months. Fieldsy, you clueless moron.*

Michael called Natsu. "Natsu, wanted to update you on two events. First, I initiated divorce proceedings against Ellie. I don't expect her to contest."

"Michael, I'm truly sorry it came to this."

"The videos you provided confirmed earlier suspicions."

"What will Ellie do next?"

"That's a good question. Don't think she and her lover will continue to conspire with Technovenia now that I've threatened legal repercussions. What do you think?"

"We learned through confidential sources that Technovenia also contacted Hakase Yamura about IPS. They will be surprised. As far as we can tell, no adversary yet realizes IPS is no longer available. Our deception worked. What was your second item?"

"Pug called to inform me he has revived his co-molded idea and has developed a new appliance application."

"Do you believe him?"

"No, but it confirms he's been working on this technology the entire time at Skunk 2. I gave him more time to pursue so we understand his game."

"Excellent. We can confirm whether he's working with Kevin McIntyre and/or others on the automotive project. Michael, I appreciate you briefing me. On a personal note, thank you for informing me and Kobayashi-sama about Debiddo's US situation. Looks like both of us have been betrayed by James men. Sayōnara."

70
THURSDAY, JULY 11
PALO ALTO

J ACKSON RECEIVED AN URGENT CALL from Howard Riley.
"Hey Jackson, sorry to bother you, but I just got off the phone
with an irate Pug James."

"What happened?"

"He asked me to review documents concerning patent ownership
and legal entity structures. Pug had already signed them, so I'm not sure
why he asked me to look at them."

"What did you tell him, Howard?"

"That these documents he executed did not reflect his understanding.
Has to do with ownership of patents and stock. But I'm not a lawyer. So,
I recommended he get a second opinion. I gave him your name."

"And what did Pug say?" Jackson knew the answer.

"When I mentioned your name, he went ballistic, accused you of
fraud, deceit, and betrayals."

"What set him off?"

"I don't know, but he mentioned something about the case study I
gave him. He hung up before I could ask for more details."

"Don't know what to tell you. Pug and I disagreed over payment for
legal services. That has nothing to do with those documents he signed.
Let's meet for coffee. I might have some suggestions."

"Thanks, Jackson. Hate to lose Pug as a client, because I really
think he's on to something special. Who knows, there may be work for
you in the future once your problems get settled."

"Let's discuss that after we meet. Thanks for the update."

Jackson immediately texted Michael about the legal documents. Once he meets with Howard, he will provide more information.

71

FRIDAY, JULY 12
NEW YORK CITY/ BURLINGAME

Pug's cell phone displayed a New York City caller ID. "Hello."

"Is this Mr. Paul James?" Doug Stiller asked.

"Yeah, who's callin'?"

"Mr. James, I'm Douglas Stiller, Ronald J. Blunt's attorney. He'd like to talk with you about investment opportunities."

"Hell yes! Happy to talk! Put 'im on."

"Excellent, sir. Please hold for a moment. I'll connect you."

Ten minutes later, Pug heard Blunt's booming voice. "Paul James, Blunt here."

"Hey, call me Pug. Loved your book about doin' steals."

"What did you love most about my book?"

"Everything! Suin' people, fightin' for what's yours, takin' no crap from nobody."

"What else did you love about it?"

"Well, you got an eye for the beautiful ladies. I like your style."

"Pug, I can tell a bunch about someone in the first ten seconds."

"Me too. What can I do you for?"

"I'll cut to the chase. This venture fund told me about a company you founded ... IPS?"

"You bet! My baby! Sold it for a huge profit to some Japs. But they're destroying my creation."

"Still own shares?"

"Yeah."

"Tell you what, how about we do a great deal together and make some quick money. You ready to rock and roll?"

"Ab-so-frig-gin'-lute-ly!"

"Doug'll call you with the details. Gotta go now."

Before Pug could reply, the call ended.

Pug sat back in his chair and grinned. He liked Blunt's no-nonsense, quick action style—a refreshing change from Michael's plodding.

Fifteen minutes later, Stiller called. "Mr. James, I'm following up for Mr. Blunt. He thinks you've created a great company. You know, he's an America-first guy who wants to keep our technology in the USA. Would you be interested in getting IPS back in the USA?"

"Hell, yes!"

"So, here's the deal. Mr. Blunt, with the help of his venture fund, would like to purchase shares in IPS and combine them with your shares to bring this company home. How does that sound?"

"Music in my ears. Whadya you want me to do?"

Stiller outlined the steps, explaining that once they got majority control of IPS, Pug would become CEO.

"Hey Doug, when you talk to Blunt again, tell him I got this new technology that will go great with my silver-lining technologies. It'll revolutionize the automotive world and be worth billions. Best part, I own the new patents one hundred per cent."

"Sounds interesting, tell me more."

"Well, to get it launched we need a company and location. I've scouted around and found an ideal spot in the East Bay where we could launch."

"Send me details, and I'll discuss them with Blunt."

"Ya got it!"

After the call, Pug remained at his desk and thought, *Get IPS back. Combine with Skunk 4. For now, don't tell Kevin or Tiff. They dumped Blunt when they kicked 'im out of that JV.*

Darnisha walked into his office. "Darni, close the door, I got great news!"

"What's that?"

"I'm gonna be rich. I'm dealin' in big leagues now. And you'll be glad you did what I told ya. Now, you can rocket to the moon with me!"

He thought she'd be more excited about his news.

72
TUESDAY, JULY 16
SSFO

S KUNK 3 OFFICIALLY OPENED ON July 16. The building was located two miles from IPS. When he regained control of IPS (with Blunt's help), Pug could now dream of Skunk 3 merging with IPS. Pug was confident he could pull it off. Skunk 4 was his safety net if McIntyres bailed.

Pug and Kevin worked closely to organize the facility. After Pug sketched out his plans for operations—materials testing, product design, proof-of-concept prototyping, and administrative functions, Kevin recruited staff, saw to equipment installation, and established support functions.

Pug and Kevin walked through Skunk 3's labs, design shop, and prototyping area. "Kevin, super job gettin' this facility up and runnin.' Couldn't have done it better! An' that's sayin' somethin' comin' from me!"

"Pug, you had the vision, so it was easy to follow your roadmap. It's been a hectic but fun journey, and I've learned a lot."

"Yeah. Now the rubber hits the road. Been thinkin' about how we run this operation."

"Commence firing as I said in the Marines."

"You cover the day shift between seven-thirty and four, then I'll come at four o'clock, we overlap for an hour, and then I supervise the evening shift until midnight."

"Pug, I can't be here full time. I hired us an operations guy to work between eleven and eight. That way he can overlap both shifts."

"Makes sense."

"As for you, that's a tough pace to keep up between Skunk 2 and Skunk 3," Kevin added.

"No sweat. Got me a cot to sleep over here, so I don't waste time. Who'd you hire as office manager?"

"The recruiter sent Darnisha Washington. She has great references. When I interviewed her, I was impressed with her computer skills, and she looks like an energetic personality who'll keep the office humming."

"That's good." *Way to go Darni!* "The next weeks are all hands-on deck."

"I agree. When do you think we can begin field trials with prototypes?" Kevin asked.

"End of August, middle September. After all, we're workin' two shifts. I've already done a ton of materials testing so we're ahead of the game. First customer orders should happen by early October," Pug answered.

"Sounds aggressive, but we can do it. When should I bring Mom by to see the facility?"

"Uh … let's see where we are in a few weeks. If we're runnin' with no hiccups, then she can come to see my handiwork." *Gotta keep Tiff away from Skunk 3 when Darni's here!*

"Good plan, Pug. See you tomorrow."

Pug remained at the facility after Kevin left. He was on top of the world and knew Kevin had done a super job. Pug now had the perfect roadmap to get the East Bay facility started.

73
TUESDAY, JULY 30
SSFO

MICHAEL FELT PUG REQUIRED MONITORING both at Skunk 2 and his after-hour activities. When Sam told him about Darni's resignation, he instructed Sam to increase surveillance. Michael and Sam met at a coffee shop near IPS's offices. It had been six weeks since Michael's last project review.

"Why did Darni quit?" Michael asked.

"Allegedly, she found a better opportunity—more money, better benefits."

"That so?"

"Let me start at the beginning. She acted strange for three or four weeks before quitting."

"Strange?"

"Every morning, she'd rush to the bathroom for about thirty minutes. Reminded me of my wife's morning sickness. But Darni didn't mention any problems."

"Pregnant?"

"Not sure, but a week before she left, she seemed better. Pug hosted a going-away lunch. She ate spicy food, drank several margaritas, and there were no rushed bathroom visits. Then about the same time, Pug started acting different."

"In what way?"

"He leaves the office around three-thirty each day. When Darni was at Skunk 2, they stayed late all the time."

Michael had theories. He could believe anything about Pug: getting Darni pregnant, maybe an abortion—but still screwing her.

"Would you believe Pug's other gig is in South San Francisco? Here's the address." Sam handed Michael a slip of paper and photos.

"I know where this is." *Sonovabitch. This is only a couple of miles from IPS.*

Sam continued, "Pug stays overnight. Leaves early the following morning and goes directly to Skunk 2."

"Good you observed all that. Any idea what's going on inside the new place? Who's working there?"

"Definitely a startup—lots of equipment being delivered, and a bunch of people coming and going through the day. Saw several delivery trucks unloading materials like the metal alloys we've tested at Skunk 2. No name on the building or indication of what's inside."

"Did you recognize anyone else besides Darni and Pug?"

"No, never saw any of them before. I saw two men in suits one day arrive in a silver Porsche and after Pug arrived. Stayed for a couple of hours."

"You catch a license number?"

Sam pulled out photos of the two men and the car's tag number. "Oh, forgot to mention, security's tight. The building has some kind of handprint recognition to gain access. One more interesting fact: some of the days I did my stakeout I saw Pug there. He was supposed to be in Chicago with customers."

Michael would examine Pug's expense reports. *Did Pug really think he could get away with bogus trips?* He sensed Sam's nervousness.

"Sam, no need to worry. I won't let on I know anything. What's the status of Skunk 2 projects?"

"More accelerated testing but with a slight twist; testing several combinations of plastic and metal alloys for thermal and acoustics metrics."

"How are these combinations prepared?"

Sam took a long sip of his latte. "Various processes like blow molding, compression molding, injection molding, structural molding, and foam molding. Pug's outsourced the molding work to various shops."

"That explains Darni's comments about molding vendors. Has he explained why he's testing these different combinations?"

"No."

"Has he ever mentioned a co-molded small oven appliance project?"

"A what? No."

"Call in sick again," Michael said. "Say you've got the flu and do a three-day stakeout to re-confirm this information. Take more photos. Check the county tax records for building ownership. At Skunk 2, after hours, make copies of all the test results. Make sure, before you copy them that the proprietary stamp is clearly visible. Also, see if you can locate that lab book with the co-molded details. See that Jackson gets this information as soon as possible."

"Will do." Sam looked uncomfortable again, like the coffee was giving him indigestion.

"You got this, Sam. Don't worry. I've got your back and appreciate all this detective work. How are Danny and Pete doing?"

"Like me, frustrated. Ready to quit, honestly."

"Okay, the three of you need to be patient for just a few more weeks." Michael handed Sam an envelope.

"Thanks, Michael. This helps now that another baby's on the way."

"Sam, you've earned every cent!"

"One more item about Darni. By chance, I met her about a week after she left. I asked how she was doing. She made a weird comment about Pug's treatment at Skunk 2."

"What do you mean?"

"She implied Pug forced her do something unpleasant but wouldn't elaborate," Sam said.

"Noted. Meantime, keep your surveillance in full throttle."

In the car, Michael prepared his to-do list: *Show Jackson photos and review Sam's findings and follow up with Kevin. Visit the SSFO site. Update Natsu.*

He knew he had to move fast. It was clear Pug wasn't wasting any time on his new project.

Besides betraying me again, who else is he betraying?

74

WEDNESDAY, JULY 31
OSAKA/SOUTH SAN FRANCISCO

N ATSU RECEIVED REGULAR UPDATES FROM Seamus, Walter, and Suzi while she oversaw Debiddo's project. Michael got regular briefings from Sam and Jackson, who in turn talked regularly with Kevin and Howard Riley. Michael and Walter Marken were exchanging frequent information.

Michael began, "Natsu, we know Pug launched a new business in South San Francisco, very near IPS. He visits this location every day and stays overnight. Considerable equipment and materials were delivered, and we estimate twenty to twenty-five employees work there. Photos of people at this site include Kevin McIntyre. Pug has stolen Skunk 2's testing data for this new operation."

"Michael, it is crucial we learn more. This looks like a serious threat to JT-IPS."

"I agree, but getting information is difficult. There's a sophisticated security system that limits access."

"I'll send special resources to help," Natsu said. She was pleased Michael did not question this.

"Jackson reports that Pug and his business mentor have parted company. The mentor claimed Pug's acting paranoid, much like he did just before his stroke."

"Pug has not changed. Our New York asset informed us that Mr. Blunt contacted Pug to buy IPS shares with Technovenia's assistance. Technovenia contacted Hakase Yamura as well," Natsu said.

"That means our deception tactics are still operative," Michael added.

"Yes, and we must leverage that advantage. Walter Marken advised me that Kevin no longer performs missionary marketing in Detroit. What do you think that means?"

"That Skunk 3 is now focused on completing development. I learned this SSFO facility operates on two shifts, so work accelerates."

"I will instruct Debiddo and Seamus to hasten their efforts to ensure JT-IPS wins this contest. When we talk next, let's review the development status at SSFO," she said.

"I agree, Natsu, but without someone on the inside of the SSFO building, this will be a difficult task ... without violating the law."

"Michael, once we have good intelligence about the SSFO activities, this will provide insight for our longer-term objective."

"Which is?" Michael asked.

"The value of combining JT-IPS with Skunk 3. We can turn a potential competitor into an ally and produce a win-win-win for us, our OEM customers, and licensees. JT-IPS will remain the technology of choice."

"Natsu, you have strategic perspective. It's a pleasure to work with you."

"Your kind words are much appreciated. It is not often my male colleagues acknowledge my efforts."

They agreed to talk within the next week unless urgent developments intervened.

75
THURSDAY/MONDAY, AUGUST 1/5
BURLINGAME/SSFO

A FTER MICHAEL'S CALL, NATSU INSTRUCTED Seamus to visit California to investigate the Skunks. She provided Seamus with generous resources and sensed he would enjoy spying on Pug after Seamus left IPS. *Revenge is often a strong motive,* she thought.

Seamus engaged ex-CIA operatives to monitor the two skunks, including tapping Pug's cell phone and placing videos in his condo. After hours, they disabled the security system at Skunk 3 and entered the building. The operatives installed clandestine cameras to record daytime and evening activities at both locations.

Seamus provided Natsu daily videos and on-site monitoring of both sites. He sent a confidential memo summarizing the findings:

Pug works two separate jobs--daytime at Skunk 2 and nighttime at Skunk 3. An African-American woman often accompanies him to his condo.

Skunk 2's work focuses on testing materials and using outside parties for technical work like 3D printing prototypes and manufacturing prototypes. The second location contains more sophisticated equipment and more personnel. The only connection between the two locations is Pug. He often carries boxes from Skunk 2 and leaves them at Skunk 3.

The development work at the second location is similar to Debiddo's project but hasn't progressed as far. I estimate Skunk 3's project is forty days behind JT's. However, patent applications indicate some novel breakthroughs regarding electronics for exhaust system.

Pug's actively engaged in business espionage. Unclear who owns the second facility. Photographs of people who come and go might provide clues. Bottom line, Pug is using the silver-lining patents in the co-molding project without JT-IPS's permission.

Pug has frequent conversations with an Italian venture fund and an unlisted New York number. They discuss plans about a new entity in the East Bay. They joke about screwing the McIntyre family. Not sure what that means.

Natsu read Seamus's memo twice. His report confirmed Michael's information but uncovered new material. Now she had documented proof of Pug's espionage and other nefarious behavior. In her mind, Pug was not the only problem. She needed to know the extent of Kevin's efforts. Blunt's and Technovenia's involvement with this East Bay location increased the stakes.

She called Seamus. "Seamus, these findings cause much concern. Come back as soon as possible. I need your guidance to finish the exhaust system project. Do not share this information with anybody including Debiddo."

"Why is that?"

"Without the proper context, he will overreact when he learns the depth of Pug's betrayal. Right now, secrecy is paramount."

"Understand. Something else you should know and I didn't include in my memo. Rumors circulate that Lawrent's former CEO and Ronald Blunt seek control of IPS. Blunt talks about suing some technology JV and its owners. This requires more research."

"Seamus, before you leave California, debrief Michael Fields."

Previously, she advised Michael to refer to Seamus as Sean.

Seamus met Michael at Nobusakas, a new Japanese sushi restaurant in the Presidio.

"Sean, it's been a long time! You look different than I recall."

"Been on a health regimen for several months," Seamus replied.

"Never had a chance to say goodbye. I'd hoped to see you at the IPS/Lawrent patent infringement trial, but Pug told me he fired you. I never bought that."

"Whatever. Take his version, divide it by twenty, and maybe it approximates fake news."

"Totally understand. It's great we're now on the same team."

They ordered the house specials and continued reminiscing while eating. At the end of the meal, Seamus opened his briefcase.

"Natsu asked me to give you a copy of the memo I sent her." He discussed the information and showed photos of Kevin McIntyre, Darni Washington, and Pug entering the second location.

"One curious item ... another person left Skunk 2 and followed Pug to the second location." He handed Michael a photo. "I think this guy is one of Skunk 2's technicians."

Michael studied the photo appearing confused. "I don't recognize this individual. Maybe Pug's hired someone without my approval." He sensed Seamus accepted his explanation. "Well, two things are clear. Pug betrayed Skunk 2 by stealing proprietary information. And worse, he stole Dave's co-molding idea for Skunk 3's automotive development project. Dave'll go nuts when he learns this. But the most interesting element of your investigation, Sean, concerns a third possible location in the East Bay. Looks like Pug's triple dipping."

"Absolutely! Pug's up to his old tricks. Could never trust that asshole," Seamus added. "My operatives will monitor that location for updates."

"I appreciate your diligence. Good luck on completing the exhaust system project."

"Michael, right now that's my primary mission. Natsu asked me to give you my report on Lawrent's treachery to destroy IPS's business with Exeter. Use it as you see fit."

"Thanks, Sean."

With that, they shook hands and Seamus left for the airport.

Michael finished a glass of wine. *Talk about the pot calling the kettle black. So just who are you right now—Sean or Seamus or both? And whom to trust?*

Michael contacted Jackson and updated him. He told him to compare Sean's information with Sam's. Michael said he would personally inspect the second and third locations.

Later that night, Michael called Natsu.

"Natsu, I appreciate Seamus's special tactics to avoid us getting involved with the local authorities."

"Agree. The conspiracies increase with this third location and the involvement of Blunt, Lawrent, and Technovenia. I suspect they're using Pug as an unwitting pawn in their attempt to control the silver-lining technologies."

"Seamus's information corroborates what Jackson and I have learned from my sources inside Skunk 2 and our off-site surveillance of Skunk 3. Pug has committed business espionage against IPS and Skunk 2 as well as committing espionage against the McIntyre family. If Pug is successful, the East Bay facility will get a finished project with little or no cost."

"We will not let that happen!" she exclaimed. "It appears that Ellie and Gordon are no longer involved."

"I believe my threats have worked."

Their call completed, Natsu glanced at a picture of a sixteenth-century daimyo. Drawing inspiration, she thought, *This woman daimyo will keep JT-IPS unified and defeat all adversaries.*

76
TUESDAY, AUGUST 6
OSAKA

NATSU KNEW THINGS WERE BAD. Kenji had sent a messenger—Shiganari.

After arriving at the Comfort Station, they ordered two glasses of Johnny Walker Blue over ice. Unlike Kenji, Shiganari quit smoking after the war. At Hondoya, he conveyed a tough, stern persona who tolerated no incompetence. His leadership put Hondoya at the top.

"Dear Natsu-chan, arigato for joining me."

She noted his sad, stoic expression. "How is Kobayashi-sama?"

"Not well. I have his letter, and he wants you to memorize its contents. Afterwards. I will destroy it."

She read it twice relying on her photographic mind.

August 6, 2002

Our Dearest Natsu-chan,

I write this farewell guidance.

She paused to take a deep breath and held back tears.

Let me begin:

Always follow your ikigai roadmap, lessons from Sun Tzu, the samurai warrior code, and Deming's quality principles. Your paternal grandfather instilled these important ideas in our lives, and you must continue them.

As a hafu woman, leverage your unique advantage. Your adversaries will always underestimate you. So far, this has proven valuable for your business career.

Trust advisors, whose actions warrant that trust. Ignore advice from those who do not have your best interests as their goal.

Regarding specifics:

Seamus Hafferty: direct him to continue assisting Debiddo in technical matters and you in commercial matters. Unfortunately, his pornography addiction has returned. If this becomes public, it creates problems. Also, Seamus engaged in past patent espionage against IPS and collaborated with competitors. I gave him a second chance, and he once more violated my trust.

She paused for a moment. Could she trust a father who betrays his guardian? Would he also betray his daughter? She would speak with her mother before rendering judgment.

Debiddo: limit his role to finishing the exhaust system project. When he left the US, he abandoned his family and never divorced; he has lived a lie for the last three years. I am sorry you faced this betrayal. This invalidates your relationship. I blame Hakase Yamura for this oversight. He assured me there were no problems in Debiddo's history.

She paused her reading. "Okazaki-sama, I too am at fault. I should have researched Debiddo's background with more diligence."

"Dear Natsu-chan, do not be hard on yourself. You had no reason to question this matter when Kenji encouraged you to form this business relationship."

"Why couldn't Debiddo have been honest with me?"

"That is for you to decide, Natsu-chan."

She continued reading:

Hakase Yamura and Ashi-kun: they are serious threats to our security, our business dealings, and the Brunei Trust. Okazaki-san will implement my plan. You will maintain plausible deniability.

"My anger and disappointment with Seamus and Debiddo are only exceeded by my disgust for Hakase Yamura and my oji-san Ashi," she said. "They have betrayed my sensei, JT-IPS, the Brunei trust, and me. For that they deserve no forgiveness. I await your instructions."

He nodded. "Sometimes, you must harden your heart so revenge is much easier."

She continued reading:

Suzi Yamamoto: Instruct her to implement necessary actions regarding our two kabuki actors—Blunt and Pug James. Natsu understood. Reading further, *Suzi will continue as a valuable asset for you in the US. She knows many wealthy investors who can partner with you on future real estate ventures and commercial endeavors. Continue to reward her. I did not judge your mother or Suzi for their past indiscretions. Neither must you.*

Ellie Fields and Giorgio Orliani: you assisted Michael in resolving this marital matter. Instruct Michael and Jackson Huntley to initiate the required US legal actions to address the conspiracies by Blunt and Technovenia.

Kevin McIntyre and Tiffanee McIntyre: as you learn more, determine the best way to collaborate on the global operations between JT-IPS, our technology JV, and the Skunks. He demonstrates a measured pace and the skills to succeed in doing business in Japan. He may be the key ally to ensure your legacy and perhaps a partner for your future endeavors. Meet with his mother as soon as practical.

She already had done more research on Kevin and felt comfortable accepting Kenji's advice.

Michael Fields: consider him an invaluable resource. You decide what role he can perform for you. Your weekly talks proved you can trust him without conditions. He possesses the attributes I most admired in Patrick Hafferty.

Finally, your grandfather understood and respected the bond between Shiganari and myself. He understood that our devotion to one another never hindered our business judgments. Shiganari and I believe you have inherited his generosity of spirit. Use your inheritance wisely and precisely.

Again, my dearest Natsu-chan, your achievements give us much pride. You will be successful in business and personal matters and achieve your ikigai destiny.

With my deepest love and affection,
Kenjiro Kobayashi
c.c. Shiganari Okazaki

Kenji's words were forever etched in her mind. She thought, *Why couldn't I see him one more time?*

Shiganari glanced away out of respect while she gathered herself.

At last, she said, "I understand Kobayashi-sama's message. Okazaki-sama, I am conflicted. What to do regarding Debiddo, Ashi-kun, and Seamus? First, Debiddo contributed significantly to IPS's and JT's technical successes. Second, Ashi-kun served Kobayashi-sama with loyalty for thirty-five years. Third, my father suffered traumatic losses for reasons beyond his control. Yet all three, for different reasons, have betrayed us. Do I have an obligation to consider leniency? What do you suggest I do, Sensei?"

She knew Shiganari was pleased she accepted his new status.

"Natsu-chan, consult with your mother for her counsel. She, like you, has been in a close relationship with a gaigin. She understands what Seamus experienced when she disappeared. And she understands her brother's motives and decisions about her pregnancy. With her counsel, you can assess if their betrayals and lies warrant punishment, forgiveness, or a hybrid solution. Kenji would advise you to be unforgiving and brutal. I, however, empathize with your dilemma. You will make the correct choices."

"Arigato for being Kenji's wise and loving *konpanion* all these years."

With tears in his eyes, Shiganari responded, "You will succeed. One day your unique heritage will be accepted and celebrated. For now, you as a woman daimyo will lead efforts to change our nation's culture. Now, dear Natsu-chan, I must attend to Kenji."

"Please tell Kobayashi-sama I love him and will follow his instructions."

An ominous feeling enveloped her. She knew she would never again experience Kenji's human presence. But his spirit would remain.

77
SATURDAY, AUGUST 10
MT. FUJI

WHEN HE ARRIVED AT MT. Fuji, Shiganari found Kenji resting on the sofa. He wore a nasal cannula connected to an oxygen tank. A half-full bottle of Johnnie Walker Blue rested on a low table along with four different pain medications.

Shiganari's heart thudded, but he leaned over and gently kissed Kenji's forehead. He searched for words. "My dear konpanion, your doctor does not approve of drinking alcohol while taking pain medication."

"Does that matter now?" Kenji asked.

Shiganari pulled up a chair and sat close. "I wish you had accepted Marken-san's offer to meet his US doctors. I cannot bear your pain and suffering."

"There is a beginning, and there is an ending, dear one. I am closing the circle. You have been my one and only true friend. I am most grateful for your enduring love and wise counsel."

Shiganari swallowed tears as he pulled a linen handkerchief from his vest pocket.

"Do not weep. I am at peace. I have lived a long, productive life. Your love has comforted me in difficult times. We co-molded our lady daimyo to sustain Hafferty-sama's and our legacies."

Shiganari began pacing and fumbled with his phone. Kenji's voice interrupted him.

"Stop! I do not want to die with strangers fussing over me."

Slowly Shiganari put down the phone, poured himself a glass of scotch, and downed it to calm himself. "I have discussed your instructions with Natsu. She will honor you."

Kenji's breathing grew more erratic. Shiganari attempted to help him sit up, but Kenji waved him away.

"You must listen carefully. I need to tell you things."

Wiping away tears, Shiganari kneeled on the floor next to him.

Kenji spoke, his voice barely audible. "I informed Michael Fields ... our plans for our lady daimyo. He understands, will support you and Natsu."

"That will facilitate our efforts."

"And ... Hakase Yamura ... what about ...?"

"Our plan proceeds," Shiganari assured him.

"As it should." Kenji, his hands shaking, gestured to the pain medicine. Shiganari handed him three pills and helped Kenji swallow them with sips of Johnnie Walker.

Shiganari sat closer. Kenji continued, "Cannot forgive ... for false information ... about Debiddo. Had I known ... never encouraged partnership. I feel responsible ... for loss of her son." He coughed and choked. Shiganari pressed the glass to Kenji's lips. He swallowed and managed to say, "Debiddo's seed is cursed as his father's."

"Do not blame yourself. At the time, we took prudent action with risks. As for Yamura, our organization friends returned our stolen trust funds and have punished the subordinates who conspired with him. Yamura does not know this."

A smile crossed Kenji's face. "Excellent strategy. Sun Tzu would be proud."

They smiled at each other, enjoying this game that had amused each for so many years, the samurai challenge.

Suddenly, Kenji's eyelids fluttered.

"Wait!" Shiganari grabbed the bottles of pain medicine. "How many of these have you taken?"

"Please respect my decision. As the most famous samurai said, 'Do not fear death' and 'Do not regret what you have done.'"

Shiganari realized Kenji had chosen when and how he would

depart. He would die like a true daimyo who had been defeated by the only enemy he could not defeat—cancer.

With eyes closed, he whispered, "Tell Natsu ... remain strong ... honor Patrick Hafferty's memory. Help her ... achieve her ikigai."

Shiganari clasped Kenji's hands and wept. He leaned closer to hear Kenji say, "Tell Yamura ... check mate."

Kenji's eyes closed.

Shiganari wrapped his arms around Kenji and choked out, "Rest well, my beloved."

He remained at Kenji's side until he could compose himself.

When Natsu answered the phone and heard Shiganari's voice, she knew.

"Dearest Natsu-chan, my faithful konpanion and your sensei has departed."

Natsu responded tearfully, "His teachings prepared me; I will honor his memory. His daimyo spirit remains in me."

"As bereft as we are, we must attend to business."

"Hai, tomorrow I will announce Kobyashi-sama's overseas travels," she said.

"As Kenji's power of attorney, you will undertake actions in his absence. You are the CEO of JT-IPS and its keiretsu. All primary adversaries are under surveillance. I will inform you when it is time. What have you decided about the three persons?"

"Okazaki-sama, thank you for your wise advice to consult with my mother. As Kobayashi-sama predicted, she has excellent judgment about people and relationships. She gave me considerable insight. She counseled to understand Seamus's history, his reaction after her disappearance, his addiction, and other transgressions. She told me Ashi-kun should be forgiven for his mistakes regarding Hakase Yamura. Ashi-kun did not understand the total situation. I should remember his years of loyal service to Japan Technologies and to Kobayashi-sama. Finally, she advised me about my gaigin relationship and to help Debiddo resolve his personal issues and to be given a second chance like Sensei did for Seamus and for her."

"Your mother gives sage counsel. What do you plan?"

She took a deep breath. "A measured approach like noh actors."

Natsu took a while to calm herself and to mentally prepare. She recalled Kenji telling her he had volunteered for a kamikaze mission at the end of WW II, at a time when the enemy could not be defeated. How Kenji chose to die made sense to her. He faced an enemy he could not defeat.

With her photographic memory, she recalled points in Kenji's farewell letter. *I must proceed without grieving. I must protect the legacy. I will do what I must. I will defend JT-IPS against all adversaries.* She looked at the second tattoo on her right arm. *I am a daimyo.*

That evening, Natsu informed Debiddo and Seamus that Kenji had left to inspect his foreign real estate properties. Blunt had invited him to visit the Big Apple to celebrate their recent transactions and to evaluate new investments.

She instructed them to finish the exhaust system project and to launch commercialization. Prototype field trials had gone well, and the product launch was scheduled for late August with orders expected in September. For Debiddo, he could confront his father's theft of his co-molding design; perhaps seek reconciliation. Additionally, she told him to resolve his marital situation and to make necessary amends. Without that, their partnership could not continue. For Seamus, he would continue his commercial intelligence activities and retire in Colorado. For Ashi-kun, she would discuss his future once he apologized for his mistakes.

The following day, Natsu instructed her executive assistant to request a meeting with Hakase Yamura. The meeting's purpose: Seek his counsel about Japan Technologies's future.

78
WEDNESDAY, AUGUST 28
HILLSBOROUGH

TIFFANEE READ THE *WALL STREET Journal's* article about WorldCom's bankruptcy. Kevin appeared on the pool patio. "Kev, did you read this article about Bernie Ebbers and WorldCom? So sad."

"Yes, Mom. He got caught up in lies and fraud. Probably worse than WorldCom is the Enron scandal. Talk about betraying stakeholders." He paused as if struggling to continue; his expression glum.

"What's wrong, Kev?"

Kevin knew the day had arrived. He waited until Pug's development work neared completion and the patent applications filed. The official applications indicated ownership belonged one hundred per cent to an offshore IP holding company owned by Tiffanee and him. Pug's copy, however, indicated he owned the Skunk 3 patents.

"Mom, I know you and Pug have a special relationship, but you need to understand certain truths before doing anything you'll regret."

Tiffanee set aside the newspaper. "I don't like the direction of this conversation."

"Sorry, Mom, hear me out. It's true Pug's divorced, but not for the reason he told you. His wife began divorce proceedings after watching videos of his affair with a Japanese lady. And the most disturbing part? This affair produced a child who is now ten. DNA proof confirmed this."

Tiffanee shook her head in disbelief. "What? Pug said his wife cheated on him with some lawyer named Huntley."

"I know Jackson Huntley, and Pug's claims are patently false. I authorized background checks on Pug and saw the video. He suffered a stroke soon after his wife confronted him. He went through months of rehab including psychiatric treatment."

"That can't be true! Pug told me he had a minor health event. He doesn't look like someone who just got out of rehab!"

Kevin knew she was struggling. "Mom, listen! There's more! Pug's oldest son, Skip, has been convicted of murdering his wife and awaits sentencing."

"Skip? This can't be right. Pug has one son, Darin, he works in Japan."

"Unfortunately, more Pug lies. His youngest son, Dave, works in Japan."

Neither spoke. Tiffany shook her head no. At last, Kevin broke the silence. "Remember when you lent Pug money for the off-site technical work?"

"Yes, and he quickly guaranteed the loan by pledging his IPS shares."

"Yet another lie. Those shares were already pledged for another loan."

Tiffanee held her hands to her forehead and closed her eyes. "Is anything he told me true?"

"Who knows? I learned he's planning to share Skunk 3's proprietary technical data with another entity without our approval. He is launching another Skunk in the East Bay."

"But where would he find the money? We've funded everything."

"You won't believe this, but Ronald Blunt and Technovenia joined his crazy scheme, thanks to none other than Gordon Orlio. Gordon was a silent partner in that firm. Apparently, this venture firm convinced Blunt we misled him about the JV's future. If he had known about Pug's development project, he would never have sold his interest. He's suing us and Kenji for damages. Doug Stiller requested a court injunction against Skunk 3 to cease all activities until this is resolved."

Furious, Tiffanee, red-faced and clenching her fists, yelled, "That'll be one very cold day in hell!"

"You're right, Mom. I've contacted K&F to respond. And if all else fails, our JV partner will make life very difficult for one Staten Island asshole."

"Can this get any worse?"

"I'm afraid so. Pug's being sued by a Darnisha Washington who claims he forced her to have an abortion."

"Wait, isn't she the same woman he hired at Skunk 3?"

"Yes, she and Pug had an ongoing relationship. She's threatening to sue us if she can get a lawyer to take her case. Claims to have a flash drive with proprietary data from both skunks and will sell it to the highest bidder if we don't pay. Mom, she'll settle once we countersue."

"Kevin, my head is spinning." She grabbed hold of a table and steadied herself. "My god, this is beyond belief. What do we do?"

"Thanks to Jackson Huntley, Michael Fields and I have been sharing information about Pug. I've been thinking a lot about this. First, I want you to meet with Michael Fields. He'll corroborate everything I've said. Now, as to specifics, here are my thoughts ... "

Kevin outlined how he would undertake all the heavy lifting so they wouldn't arouse Pug's suspicions. When all the gritty details became public, they would get a restraining order against Pug and take other legal actions. "For the time being, you and I should avoid talking with him."

"Won't that make him suspicious?"

"Probably, but that's a risk we take. Tell him you're sick. Mom, I'll be traveling."

"Excuse me for a minute, Kev." He watched her walk to the kitchen and open a bottle of wine. She returned with two glasses and sat. After taking a long sip, "Kevin, I let loneliness cloud my common sense. Can you ever forgive me for such poor judgment?"

"Mom, don't be so hard on yourself! There's no way you could have known he was lying. For a while, he had me convinced with his plans and enthusiasm. You and I tend to look for the best in people."

"Thank God, Pug didn't move in with me."

"In short, Pug betrayed us. We have enough dirt to keep him in court or even jail if he chooses to fight. He'll drag down Blunt and the Italian firm too. He'll be fired very soon, and his East Bay facility will be visited by law enforcement."

Tiffanee was on her feet again. "Let's take the bastards down!"

79
FRIDAY, AUGUST 30
BURLINGAME

PUG WAS TRANSFIXED BY THE TV's early morning news. The reporter announced Skip James's guilty plea and reported the police investigation found no exonerating evidence to dismiss murder charges. Skip waived a jury trial and pleaded guilty due temporary insanity. The judge, unconvinced, found the prosecution's case credible. He sentenced Skip to life without possibility of parole.

Enraged, Pug yelled to the empty room. "Godammit! Marcy caused every single one of Skip's problems! Spoiled him rotten. If he'd listened to me, he'd had dumped that Burr slut! She seduced him to steal my company. He's weak like Marcy. Didn't have the balls to fight like a man."

He checked his watch. *Oh, shit. This is the morning for a meeting with Fieldsy. Gonna tell 'im to shove Skunk 2 up his ass.*

Pug and his techs assembled at seven-thirty. He noticed Sam's nervousness. "Hey Sammy, relax. Not gonna fire ya today. Now that Darni's gone, ya got your old job back."

No one smiled or reacted. Sam stared at his notes.

At eight o'clock, Michael appeared. Pug shouted, "Fieldsy, about time! We start work here at seven-thirty. Ya not get my memo?"

"Apologies to Danny, Pete, Sam—traffic accident on 101."

Pug slapped the table with his hand. "Let's get this road on the show! Pete, you're up."

Michael interrupted, "I want to say a few words. Pete, Danny, Sam, you've done an admirable job given this difficult environment, and your positions are secure."

Pug shouted, "What the fuck ya talkin' about? An' who the hell are them jerks standing outside?"

"Pug, you're fired!"

Pug was on his feet, his face beet red. "What the fuck?"

"Get your personal stuff and leave! Pete, make sure Pug doesn't steal any more proprietary materials. Don't hesitate to use your martial arts skills."

"Nobody fires me! I quit! After all I did for ya, made tons o' money for ya and MatraScience! Saved your sorry little ass when I gave ya a job at IPS. Ungrateful bastard!"

Michael, calm, showed no emotion. "Pug, you betrayed me, your former company, and now this skunk. Leave!"

"You don't tell me what to do, ya technical moron and shit-ass manager! Ya never 'stood my inventin' talent!" Pug pointed his finger at Michael. "You, Michael fuckin' Fields, betrayed me after all I did for ya—all these years. Sonovabitch! This is the thanks I get?" Perspiring and furious, he grabbed his coffee mug and threw it at Michael's head. As Pug lunged at him, Pete jumped forward, wrapped his wrestler's arms around Pug's neck, and dragged him toward the door.

"You've got five minutes to vacate!" Michael yelled.

Corralled by Pete, Pug struggled and yelled. One security officer handcuffed Pug while the other restrained him.

Pete gathered up Pug's jacket and phone, and the guards escorted Pug to his condo.

At his condo door, the guards unlocked the cuffs. "Mr. James if you return to Skunk 2, you will be arrested by the police for trespassing. Here's the court order that prohibits you from returning or communicating with any of the employees."

"Fuck you guys!" Pug tore up the document, tossed it back at them, and slammed the door. He strode to the fridge, opened a Patrick Henry, and gulped it down.

"Fieldsy, ya screwed up big time! Fuckin' don't-know-shit. I'm takin' your ass to the cleaners! When ya find out I got Blunt on my side along with Technovenia, you'll root the day ya messed with me. No one fires me! I fire them!"

Back in the conference room, Michael exhaled and pressed his hands to the table.

"What the hell just happened?" Danny asked, flopping back into a chair.

"Simply put, Pug has engaged in a series of betrayals against this company and you guys. He stole intellectual property, trade secrets, proprietary test data, and has violated his employment contract and confidentiality obligations."

"Somehow, I'm not surprised," Sam remarked.

"Yeah, he just ran us around in testing circles, and we never completed any of the projects. Frankly, I was quitting today after this review." Danny added.

"Rest assured, each of you has full-time employment going forward both here and at Japan Technologies and at International Protected Solutions."

"Japan Technologies and International Protected Solutions?" Danny asked.

Michael explained the two entities and their relationship to the Burlingame skunk. He noted that the IPS technical director would assume management of the skunk until it could be fully integrated.

"What's Pug planning?" Pete asked.

"He's started at least one other operation similar to this skunk works—and—possibly a third one."

"Three skunk works?" Danny asked, incredulously. "That's why he changed our working hours."

Michael nodded in agreement.

"You think Pug took technical information to these new places?" Sam asked.

Michael rolled his eyes and raised both hands. "Pug's been involved with some unsavory characters. We'll thoroughly investigate and may file criminal charges."

"What happens now?" Pete asked.

"Tell my technical director what testing and analysis you're doing—particularly with regard to co-molding metal alloys with plastic materials. Get him up to speed on what's done and isn't. And, hey guys, I just want to reassure you your jobs are secure. There'll be some excellent career opportunities for you. Stay the course. Thanks for all your hard work. Each of you will get a nice bonus for the outstanding work you did under difficult conditions."

In the car, Michael called Jackson. "Hey Jackson, Pug's history."

"Have to admit I feel somewhat vindicated."

"Absolutely. As you would expect, he claimed he quit after I fired him."

"Pug could never admit losing," Jackson replied.

"It's time we visit the South San Francisco location."

Jackson added, "I'll alert Kevin to expect us next week once he gives the okay."

80
SATURDAY, AUGUST 31
HONOLULU

THE RAPIDLY UNFOLDING EVENTS NECESSITATED a meeting. Michael and Natsu arrived at Honolulu's International Airport within an hour of one other. They met in a conference room at American Airline's Admiral Club.

"Natsu, a pleasure to finally meet you in person," Michael said, motioning her to a chair.

"For me as well." She sat and waited for Michael to speak.

"I'm truly sorry for your recent loss. Kenji was a very special person," Michael said as he sat across from her.

Natsu sensed his sincerity. "Thank you, Michael. Only you and Kobayashi-sama's long-time colleague know the truth. Please keep it confidential until an official announcement." She shared how that would occur.

"I understand," Michael said.

"Kobayashi-sama thought very highly of you."

"Honestly, without Kenji's support, IPS would be bankrupt and its silver-lining technologies lost. The merger with Japan Technologies was a lifeline. Unfortunately, our Skunk 2 plan for Pug failed. I underestimated my ability to rehabilitate him after his medical and personal problems. Ironically, my former wife was right about Pug's depravity."

"As Kobayashi-sama advised, you have to take risks, learn from mistakes. Your plan made sense at the time. In fact, think about it this way: the development work at Skunk 2 and Skunk 3 produced technical innovations that integrate with our work at JT-IPS. We have multiple and viable solutions for exhaust systems. Thank you for sharing the Skunk 2 test data with JT-IPS. It accelerated our project. As for your former wife, she may have predicted Pug's collapse, but she underestimated me."

"That she did."

"Kobayashi-sama stressed that the difference between a master and a beginner is the master has failed more times—a samurai principle. So, as you can see, taking a risk on Pug produced long-term benefits in spite of the failure to rehabilitate him."

The attendant brought a bottle of Johnnie Walker Blue, ice, and light snacks. Michael poured. "I know Kenji always enjoyed his scotch."

"And I as well," Natsu replied. "How are things at IPS?"

"Calmer. The Delaware Plan, IPS's management team, and the merger with Japan Technologies are complete." Michael opened his briefcase and handed her a document outlining each completed action. "I think you'll find Jackson Huntley's report quite comprehensive. This summarizes information we've discussed in our weekly conversations."

"Our several conversations have helped strategize and to act in a timely manner. I am authorized to approve any remaining steps." She handed him a power-of-attorney document. "Hakase Yamura no longer represents JT's interests. My personal lawyers will work with Mr. Huntley." She handed him their business cards. "What is the latest information about Pug James?"

"As you know, he violated his three-year employment contract and confidentiality agreements with Skunk 2. We have evidence he gave confidential information to the SSFO location—for testing thermal and acoustic performance of high temp plastics and metal alloys. Yesterday, I fired him from Skunk 2. Pug's been working after hours and weekends at the SSFO and East Bay locations. The East Bay entity looks like a copycat version of the SSFO location. Seamus confirmed Pug took information from SSFO operation to the East Bay facility. But, we don't think Kevin McIntyre knows about this. Pug probably betrayed Kevin with the help of Blunt and Technovenia. In short, Pug has committed business espionage against Skunk 2, Skunk 3, and JT-IPS."

"We have enough information to discuss with Kevin how we can cooperate going forward. Do you agree?"

"Yes. We'll explore how to coordinate with Kevin McIntyre."

"Michael, if Pug retaliates by creating a storm, we will support your efforts to defeat him."

Natsu thought about the word *storm*, reminding her of her favorite Shakespeare play, *King Lear* and the storm scene on the heath. *If Pug were King Lear, who would play his fool? Who could point out Pug's many faults in a sarcastic and humorous fashion? Perhaps, Debiddo could play the fool, the father-son, love-hate dynamic and competition.* In any case, she wished Kenji were still alive. *We would debate this metaphor.*

She sipped scotch and added, "I will explore how we can leverage our mutual interests using our technology JV. I suspect Kevin had already considered this."

"Makes perfect sense. From my brief interactions with Kevin and Jackson's opinion, you two may have much in common. He appears thoughtful, extremely bright, and analytical. He definitely could be an excellent business partner."

She appreciated his comment as it agreed with Kobayashi-sama's assessment. "Michael, I hope the SSFO technical team can work in parallel with JT-IPS's to strengthen the development and market strategies. This would give the appearance of competition and preclude others from entering this domain. Kevin will take the right actions when I explain the entire picture to him. When we purchased Blunt's interest in a JV, we became partners with the McIntyre family. Simultaneously without our knowledge, Pug initiated contact with Kevin about his new co-molding idea."

"And Pug's 'new idea' was Dave's original co-molding idea," Michael added.

"Yes! Thanks for alerting us to that. When Kevin visited Osaka, he alluded to a project that sounded similar to Debiddo's project. Kenji asked Walter Marken to investigate Kevin's Detroit work, and later I asked Seamus to investigate. We soon realized the two projects were parallel efforts directed towards a mutual objective. How did Pug meet Kevin McIntyre?"

"Tiffanee, his mother, introduced them. Pug and Tiffanee ...uh ... were lovers when they worked at MatraScience in the late eighties."

She laughed. "Pug James is quite the lady's man, indeed. Kenji told you about Pug's liaisons with Japanese hostesses." She noted Michael's agreeing nod. "Speaking of affairs, I know we shared unpleasant news with you."

"Yes. That was about the time our weekly phone calls started. In truth, I had my suspicions about Ellie. The videos and conversations you furnished were final confirmation. I initiated divorce proceedings so I controlled the process. On reflection, I'm partly responsible for my wife's betrayal. Let's put it this way, Gordon Orlio was in the right place and time when she needed change. I can only wish her good fortune."

"Do you mean Giorgio Orliani?"

"One and the same. That's his Italian alias."

"Oh, dual citizenship. Michael, I admire your generous understanding. It takes courage to face a personal betrayal, to forgive and to move forward." *As a lady daimyo, I must learn forgiveness.* She paused for a moment. "I look forward to working with you. Perhaps in the future, you can counsel me about moderation and forgiveness."

"If I can assist you in any way, let me know," Michael said.

"You treat me as an equal, and I sincerely appreciate that. In Japan, it is not the accepted custom." She looked at her watch. "Time passes, and we have to get to our departure gates. There are other points I want to share. First, JT-IPS's exhaust system project is nearly finished and ready for commercialization. Our team has done an amazing job."

"Are you satisfied with the IP protection and patent positions? Jackson Huntley is impressed with your IP lawyers' work."

"Yes, but there are issues with Debiddo and Seamus." In quick succession, she described Debiddo's marital lies and Seamus's addiction. She continued, "I want Debiddo to return to the US and atone for betrayals of his American wife. He may choose to stay in the US. If he does, I will consider Jun Ashi to replace Debiddo. As far as Seamus, he will retire and return to Colorado where he grew up. He has earned a bonus for his recent efforts."

"There he can resume his Sean persona," Michael added with a smile.

She retrieved a file from her briefcase. "This last document is my draft plan to intersect JT-IPS's business activities with the McIntyre family. Please give me your assessment once you have read it. I hope to share this with Kevin in the near future."

"Natsu, this has been an informative meeting."

"Michael, I value what we have started. Kobayashi-sama was a wise judge of people, and his legacy will guide our futures."

"I have two more suggestions for your consideration. Kevin's an impressive person with a lot of potential. He could benefit from working with a person of equal intelligence and drive. But he needs more exposure to Asian history and philosophies."

She smiled. *Kobayashi-sama had similar thoughts.*

"One more item. The merger between Japan Technologies and IPS must go well. I know an American professor who studied Japan and American companies. He wrote a book, *Theory Z*."

"Michael, I have read that book; most informative."

"Perhaps he could consult for our combined companies. Our IPS team needs to learn why Japanese business has been so successful on productivity and quality." Michael said.

"An excellent suggestion. This may be a good role for Ashi-kun to oversee," she said. "Perhaps you could arrange a meeting with the professor when I travel to the US. Kenji advised me to listen carefully to you." She took another document from her briefcase. "Please review and call me when you are ready to discuss."

She stood and before shaking his hand, "Michael, I want to show you something. You are the only one who has seen these." She rolled up both sleeves and showed him the two tattoos.

On the plane back to Osaka, Natsu recorded her follow-up: *Continue monitoring Pug's activities at the East Bay location. Debiddo and Seamus trips. Initiate corrective action to close East Bay facility. Resolve Technovenia, Lawrent, and Blunt.*

Aboard his flight to SFO, Michael studied the five-page document. Natsu made it clear she admired his business judgment and interpersonal skills. She requested he become her confidential sensei for business and personal matters. She also proposed him as the Non-Executive Chairperson of JT-IPS. The last page outlined lucrative compensation and benefits if he accepted. He thought, *Perfect timing. Ellie's gone; I can spend more time in Japan. I am truly honored. Maybe I can teach Natsu to relax and adopt a softer view of people. Ellie, too bad for you. You've lost our marital shogi match. The Lady Daimyo is in my corner.*

He checked emails and read a news release that Skip James was found dead in his jail cell—suicide.

Sadness swept over Michael. He remembered working with Skip when he first joined IPS. He watched the relationship between Pug and his son deteriorate over the years. *What will Marcy do now?*

81
SUNDAY, SEPTEMBER 1
HILLSBOROUGH

ICHAEL ARRIVED AT TIFFANEE'S HOME and was escorted to the outdoor terrace.

"Ms. McIntyre will be with you shortly. May I get you a beverage?" the maid asked.

"Yes, I'll have a scotch and soda." Michael surveyed the surrounding views of the pool and tennis court. *Very impressive. She's done well!*

Tiffanee joined him and extended her hand. "Michael Fields, it's been a long time since MatraScience. Please sit. We have a few moments before dinner."

"Thank you. May I call you Tiffanee?"

"By all means! I've heard a lot about you from our common acquaintance!"

"That could be bad or good." He saw her knowing smile.

Drinks arrived, and Tiffanee immediately raised her glass. "Welcome to Maison du McIntyre."

Michael raised his glass to her. "Merci."

"I understand you and Kevin have talked," Tiffanee said.

"Correct. Jackson Huntley facilitated our discussions. The common catalyst was Pug. Once we realized what Pug had done, we quickly developed mutual interests."

He saw Tiffanee's face register disappointment. "Pug betrayed Kevin, and…me. He was not the close and fun friend I remembered in 1987."

Michael sighed. "Tiffanee, over the years I worked with him at

MatraScience, at IPS, and later at the Skunk. I believed in his creative and innovative mind. That's why I continued to help him. But alas, I completely failed. While he was IPS's CEO, the company nearly went bankrupt. Thanks to the JT merger, the company will survive."

"He never mentioned your role at IPS or at Skunk 2."

"Not surprising."

The maid interrupted. "Ma'am, Chef Sergio says dinner is ready."

Tiffanee stood and invited Michael to accompany her. "We have much to discuss, don't we?"

"Indeed, we do," Michael replied.

During a five-course meal, they shared their Pug stories and his betrayals.

Michael recounted in detail working with Pug at MatraScience, and then IPS. He described Pug's marital problems, his stroke, and the efforts to rehabilitate him at Skunk 2.

"And one of the saddest events involved Pug's horrible treatment of Skip at IPS. I believe that's why Skip betrayed Pug and began an affair with the lady who was murdered. The newspaper account said they found Skip dead in his jail cell. Suicide, most likely."

"So sad … Pug never acknowledged that son. Now, I understand why."

Michael could see that Pug's disastrous relationship with Skip clearly bothered her. In his mind it was critical she understand Pug's total depravity.

Tiffanee continued, "From the moment we reconnected at Kuletos, I believed Pug about his family, his career, his great plans. Lies … all lies." She was near tears. "I was so gullible."

"Pug can draw you in with his outsized personality, incredible energy, and enthusiasm."

"Michael, your perspective and rational view are a refreshing change from Pug."

After dinner, they returned to the terrace to drink Cognac. "Guess it's fair to say, you and I are cross-linked by Pug's betrayals." Michael observed Tiffanee's smile at the reference to one of MatraScience's technologies.

"Or as Pug would say, we've both been 'Pearl Harbored,'" she added. "So, Michael, tell me about you and your family."

Michael shared his business and personal story. "You could say my passion to save IPS and to rehabilitate Pug cost me my marriage. Ellie had sufficient reasons to seek happiness elsewhere. The divorce would have been amicable, but now I've learned she and her lover, Gordon Orlio, conspired to disrupt the merger between IPS and Japan Technologies. They wanted control of the silver-lining technologies. All this changed my divorce calculus."

"That explains why Gordon kept asking me what Pug was doing. The betrayal dots are clearly connected."

"True. Gordon got Technovenia to encourage Pug and Blunt to work together." He reached for the Cognac and refilled their glasses. "But now I look forward to working with Natsu Nashakatani at JT-IPS. And I'm excited to work with Kevin—to build new, innovative technology for automotive."

"Michael, I appreciate your honesty and look forward to working with you. I know Kevin does as well."

"Thanks, Tiffanee. On that note, I suggest you invite Ms. Nashakatani to visit and to discuss how the McIntyres can work with the merged entity. It's important mutual trust be established between the JV partners."

"Would it be a conflict to serve as an advisor for me?" Tiffanee asked. "You could facilitate our mutual interests."

"When we meet with Natsu, let's see what makes sense."

"I appreciate that."

"It's really late. I need to get back to the City."

"I don't want you driving now. I have plenty of spare rooms. Please stay, and Sergio will prepare a good breakfast before you leave."

Michael looked at his watch. "A very kind offer, but I need to get going very early in the morning. I'll take a rain check."

"Of course, Michael ... I look forward to our meeting again. Please drive carefully."

As Michael drove back to SFO, he was impressed with Tiffanee's honesty about Pug's deceptions. He was pleased to facilitate a meeting between the two women.

His last thought before falling asleep, *The years have been very kind to Tiffanee. Wonder what's her secret? Look forward to seeing her again.*

82
MONDAY/FRIDAY, SEPTEMBER 2/7
BURLINGAME

EBIDDO WANTED IMMEDIATE CONFRONTATION WITH Pug, but always deferred to Natsu's insistence that he first complete the development project. Based on information from Seamus and Michael, Debiddo knew his project was ahead of Pug's. Natsu authorized his visit during first week of September.

During the twelve-hour flight, he read Natsu's memo instructing him to accomplish two things. First, he would confront Pug and threaten legal consequences if Pug refused to stop his co-molded project. Second, Debiddo meet with his wife and settle their marital issues. He was surprised Natsu didn't act upset after learning he was still married.

But, he knew if he didn't resolve the marital issue, his relationship with Natsu was over. Early signs had appeared. Since her miscarriage, Natsu had become remote, focused only on business, increasingly impatient, and they had ceased intimacy.

In the passport queue, he thought about his wife. *Maybe I can offer her money, and we can have a friendly divorce. I'll make it worthwhile if she agrees.*

The agent eyed him and then the passport photo.

"What's the purpose of your visit, Mr. James?"

"Business and family."

"How long will you be staying in the US?"

"About five-six days."

He felt this agent took too long to process his documents, but relieved when he heard, "Welcome home, Mr. James."

That evening, after checking into a hotel in South San Francisco, Debiddo headed to Kuletos for dinner. He sat at the far end of the bar, gazed around, and immediately understood Pug's attraction—cute and flirtatious female servers and lively atmosphere. He sipped a Corona and glanced at the TV screen. The San Francisco Giants were getting clobbered by the LA Dodgers.

As he motioned to the bartender for another beer, he saw a couple enter the restaurant. *It's him!* He saw Pug holding hands and whispering to a tall, attractive African-American woman who looked about twenty-five. *Pop's taste in women has changed.*

He watched them be seated as his feelings alternated between disgust and amazement. After the second beer, he ordered take-out and returned to the hotel. Jet lag convinced him to postpone a confrontation.

From Michael, Debiddo got the address of the Starbucks near Pug's condo. His last phone call with Michael summarized all the co-molded test data and a status report on Skunk 2's development progress. He was unaware of the other skunks.

The next morning, he parked his car at Starbucks and waited. He saw Pug amble into the coffee shop. Debiddo waited five minutes before entering and found Pug sitting in a booth.

Pug looked up from his cell phone. "I'll be fucked! It's the traitor himself."

"Hey Pops, great to see you too." He sat down across from Pug. "I hear your current lab's a big downer from your IPS digs."

"Davey, my boy, already got me a new, bigger, better location. Come back in six months; maybe I'll offer you a job. But enough about me, why the hell you here? Lemme see, things not working out in Jap Land? Kenji betrayin' you like he did me? Oh no, don't tell me, you've been fired by the slopes and want your old job back."

"Nope, not looking for anything. Work's going quite nicely in Japan, Kenji treats me with respect, and unlike you, I haven't got fired."

Pug looked surprised at the last comment. "So why ya here?"

"By the way, who was that young lady I saw you with last night?"

"What?"

"Scratch that. Mom divorced you so why should she care?"

"Bingo! None of your fuckin' business. And for your information, I divorced her. So, why ya here?"

Dave stared at Pug. "Whatever, why the hell did you steal my co-molding idea?"

Pug glared back. "Davey, it's my idea, an' you damn well know it! I discovered it!"

"Oh, I'd love to see your original lab notes."

"That'll be one cold day in hell! I'm not showin' you shit!"

Dave stood, "Afraid you'll be caught in a big lie? Or did your stroke affect what's left of your brain?"

Starbuck's patrons were turning heads and watching them.

"Don't give a damn what you think!" Pug yelled. "You can't prove shit! An' since IPS owned all lab notes done at my company, tough titty for you. 'Sides, your idea wasn't worth a damn so I shit-canned it."

"Interesting. You stealing my idea reminds me when you stole Seamus's and my invention of the IPS 10000. Your name never belonged on our patent. You threatened to fire Jackson if he didn't include you as one of the inventors."

"There you go again, making up fake stories! I owned IPS and all the patents. You owned zilch! Now get the hell out of here an' go back to your slope-eye buddies in Jap Land."

An Asian gentleman in the next booth stood up and approached the manager.

"Kenji nailed it when he said you'd put a curse on the silver-lining technologies! It's true! All your treachery, all your stupid actions against Mom, Skip, Michael, Seamus, Jackson, and me. Soon you'll be gone, and then I'll lift the curse! When I'm back in Japan, I'll make a success of the silver-lining technologies and my co-molded idea!"

The Starbucks manager approached them. "Gentlemen, take your argument outside. You're disturbing other customers!"

"You'll be hearing from my lawyer, Jackson Huntley," Debiddo said. "He can't wait to sue your ass again!"

"Big fuckin' whoop! Bring 'im on."

"And one more thing, Mr. I-Know-Everything, IPS settled its lawsuit with Dexter-Foresman!"

"Get the fuck outta my sight!"

He gave Pug a middle-digit salute, then turned to the manager. "Sorry for the trouble, sir."

Pug sat back down at the table. "Barrister, gimme 'nother grand cup of this java americano?"

The manager threw up his hands. "Sure, why not?"

Debiddo sat in the car knowing he had surprised and confused Pug. He could see it in his face. *Probably wondered how I knew about his development project, who is Seamus and what's this silver-lining curse?*

His call to Tina went to her voice mail. "Hey Tina, it's Dave. It's about eight-thirty now. I'll stop by around nine-thirty and buy you breakfast. Got great news for you."

He returned to his hotel. At reception, the clerk handed him a package. It contained legal documents explaining Tina's legal action for child support and family abandonment.

He panicked. An hour later, he arrived at San Francisco Airport. At the counter, the agent processed his ticket and scanned his passport. She motioned to her supervisor who examined Dave's documents.

"Mr. James, there seems to be a problem. Could you step over to the next counter?"

"What?"

"We're not sure. Your passport is no longer valid for travel to Japan."

"What? I just arrived two days ago, and it was fine then!"

"I don't know, sir."

"What the hell do I do? I need to get back!"

"You'll have to contact the Japanese consulate in SFO to resolve this. Apparently, they have notified the US you're not allowed to travel to Japan."

"Shit!" Debiddo grabbed his bags and stomped away. He dialed Natsu. After several rings, she answered.

"Debiddo, do you realize what time it is?"

"Of course, I do! I wouldn't be calling if I didn't have a problem." After back-and-forth about the situation, Natsu promised her lawyer would contact the Japanese authorities in the morning.

"Were you able to resolve your marital issues?" she asked.

"Won't be a problem."

"Glad to hear that," she replied.

Over three days, Debiddo called Natsu several times. She did not return his calls.

On September 7, a loud knock on the hotel door awakened him.

"Who is it?"

"San Francisco County Sheriff's office. Open the door, sir!"

"Okay, Okay. Keep your pants on." He opened the door.

"Mr. David James, we have a warrant for your arrest."

"What?"

"Bigamy, child abandonment, failure to provide child support, and theft."

"What the hell?" Debiddo grabbed for the warrant papers but was constrained by the other officer.

The second officer said, "Mr. James, we can do this peacefully, or we can do this the hard way. Your choice."

"Okay! I hear you! I want a lawyer!"

"There'll be plenty of time after you're processed. Get dressed, sir."

In the police car, the officers let him read the warrant charges. Zach Binder, Tina's lawyer, had filed papers on her behalf. Debiddo seethed as he examined the document. *Just a goddamned ploy to get my money. No way in hell!* Then he remembered. Michael had told him Binder was Skip's public defender. *That guy did a shitty job defending Skip.*

At the sheriff's office, they escorted him into a holding room, read him his Miranda Rights, and allowed him to use his credit card to make one call. He called Natsu, and this time she answered.

"Natsu, Natsu, thank god I finally got through. Where in the hell have you been the last three days?"

"I have been ill and resting at Mt. Fuji."

"Sorry, but I got bigger problems. I've been arrested on some trumped-up charge by Tina, my ... uh ... former wife. Did your lawyer resolve my passport problem?"

"He's in the hospital. What are the charges?"

"Some crap about bigamy, child abandonment, not paying child support. I wanted to have a rational conversation, and she hits me with this phony lawsuit."

"I am sure you will be able to resolve this with calm discussions."

"I have to post a $50,000 bond to get released. Wire me the money!"

"A lot of money for such frivolous charges."

"No kidding. When can you wire it?"

"I will do my best. Be patient, and you will be home in no time. You shouldn't return until you have resolved your marriage issues. I suggest you engage a US lawyer familiar with divorce laws."

Debiddo waited two more days. No wire, no calls, only silence. Natsu's lawyer processed documents to terminate their business relationship.

83
SUNDAY, SEPTEMBER 8
SSFO

P UG ARRIVED AT SKUNK 3 at eleven o'clock at night to retrieve papers and proprietary data. This was the last batch of documents he needed to transfer to the East Bay location. This new facility would become operational in record time, thanks to Kevin's meticulous planning for Skunk 3. Skunk 4 would be Pug's ultimate jackpot. Next would be going public.

Pug knew he had to work fast. When his business mentor questioned his patent ownership, he suspected Kevin and Tiffanee betrayed him. For the last two weeks, neither returned his calls. The confrontation with Dave was one more data point. *Fieldsy's in the middle of all this shit, somehow!*

Blunt's unexpected call had given him the idea to establish a separate facility in the East Bay. When he told Blunt that the McIntyres dumped him from the JV, Blunt was pissed. What he didn't know was the others who conspired with Blunt—Lawrent, Gano-Nippon, Technovenia, and Gordon Orlio.

Pug approached the front of Skunk 3 to find an envelope taped to the door. His name was scrawled in large print. He tore it open and read a letter announcing his termination and that law enforcement had been notified about his business espionage and conspiracy to defraud. He read another document, a restraining order preventing contact with Tiffanee and Kevin.

"Fuck them! They can't do this!" he yelled out as he tried to enter the building. His passcodes and fingerprint IDs were blocked. A security guard motioned for him to leave the premises. Pug responded with a middle-digit gesture.

"Them McIntryes think they can screw me!" he yelled at the guard, who turned away. "Do I have a surprise for them when they find out about my new skunk!"

Pug stalked off, yelling. "Blunt and I'll take 'em to the dump."

84
MONDAY, SEPTEMBER 9
BURLINGAME/NEW YORK CITY

MONDAY MORNING, PUG CALLED BLUNT.

"Hey Ron, we need to move fast now. I'm workin' full time at the East-Bay Skunk. Ya got the rest of the IPS shares so we can merge IPS with our new entity?"

"Slow down! Stiller couldn't nail down the IPS shares. Also, had to sue some Japanese bastards to recover my interest in a JV. I was betrayed by them and that bitch, Tiffanee McIntyre. Until the judge issues an injunction, can't do anything."

"What the hell does she have to do with this?"

"Where the fuck have you been? You're the one who told me she was in bed with those Japs and had betrayed me. Keep your pants on!"

"What the hell?" Pug yelled. "Look, you told me this would be a piece o' cake and go like blazes. Dammit, you're supposed to be a get-er done guy! Remember I own the patents and without them the East Bay operation is worthless! You and your foreign buddies can piss your investment goodbye."

"Keep talking like that, and you'll hear from my lawyers!"

"I shoulda known I couldn't trust a draft-dodgin' asshole! How'd you get outta servin'? Ingrown toenail?"

"You were in military like all the other losers? One more reason not to trust you! And I don't need you in my deal anyway, you two-bit piker."

"Fuck ya and the daddy ya rode in on! Just try to run Skunk 4 without my patents!"

Blunt hung up. Pug sank to the floor. After a while, he finally hauled himself up and asked himself, *What now?*

He turned to a pile of mail on a table. *Who the hell are Bannon and Miller, Attorneys at Law?* He tore open the envelope. *What the fuck? Darni's suin' me? Sexual harassment? Forced her to get an abortion?*

Another envelope contained a summons for a discovery deposition for Jackson's latest lawsuit. *That's what Dave was yakkin' 'bout!*

Pug needed a new lawyer.

85
TUESDAY, SEPTEMBER 10
OSAKA AIRPORT

SEAMUS STOOD IN THE PASSPORT queue before heading to the United Airlines departure gate. As he waited, his thoughts rambled. He and Natsu had conversations about his future roles. She expressed appreciation for his technical and marketing intelligence. She now had given him one more assignment to return to the US and finish the intelligence work about Lawrent and Technovenia. They agreed he would then retire and return to Colorado. She gave him a severance bonus for his work and thanked him for facilitating conversations with her mother.

Seamus presented his documents to the ticket agent. *This is taking too long.* After the standard, perfunctory questions, the agent excused himself. Three minutes later, two airport security personnel approached and asked him to step away from the agent's window. "What's the problem?" Seamus asked.

"*Mizu* O'Leary, you come with us." No other words were spoken as they escorted him to a nearby room. A third person, more senior, joined them.

The supervising agent said, "Mizu O'Leary, please sit. Do you prefer we speak in English or Japanese?"

"I'm a US citizen returning to my country. What the hell's going on?"

"We have questions."

"Make it quick because my flight leaves in fifteen minutes." Two police officers waited outside the door.

The officer continued, "US customs officials send evidence to local authorities that Sean O'Leary engaged in production and distribution of illegal pornography in US and Japan. Authorities in both countries request your detainment. You are Sean O'Leary from the United States?"

"I already told you I'm a US citizen returning to my country! I've done nothing wrong!"

"We have regret for you, Mizu O'Leary, but we required to arrest you for illegal business. You will come to police station."

The police officers took him into custody.

Two hours later, Natsu received a call from Shiganari. "Natsu-chan, Seamus Hafferty and Sean O'Leary have been detained. I know you must be sad."

"I am. We had a good understanding about his future before he left for California."

"According to the authorities, his illegal activities crossed the line in both Japan and the US. We underestimated how extensive they were and that he had been under long-term surveillance. I doubt Japan will honor the US extradition request," Shiganari said.

"I agree." She was sad he had not honored his vows to Kenji.

"Sensei, his intelligence reports have provided us weapons to deploy against Lawrent and Gano-Nippon. We can leverage this to obtain their future market cooperation with our licensing proposals. For that I am grateful. I hope Seamus can successfully resolve his legal matters. Please see that Seamus has access to competent legal representation."

"Natsu-chan, that is most admirable. You demonstrate appropriate forgiveness."

"I thank you for that. You have taught me more balanced thinking."

"Kenji told me that would be an important task for me when he was not available."

"I understand, but my ability to forgive will not extend to everyone who betrays us." In her mind, Hakase Yamura did not qualify.

86
WEDNESDAY, SEPTEMBER 11
OSAKA

HAKASE YAMURA SAT IN HIS Osaka office. He called Jun Ashi. When Jun answered, he announced, "Ashi-kun, your hafu niece requested to meet at my office. This is good news."

"Why do you say that?"

"In her phone call, she sounded worried. She talked about ominous events that were unfolding and implied she had lost faith in Kobayashi to continue as CEO of JT. I suspect she will ask for my assistance."

"That is good to hear," Jun replied.

"How are things at JT?"

"Until a few weeks ago, I worked on various projects to improve the efficiency and cost reduction for manufacturing; busy work to distract me," Jun said.

"With Kobayashi away on extended travel, she said that JT has serious problems and needs help. When she learns of Kobayashi's unfortunate accident, she will panic. Her protector will be gone. She will be receptive to our assistance and authority."

"When do you plan to meet with Natsu?"

"She will come here on September 16. At that time, I will be interrupted by an urgent phone call and informed that Kobayashi has perished in a tragic boat accident off the Florida coast. When I convey the sad news, she will be receptive to my offer to help during this difficult transition period. She will reach out to you as well."

"That is wonderful news, Hakase Yamura."

"Correct. I will become chairman of Japan Technologies, and you will become the CEO. Then we can begin the merger with Gano-Nippon with General Appliance's blessing."

87
MONDAY, SEPTEMBER 16
OSAKA

HAKASE YAMURA RECEIVED NOTIFICATION THAT Natsu would arrive at ten o'clock, so he made sure Jun Ashi came earlier. They met in Yamura's office and reviewed the morning's plans. Yamura announced, "Ashi-kun, today our fortunes change. My associates confirmed Kobayashi perished."

At nine-thirty, they finished their coffee as the secretary delivered the morning mail along with two FedEx packages marked "CONFIDENTIAL."

"Ashi-kun, please excuse me while I attend to this mail," Yamura said.

Jun departed to the restroom.

Yamura examined the mail and the two packages. The sender's addresses indicated Gano-Nippon and General Appliance. He couldn't wait to open. *These are the documents for the merger plans and future business agreements among JT, Gano-Nippon, and General Appliance.*

He tore open the Gano-Nippon package. An enormous explosion rocked the premises. The second package detonated immediately after. Smoke and debris engulfed the office.

In the bathroom stall, the explosive shock threw Jun off the toilet seat and into the wall. He lay there with loud ringing in his ears. Slowly, he gathered himself. In the hall, he could hear people screaming. Somehow, he staggered from the building.

Later, as he sat outside with others and emergency workers

examined him, a police officer approached. "I am Detective Inspector Nagasura. I must ask a few questions."

"How is Hakase Yamura?" Jun asked.

"Unfortunately, he did not survive."

Jun put his head in his hands. "My friend ... "

"You were the last person in his office before the explosion. Is that correct?"

"Hai, we were preparing for a meeting at ten o'clock. He excused me to review his mail. I was in the restroom when the explosion occurred."

"How long had you been gone?"

"I am not sure. I hit my head on the restroom wall."

"Ashi-san, did you notice anything unusual about Yamura's actions or words before you left?"

"No! He was happy. He looked at the mail and seemed pleased. That is when he excused me."

The detective asked, "Do you know who sent the packages?"

"He mentioned two names: Gano-Nippon and General Appliance of Japan."

The detective noted the names. "Tell me about the meeting he would attend."

"Ms. Nashakatani was arriving to discuss business matters."

"Ms. Nashakatani?"

"The chief operating officer for Japan Technologies."

The detective looked surprised and flipped back pages on his notepad. He noted the name corresponded to the receptionist's appointment calendar.

"What can you tell me about the business matters Yamura planned to discuss with this, this ... woman?"

"They would review business transactions affecting Japan Technologies and related entities. Hakase Yamura was legal advisor to this company ... before he was terminated."

"Terminated?"

"Kobayashi-sama, the CEO of Japan Technologies, recently terminated Hakase Yamura's employment contract without cause."

The detective made notes. "Do you have reason to suspect foul play?"

Jun's eyes twitched, and his voice softened. "Detective Nagasura, Hakase Yamura served Kobayashi-sama for 35 years as a loyal and respectful advisor. All that changed during the last months. In fact, Kobayashi-sama also treated me badly causing deep hurt."

"Why do you think that occurred?"

"All I know is that this whole unfortunate experience began when Kobayashi announced that this ... woman ... would become the chief operating officer, a position he had promised me."

"Where can we find Kobayashi-san?"

"He is currently on an extended foreign business trip. I have no itinerary details."

The detective scribbled more notes, "Do you know if Yamura had enemies who wished him harm?"

Jun grimaced at the question. "Hakase Yamura aggressively represented his clients. He probably made enemies. However, I can't imagine what would motivate someone to kill him."

"Okay, Ashi-san, here is my card. If you think of anything else regarding this incident, please contact me. Until this investigation is complete, do not travel without advising us. One more question. We found a scrap of paper outside Yamura's office with the word *Checkmate* on it. Any idea what it means?"

"No."

A concerned look spread over his face. Jun knew his future was uncertain. With Yamura dead, his plan to become JT's leader was gone. What will Natsu do now with both Kenji and Yamura gone?

Surely, she will reach out to me.

Mt. Fuji

Shiganari called Natsu at the lodge. "Natsu-chan, you have heard about the unfortunate event in Osaka?"

"No, I have been in mourning at the lodge as you instructed."

"Hakase Yamura died in an explosion at his office."

"I planned to meet him at ten o'clock but postponed given the news about Kobayashi-sama."

"Correct, Natsu-chan. Hakase Yamura was informed as you were also, that Kenji had perished. This happened before the office explosion. Anonymous informants provided information to the police that implicated Hakase Yamura and his associates in causing Kobayashi-san's death. In any case, the accident—or murder—of a well-known and respected Japanese businessman will be fully investigated."

The notification of the "yacht explosion" off the Florida coast revived her memories of Kenji's actual passing. However, she took comfort knowing this was part of Kenji's final deception.

From initial reports, determining causes of the yacht explosion and recovering the bodies would be nearly impossible. Shark-infested waters, strong ocean currents, and an approaching hurricane compounded the difficulties. She knew Hakase Yamura's death would complicate the ability to discover the truth.

"What will happen next, Okazaki-sama?"

"Expect follow up investigation from the police."

"Why?"

"We learned Ashi-kun was at the office before the explosion. Fortunately, he was unhurt. We assume he told the police about the disagreements between Kenji and Hakase Yamura."

"Understand, I will be ready. I'm grateful Oji-san is safe. I will talk with him about his future. This will be another test of my ability to forgive."

88
FRIDAY, SEPTEMBER 20
OSAKA

NATSU SAT IN KENJI'S FORMER office and surveyed the decor. *I am honored to occupy his office—a living memorial.* She retained the same ambiance *but with a few changes. On a nearby credenza, a picture of Kenji with Patrick Hafferty rested alongside Kenji's favorite books by Sun Tzu and Deming. She replaced Kenji's painting of Miyamoto Musashi with an artistic impression of three famous daimyos—Nobunaga, Hideyoshi, and Tokugawa Ieyasu— all known as unifiers of Japan. Her message was clear. This lady daimyo would unify JT, IPS, PSW II, PSLW III and the JV. A six-foot ficus benjamina tree stood at the left of her desk. Its soil contained some of Kenji's ashes. She had spread the rest at the Mt. Fuji lodge and in the gardens of his Osaka residence.*

The phone rang and her assistant transferred the call. Natsu flipped a switch to encrypt the call.

"Good morning, Sensei. It's comforting to hear your voice in these stressful times."

"Likewise. How did your police interview go?" Shiganari asked.

"Very well. Just spoke with a detective. I conveyed my deep condolences about Hakase Yamura."

"What did he ask?"

"The usual—what was our scheduled meeting about, did I know anyone who might have a motive to harm him, and what services did he perform for JT and trust, etc. I showed him Hakase Yamura's resignation letter indicating his retirement."

"Any concerns?"

"No. I doubt they will talk with me again."

"Did they question you about Kobayashi-san?"

"Specifically, they wanted to know where he was and when would he return. I suspect the detectives were comparing my answers with those given by Oji-san Ashi. When I told them about Kobayashi-sama's tragic death, this confused them. The Florida accident will eliminate further inquiries."

"What did they ask about Ashi-kun?" Shiganari wondered.

"I told the detectives Ashi-kun would assume more responsibilities at JT. I stressed he was a valuable part of our company."

"Natsu-chan, you have performed your role according to Kenji's wishes. He would be proud."

"Arigato. After talking with my mother, I understand my Oji-san's situation and how Hakase Yamura manipulated him. Perhaps, Kobayashi-sama could have been more candid with Ashi-kun about the future of Japan Technologies."

"Natsu-chan, a sensible conclusion. Kenji and I often argued about this. We should not forget Ashi-kun's loyalty before Hakase Yamura misled him."

"I will reach out to him and discuss how we can work together now that Debiddo is no longer with us. You have counseled me to be more understanding. For that, I am indebted."

89
FRIDAY, SEPTEMBER 20
SAN MATEO

MARCY JAMES TOSSED ASIDE THE *San Mateo Times.* She felt as if a load of bricks rested on her heart.

Surely, my so-called daughter-in-law could have confessed she killed Annie Burr. Oh, Skip! They gave you a life sentence for a murder you didn't commit! And your so-called wife confessed after you committed suicide!

Marcy poured a drink as tears rolled down her cheeks. Despite her disappointment at her son's behavior, he didn't deserve this.

She spoke to no one in particular, "Always knew in my heart Skip didn't kill Annie. It's all Pug's fault. He mistreated Skip when he worked at IPS, encouraged Skip's affair, and then accused Skip of betrayal."

A loud knock interrupted her thoughts. It was 9:30 in the morning. She opened the door and saw Pug.

He stared back with a big grin, as if he were really happy to see her after all these months. It was clear to him she wasn't pleased. Her slovenly appearance shocked him. She reeked of alcohol.

"Marcy, gotta talk with ya!"

"What for?" she asked.

"I got problems."

She held the door open. "Looks like you could use a drink."

"Just water." He entered and noticed the almost empty bottle of Jack Daniels. *She's snockered already.*

She brought him water and he watched her refill her glass, take a long swallow, and light a Marlborough.

"When'd ya start smokin' again?" Pug asked.

"Not that you really care; but let's see, after I saw that video of you screwing some Japanese babe like you used to screw Tiffanee."

"Hey, that wasn't me! I was ... uh. . . photoshopped!"

"Didn't look that way to me ... you were groaning out, 'oh, baby, oh, baby.'"

"Look, I wanna move forward. Got me some serious problems."

"What? You got problems? How about Skip killing himself in jail, and then his wife confessing to the murder? And don't forget Dave, your favorite son. He's arrested for bigamy and child abandonment. Like father, like sons. You can be proud of your fucking legacy!"

"I wanna talk 'bout gettin' back together. I could move in ... see a marriage counselor."

She laughed. "As you always said, 'Do my ears hear me?' You encouraged Skip to cheat on his wife, and you drove Dave out of the country. And to make matters worse, you forced Michael Fields to quit IPS and ignored his advice to save IPS. You've put a curse on everything you've touched. Hell, you don't need a marriage counselor, you need a psychiatrist!"

"Damn it! I fired Fieldsy's ass. That ain't fair. He deserved it. Come on, let's talk like adults."

"What's in it for me?"

"Look, I haven't felt this bad since Mom died."

"You should be crying for our two sons and your ten-year old daughter."

"What daughter? Has that Jack gone to your head?"

She handed him photos and a note. "Got these in the mail a few days ago. Take a gander while I go pee."

He stared at the photos. Duplicates of the ones he received.

Five minutes later, she returned. He was looking at the *National Inquirer's* cover page showing Ronald Blunt's photo and the quote, "Our Next Commander-in-Chief?" She heard him mumble something obscene about Blunt. He turned to look at her. The gun was pointed at his head.

90
MONDAY, SEPTEMBER 23
SSFO

MICHAEL REFLECTED ON FRIDAY'S NEWS in the papers and on weekend TV. The murder/suicide of Pug and Marcy James garnered considerable coverage. The San Mateo police contacted Michael for information to shed light on the motives. They showed Michael a copy of Marcy's suicide note addressed to him.

Michael wanted to get ahead of the curve and contact individuals who deserved a full explanation.

His first call went to Natsu. It was evening in Osaka when she answered.

"Natsu, you may have already heard the news. Pug James was killed by his wife in an apparent murder/suicide."

"Michael, that is indeed sad to hear. What are the police saying?"

"From preliminary indications, it looks like Pug's wife murdered him for his betrayals against her and the two sons. Marcy had been depressed about the divorce, her one son's suicide, the other son's arrest, and her financial problems. Her suicide note suggests she blamed Pug for everything."

"Michael, such dreadful news. What now?"

"I'll contact Jackson, then he will call Kevin McIntyre. I'll talk to Tiffanee."

"I will see Kevin in Osaka in a few days. It occurred to me when you were telling me about this tragedy, that with Pug now gone, one could say the curse on the silver-lining technologies has lifted."

"Why do you say that, Natsu?"

"If you think about it, all the inventors whose names appear on the original patents are gone—separated from the technology."

"You're right. Goodbye for now. See you in California soon."

"Sayōnara, Michael."

Michael's next call was to Jackson.

"Michael, what a tragedy! Pug did a lot of damage to many people and companies, but no one would imagine this outcome."

"Jackson, I agree. Somehow, I'm not surprised. Marcy was very depressed, and I suspect Pug finally pushed her over the edge. Regardless of what would happen to Pug, her future was bleak. She probably felt life wasn't worth living."

"Anything I can do for you about this?"

"Would you contact Kevin and update him about Pug?"

"Will do." Jackson replied.

"I'll contact Kevin's mother and do likewise."

Michael's next call was to Tiffanee.

"Hello Michael, I was expecting your call. Terrible what happened to Pug and Marcy. I wouldn't wish that on anyone, regardless of what they'd done."

"Tiffanee, true, but we have to move forward and not dwell on the sad stuff."

"What happens now that Pug is gone from the scene? Does it affect anything we've discussed?"

"Not really. Jackson Huntley will talk with Kevin and update him on any impact on our business decisions. When you meet with Natsu and me, we can adjust our plans if required. In a way, Pug's departure clears up a lot of confusion and distrust he precipitated. I believe we're on a good course for an exciting future. Talk with you soon."

"Goodbye, Michael. Thank you for calling."

91
THURSDAY, SEPTEMBER 27
OSAKA

FTER HER EARLIER PHONE CALL from Michael about Pug, Natsu considered that all known problems had been solved or neutralized—Pug, Debiddo, Giorgio, Ellie, Seamus, Hakase Yamura, Jun, Technovenia, and Blunt. Others like Lawrent and Gano-Nippon would be pressured to cooperate. She invited Kevin to Osaka to discuss the future of their companies. He arrived for a four-day technical and marketing review.

After an early dinner and restful night at Hotel Osaka, he arrived at Japan Technologies the next morning. He saw that Natsu now occupied Kenji's office. The space still reflected Kenji's strength and determination.

"My pleasure to welcome you again to Osaka," Natsu said.

"Arigato, Ms. Nashakatani."

"Please call me Natsu." She was pleased Kevin used a few words of Japanese.

"Only if you call me Kevin."

"Excellent, we are off to a good start." To Natsu, this confirmed that Kevin treated women as equals.

"Hard to believe a year has passed since 9-11."

"Yes, we in Japan are very sad your nation suffered this calamity. I hope the US can avenge the terrorists."

"I agree, but President Bush and Secretary Rumsfeld are threatening Iraq. That could be disastrous."

"You are most perceptive."

"On a personal note, I received the notification about Mr. Kobayashi's accident. My sincerest condolences."

She glanced at the tree. "I truly miss him. His presence remains with me along with his guiding principles of ikigai."

"I hope to learn more about that philosophy. Just haven't had the time."

She smiled. "Perhaps I can address that if we have spare moments while you are here. Before we talk business, I wish to discuss a personal matter."

"What is that?"

"Kobayashi-sama and Michael Fields suggested I explore a closer business partnership with you." She recalled Kobayashi-sama telling her that she and Kevin displayed harmony between their minds. *Perhaps this could spill over into our hearts as well.*

"Natsu, I look forward to knowing you better."

"Anticipating that, I will arrange a brief trip to Kyoto if you can spare a few extra days?"

"Definitely! I will adjust my schedule."

"Wonderful. Now to business: first, I must comment on the status of Debiddo James and Sean O'Leary who are no longer with JT-IPS. Both were instrumental in the technical progress for the exhaust system project. They co-invented the silver-lining technologies."

"Yes, I recall their names on the patents along with Pug James."

"Correct. Debiddo returned to California to address personal matters." She knew Kevin made the connection between the names, Debbido and Dave.

"Forgive me, Natsu, I assumed you and Debiddo were married."

"He served as my technical manager for new product development. As for Sean O'Leary, he will retire in Colorado after resolving some personal issues."

"Did both execute non-disclosure and non-compete agreements before leaving?" Kevin interjected.

"Yes. Michael Fields informed me of related matters. You are aware Pug James and his wife are deceased?"

"Jackson Huntley contacted me about Pug. Michael told my mother as well. Pug's death happened shortly after I terminated him from the SSFO operation. I hope that didn't contribute to this tragedy."

"Pug betrayed you, and his termination from Skunk 3 was justified. What happened to him has nothing to do with your actions."

"Natsu, I appreciate your understanding. In truth, Pug betrayed us all. You're right; I should not feel guilty."

"With the original inventors of the silver-lining technologies gone, the curse on this technology is lifted," she said. She noticed Kevin's confused look.

"What do you mean by 'curse?'"

"Kobayashi-sama first recognized the curse. He said each of the inventors had committed many betrayals. Now that these three are no longer associated with the technology, the curse has been lifted."

"Hai. Pug's betrayals extended to conspiring with Ronald Blunt and Lawrent to regain control of our technology JV and IPS's silver-lining technologies."

"That is my understanding."

"It disappointed me to learn that one of my law professors, Gordon Orlio, conspired with Technovenia to control the technology. The venture fund wanted control of IPS to sell to the highest bidder or combine it with the East Bay organization. Jackson told me Michael Fields's wife participated in this conspiracy. Fortunately, neither Gordon nor Ellie pose future threats. They're both under investigation for conspiracy to defraud. I understand Technovenia will no longer be a problem either. The Department of Justice and SEC will charge the principals for securities fraud, tax evasion, and racketeering. I think this fund will disappear along with its principals."

"Why do you think Mr. Blunt got involved?" Natsu asked.

"We're not sure, but Blunt claimed we misled him about the value of the JV. He hated losing. Therefore, as is his normal practice, he sued the McIntyre family."

"Kobayashi-sama once said that Blunt and Pug had much in common—narcissism, paranoia, penchant for litigation, and using other people's money. In the end, Blunt got out of the scheme and abandoned Pug," Natsu said.

"No honor among thieves," Kevin said. "When I first met Pug, he appeared to be an ally who wanted to work with us. I admired his innovation skills, and my mother enjoyed reconnecting with him after fifteen years. We were very disappointed at his many betrayals."

"I understand. I too suffered similar disappointments. But we learn from our mistakes. Kobayashi-sama had good advice for such situations. 'Verify one's actions before trusting one's words.'"

"I'll keep that in mind. Will Blunt continue to be a problem?" Kevin asked.

"Kevin, you need not worry."

She handed him an agenda. They would cover their respective technical and marketing subjects. Kevin would discuss proprietary and patent issues. After that, they would discuss the commercialization and confronting potential competitors.

"Kevin, I'll begin with JT-IPS technical and marketing status." After presenting the update, she concluded, "The brand name for products using this technology is—SLATES—Silver Lining Acoustic Thermal Exhaust System."

"Japan Technologies has achieved significant breakthroughs," Kevin observed. He then presented the South San Francisco project status and remaining tasks.

Natsu listened carefully and was struck by Kevin's contribution. "Your electronic enhancements are far superior to ours. They should be immediately incorporated into our project."

"Thank you. We've named our technology—TASLEE—Thermal Acoustic Silver-Lining Electronics Exhaust."

She smiled at the reference to silver lining. "That definitely reinforces our joint brands."

At the meeting's conclusion, they both seemed pleased. The synergies would produce even stronger proprietary positions. The next two days would focus on marketing opportunities, commercialization strategies, and controlling competition.

After their business meetings concluded, Natsu spoke with Shiganari before leaving for Kyoto. He asked, "How did the meeting go?"

"We've made excellent progress on both projects; commercialization can start. We will prioritize the beachhead customers and decide which segments to pursue. But with limited resources, we have to choose which project to do first."

"Natsu-chan, which do you support for initial commercialization?"

"Definitely JT-IPS's project."

"Why?"

"It has stronger technical progress and patent applications, is better organized and commenced earlier. Although Kevin's project made significant progress, Pug's chaotic involvement caused delays. Also, the McIntyre family funded the second operation; they chose a more conservative approach and demanded accountability which frustrated Pug. That's probably why he sought alternatives like Mr. Blunt and Technovenia."

"Excellent observation. How did Pug know about Blunt?"

"Kevin said his mother may have mentioned him to Pug since her husband did property deals with Blunt. And Suzi confirmed Hakase Yamura communicated with Blunt."

"Other reasons?"

"The second reason is politics. As you and Kobayashi-sama taught me, never underestimate the importance of balancing politics and technology. JT-IPS knows how to optimize this equation. The McIntyre family has yet to fully appreciate the importance of balancing these variables. But, I will begin coaching Kevin while we are in Kyoto."

"The perfect city for such a task."

"Do you have other advice on how I interact with the McIntyre family as we move forward?"

"Your trip to Kyoto and scheduled visit to California will be good starts. Understand Kevin's mother and you will understand Kevin. There will be plenty of opportunities to coach him in balancing politics and technology, Sun Tzu's principles, ikigai, and the samurai code."

"Kevin seems very business-like, understands technology, and is excellent at legal matters. With his keen intellect, I have no doubt that he can absorb our lessons. He has an excellent vision for the future of automotive developments."

"Please explain."

"He realizes our current projects only take us forward for fifteen years. Therefore, we need to develop new technologies when fossil fuels no longer are the dominant energy source. We have to invest in technologies that will accommodate the transition to alternative power like electric and solar."

"That is quite futuristic."

"Hai, Sensei." She knew the Kyoto trip would determine how she and Kevin would cooperate both on a business level and on a personal one. She would have to utilize all the training and knowledge she had acquired to ensure a successful outcome. She would not repeat the mistake she made when she agreed to cooperate with Debiddo. She would verify actions before trusting words.

Kyoto

Natsu gave Kevin a tour of historic Kyoto, its shrines, culture, and cuisine. She hired a local university professor to explain the Sun Tzu principles and the samurai code and their applications to business and life. One evening, she arranged for a private showing of *Ran*. Later, she would introduce him to noh and kabuki theater. She did not want to overwhelm him like Kobayashi-sama had overwhelmed her.

Another evening over dinner, she gave him an introductory tutorial on ikigai. She followed Kenji's process using the schematic to explain how the eight elements in the four circles apply. The fact that both had lost parents at an early age gave them a special bond.

Over coffee and cognac, they played four shogi matches. Kevin liked learning a new type of chess.

On the last day, she accompanied him to the airport. "Kevin, I have truly enjoyed these last few days."

"Natsu, this has been a great experience. As someone trained in engineering and the law, I've found a whole new perspective. When you come to California, I'll return the favor. I'll arrange a meeting with Elon Musk, the innovative technologist who recently launched Space X. He can talk about his vision for an electric vehicle."

"Why is that important for us?"

"This means our exhaust system technology based on fossil fuels has a limited life in the marketplace. We have to search for the next technology to accommodate this trend."

"I understand. The electric vehicle will eliminate the need for the traditional exhaust systems."

"Exactly. We have to stay ahead of the curve like Steve Jobs does at Apple. We need new technologies for cars of the future."

"Kevin, I can't wait to meet Mr. Musk and look forward to visiting California. Safe journey, and practice your shogi skills!"

"Challenged accepted!"

As Natsu left the airport terminal, she knew they had bonded intellectually. She looked forward to strengthening their links in California. That is why she had shown him her two tattoos. He could verify her actions first.

Natsu called Shiganari after Kevin left. "Sensei, I want to brief you on Kevin McIntyre. We had excellent business discussions in Osaka, followed by a wonderful time in Kyoto."

"Dear Natsu-chan, what are your impressions?"

"I felt a silvery sparkle inside my head while we were in Kyoto."

"What do you mean?" Shiganari asked.

"I believe with Kevin as a long-term partner in business, I can truly achieve my life's purpose. Using the silver-lining technologies, I can unify the global appliance dissipater industry and the automotive exhaust system industry. I envision combining JT-IPS, Skunk 2 and 3, and our JV to achieve this and to dominate our competitors." *I regret I cannot have children with him.*

"Sounds promising but remember Kenji's advice, 'Make haste slowly.'"

"I have accepted Kevin's invitation to visit California. I will meet his mother in Hillsborough and spend more time with him."

"Natsu-chan, proceed in a measured manner as Kenji advised."

"I will, Sensei."

On the flight back, Kevin thought about the Osaka meeting and the personal time in Kyoto. He was pleased with the business developments and the future outlook for the automotive business. This latest visit to Japan confirmed his initial instincts about Natsu. He had found the first woman who met his expectations on many levels—intellectual, emotional, and maybe physical; all important criteria for establishing a long-term partnership. He knew Tiffanee would support his decision.

92
MONDAY/THURSDAY, OCTOBER 7/OCTOBER 10
HILLSBOROUGH

NGRAVED INVITATIONS WERE SENT TO selected guests. They would celebrate the completion of the exhaust system projects and the commercial launches. Invitees would stay at Tiffanee's home.

Natsu arrived two days before the formal event. The morning after her arrival, Natsu joined Tiffanee for breakfast on the terrace.

"Good Morning, Natsu. I hope you rested well."

"Thank you, Tiffanee. A most comfortable and luxurious bed. I appreciated the copy of *The Osaka Times*."

"That was Kevin's idea. You slept in his former room. He personally selected the bed based on his engineering perspective. He threatens to take it with him one of these days ... if he ever finds his soul mate."

Natsu laughed. "He made a wise purchase. Please tell him I rested well." She thought, *Maybe I am that soul mate.*

"I am sure he'd love to hear that from you."

"I admired his collection of trophies from his swimming events. I didn't realize he was an accomplished athlete."

"He has little time for the sport now. He plays golf with clients."

"Hai. My mentor, Kenji Kobayashi, did as well. I am learning the game."

"Kevin tells me he's taking you to the wine country while you're here."

"Yes, I look forward to that."

Natsu found Tiffanee's demeanor interesting. She did not appear upset about Pug's death. Michael had observed Tiffanee expressed regret but had not mourned Pug's passing. A good sign.

Tiffanee motioned to the maid to bring coffee and tea. "Natsu, please tell Linda what you'd like for breakfast, and Sergio will prepare it. Kevin advised me to have Japanese dishes available for you."

"Very considerate of him! May I have miso soup and green tea?"

"Of course! Michael will be here soon to talk business."

"I appreciate Michael suggesting we meet."

"Michael has been so helpful with the South San Francisco skunk and other business matters. I understand he's also assisting JT-IPS?"

"Kobayashi-sama advised me to have Michael assist wherever needed. He has become my business mentor. In Japan, we call one's teacher or advisor, sensei."

"I too would like to have Michael as my business mentor. But only if it doesn't pose a conflict for you."

Natsu thought for a moment. "Let's ask him what he thinks. If he has no problem, I see no obstacle." She could predict Michael's response.

"I appreciate that," Tiffanee said.

"Tiffanee, my willingness comes from believing in ikigai. Kevin tells me you follow this philosophy."

"Absolutely. After my husband's premature death, my spiritual advisor introduced me to this concept, and I have practiced it ever since. How did you learn this?"

"My guardian stated that my paternal grandfather instructed him in ikigai. Further, I believe Michael Fields supports this principle. His actions are consistent with its principles."

"I see your logic."

"Michael understands what we are good at by understanding people and relationships. He knows constant innovation is the key to addressing what the world needs. He is realistic about what one can be paid for by balancing politics and technology. And most important, this satisfies what we love."

"And that is winning with humility," Tiffanee added.

Natsu smiled. "I could not have stated it better. For me, it starts with defining what one loves which then drives the other three circles of ikigai. It is my passion and mission to become a role model for Japanese women who want to succeed in business."

"Natsu, my husband encouraged me to excel in business and continually supported me. I want Kevin to adopt this philosophy, but … perhaps he'll listen to a younger person."

"I gladly accept that challenge. When we were in Kyoto, I began to show him how ikigai has a silver lining for him."

"He told me about that. I'm happy you've begun his education!" Tiffanee poured herself another cup of coffee. "I must confess something. When Kevin first met you in Osaka about the JV investment, he told me if you weren't in a relationship, he would have considered his options."

Natsu did not reply but looked pleased. When she saw Tiffanee's knowing smile, she knew Tiffanee endorsed a closer relationship with Kevin.

Later, Michael arrived. "My, this is a most beautiful day and setting for discussing common interests with two savvy business women! Ladies, I am at your service."

Natsu smiled. "Michael, please give us an overall update before we address specifics."

"Happy to. First, I'm pleased to announce that Ronald Blunt ceased all legal actions against the JV and SSFO skunk. His frivolous claim is no longer an issue."

Natsu asked, "What happened?"

"According to our lawyers, he received extremely embarrassing material he didn't want publicized or discovered in depositions. He doesn't want his personal interests open to public scrutiny. Tabloid rumors suggest he has political aspirations."

Tiffanee asked, "What embarrassing material?"

"Serious enough to convince him to cease litigation," Michael said.

"Knowing his past history, he knew he would lose in court and would have to pay," Tiffanee replied.

"Please update Tiffanee about the merger status," Natsu requested.

"Japan Technologies and IPS have successfully combined, and

the merged entity aggressively pursues the global appliance business," Michael said. "The merger ensures JT-IPS controls the silver-lining technologies. Kenji's colleague, Walter Marken, has been an enormous help at the OEMs. Now we can successfully compete against Lawrent and Gano-Nippon. When these two competitors realize their dilemma, they'll cooperate, not compete."

"Michael, you are to be commended for managing this difficult transition period," Natsu noted.

"Kind of you to say, but it has been a team effort."

"How about the automotive JV?" Tiffanee asked.

"Several items to report. The JV will operate as a stand-alone entity. It will oversee the innovation process with technical resources from the two skunks and JT-IPS. Natsu will lead the Asian JV activities while Kevin directs the US JV activities."

"What about patents for the exhaust system projects?" Natsu asked.

"Our patent lawyers, led by Jackson Huntley, have filed strong patent applications both in Japan and in the US. Jackson's optimistic about receiving final approvals. Once granted, we'll implement a strong licensing program to ensure the OEMs have multiple supply sources. This will forestall serious competition. Of course, we'll enforce our intellectual property."

"I understand you and Kevin adopted Pug James's licensing model," Tiffanee said.

"Yes, this model will balance technology with the politics of customer relationships."

Natsu smiled broadly. "Kobayashi-sama would be most pleased."

"Unfortunately, Pug never learned this when he ran IPS. He was more interested in accusing Kenji of stealing his silver-lining technologies. If Pug had listened to Kenji and Walter Marken, IPS would have been successful from the start."

"Michael," Natsu said. "you serve as the non-executive chairman of JT-IPS as well as the automotive JV. You oversee all operations. In addition, you've agreed to serve as my business mentor on a variety of matters. I appreciate your support."

"Happy to do it!"

"Michael, would you consider acting as business mentor as well?" Tiffanee asked. "I've discussed this with Natsu."

"Honored you'd consider me. Natsu, would this be a conflict for you?"

She laughed. "Not at all!"

Michael paused for a moment. "Well, by now you both know me pretty well. I am truly honored to be working with two aspiring and inspiring women."

In the early evening, the guests assembled in the enormous great room. Sergio and his assistant put finishing touches on a five-course meal. An Italian sommelier poured wines from Tuscany and Umbria, explaining the floral, fruit, and oak notes.

Tiffanee had special menus printed with the ikigai symbol prominently displayed. In front of each place setting were samurai dolls, two lady daimyos for Tiffanee and Natsu, and men samurais for the other guests. In the table's center rested three books authored by Sun Tzu, W. Edwards Deming, and Miyamoto Musashi.

Natsu knew Kevin had suggested Tiffanee add these touches. Her Kyoto tutorial for Kevin had been successful. This was another excellent sign for their futures. In a way, she considered herself as Kevin's sensei.

Natsu and Tiffanee sat at opposite ends of the beautiful oak table. An ikebana arrangement of California wildflowers rested at the center, and the glassware and china reflected soft light from numerous candles. On Natsu's immediate right was an empty chair. The place card read *In Memory of Kenjiro Kobayashi*. To her left sat Walter Marken, Sr. At Tiffanee's end of the table, Kevin sat on her left. On her right side was a second empty chair. The place card read *In Memory of Alan McIntyre*. Jackson Huntley and Michael Fields sat across from each other.

Despite Natsu's pleas, Shiganari chose not to attend. She recalled his words, "Natsu-chan, everyone at this celebration must know you are now in charge. My presence detracts from your role."

The sommelier poured kir royales. Tiffanee stood and raised her glass. "I wish to toast all—and to thank everyone for your hard work! If my Alan were here, he would greatly enjoy this celebration. His spirit is with us. To our continued prosperity!" Everyone raised their glasses. "Now, Natsu would you say a few words?"

Natsu raised her glass. "On behalf of Kobayashi-sama, my sensei, who gave me the gift of ikigai, I thank everyone here for your dedication and hard work." She nodded towards Michael.

Michael, looking relaxed, stood and surveyed the table. "First, a toast to Natsu, Tiffanee, Walter, Jackson, Kevin. I want to acknowledge the outstanding work by everyone at this table. We've had a challenging journey but have made terrific progress. Thanks to Japan Technologies for facilitating the merger and progress of the automotive JV. Here's to more success!"

Natsu and Tiffanee stood and joined Michael who seemed a bit surprised.

Natsu announced, "Tiffanee and I would like to now acknowledge Michael Fields. He has been our bedrock foundation, past, current and more importantly for our future. To Michael Fields! May he always retain his wisdom to never judge before listening, to encourage the right solutions, to teach others to practice ikigai, and to encourage our aspirations at all times. Arigato, Michael for everything you have done!"

Michael, blushing, raised his glass in response. "Arigato, Natsu and thank you, Tiffanee, for the opportunity to be part of your team. It's been my honor and pleasure, and I look forward to working with these extremely talented women who excel at overcoming obstacles and aspire to higher goals. Truly inspirational! A final note, I can state unequivocally the silver-lining curse has been lifted."

Everyone applauded.

Dinner concluded, they adjourned to the patio for cognac.

Kevin sat next to Natsu. "Looking forward to our visit to the wine country. This is my thank you for Kyoto." He leaned closer, took her hand, and kissed her.

She smiled. *This lady daimyo awaits ...but will not make King Lear's mistake.*

~ The End ~

ABOUT THE AUTHOR

S. J. Fairchild began his business career working in family businesses where he observed dysfunctional behavior and learned "how *not* to run a business." Later in his professional career, he lived and worked in five states, Europe, Asia, and Australia.

He held senior management roles in both public and privately-owned companies. With his experience in finance, sales, marketing, product development, operations and international business, he successfully commercialized new technologies in culturally diverse environments.

Currently, he consults and mentors new startups. He coaches students at the University of North Carolina business and medical schools.

He and his wife, Katherine, live in North Carolina.

Visit S. J. Fairchild at www.fairchildsj.com

Connect with him on:
Linkedin.com/in/stephen-fairchild-02201a14
Twitter: @Stephen18429957
Instagram: s.j.fairchild8

F.165-1B02-A7ED-46B0

Made in the USA
Columbia, SC
31 December 2021